Flood

MORE BY THIS AUTHOR

The Anniversary
The Travellers
A Running Tide
The Testament of Mariam
Betrayal
This Rough Ocean
The Secret World of Christoval Alvarez
The Enterprise of England
The Portuguese Affair
Bartholomew Fair
Suffer the Little Children

Praise for Ann Swinfen's Novels

'an absorbing and intricate tapestry of family history and private memories …
warm, generous, healing and hopeful'
VICTORIA GLENDINNING

'I very much admired the pace of the story. The changes of place and time and
the echoes and repetitions – things lost and found, and meetings and partings'
PENELOPE FITZGERALD

'I enjoyed this serious, scrupulous novel … a novel of character … [and] a
suspense story in which present and past mysteries are gradually explained'
JESSICA MANN, *Sunday Telegraph*

'The author … has written a powerful new tale of passion and heartbreak …
What a marvellous storyteller Ann Swinfen is – she has a wonderful ear for
dialogue and she brings her characters vividly to life.'
Publishing News

'Her writing …[paints] an amazingly detailed and vibrant picture of flesh and
blood human beings, not only the symbols many of them have become…but real
and believable and understandable.'
HELEN BROWN, *Courier and Advertiser*

'She writes with passion and the book, her fourth, is shot through with brilliant
description and scholarship...[it] is a timely reminder of the harsh realities, and
the daily humiliations, of the Roman occupation of First Century Israel. You can
almost smell the dust and blood.'
PETER RHODES, *Express and Star*

Flood

Ann Swinfen

Shakenoak Press

Published in Great Britain by Shakenoak Press, 2014

ISBN 978-0-9928228-0-4

Cover design by JD Smith www.jdsmith-design.co.uk

For

Heather, Falco, Hazel and Willow

Chapter One

We are known for troublemakers in my family. Some fifteen years ago my grandfather led two hundred commoners in an attack on Lord Bedford's drainage works in the Great Level. They made songs about him – sung to this day around the fenlands – and his very name is still famous hereabouts. In my earliest memory I was taken, with my brother Tom, to see him where he was kept in a filthy pit in Cambridge Castle. I know that I screamed, sure that the monstrous shape crouched in a corner was not my grandfather, but one of those fearful boggarts who haunt the Fens in darkness and in fog. I was three years old and impressionable.

My mother carried me outside and I remember the smooth lawns and the students in their gowns, all of which was as baffling to me as the prison. My brother Tom, nine years old and stout of heart, stayed behind with my father and the basket of food we had brought for my grandfather. He told me years later that he'd also been afraid of the gaunt figure with its wild hair and unkempt beard.

'I wanted to run,' he said, 'but I wouldn't shame myself before Father.'

I never saw my grandfather again, for he died soon afterwards, still waiting for his chance to appear before a court and demand justice, yet his fame in the eyes of fenlanders has never diminished and washes over us still. A chancy legacy.

Not that you would think it now. Here sat my father, who made one of those two hundred rioters all those years ago. He was a young man then and filled with outrage at the theft of our lands by the projectors and drainers – King and courtiers among them. Our own lands were not threatened then, it was away to the south, but we people of the Fens have strong loyalties and never much loved the King.

Yet here my father now sat with his cronies beside the fire, in our farm at Turbary Holm, like any contented old man wreathed in the tar scent of the peat, and I had just gone round again with a jug of my mother's best ale. That would be the third time and they had hardly started yet. They would pause in their drinking to eat, then carry on well into the night, for there is nothing like a belly full of food to make a man savour his drink.

'Here's thanks to you, Nehemiah,' said my father, raising his cup, 'for the gift of those eels. Mercy, our neighbour needs more ale.'

I obliged, though the stink on my hands from skinning the eels must have wafted a distinct flavour over the drink. Probably Nehemiah Socket wasn't aware of yet another layer of eel added on top of his permanent cloak of the smell. He was the most successful eeler in the village and spent more time weaving his traps and harvesting his catch than he devoted to all his crops and beasts together. Still, when he had more than enough sticks of eels to sell in Lincoln market, he was generous to us and in return my father and Tom kept an eye on his cattle and sheep out on the commons.

'Over here, Mercy.' Joseph Waters waved his cup at me. An old man whose watery eyes were still sharp enough to detect when there was a free meal to be enjoyed, he was one of the poorest of our neighbours, living by day labour on the farms. When he followed Nehemiah and his eels through the door, my parents had not the heart to turn him away. In any case, he was like to turn up here at least once in every week, eels or no, bringing with him the earth and sweat of his clothes which I swear had never been washed since his wife died. Aye, they were an odoriferous company.

'Test those eels, to see if they're cooked,' my mother called across from the table where she was sawing great hunks of bread off a loaf I had baked that morning. We would soak up the juice with it, chasing every last drop around our bowls.

'Done,' I said, when I had prodded them with the tip of my knife. Cut into short lengths, the eels were no longer swimming in the pure waters of Baker's Lode but in a rich brew of onions, carrots, parsley and ale. The meat was falling into soft flakes and the rising steam filled my nose with anticipation. My stomach groaned so loudly I was afraid the others would hear it, so I made a great clatter as I lifted the stewpot off its hook over the fire and carried it to the table, where I stirred in a jugful of rich cream.

'I'll fetch Tom.'

My mouth was watering as I crossed the yard to the cowbarn. Times had been somewhat lean for the last two years, with cold winters, late springs and sodden summers. My family was comfortable enough, but several poor harvests had meant starvation for some and we had gone short ourselves to help our neighbours. Nehemiah's eels were a welcome addition in these hungry months of spring, when the winter stores were nearly exhausted.

I leaned through the cowbarn door, drawing in the sweet meadow scent of the cows' breath.

'Supper, Tom.'

'Coming.' He hung the milking stool on a peg and patted the rump of Blackthorn, our favourite cow ever since the two of us had raised her by hand after her mother died.

'I can smell the eels.' He grinned as he wiped his hands on the seat of his breeches. 'Did I see Joseph Waters sidling in?'

'You did. That man will never miss a free meal.'

I turned as my eye was caught by a figure briefly silhouetted again the setting sun in the lane.

'Master Clarke!' I called, 'will you come sup with us?'

'Is there enough?' Tom whispered.

'Aye, plenty. I know Mother would want us to ask him. Since his housekeeper died she thinks he hardly eats.'

'I thank you, Mercy.' The rector opened the gate and came across the yard to us. 'Do I smell eel pottage?'

An uncharitable thought crossed my mind that perhaps Gideon Clarke, like Joseph Waters, had seen Nehemiah arriving with his basket of eels, but I dismissed it. The rector was bound to be hungry, but he was too uncomplicated a man to be so cunning.

His simple faith and unworldliness would get him into trouble one of these days. Still, I had a great affection for him. It was Gideon Clarke who had taught me to read and write, when my father sent me to be schooled by him at the age of twelve. And it was to him that I owed my love of books. Even when I was a child he had let me borrow precious volumes of his own.

Around the table we were a more sober company now that Gideon had joined us and said a blessing over the meal, but we were all soon spooning up the stew eagerly and wiping out our bowls with my good bread until they gleamed in the candlelight as if fresh come from the kiln.

I glanced round at the comfortable faces, a little shiny from grease, a little flushed with drink. No, you would not have suspected that we were the kin of the local hero and troublemaker Nathaniel Bennington. During these late war years, we had kept our heads down in this corner of the Fens, though a few young men went for Parliament, and the son of the manor went for the King. It was our fellow fenlander, Cromwell, who was come to power now, and my father had left off rioting and attacks on the drainers. In any case, those fine gentlemen, courtiers and landowners, who were bent on stealing the Fens before the War, had gone into exile now, or were lying low, watching to see which way Cromwell's wind would blow.

With a stomach warmed by eel pottage and mashed turnips, followed by a pie I had made from last year's dried apple rings, I slumped sleepily on the bench for a few minutes before I needed to clear away the litter from the table.

'I was in Cambridge today,' Gideon said slowly, gazing down into the dregs of his ale as if he was reluctant to look at the other men. 'I wanted to make sure that what I had heard about the new rules was true.'

So that was why Gideon's clothes were dust-stained and he looked weary. It is a long ride back from Cambridge.

'What rules?' Tom said. He always pricked his ears at the mention of Cambridge, where he had gone to school until the War put an end to his studies.

'We are no longer allowed to marry in church, or to baptise our infants.' Gideon's voice broke on the words, but looking up I noticed a flash of anger in his eye and felt a lurch in my stomach.

There was a sharp intake of breath from my mother, but it was my father who spoke.

'What? Are our young couples to live in sin? And our children to be exiled from holy church?'

'They have devised some ungodly rites.' I had never heard Gideon's voice so bitter. 'Which they, being Saints here on earth, claim are more godly that the rites of our English church. And as well, there is to be more destruction of our churches.'

In the moment of silence I remembered what had happened in Suffolk. Beautiful windows of ancient glass smashed to powder. Ancient statues of the Virgin and the saints, which had survived the other Cromwell's destruction, decapitated. Altars axed to splinters. Altar rails thrown on bonfires. The man sent to direct all that destruction, one William Dowsing, had gone off, no one knew where, but there were plenty more of like mind.

I knew we were all thinking of our own church. It was a simple cross with four small side bays, a square tower and a single bell, but there was one window of singular beauty at the east end, put up three hundred years ago to the memory of his wife, who died young, by Sir Anthony Dillingworth, ancestor of our local gentry. I had known that window all my life. The Virgin, in a robe as blue as a hot summer sky, was holding out a white dove to the Christ child, who was a toddler on fat legs, clutching a handful of daisies. Just ordinary daisies. I had loved that, ever since I was small. A bunch of daisies like the ones I could pick myself from the hem of the churchyard. At morning services the window glowed like the jewels of fabled Arabia, but I liked it better at evensong when the branches of an old oak, shivering in the diffused light, made the Virgin and Child stir into life, as though they would step down from their stone frame and walk amongst us.

'They would not dare to come here.' Tom voiced all our thoughts. 'Not with the Dillingworths still in the manor.'

Gideon shrugged. 'Sir John may be for Cromwell, since he's some sort of distant cousin, but Cromwell and his men will not forget that Edmund Dillingworth fought for the King.'

5

That silenced us again.

'And I heard something else in Cambridge.' Gideon glanced up at my father, then down again at his empty cup.

I rose to fetch the jug and fill it. For some reason my stomach had clenched again at his words.

'Something of more concern to you, Isaac. Indeed, to all the commoners.'

'You're a commoner yourself, Gideon,' my father said.

He nodded, but did not allow the acknowledgement to put him off his stride.

'I heard that there is a new projection got up, to drain and enclose our lands.'

'Our own village commons?' Tom shot up from his seat. 'Here? If they enclose our commons and destroy centuries of our work with their useless drains, people will starve. Even our family is not secure. We need those lands. Without them, we'll be brought to beggary.'

'Furthermore,' said Gideon, looking keenly now at my father, 'it seems that Cromwell himself is behind the scheme.'

Then the talk exploded.

'I do not believe it,' my father said, thumping the table with his fist. His face was red now with more than drink. 'Cromwell has always said he will support the fenlanders against the drainers. He would not betray us.'

'He was not the almost-king then, Father,' said Tom. He would have been wiser to keep his tongue behind his teeth, for Father turned on him.

'Mind your manners, boy!' he shouted. 'You know nothing of such a man as Cromwell.' He turned to Gideon. 'Where did you hear such lies?'

Tom kept silence, but I could see him biting back his anger at being called 'boy'. At four and twenty, he now carried most of the burden of labour on the farm as our father grew older.

Gideon shrugged again and sighed. I think he wished he too had stayed silent on the matter. He must have forgotten the strength of my father's belief in Cromwell.

'The news was everywhere. But I was told it as a fact by a friend of mine who is a magistrate. We were lads together at

Trinity and he's not a man to spread gossip. He has seen the plans for the projection. It takes in the whole of our commons and beyond.'

Nehemiah ran his hand through his unkempt mop of hair.

'They will destroy us for sure, whoever is behind it. Look what has happened to those schemes from your father's day, Isaac. The natural winter floods drained away from the croplands, so they're not fed with the washings. The peat moors sucked dry till they cave in like an old man's toothless cheeks. Useless now. The peat turned to dust instead of fuel.'

'Our rushes and sedges dying away for lack of water in the Fen.' Tom could not stay quiet. 'Whole villages on safe ground flooded, homes destroyed. People drowned.'

Before my father could chide him, Joseph Waters joined in mournfully. 'That will be an end to your eel fishing, Nehemiah. And we'll lose the water fowl. And the fish. And I've heard they steal the commoners' cattle if they find them straying on to the land they've enclosed.'

I was sitting there with my mouth agape, but now I saw my mother, her face tense with distress, signing to me to help our little maid, Kitty, clear the dishes and broken meats from the table. There was a general movement of the men back to the fire and as I was sweeping the crumbs into my apron, Tom murmured to me, 'Come out to the yard.'

I nodded.

'We'll just shut up the stock, Father,' he said.

Father waved a dismissive hand at him, for he was deep in argument with the others. I pouched my apron and added a few more scraps for the hens, then followed my brother outside.

After I had shaken the scraps into the hen-hus and shut the hens away, Tom beckoned me into the cowbarn. It was warm and quiet in there, out of the niggling March wind that had sprung up at dusk, plucking at my skirt and cap. The only sounds were the familiar rhythmic chewing of the cud and the rustle of straw as one of the cows shifted or else some small creature – rat or mouse – made its stealthy way through the barn in search of food.

'What is the matter?' I asked. 'Secrets or mischief?' My brother was known for both, though Cambridge had sobered his mischief somewhat. However, his six months at Grey's Inn in London, soon after Parliament and King locked horns, had increased his appetite for secrets.

'I believe what Gideon told us is true.'

'About the ban on church marriages and baptism?'

'That too. There's no end to the tyranny of these Puritans. No, I meant Cromwell and the projectors.'

'Father doesn't believe it.'

'Father is blind to what that man has become. He wooed us when he wanted a seat in Parliament. Now he has got it, and made himself king in all but name, he is greedy for our land to support him in fine state.'

I looked at him dubiously.

'We still have a king.'

'A king without a throne, without power, prisoner of Parliament.'

'But– '

'Oh, I've no love of Charles, but I'm not such a fool as to trust Cromwell either. I saw what they are like, these new men scrambling for power, during those months I was in London. They are no more friends of the common man than the King. Did you read those pamphlets of John Lilburne's that I gave you?'

'Aye. And what he says is a fine dream, but when will such a dream become reality in England? And besides, Father is no fool either.'

Tom picked up a hazel branch from the floor and began swishing it angrily against his leg.

'I don't say he is a fool, but he has put his trust in a man who shifts like fog. They say Cromwell acts always as God's voice directs. Perhaps he even believes that. But why does the voice of God forever prompt him to work for the greater glory of Oliver Cromwell? If he has it in mind to drain our Fens and enclose our commons for his own possession, is that God's will? It seems to me it is Cromwell's will.'

I did not answer him at once. Because he was so much older than I, Tom had always led and I had always trotted along behind, trying to keep up. When I was small, I had believed him wise and invincible. And my father? He was a man of standing in our village, a substantial yeoman farmer, held in some awe by the poorer cottagers and labourers. Besides, he was Nathaniel Bennington's son. Troublemaker and hero. The quarrels that had flared up recently between my brother and my father had left me floundering. They could not both be right.

Still, there was no sign yet of surveyors laying their cordon of instruments around our commons. And until there was . . .

'You will see,' Tom said, reading my thoughts, as so often he did. 'Once the surveyors come, you will see the truth of it.'

'And what shall we do then?

'What shall we do?' He stepped out into the yard and I followed him. 'What do you think?' He leaned over to close and bolt the door.

Then he turned to me and gave an odd smile, half rueful, half eager.

'Why then we will fight!'

We had not long to wait. March blew itself out on a wet wind and, as the feeble April sun came in, the winter-flooded fields dried out. We drove the cattle and sheep and horses out on to the lay-lands delegated for pasture this year, and the pigs into the copses. As soon as the ground was fit, we ploughed the remaining fields, turning in the rich silt washed down from the inland wolds, which nourishes our land and makes it, so I've been told, the richest arable in England. The air was full of the scent of the tilth, heady as a Christmas plum cake. The blackbird and the mavis were building their nests in the hedgerows, while herons high-stepped along the runnels and the lace of meres that stretched across the peat moors, dignified as magistrates strolling to a Lincoln courthouse. Until an unlucky fish or frog caught their eye and they swooped, sudden as a blue hawk.

After Gideon Clarke's announcement, the matter of Cromwell's projection was not mentioned again in our house, as if an unspoken truce held between Tom and Father. Still, there was a kind of quivering tension in the air. As for marriages and baptisms, the rector carried on just as before. A quiet, gentle man, he could be stubborn as a pig in defence of what he believed. Unless he could perform the traditional rites of the church, he would not consider a couple married in God's sight or a child accepted into the holy company of Christians.

The first marriage to take place in the village after the Puritan decree was to be between my friend Alice Morton and Rafe Cox. And, because Alice had whispered it to me, I knew it would not be long before there would be a baptism too. The wedding would be held after the ploughing and the planting of the spring wheat. When the common field was harrowed after sowing, to spread and bury the seed wheat, Alice and I sat side-by-side to weigh down the flint-toothed harrow as we had done since we were six years old. Jealous of our rights as the harrow girls, we had not yielded our place to the youngsters of the village, but this would be our last year, and we knew it. Two great girls sitting, knees up, our skirts gathered about us, barely finding room on the harrow unless we clutched at each other, we giggled at our own folly, but felt a touch of melancholy at the passing of our girlhood. It was as we bumped across the field, drawn by my father's yoke of plough oxen, that Alice confided to me that she was gone with child, who would be born in the summer. Her plump form, snug and homely as a new-baked loaf, concealed any sign of the baby yet, but I could see in her eyes a faraway look, as though she was watching something I could not see. Marriage would put an end to our closest ties, warmer than sisters.

'Will you stand for the babe, Mercy,' she whispered, 'when he is baptised?'

'Of course I'll be his gossip,' I said, giving her arm a small squeeze. 'So, it's to be a boy, is it?'

She grinned. 'That's what Rafe hopes. His father is so bent with rheumatism that he wants to see an heir growing up for the farm. I'll hope to satisfy him. But for myself, I'll be as happy with a girl.'

'We work as hard as the men,' I said. 'In the fields as well as at home. A girl could be as good an heir for Master Cox.'

She smiled and shook her head. She knew I read pamphlets and entertained some of the dangerous ideas brewing in the air, but she could not read, nor could she agree with me.

'And will you attend me on my marriage day?'

'Would you dare to ask anyone else?'

We fell to discussing the wedding, to take place the following week, until the harrow reached the end of its last turn at the adland and we climbed off, stiff and dusty, and a little ashamed of our childish behaviour. Let the young girls take over the task in future. Our lives were changing.

I went early to Alice's house on the marriage day and helped her into her best bodice and skirt, noticing as I laced her in that they were both tighter than they should be. We had gathered flowers the previous evening and kept them overnight in water in her mother's stillroom. It was too early for many to be found, but I wove together forget-me-nots, and pale ladysmock, and a few hearts-at-ease to make her a crown, which I pinned in place on her piled-up hair. This one day she would let the full glory of its red-gold curls be seen. I had always envied it, a burst of dawn sunlight compared to my dun brown hair of dusk. Still, when she persuaded me that in my role as attendant maid I should uncover my hair and dress it with the leftover flowers, I felt a curiously guilty pleasure in laying aside my headcloth and cap, and feeling freedom like a soft wind on my head.

Around her shoulders I draped a silk shawl of my mother's, which had once belonged to her grandmother, born a Dillingworth and therefore gentry. The colour feasted the eye amongst our village greys and browns; it was the very shade sported on the breasts of the peacocks which strutted on the manor lawn. I stroked it delicately with tender fingertips. Usually it was kept hidden in my mother's coffer, layered with lavender and rosemary, whose scent filled the air around us as I tucked the points into Alice's too-tight waistband.

'One day you'll wear this yourself,' Alice said, 'when you marry.'

'If I marry.'

No young man of the village meant anything to me.

Alice and Rafe were married by custom at the church door, and then we all processed inside for the service of blessing. Alice was lovely as apple blossom, while Rafe looked like a smug fireside cat at having secured the prettiest girl in the village. In the usual fashion at every wedding, some of the mothers wept a little and the men shifted uncomfortably in their Sunday clothes, surreptitiously loosening their shirt strings at the neck and turning their felt hats on their knees while Gideon preached a brief sermon on the joys and responsibilities of marriage. He had not, I was sure, noticed Alice's increased plumpness.

After the wedding, we gathered in the village tithe barn to celebrate. Empty now except for a few piles of hay and straw, and the sacks of seed beans and peas and barley we would be planting next week, it was our largest covered space, apart from the great hall of the manor house, but the Dillingworths had no part in the wedding of Alice Morton and Rafe Cox.

Every one of our neighbours had contributed what they could. The last of the dried fruits had been baked into pies, the first of the spring-rich cream had been curdled into syllabubs, and sweet frumenty had been flavoured with almonds and orange-flower water. Alice's father had brought his final and finest ham from last autumn's slaughtering. Even Joseph Waters had trapped a wild duck, and old Hannah Green, who lived by herself out on the edge of the Fen, had brought a pot of her precious honey.

After the bulk of the feasting, there was dancing. Alice's brother Robin played the fiddle, while Johnny Samson was the best piper in the whole hundred round about. They struck up with *Fair-Haired Maid* in honour of Alice as Rafe led her into the space which had been cleared in the centre of the barn for round dances.

No doubt our country gambols would seem like the clumsy clod-hoppings of peasants, with no more grace than cattle, in the eyes of the grand folk Tom had mixed with in Cambridge and London, but I doubt whether their fine marriage feasts could have showered more love and generous hope on the bridal pair than was in the air that evening.

I joined in with the rest, dancing with Tom and some of his friends, until Gideon Clarke approached me. His clerical bands were slightly askew and in the friendly candlelight he looked younger than his near thirty years, closer to Tom and the others. He adjusted my garland, which had slipped down, and held out his hand.

'Will you dance with me, Mercy?'

'I will, gladly,' I said, taking his hand. My heart jumped at its touch, cool and strong in mine. We have no mincing manners here. A grown girl may dance with whom she chooses, even the rector, let the godly Saints frown how they will. We danced to fiddle and pipe till we gasped for breath, and Gideon trod on my toes as readily as the rest.

'Pax!' I cried at last. 'Give me to drink of beer before I melt like butter in the sun!'

He brought wooden cups of beer for us both – a somewhat strong brew from Mistress Cox's still room – which we drained thankfully as the figures spun across the barn and out into the moonlit night. Setting our cups aside, we followed them, out under the clear sky where the stars throbbed to the beat of the music flowing from the barn and our feet moved noiseless over the grass of the village green. Gideon's arm around my waist whirled me away under the trees until the milk-white gleam of the moon above and its shivering reflection in the village pond seemed to join into one shaft of silver light spinning around my head.

Was there something frantic in our merriment? Did we sense, somehow, that this was not a beginning, but an ending? That after this night, when we had roared and teased Alice and Rafe to bed by lantern light, then blown out our frugal candles to make our way home through familiar lumps and shadows in the dark, nothing would be the same when the sun rose in the morrow on our thick heads and heavy limbs?

Chapter Two

No, we had not long to wait. We made a sluggish start, the morning after Alice's wedding day. Heads were sore and not a little fogged. It was a few days until we planned to sow the barley and after the barley, the beans and peas. No need to rush out into the unfriendly brightness of day. I took my time letting out the chickens and cleaning the hen-hus. My head and stomach lurched at the stench of the dirty straw, so I was glad to escape to the morning milking. Tom had driven the cows in from the common, but then gone out again with Father and the other men to take a leisurely look at the barley field. There was no need for this. It was ploughed and ready, unchanged from yesterday, but it gave them the excuse to seem busy, while airing their boozy heads. For us women, the daily chores went on.

I had milked four of our ten cows, glad to be sitting down, leaning my head against the friendly flank of the fifth cow, Elderberry. My eyes crept shut, the rhythmic movements so schooled into my fingers that I could half-sleep and still continue milking. When Tom burst through the door with a clatter that made Elderberry jump sideways, I opened my eyes with a start to see my hands spurting milk into the straw.

'Tom! What are you about?' I was angry at the wasted milk and the frightened cow. It would take me time to persuade her to let down the milk again.

'Come with me.' Tom was shaking my shoulder. 'Leave the milking.'

'I cannot–'

'This is important.'

There was something in his voice that made me lift the milk pail on to a shelf and follow him across the yard and out of the gate. He was striding so fast ahead of me that I broke into a half run to keep up with him. We took the path from the farm in the direction of the common fields, not the barley field, as I had expected, but the newly sown wheat field where Alice and I had so recently perched on the harrow. In the week and more since then, there had been two nights of soft rain and several days of surprising April warmth, which had nursed the grain and drawn it into life. In the morning light, with the sun still low in the sky, a faint blush of yellow-green lay over the soil, like the shimmer on a flooded field when a breeze passes over it. A promise of bread for our future.

'Wheat's sprouting already,' I called to Tom's back.

'Little gain that will be for us.' He spat the words over his shoulder.

'What do you mean?'

He gave no answer.

'Tom, wait.' I was wearing my light house shoes of felt and hobbled over the clods and stones of the lane like a cripple.

He stopped abruptly, not in response to my plea, but because we had reached what passes for high ground in a our fenlands, the bank beside Baker's Lode where it skirted the edge of the wheat field. This bank was built to hold back the winter floods to the beneficial depth and allow the soil washed down from the wolds to settle. When the water reaches a certain level, the excess drains away into the Lode, leaving the watery porridge to feed the field throughout the winter months until it soaks away in the spring. We jumped the small sock-dike, which was dry at this time of year, and climbed the bank. From the top we could look across the wheat field with its greenish wash brushed over the chestnut brown of the soil.

Tom pointed, wordless.

Following the line of his finger, I could see, on the far side of the field, a group of six or eight men. I shaded my eyes with my hand and squinted into the distance. Even across that wide reach of land, I could tell they were not local men. There was something unfamiliar in the way they moved, stiff and precise, without the loose, easy gait of the Fens. And instead of our broad-brimmed hats of straw or our knitted caps, both of which we women make in the long hours of winter, these men wore dark, high-crowned hats, which looked – as far as I could make out at this distance – as though they were made of felt. There was something strange, alien, in their tall shape.

The men were not standing idle. They were busy about some contraption of poles, and then two began to walk towards us, across the new-planted wheat, while another two set off at a right angle, also stamping their heedless boots amongst the tender shoots, walking parallel to the far edge of the field.

'They're walking across the wheat!' I was so shocked, I cried out what any child could have seen. 'Trampling it down. We must stop them.'

'That is the least of what they will trample under foot.'

'But who are they? What are they doing?'

'They are the enemy,' Tom said. 'And they are surveying our land, to work our destruction.'

'We must stop them,' I said again.

He shook his head. 'They will pay you no heed. We have challenged them already, but all they did was shake a parchment under our noses, got up in a finery of ribbons and seals of red wax. I glimpsed only a word or two written on it, but it is an authorisation from a company of projectors to survey our commons for the "better improvement of the land". Father and the others have gone off to Sir John for help. He must have a lawyer in his pocket, they think, who will act for us.'

'So we need not fear?'

'What aid did the law give our grandfather? The only thing these robbers understand is force.'

'Why do they look so strange? Their clothes . . .'

The men were approaching nearer now, and I could see that besides their odd tall hats, they wore breeches much baggier than those our men wore, and waistcoats with long skirts, like a woman's bodice.

'They're Hollanders, brought over because of their knowledge of draining land. Half their country, it's said, is reclaimed from the sea.'

16

'But we're ten miles from the sea. We already own our land, solid land, and farm it. What has the sea to do with us?'

'What indeed?'

The men approaching us looked up, but never slowed their pace. One, bigger and somehow more affluent looking than the other, even raised his hand to the brim of his strange hat and gave us a smile. I did not care for that smile. There was something condescending about it, as if he were already in possession of our lands and we were his serfs, awaiting his bidding. I tugged at Tom's sleeve.

'Let us go home.'

He nodded and we turned away.

All the way back we were silent until we reached the farm.

'What shall we do?' I would not have voiced my thoughts, but that careless smile had alarmed me more than any threat, compelling me to speak.

Tom stopped with his hand on the latch of the gate.

'There is nothing we can do. Yet. They have dug no ditches, erected no fences, built no pump mills. They merely have a parchment in their hands and they are wielding their surveying instruments.'

'They have damaged our young wheat!'

He shrugged. 'A few strides along the borders of a field? No law court meeting months from now will care a farthing for that.'

He thumped the gatepost angrily.

'No, we must wait until there is some solid evidence of what they intend.'

'Then take them to law?'

He gave a bark of impatient laughter. 'Have you no eyes and ears, Mercy? No memory? You know what happened before the War. Now that the fighting has ceased and the King is in custody, a new breed of scavenger rats has arisen to prey on our land.'

'They won't have the power of those other projectors,' I protested, trying to push away the thought of what drainage and enclosure would mean for us. 'They were noblemen and courtiers, with the law courts at their bidding.'

'You think that Cromwell and his fellows will play by the law? I think not.'

'Perhaps Sir John will help.' I clung to the belief that the Dillingworths, the greatest family in the neighbourhood, would have the power to overcome half a dozen Hollanders.

The milking was done, the cows driven out to pasture, and we had broken our fast by the time Father and the other men returned. They gathered in our kitchen, crowding in, their shoulders jostling our hanging pans, their boots casting gobbets of mud over the flags I had just scrubbed. Not everyone was there. Not the old and feeble. Not Nathaniel Sprocket who would have been away at his eel traps a mile or two along Baker's Lode before dawn.

Tom folded his arms and confronted Father.

'What help from Sir John?'

Father smiled broadly. 'He writes to his London lawyer today. And to Cromwell himself. There will be no enclosing our land, you may be sure. Sir John knows that Cromwell will put a stop to it, as he promised us, years back. His *cousin* Cromwell.'

Tom flicked a glance aside to me. This cousinage was much talked of, but no one was quite sure how close it was. Not close, Tom said. But of importance to Sir John since Edmund Dillingworth had fought for the King and come home a beaten pup, tail between legs. I wondered how much Sir John dared trade upon this thin cousinage. The safety of his son would outweigh all else.

It seemed some of the men shared Tom's doubts, for they looked at each other uneasily, but nothing could mar Father's confidence. His smile warmed the room.

'Come, Abigail, we've had a hungry walk to the manor. What can we give our neighbours? Mercy, fetch the good beer.'

My mother and I hurried to bring out bread and hard cheese, and Tom rolled the beer cask into the kitchen for me.

'Father seems hopeful,' I said as I filled a jug from the spigot.

He turned his mouth down. 'We shall see. Sir John is full of fine words, but his father never came to the aid of our grandfather. I shall believe in him when I see those Dutchmen sent packing back to their own dykes and ditches.'

It was decided by common consent that morning that nothing should be done against the surveyors while we awaited word from

Sir John's lawyer. However, Father did approach the leader of the Dutchmen, who was called Piet van Slyke, to ask him civilly not to walk across our crops. I do not know what van Slyke answered, for Father would not say, but he looked grim afterwards.

Barley was sown for beer and beans and peas for the pot. The medlands were filled with the carefree scamperings of the new lambs, while the young calves, one moment quietly following their mothers, would suddenly flick their tails in the air and gallop across the grass in joyous freedom of their youth, innocent of the heavy bodies and lumbering gait that would burden their mature years.

'It will be the first of May next week, and soon after that Rogationtide,' Gideon Clarke reminded my father, as they sat on a bench, leaning against the warm southern wall of our house and smoking their long pipes while I cleared weeds from my rows of onions and carrots.

'And have the Puritans banned that too?' Father asked.

'No doubt. I have not heard. In any case, I mean to beat the bounds with all who will accompany me.'

'We will come. The whole village.' My father had no need to ask the rest of us. We had not missed the beating of the bounds even during the War.

I stood up, easing my back and dusting the soil from my hands.

'And shall we have a Maying?' I asked.

'Fetching in the May, and a maypole, and a summer queen? Every bit. Would you be our queen, Mercy?' Gideon was laughing and I blushed, with his eyes on me. For the last few years Alice had been the queen, but she was a married woman now.

'That would be for the village to choose,' I said with a fine show of modesty. 'But I do think we should have a Maying. Beat the parish bounds to show that we are not afraid of these men who would steal our land. And hold a Maying to show we are not afraid of the godly Genevans who would put an end to all joy.'

'The surveyors have been gone these three days.' Tom had come out of the barn and joined us. ''Tis to be regretted. I would have liked to lift two fingers to them as we beat the bounds, but – surveyors or not – I agree that we should have both the Maying and the beating of the bounds. Let them think what they will.' He did not say who he meant by 'they', but we understood him well enough.

Preparations went ahead swiftly. Before dawn on May Day, all the young people of the village went out to fetch in May blossom from the hedgerows, to deck our houses and the church. It was the first time in my whole life that I went without Alice, but I took our little Kitty with me. She was one of the village paupers, a church-door foundling, though it was whispered she belonged to Joseph Waters's daughter, who had gone off, soon afterwards, with a travelling pedlar. Kitty had scrambled up, hand-to-mouth on parish charity, and had come to us, at eight years old, as general servant. She was eleven now. Not a stupid child, and willing. She had never been a-Maying before and skipped along at my side, her eyes bright with the excitement of a few hours away from washing greasy pots and muddy flagstones.

'Is this what we want, mistress?' She broke a cluster of whitethorn blossom from the branch and held it out to me.

'Aye, but not like that. We need long stems so we can weave them round the pillars and altar rails in the church. But take care! The thorns are sharp.'

'I remember last May.' Her face glowed. 'And we will have some for the master's house too?'

I laughed. Kitty was in awe of Father. In her eyes our house belonged solely to him. The rest of the family counted for little.

'We'll gather plenty, then we can pin it up round the doors, and along the mantel.'

'Can we put some over the barn door too? I know the beasts will love to celebrate May Day. Especially Blackthorn and Blaze.'

I smiled at the thought of the staid cow and our quiet gelding rejoicing in the Maying. 'Aye, if we gather enough. We need sweet eglantine as well. There's a hedge of it further along. And sops-in-wine.'

'Is that a flower?' She laughed. 'I don't know it.'

'It grows in low clumps. A deep red flower with white patches. So it looks like red wine with sops floating in it, such as rich invalids are given.'

'Like the bread sops we put in pottage?'

'Aye, like that.'

The heady scents of spring followed us along the lane. The young people of the village, all those unmarried, had turned out every one. Parliament might try to ban our merry-making, but for this last year at least we would have our Maying. There must have been twenty of us, all who had grown up together within the boundaries of this parish, and later in the month we would follow Gideon with his cross and prayerbook, and beat the young children at the parish bounds, that they would know their land and their rights and never forget them.

From time to time some of our companions would pair off and slip away behind a hedge, for May is the time for courting. And if we heard squeals and laughter, we smiled and passed on along the lane. There would be new babes in the village, come the turn of the year, and perhaps a few hasty weddings beforehand. Though I was fond enough of the village boys I had known all my life, none could tempt me away to tumble in the young grass, despite hints and a few stolen kisses.

The lads were collecting supple young birch branches, just coming into leaf, which would provide a strong framework for our garlands and wreathes. Tom, with his friends Toby Ashford and Jack Sawyer, cut down a straight young beech to make our maypole, and carried it back between them to set up on the green, accompanied by the blowing of horns and beating of drums. While they dug a hole and set the maypole, firming it in with the edge of their boots, the rest of us decorated the church, winding the branches through the carved openings of the ancient altar rail, garlanding the font and pillars, and draping swags of blossom across the altar. By now the sun was fully up and we went home to decorate our doorways and eat our breakfasts. I gave Kitty the rest of the branches and flowers to swag the animals' quarters, while I joined Tom in the kitchen for a hasty meal of porridge and ale. As we were eating, Gideon came in, his eyes lit with laughter.

'So, it is to be your turn this year, Mercy. The village has chosen you our summer queen.'

He took my hand and kissed it, dropping on one knee. 'Your humble servant, Your Majesty!'

I looked down at his thick curls and felt my breath catch in my throat. I feared he was merely humouring me, as he used to do when I did well in my lessons, but he held my hand tightly, and his lips lingered on my skin. Then he turned my hand over and kissed the palm, so that a shudder ran through me.

'So many years in Alice's shadow,' I said, as lightly as I could. 'At last I will lead the revels! I hope I will not disgrace the village.'

Gideon stood up, and released my hand slowly.

'You will wear your crown with beauty and dignity,' he said, looking at me intently.

I could not hold his gaze, but dropped my eyes and felt the heat of my skin burn from my neck to my hair.

After we had eaten, I changed into my best bodice and skirt, then the whole family walked down to the village, where I would don the summer queen's cloak, which was kept for safety from year to year in a chest in the church vestry. In our grandparents' time, the May celebrations had included a church ale, when the village gathered in the churchyard for feasting and games, everyone contributing a few pennies to parish funds, but church ales were banned now. And even when my father was young there had been a summer king as well as a queen. He would choose a band of followers and they would travel to all the villages for miles around, accompanied by pipe and drum, the purpose being to visit every yel-hus within walking distance. The kings of the other villages would return the visits and an uproariously drunken time was had by all, over several weeks. My father had twice been chosen king and spoke of it with a certain gleam in his eye that sat ill with his present dignity.

The May queen's cloak was grown threadbare by now, for it dated back to the old Queen's time, Queen Bess, whom Hannah had once seen making a progress. Gideon lifted it carefully out of the chest and as he did so I saw how fragile it was. The spring sunshine slanting in from the window shone through the bare patches in the velvet and picked out a random lace of tiny holes. Gideon draped it about my shoulders and pinned it together at my throat. I scarcely dared to draw the edges together.

'I hope it will not fall apart while I am wearing it,' I said.

'I think it will survive for one more ceremony,' he said. 'But after this year – who knows? As with so many of our customs, we may be forced to abandon it.'

'We have made you a fine crown, Mercy.' Alice held it out for me to see.

Alice and the six girls who were to be my May maidens had shaped a crown framework out of supple willow twigs, then bound in roses and May blossom. It was a beautiful thing and I held my head steady while they pinned it in place.

'Now, Your Majesty!' Gideon took my hand and led me out of the church, down the steep path and across the green to a seat beneath the maypole. 'May you preside in peace over your subjects' revelry.' His tone was mock-heroic, but in spite of his vocation I knew that he loved these old festivals as much as we all did, and would be as sorry as the rest of the village if the new powers of Puritans put an end to them.

Many of the villagers joined hands in a ring around the maypole and began to dance to the music of fiddle, pipe, and drum. Circling first to the right, then the left, forward then back, they went through the steps of the traditional maypole dance. Around the green the older folk were already drinking beer and nibbling at cakes and suckets. When the dancers tired, they joined them and I wondered whether it would be consistent with my royal dignity to fetch myself a drink.

'Here.' Alice appeared, carrying a tray with two cups of beer and a plate of sweetmeats. She sat down on the grass beside my chair.

'It is all very well to be dressed up in finery,' she said, 'but I remember how hot and thirsty I was, sitting there.'

'You are an angel sent from heaven,' I said, drinking deeply. 'This velvet cloak is a little too heavy for a fine spring day.'

She brushed it gently with her finger. 'Poor old thing. It cannot last much longer.'

'No. I wonder how much longer we will be allowed to bring in the May.'

'If they knew of this in London, they'd clap us all in fetters.'

'It's a sad, dreary world they would condemn us to, these ardent reformers,' I said. 'As well as cutting up our lands and giving them away to rich men.'

Our festivities went on all day and I was glad when I was allowed by custom to leave my throne under the maypole and join the rest. The children played at hoodman-blind and skipping games, the young men wrestled and ran races. Even the young girls kilted up their skirts and batted a ball with gloved hands. It was my task to award prizes: a sucking pig to the victor of the wrestling matches and a silver spoon to the girl judged the winner of the ball game, whose rules I had never been able to fathom. In the evening, as I took off the ancient cloak and gave it back to Gideon, I felt some of it come apart in my hands.

'Oh, no! I did not tear it, it just fell in two pieces.'

He folded it carefully and laid it in the chest.

'It could not have lasted any longer. It belongs to the past. As, I fear, does our Maying.' He smiled at me, rather sadly, I thought. 'At least you had your chance to be our queen, Mercy.' And he touched my cheek lightly with the tips of his fingers.

Early on the Monday morning before Ascension Day, we set out to beat the bounds, Gideon at our head reading the Rogationtide homily, prepared to bless the fields, crops and animals. I followed next with my May maidens, and behind us every villager who was sound in wind and limb. The children who were to be beaten, mostly five or six years old, looked suitably solemn and important. All the youngsters carried sticks.

Our first boundary stone lay where Baker's Lode met a stand of sallows which we coppiced regularly for baskets and hurdles. First the children beat the stone with their sticks, then lined up and one by one had their heads gently knocked against the stone and held out their hands to be beaten. Father, foremost of the villagers, tapped their palms lightly with a willow wand, and then Hannah Green, the oldest of our neighbours, gave them each a honey sweetmeat.

On we went to the next boundary marker, an oak so ancient that its hollow centre could hold five men, yet whose outer skin and branches, knobbled and gnarled like the arms of an ancient labourer, were hard as iron. Always the last of trees to raise its sap along those mighty limbs, it was just putting forth the first tips of its leaves. Beneath our feet the few acorns overlooked by the village pigs crunched and crumbled. I picked one up, smoothing its golden shell with my thumb, then slipped it into the pocket of my apron. The children were tapped against the rugged trunk, Father made a pretence of beating their hands, and Hannah doled our her sweetmeats. No wonder we had always looked forward to the year when we would be old enough to beat the bounds!

It took us until sunset to make the circuit of our entire parish, though we stopped at midday on the boundary of the Fen, near Hannah's cottage, to eat the eel pies and gingerbread we had brought in our baskets. We drank our ale straight from the leathern jacks, passing them from hand to hand, and dabbled our tired feet in the small mere that provided Hannah with fish. By the time we reached the village I was ready to fall into my bed, but there were still the cows to be milked and the eggs collected. I sent Kitty to fetch the eggs, while I milked. Before I had finished, Tom joined me and milked the last two.

'A good day,' I said, stretching my arms above my head.

'I hope it will not bring trouble down on us.'

'Why do you say that?'

'I saw that we were watched from the next parish, beyond the oak. Villagers from Crowthorne. There's a nest of godly Puritans there, who like nothing better than to sour the happiness of their fellow men. And their preacher is a rampant Genevan, bent on rooting out all who take a kindlier view of mankind.'

'I've heard the talk. Why should they care? In their eyes we are already the Damned, are we not?'

'Damned indeed.' He lifted his pail of milk to carry it into the cool, stone-walled dairy next door, and gave a sharp sigh. 'Sometimes I do not know which way to turn, Mercy. I do not love the Stuart monarchs, who think themselves God's Appointed, nor do I love the Puritans, who think themselves God's Chosen. Why can we not be left to ourselves, here in the Fens, to grow our food, and rear our animals, and mend our houses, troubling no one? We need no courts or kings or Parliaments.'

'Or drainers,' I said.

'Them least of all.'

As if conjured up by our thoughts, the drainers returned the following week. This time van Slyke was accompanied not simply by his small group of surveyors. Hordes of labourers followed them, more of the Dutchmen, but Englishmen too, of the poorest sort, clad in rags and with the pasty skins of townsmen who have never walked across a field or snared a rabbit or ploughed a furrow. There was also a miserable group of men wearing nothing but rough cloth wrapped about their waists, and no more than three shirts amongst the dozen of them. They clanked in the rear of the company, chained together, right ankle to right ankle. Word soon flew round the village that these were Scotsmen, prisoners captured in the War.

'Savages!' the whisper went round, 'worse than the Hollanders. If they are unchained they'll slit our throats while we sleep.'

Fear stalked abroad, and fear of the Scots was but the beginning of it. It served as a cover for the true underlying fear: What is to become of us?

There had been no word from Sir John's lawyer.

The company of drainers set up camp in one of our common pasturelands, amongst our grazing beasts, building themselves rough huts out of our timber, gleaned from our woodlands, covered with rough canvas cloths. They fed their open fires from our firewood, their smoke rising mockingly into the spring sky, and it wasn't long before chickens disappeared from our runs, and then one or two of our sheep. Like the soldiers of both armies during the War, these men were bent on foraging off the land. Our land. And the War was over. When a group of our villagers went to protest to van Slyke, he pointed to sacks of meal and onions and turnips.

'We provision our men ourselves. They have not touched your goods. You should shut up your chickens away from the fox, and keep your sheep from wandering off over these desolate marshes. Little wonder that they drown or are swallowed by the bog.'

And he smiled his superior smile.

The men came back muttering angrily into their beards, but no one was quite sure how far these invaders could be challenged.

A few days after their arrival, I made my way round the far side of the pasture where the strangers were camped, keeping a wary eye on their activities. Van Slyke and his surveyors were ordering some of the labourers about and the men were laying out lengths of rope along the ground. I did not approach so near to them from choice, but I was worried lest any harm come to Hannah Green, whose cottage stood at the far edge of the pasture, where it met the Fen, embowered in the constant murmur of sedge and rush. Her home was dangerously close to the enemy and distant from help in the village.

'Hannah, I've brought you a basket of goods.' I called out ahead of myself, so that she would know who was approaching.

As usual, when the weather was warm enough, her door stood ajar. She had not yet been troubled by the strangers, then.

'Mercy! Come in, child.'

Marriageable in age I might be, but I would always be a child to Hannah, who had nursed me through childhood illnesses and comforted me with spoonfuls of her honey when I grazed my knees or fell from a tree. I was forever trying to emulate my brother.

As I unpacked my basket on her table, I looked about me. The one-roomed cottage was a place I had always loved. Unlike our rambling farmhouse, with its jutting wings added on willy-nilly over the generations, Hannah's home was a simple, plain square, like a child's toy house, everything clean and in its place. A low settle, serving as her bed at night, was cleared of bedding by day, which she stored in the cupboard beneath. Her wooden cups and platters stood regimented along a shelf with her one pewter tankard, polished till it caught the beam of light from the door, standing proud in the centre. Bunches of herbs, a plait of onions, and a necklace of apple rings dangled from the low rafters, so that I had to duck and dodge as I laid out the bread and beer and eggs I had brought. As quickly as I unpacked them, Hannah swooped down and tidied them away.

'You had no need to bring me eggs, Mercy. My Polly lays enough for me.'

'Our hens have gone mad with their spring laying,' I said. 'We have more than enough. And these are fertile. You could brood them.'

Hannah had no rooster and I thought she might be glad of some young pullets, for her Polly was growing old.

'Aye, that's well thought on.'

She picked up the eggs, which I had wrapped in raw wool to keep them warm, and took them out to her hen-hus.

'Polly's looked fair broody of late, trying to make a nest of her own eggs,' she said when she returned. 'She should do well with them.' She tucked the swags of wool back in my basket. 'You'll take a cup of my cider.'

It was an order, but I was happy to comply, for it was a good walk from home and the weather had turned warm. I pulled up a stool to the table, scrubbed almost white with Hannah's fierce housekeeping, and accepted the turned wooden cup. She did not brew ale or beer, but her small plot held a venerable cider apple tree, whose juice she pressed and preserved every year. We are not cider country here in the Fens, and the tree had been planted so far back it was beyond all memory, but there it stood, just beginning to burst forth in pink blossom like a young maid dressed for a wedding. It was a novelty for us, and we never refused a drink of Hannah's cider. Some of the village dames urged her to make mead with her honey, but she preferred it in its natural state. Whenever Nehemiah went to Lincoln market, he would sell a pot or two for her. The coin they earned paid for the few things she could not grow or make for herself.

'They haven't troubled you, have they?' I jerked my head in the general direction of the drainers, whose voices we could hear in the distance.

'Not yet. What are they about, do you know?'

'It is another of these schemes like those before the War on the Great Level and Deeping Level. But Father thinks Sir John's lawyer will be able to stop them. Or even Cromwell himself.'

'They'd best make haste, then. I saw them unloading a cart full of picks and shovels this morning.'

My heart jerked, and I felt a prickle of sweat along my spine. 'Are you sure?'

'I haven't lost the use of my eyes, even if my back is bent, young Mercy.' Her voice was tart. Hannah would never yield an inch to age, and did not care for anyone else to mention it. She was as sensitive to any such remark as a horse to a buzzing fly.

'I'm sorry. I was alarmed. We did not know things had come to such a pass so soon.'

I stirred uneasily. I mustn't linger. This was something Tom and the others needed to know at once. Setting down my empty cup, I picked up my basket and rose to leave.

'Here's a pot of honey for you.' Hannah reached one down from the shelf above the settle. She would never accept a gift without making a return, her pride demanded it.

'Thank you. You know we'll savour it.' I tucked the jar into my basket.

As I ducked out through the low doorway, I saw that the drainers, having laid out a double line of ropes were now driving pegs into the turf alongside.

'Hannah,' I said, 'if anything happens, if those men trouble you, promise me that you will come to us.'

She gave me a shrewd look.

'You think they mean trouble.'

'I know it.'

'I'll not let them disturb me. Now, get you away home. I've the pig to feed and the goat to tether on a fresh patch. If those eggs hatch, I'll send word.'

The eggs never hatched. Nor did the pig eat many more meals at Hannah's hand. I went home that day deeply troubled by what Hannah had said about the shovels and picks and by what I had seen of the purposeful activity of van Slyke and his men. The most direct way to our farm would have taken me right past their encampment, but I took care to skirt the far edge of the meadow, stopping once to scratch the head of one of our own ewes who came ambling up to me, followed by her twin lambs skittering about, leggy and shy. I passed the cottage belonging to Nehemiah, who was Hannah's nearest neighbour. He was not at home, but the smell of eels hung about the place. His holding nets, bobbing about in the small mere where we had stopped during the beating of the bounds, squirmed in a tangle of eels, their silver-black sides coruscating in the sunlight. I wondered whether the invaders had discovered this source of food yet. The townsmen and the Scots might not take to them, but I guessed that the Hollanders, being a watery people, would probably relish the meat of a fat eel to vary their diet.

When I told Tom of the drainers' activities, and the arrival of their picks and shovels, he went off at once to his friends in the village. As soon as he returned, he and Father began to argue.

'We must act *now*!' Tom strode about the room, thumping his fist into his palm. 'We have waited long enough for Sir John's lawman. And Cromwell.' He spat out the name as though it was bitter on his tongue.

'You will do nothing, do you hear?' Father was slower to anger than Tom, but when he was roused he could be formidable. 'You and your wild young friends. If we do any act of violence against the drainers, we will have no case in law.'

'Law! How has law ever protected the fenlanders? In your father's day, the men of the Great Level took the ancient charter to London, which laid down their rights to the common land of the Fens. Inalienable, they were meant to be.'

'That was another part of the Fens, and there was some doubt about the wording of the charter. Ours is clear, Sir John says, on good authority. But these matters of law take time. And since the War, all things are unsettled, even the courts in London.'

'And Cromwell will protect us.' There was contempt in Tom's voice.

'Do not speak of that great man with disrespect, you puppy!' Father was on his feet now, confronting Tom.

Like a punctured wineskin, Tom sank down on the bench beside the table and put his head in his hands.

'If we do not fight, they will slaughter us like sheep,' he muttered through his fingers.

Mother and I crept away to bed, but I lay awake far into the night, hearing their raised voices through the floor.

Two days later, at dusk and just as we were lighting candles, there came a frantic scratching at the kitchen door. When I opened it,

Hannah Green fell into my arms. Her cheek was bruised and bloody, her cap torn half off so that her white hair fell about her shoulders. Her skirt was ripped, wet and muddy. She dragged a small sack over the threshold and under her arm her hen Polly thrust out a frightened head. A swift dark shape darted in behind her, her cat Tobit.

'Hannah!' I half carried her to a chair by the fire. 'What has happened? Here, give me the hen.'

But she would not loose her grip on the hen or the sack, and stared about as we crowded round, as if she did not know us.

'The men,' she said. 'The men.'

She seemed unable to say more. Tom fetched her a cup of beer and I laid a quilt over her knees. I prised her fingers from the strap of the sack and folded them around the cup. They were frozen, for a cold wind had been blowing all day from the east.

'Drink,' said Mother. 'You can tell us more when you are ready.'

It must have been half an hour before Hannah stopped shaking. By then Polly had settled herself on her lap in the warmth of the fire and tucked her head into her feathers in sleep. I brought a stool up to the chair and took Hannah's hand between mine.

'Can you tell us what happened?

She turned her face toward me. Slow tears welled up in her eyes and rolled down her lined cheeks. I had never seen Hannah weep. She was the strongest person in my world.

'The Dutchman, he came and said I must move out of their way, because they were going to dig a drain right through my land. When I said him nay, said he had no right, he said he had every right. I tried to close the door in his face and then he hit me.'

She raised her hand and tenderly touched her bruised cheek. Her fingers caught in her hair and she looked surprised, then pulled her other hand from mine and tried to stuff her hair back under her cap, but her hands were shaking too much. Quietly I stood up and settled her hair, then tied her cap in place.

'Thank you, child.' There was still a vacant look in her eyes, as though she did not quite know me.

'The Dutchman struck you,' I reminded her gently, 'then what happened?'

'I tried to bolt my door. You know I never bolt my door, and it was too stiff for me. I heard the men outside, and my pig squealed. I heard them dragging him away. I didn't know what to do. Then I remembered you had said to come to you, so I was putting some things in a sack, my salves and my honey . . .' she looked down at the sack by her feet, as if she wasn't sure if it was hers.

She was silent again, and this time Tom prompted her. 'Did the men come back?'

She nodded. 'I could hear them striking at my house with their pickaxes. One splintered the wall above my bed and my shelf of honey fell down. I saved some of it. And Polly.' She stroked the sleeping hen, who stirred but did not wake. 'Then I thought I'd best run. When I went out of the house, they came after me, swinging their pickaxes. I don't think they would have struck me, but I was afraid. My goat was gone and my hives overturned, the bees everywhere.'

'I hope they stung the drainers,' I said, furious.

She gave me a weak smile. 'I think they did. I made my way here as fast as I could, but it was beginning to be dusk, and I was frightened, and I fell a few times.'

She had taken my hand again, and I could feel fear running through her fingers.

'My bees gone, my home, my goat, my pig. I don't know what has become of my cat.'

'He followed you here.' I pointed to where Tobit had curled up just within the warmth of the fire, but away from our dog, Jasper, who eyed him from time to time, but made no move to approach.

'Now do you see?' Tom had drawn Father to the far side of the room, away from our group by the fire. 'These men mean our destruction. How could they treat an old woman so? An old woman out on the Fens by herself, doing no harm, and they have struck her and destroyed her home and stolen her livelihood. You must see that we can wait no longer for word from Sir John's lawman. We must act ourselves.'

I glanced across at them. My father ran his hand over his face and looked at Hannah. His eyes were troubled and for once he spoke hesitantly.

'It is unforgivable, what they have done. I will go myself to Sir John in the morning. If he has heard nothing from London, perhaps he will come and speak to Meneer van Slyke himself, put a stop to this and restore Hannah's home.'

In my mind's eye I could see that neat little cottage, now a heap of broken timbers and scattered bedding. I could smell the bonfire they made of it, and hear the crackling of the roasted pig, turning above it on a spit. Hannah's home would never be restored.

Chapter Three

The village was beginning to divide into two factions. The younger men, with Tom at their head, were all for attacking the drainage works at once, before they could do any more damage. Not only was Hannah's cottage destroyed and her stock stolen, but the other beasts grazing at common on the pasture were disturbed and fearful. They crowded to the far side of the large meadow, as far from the drainers' camp as they could get, and stayed together for safety. There were perhaps two hundred sheep, about seventy cattle, two pairs of working oxen, and five mares with foals running at heel, as well as two geldings, a stallion and three yearlings. With so much stock confined to one area of the pasture land, the grass soon grew thin and poached, and we saw that they would need to be persuaded to spread out or else moved to the hay meadow, which would mean no hay harvest for the winter.

At the same time, a number of the older men, the elders and leaders of the village, headed by my father, clung to the belief that Sir John would save the day. Sir John had indeed ridden over, not long after Hannah had sought sanctuary with us, and spoken to van Slyke. As a result, the drainers drove their ditch southwards only as far as the peat moor behind Hannah's cottage. This was designed to drain the Fen and run the drained water off into Baker's Lode. Once they had reached into the Fen and dug some cross-ditches, they worked back north from the beginning of their original ditch, across the pasture – thus cutting it in half and confining the grazing stock still further – and out through a corner of the wheat field to the Lode, destroying a quarter of the new crop as they went.

Bread would be short this winter.

They built a sluice gate where the new drain met the Lode, and began to construct a wind-driven pumping mill where Hannah's cottage had stood.

My mother owned a few pieces of blue-decorated Delft pottery, including a large platter which had been my grandmother's. It was used for high days, when we had a large ham or leg of mutton, and entertained friends. I had never taken much heed of the picture before, but now I was drawn out of curiosity to examine it where it was propped up on the kitchen dresser. The scene depicted was clearly Dutch: a canal in the foreground, with disproportionately small wherryboats plying to and fro, while a Dutch family looked on, twice the height of the boats, the man in baggy trousers and a tall hat. Beyond the canal was a cluster of houses, a village I suppose, and a tall windmill which (unlike the boats) was disproportionately large. In the past I had always assumed that the windmill was for grinding grain, like our English windmills, but Tom said no, that it served to pump water out of the Dutch farmland and deposit it in the canal.

The drainers' new windmill grew quickly on the edge of the Fen. They worked quickly, those men. Not for love of the work, I suspect, but because van Slyke was a ruthless master. It was built of timber (our timber) and before we knew what was afoot, a strange machine had been hauled in which Tom said was the pump. Soon after that they were constructing the sails. Laid flat out on the ground they seemed huge.

Still the older men forbade Tom and his friends from interfering with the work, clinging to the hope that Sir John would act on our behalf.

Then one night we saw fire over on the Fen.

Tom, coming in from driving the cows out to pasture, paused in the doorway, drawn to the flickering light.

'That's no cooking fire,' he said.

We crowded behind his shoulders, trying to decide where it could be. Sometimes odd flames would burst out on the marshes. Boggarts' fire, the old people called them, or jack-a-lanthorn or sometimes jenny-burnt-arse, set to lure folk astray to their doom in the quag. Gideon, who read books of the new natural sciences, said they were due to gases escaping from the marsh. This, however, was too big to be a marsh fire.

'That's near Nehemiah's place,' my father said.

'It couldn't be his cottage, could it?' My mother twisted her hands in her apron. Nehemiah liked his beer of an evening, and might have overturned a candle. Without another word, we hurried to gather up buckets, the five of us, my family and Kitty too, and set off at a run, leaving Hannah to mind the house.

As we drew nearer, stumbling through the dusk, we could see that it was indeed Nehemiah's cottage afire, and the blaze had taken vicious hold. The reed thatch set a fiery crown on the house, and fingers of flame were creeping down the timbers, making orange frames for the clay daub between. We rushed to fill our buckets in the mere and throw water helplessly over the cottage, but it was too much for us. More of our neighbours arrived and someone found a pitchfork and a rake, with which the men tried to drag the flaming thatch off the roof. Others formed a bucket chain, but we knew it was useless. Tom stripped off his shirt, soaked it in the mere, and tied it round his face.

'Be careful, Tom!' My mother clutched at his arm as he made for the cottage.

He put her hand aside. 'Where is Nehemiah? He may be within.'

Tom fought his way through the flaming doorway, but there was no sign of the eel-fisher. He emerged scorched but empty-handed.

By now it was growing full dark, with an overcast sky, moonless, starless. The only light came from the burning cottage. I groped my way further along the bank of the mere, beyond where our feet had slurried the mud of the shore. I must have been near the spot where Nehemiah moored his holding nets when I stumbled and fell over something in the dark. I reached out my hand and felt rough cloth. And smelled the unmistakable stink of eel. My heart tripped over like my feet as I pushed myself up and felt around me. My hand met something warm and sticky and I knew at once what it was. Bile rushed into my throat and for a moment I could not make a sound, then I croaked out, 'Nehemiah is here. He's hurt.'

Or dead, I thought. Poor old man. Heaven help him.

They came running to my side, my neighbours, dirty and tired, some of them with scorched hands or singed hair. Someone had had the sense to bring a candle lantern, which he had lit from a fragment of burning thatch. Nehemiah was lying face down in the muddy turf, his right arm outstretched toward the mere, the back of his head a mass of bloodied and tangled hair. Gideon knelt down opposite me and felt beneath Nehemiah's ear.

'He is still alive, though his heartbeat is weak. Help me to turn him over, Mercy. He could suffocate with his face in the mud like this.'

We eased him over on to his side with some difficulty, for he was a big man. He was limp in our hands like a child's rag doll. I pulled back my cap and tore off my head cloth so that I could bind his wound. It was a clumsy dressing, but the best I could do, in darkness with my knees in the mud and half my skirt in the mere. At least it would keep out the dirt and staunch the blood until we could carry him to shelter. As I tightened the bandage, Nehemiah moaned.

'What happened?' Gideon leaned over him. 'Can you tell us?'

But he did not respond.

Tom's friend Toby had taken the lantern over to the mere.

'His holding nets are gone.'

Gideon and I exchanged looks over the prone form of the eeler. I knew what he was thinking. The drainers' men had stolen them. Had they also attacked the eeler and fired his cottage? I pushed back the hair which had fallen over my face, and opened my mouth to speak, but Gideon shook his head and laid his finger on his lips.

The men contrived a sort of hammock from the oars and sail of Nehemiah's boat, a skerry which still lay undisturbed further along the shore of the mere, near the delph that led down to Baker's Lode. In this they carried him back to our house. It was not the nearest, but Hannah was there and we all knew that she was the most skilled woman in the village at caring for the sick and injured.

The following morning Nehemiah, salved and bandaged, had regained his wits, though his speech was slurred and he kept falling asleep. Tom and Father, and several of Tom's friends, who had come to us early, crowded into Kitty's small room off the kitchen, where Nehemiah had been put to bed the night before, while Kitty slept on a pallet in my room. I busied myself in the kitchen near the doorway, so that I could hear what was said.

'They came stealing my eels.' Nehemiah's voice was weak but indignant. 'I told them to bugger off. I'd see them in Hell first. There was five of them, three Dutchies and two Englishmen. Not any of them Scots. They keep them Scots chained up at night or they'd run off home. I'd have taken them all on.' His voice faded.

He would have fought them, I knew. Even though he was an old man now, past fifty, he had been a fighter in his youth, and he was still powerful.

'Did they fight you?' Tom asked.

I heard Nehemiah clear his throat to spit, then, no doubt remembering where he was, he coughed instead. There was a pause and I could hear someone giving him a drink.

'Not them, the cowards. They just grinned at me and went on hauling in my nets, when something hit me from behind. I didn't see them, but there must have been more coming up.' He stirred impatiently on the bed and the straw mattress rustled. 'I need to get back home and fetch in my traps. I'm due at Lincoln market today. I'll need to go down to the Lode.'

'You're going nowhere, with a wound the breadth of my palm in your head.' My father's voice was firm but kind. 'Hannah would roast us all alive if we let you out of that bed. You sleep a while. You'll feel better tomorrow.'

They trailed out of the room, shutting the door behind them, and I guessed from their uncomfortable looks that they had not told Nehemiah that he had no home left to go to. Or nets of eels to fetch.

Tom beckoned his friends Toby and Jack outside and through the window I watched them in a huddle beside the yard gate, arguing and gesturing. Then they seemed to come to some agreement. Tom raised his hand to the others as they left, then went away whistling to fetch in the cows for milking.

As soon as I had washed the dishes which had been neglected while our visitors lingered, and sent Kitty to fetch in water from the well-hus, I helped Mother mix up the day's batch of bread dough. When I had laid it in the bread trough with a cloth over it to prove, and my mother was sitting at her spinning, I went out to the barn, where Tom had just finished milking. We carried the pails through to the dairy and poured the cream off. I stirred rennet into a large tub of milk and left it to curdle for cheese-making.

'Well,' I said, leaning my back against the bench and looking up at Tom, who was smiling secretively to himself. 'What have you and the others been plotting?'

He hesitated, then could hold back the words no longer.

'We will not wait another day for Sir John's invisible lawyer. We will act tonight.'

I felt a lurch of fear in my stomach, and yet I caught a little of his excitement too.

'What do you mean to do?'

'You must say nothing. Not a word to Father.'

'I can hold my tongue.'

'We'll ride over tonight and cast their earthed-up banks down into the ditches they have dug. Break up the sluice gate. If we can, we'll fire their mill. They are not the only men who can set fire to others' property.'

'It will be dangerous.'

'Aye. But no more dangerous than sitting here like sheep, waiting to be slaughtered.'

No. I remembered the feel of Nehemiah's bloodied scalp under my hand, and Hannah stumbling into our kitchen with her old hen and a few pots of honey. Both of them with their homes burnt to the ground, their few possessions gone, beggared in their old age. What would become of them? We had taken them in for now, but our farm could barely support us these last few years – years of mouldy crops and grain withered in the ear. How could we feed two more mouths?

39

By afternoon, Nehemiah had insisted on getting out of his bed, though his trembling legs would carry him no further than the bench by the vegetable garden. He had persuaded Tom to cut him a sheaf of withies and begged a ball of twine from me. Now he sat from dinner until the light faded, weaving new eel traps and holding nets. There was a grim set to his mouth, so I guessed someone had told him of the fire.

After we had supped I took my candle to my room, but did not undress. Instead I sat on the edge of my bed, straining my ears to the sounds of the house. Kitty, clearly feeling out of place on my floor, had dragged her pallet up the ladder to the attic room where Hannah slept. I could hear them moving about overhead, and the soft murmur of their voices. My parents came upstairs next and were soon silent, exhausted after the troubles of the last two days. Tom was still downstairs in the kitchen. I heard him throw another log on the fire and kick it into place, then the creak of the chair as he sat down.

I made up my mind. I blew out my candle, picked up my shoes and crept out of my room. Heavy breathing came from behind my parents' door, with an occasionally snort from Father. Nothing could be heard from the attic. I stole down the stairs, keeping to the inside edge which I had known from childhood would not creak. Tom and I had had our night-time excursions in the past.

In the kitchen Tom was moving about purposefully now. He had taken down the short sword that hung on two pegs over the door and strapped it to his waist. He was fitting a tallow candle into a lantern as I crept in.

'Tom,' I whispered, making him jump so that he nearly dropped the lantern.

He shook his head and pointed to the room where Nehemiah lay. There was no sound of heavy breathing, so perhaps he was still awake. I put on my shoes, then took down my cloak from its peg by the door. Tom frowned and shook his head again, but I ignored him. I looked around the kitchen. We possessed only that one sword, an ancient one, come down the family, but I would not go unarmed. I took the largest kitchen knife from the rack and tucked it into my sash, where it pressed uncomfortably into my side. Then

I walked out into the yard. My heart was beating fast and my breath caught in my chest. We were about to break the law.

Tom followed me, pulling the door to behind him with great care. It gave its usual small squeak and we froze, but there was no sign from the house that anyone had heard. Tom seized me by the elbow and steered me toward the barn.

'What are you doing? Why have you taken that knife?' He was keeping his voice down, but I could see he was angry.

'I am coming too. And I thought I should come armed.' I knew I sounded foolish.

He sucked in his breath, then gave a soft laugh. 'Very well. I suppose our women and girls have as much right as we to be avenged. Our grandfather had women amongst his followers. But you must keep out of our way.'

He headed into the barn.

'Why–?' then I saw our gelding Blaze tied up in his stall. So that was where Tom had slipped off to after supper.

'You are going to ride? But it isn't far.'

'We may need to come away in a hurry. They cannot pursue us on horseback. They have no horses but the two ponies who draw their carts.'

'Then we must needs ride two to a horse.'

'Very well, if you are sure you want to come. There may be fighting. No place for a girl.'

I shrugged, but I licked my lips, which suddenly felt dry. 'As you say, I have as much right as you.'

It was strange, that ride through the night, as I sat bareback with my skirts hitched up and my arms around my brother's waist. Darkness and dew had brought out the spring scents along the lane, green scents of new growth, and the horse's shoulder brushed the last petals of cherry blossom over us. After the cold spring, the apple trees were only now in flower, and we were soon be-dabbled with pink and white petals. There was the merest sliver of a new moon, barely enough to see our direction, but the horse knew the lane and made his way confidently, though it was mired and muddy from the drainers' heavy traffic. I could hear courting frogs in the Lode, which lay here on our right, and an occasional murmur from birds half asleep in the hedgerows. A hoolet swooped suddenly close overhead, busy hunting for mice, and the horse jinked sideways, but he was a steady beast and soon calmed. As we reached the edge of the village I was aware of dark shapes looming up near us, a jingle from a bridle, and a whoosh of breath from an unseen horse. The darkness of the night seemed warmer from the press of bodies around us.

Tom murmured a greeting and there were soft words in reply, amongst which I heard 'your sister'. He reassured them that I would not be a hindrance as we turned our horses and made first for the section of the ditch in the pasture which was furthest from the encampment, where we dismounted and the men found me suddenly useful as horse-minder. Along with the others, Tom had brought a shovel, and soon they were working eagerly, lined up along the ditch and shovelling back the banked up earth so recently dug out. They did not try to return every morsel of earth to its rightful place – there would not be time and dark enough for that – but concentrated instead on blocking the ditch so it could not carry water.

We worked our way down the end of the pasture and across the wheat field to the new sluice gate and the Lode, the men shovelling all the way, and I bringing up the horses in relays.

'Why have they put a sluice here?' I asked Tom, as he paused to wipe the sweat off his face with his sleeve and to take a swig from the beer jack someone had brought.

He shook his head. 'They don't understand our natural flooding and drainage. If a lot of water comes down from the Fen through this ditch, and they close the sluice, the water will back up and flood the village. They are fools! They may have great skill at keeping the sea at bay, but our Fens are very different.'

A voice hailed us from the Lode. We were less careful to keep our voices down, now that we were some distance from the camp. The Waters twins, Joseph's nephews, had poled an old leaky punt down the Lode and were now tying it up to the sluice gate. They jumped out, their feet and stockings wet through.

'It's too wet,' someone called. 'It won't burn.'

'Dry enough except the bottom six inches,' said John Waters. 'Who has the hassocks?'

There was a great noise of crackling and snapping, as some of the lads dragged great bundles of dried marsh grass out from under the hedge, where they must have hidden them earlier. These they passed down to John's twin, Dick, who piled them up in the punt until they formed a teetering mound four or five feet above the gunwales. We all stood back to admire their handiwork. I understood now what they planned to do.

'As soon as that flares up, someone will see it,' I said. 'The drainers will be down on us.'

'Mercy is right,' said Toby. 'Those of us going to the mill had best be off. Give us a few minutes' start.'

Tom mounted Blaze and reached down to give me a hand up. Toby and three or four others mounted as well. While the rest of our party remained behind at the sluice, we rode as fast as we could back up the lane, then cut across the pasture to Hannah's old cottage plot, where the half-built mill reared up against the sky. There was still little moonlight, but I had been out in the night long enough now that even the starlight seemed bright. It was a world of blue-black and silver, with the outline of the mill looming in dark menace ahead of us. There was something missing. I realised then that Hannah's ancient cider tree had been hacked down, not even its nubbin left standing. The new-flowering branches lay broken and sprawled in the mud. Over to our right I could make out the dull gleam of the drainers' cooking fires damped down for the night, but no one seemed to be stirring there.

Then suddenly the night was lit up by a vast tongue of fire which rose up behind us in a column of scarlet and yellow. The others had been too impatient to fire the sluice and we were not ready.

'Quick!' Toby shouted. There was no use keeping silent now.

Tom and the others leapt from their horses and ran towards the mill. I slid down and led Blaze nearer, peering with eyes half blinded by that sudden burst of light. There were shouts from the encampment, while nearby I could make out Toby striking flint and cursing. A small flower of flame budded and caught, and they were all making twists of hay for torches. Hannah's hay, I realised,

43

still left lying here when everything else was gone. There was something grimly satisfying in that.

I was no longer prepared to stand by and watch. I dropped Blaze's reins and ran forward to make my own twist of hay.

Tom saw me. 'Here!'

He held his torch out towards me and I lit mine from the tip of his, then we ran forward together to thrust our flaming brands in with the others, between the joints of the half-built mill. The wood was dry and crisp and caught at once. We could hear pandemonium from the encampment and make out the flash of swords as a stream of men headed towards the sluice.

'Back to the horses!' Tom shouted and we began to run.

But not all the drainers had headed to the Lode. Suddenly there was Piet van Slyke, not twenty yards away, and in the light from the mill, now well ablaze, I saw him raise a gun and fire.

Tom gave a shout of pain and stumbled against me, then collapsed on the ground. I could not lift him. Cold panic seized me. Was he dead?

'Help me! Toby! Jack! Tom is shot!'

They ran to me and hauled Tom to his feet. He gasped. 'My leg. Can't. Stand. My leg.'

We could all see the blood pouring from his thigh. Already his breeches were blackened.

'He can't walk,' said Toby. 'Can he ride?'

'Help me get him on the horse,' I said, 'I'll manage. Quick. Van Slyke and his men are coming.'

Somehow we got Tom on to Blaze and Toby gave me a leg up behind him. I reached round Tom for the reins, holding him in place as best I could. As I kicked Blaze and urged him on, I could see the others scrambling on to their horses. In a pack, we wheeled our mounts and galloped down the field, scaring a few sheep who had wandered from the main flock. Something whizzed past my head and at the same moment I heard the crack of van Slyke's gun. He was still firing at us, but we were gaining on our pursuers. In the lane we passed the other drainers running toward the sluice. One burly Dutchman stepped into our path to try to stop us, but we rode him down and he jumped out of the way. I heard Tom give a triumphant croak, then he went slack in my arms. I struggled to stop him sliding off.

At the village boundary where we had gathered earlier, we paused briefly.

'Better disperse,' said Toby. 'Rub down your horses so they don't give you away. And hold your peace. Everyone in the village will have seen the fires by now. Not everyone will keep their tongues behind their teeth.'

'Fires?' I said recklessly. 'What fires?'

Someone laughed and I felt a surge of excitement and pride. We had succeeded. Tom was hurt, but surely the wound would not be serious.

'Can you manage Tom the rest of the way?' Jack asked.

'Aye,' I said, 'I can manage.'

And so we ended our first attack on the drainers.

There was no hiding Tom's wound from the rest of the household. Father heard Blaze clatter into the yard and came out holding a lantern above his head to see what was afoot. Our dog Jasper was at his heels, but gave a welcoming bark, not a warning against intruders. Father raised the lantern and looked up at me, shock and anger chasing each other across his face.

'Mercy? What are you about? And what is wrong with Tom?'

Tom by now was slumped sideways against my arm and it was all I could do to stop him slipping to the ground. Explanations could wait.

'Help me, Father. Tom is hurt and I can't hold him.'

My father steadied Tom on Blaze's back while I slid to the ground, then between us we lifted Tom down. By now the rest of the household was out in the yard in their night clothes, Mother white with fear, Kitty hiding behind Hannah. Despite his broken head, Nehemiah helped us carry Tom into the kitchen and lay him on the settle.

'Kitty,' I said, 'take Blaze into the barn and hang up his bridle. He'll need to be rubbed down and given some feed. He's worked hard tonight.'

She dipped her head in acknowledgement and ran outside. She was a little afraid of horses, but I knew I could trust her to do her best. I turned back to the kitchen, where Mother had stripped off Tom's jacket and Hannah was leaning over him, examining the wound.

'That's a bullet wound,' she said, 'and a nasty one. It's not come out 'tother side. It'll be lodged in his flesh.'

She rolled up her sleeves and turned to me. 'Fetch me a bowl of hot water, Mercy, and rags. This'll bleed a fair bit. And I'll need . . .' Her eyes lit on the knife at my side. I had forgotten it was there and glanced nervously over my shoulder, where my mother was sitting in her chair, her hands over her face, weeping.

'I'll have that.' Hannah pointed to the knife and I handed it to her. What was she going to do?

I fetched water and rags, then climbed up to the attic for a pot of Hannah's salve.

'Unfasten his belt,' Hannah said, when I handed her the salve, 'And lay aside that fool sword.' She clucked her tongue in irritation as I laid the sword on the floor and rolled up Tom's belt. Carefully I eased his breeches down until his whole thigh was exposed, a mass of broken flesh and fragments of cloth.

'He'll be wanting that,' she said, nodding at the belt.

Suddenly I realised what she was going to do and felt sick, but my mother was in no state to help her. Tom moaned and opened his eyes.

'My leg,' he said.

'Never fear,' I said, patting his shoulder. 'Hannah is here and she's going to take the bullet out.'

His mouth screwed up as he took in my meaning. Silently I handed him the belt and he gripped it between his teeth. Hannah pulled away the torn pieces of cloth from his leg, then picked up the knife and made two swift slashes across the mangled flesh of his thigh. Tom gave a muffled yelp through the leather of the belt and gripped my hand so hard I thought the bones would break. Hannah probed into the wound with the point of the knife, then something flew across the room and landed with a clink in the hearth. Blood was pouring out of Tom's leg and with my free hand I tried to staunch it with the rags, but they were soon sodden.

'I have to fetch more rags,' I whispered in Tom's ear, drawing my hand from his. His face was grey with pain and he nodded as the belt slipped from between his teeth and fell to the floor. Then he became very still.

I found I was weeping.

'Oh, Hannah, he isn't dead, is he?'

She shook her head. 'Just lost his wits with the pain. Wash out the wound and salve it, Mercy. Then bind it up.'

I realised that Hannah herself was pale and shaking. She sank down on a bench beside the table and laid her head on her crossed arms. As I washed Tom's wound, which looked even worse now, I heard Father pouring ale for Hannah and Mother. My own hands were trembling, but I managed to smear Hannah's salve over the torn flesh, though my own flesh cringed as I did so. I wrapped a length of cloth torn from an old sheet around and around Tom's leg, but the blood continued to seep through it.

Hannah must have raised her head and seen my face, for she said, 'It will stop bleeding soon. There's herbs to dry the blood in the salve.'

I nodded. I felt too sick to speak. When I had done my best with the bandage, I cleared away the bloodied water and rags. There was a dull glint of something on the hearth and I picked it up. It was a lead bullet, smeared with blood, once round but now flattened and distorted.

'It must have hit the bone.' It was the first time Father had spoken since we had carried Tom into the kitchen. He picked up the bullet from my palm and turned it around between his fingers. 'That's what has pushed it out of shape. He's lucky it didn't break his thighbone.'

He sighed deeply. I had expected him to be angry, but he merely looked defeated.

'Tomorrow you will tell me what happened. Tonight we must go to our beds.'

'I'll stay with Tom,' I said. 'He may need something when he wakes.'

He nodded and dropped the bullet back into my hand.

When they had all gone, I made up the fire and brought the coverlet from my bed to lay over Tom, who lay lost in some silent world, his face drawn. I could see in the lines of his face how he would look when he was old. Drawing up a chair close beside the settle, I sank down, finding my legs suddenly weak beneath me. How had it ended like this? These intruders brought us nothing but pain and suffering. And I feared there would be retribution.

In the light from the fire, I turned the flattened bullet over and over in my hand.

Chapter Four

Father and I faced each other across the table. Tom still lay on the settle, grey-faced but awake, after a night of pain and bad dreams. Now was the reckoning. I drew breath to speak, but Tom forestalled me.

'You must not blame Mercy, Father.' His voice was weak, but firm. 'Without her I would have died.'

Father flicked him a cold glance. I rarely feared my father, but I knew that this time his anger, held back and damped down, would be scorching when it broke out.

'I blame you both,' he said. The calmness of his voice was more frightening than any shouting. 'These drainers will not be defeated by riots and fires. They must be defeated at law. What you did last night makes our case worse.'

'Father.' Tom struggled to sit up, but sank back again. 'We have a royal charter declaring our commons inalienable. Yet this projection of drainage and enclosure – whether or not Cromwell is responsible – marches on with no one to say it nay. Sir John made us promises two months ago, yet nothing has come to our aid.' His voice faded and he closed his eyes.

'They have attacked our people.' I knew my father would think I spoke out of turn. This was not women's business. But sitting awake beside Tom all night, I had had time to think. Last night I had acted spontaneously, following in Tom's wake as so often in our lives, but now I needed to make clear to our father why I believed Tom was right to act.

'Hannah and Nehemiah – their homes have been burned to the ground, their goods and stock stolen or destroyed, their livelihoods taken from them. How can we stand by and do nothing? We know, all of us, what has happened in the Fens where these foreign drainers have been at work. Land ruined, homes washed away yet peat dried to dust, whole villages which used to prosper turned to beggary.'

I held out my hands to him, pleading. 'It will be the same for us, surely? Their misguided works will flood the village at the next great storm. We could lose the farm.'

Father stared at me.

'Do you believe that, Mercy?'

'Aye. Truly I do believe that. We must act.'

'Mercy is right.' Tom's voice came weak from where he lay.

Father passed his hand over his face and I saw that his anger was ebbing away, leaving him tired and perhaps a little frightened.

'You are right that we have waited too long for word from Sir John's London lawman.'

It was a concession. Unusual from him.

He got up and walked to the door. Throwing it open, he stood framed in the doorway, looking out across our land, with its rich level fields and the wide arched skies of these eastern counties. For a long time no one said anything. At last he came back and sat down again at the table.

'It seems we must act for ourselves, but not by breaking down banks and setting fire to sluice gates and pumping mills. I will take our case to the authorities in Lincoln. It may be that our local magistrates will take more interest in local affairs and local charters than the courts away in London.'

Tom and I exchanged a look. I knew that he had little faith in the workings of the law, but a faint hope stirred in me at Father's words. Perhaps our land could be saved after all without further violence.

A shadow passed over the floor as Gideon stepped into the doorway.

'So,' he said, soberly, taking in the sight of Tom's sickly pallor and heavily bandaged leg, 'what they are saying in the village is true.'

I looked at him in alarm. 'It is being spoken about?'

'Only amongst ourselves. But van Slyke is bent on hunting out the miscreants who burned down his mill and his sluice and filled in more than half his ditches. He is on the hunt, moreover, for one whom he winged last night, although he escaped.'

Tom gave him a shaky smile. 'Mercy carried me home on Blaze, else I had been left to his thugs to finish me off.'

'Mercy was there!' Gideon was startled. He looked at me in concern, but I avoided his eyes. I was not sure whether I was pleased or annoyed. 'Well, I came to warn you. It would be best to keep Tom out of sight just at present, in case van Slyke and his men come ferreting about.'

'They cannot enter our homes. They have no right!' Father stood up indignantly.

'No right, indeed. But they are armed. They are many. And they are, I imagine, unscrupulous. You had best hide Tom until that very unpleasant wound is healed.'

We looked at each other. Where could he be hidden? The house was easy to search.

'The hay loft?' I suggested hesitantly.

'I could never climb up there.' Tom shook his head.

'The hay loft seems a wise suggestion,' said Gideon. 'I can carry you.'

Tom protested, but Gideon was adamant. Despite his clerkly calling, he was strong and in the peak of life. Tom had always been slight, but even so I was surprised at how easily Gideon lifted him. I went ahead of them to the barn, carrying the coverlet and cushions, and climbed the ladder to the loft. In the far corner I made up a crude bed and watched as Gideon climbed awkwardly after me, with Tom over his shoulder and Father steadying him from behind. We laid Tom down in a nest of straw and I tucked the coverlet around him. He was sweating with pain, but kept his lips compressed against the escape of any sound.

When he was as comfortable as we could make him, we piled up hay to form a low wall, to conceal him as best we could.

'You must stay very quiet,' I warned.

'Teach your grandmother.' Tom's voice was faint but defiant.

'I'll bring you dinner later.'

'Good. I'll sleep till then.'

We climbed back down into the barn and looked at each other as we brushed the wisps of hay from our clothes.

'Sleep is the best thing for him,' Gideon said.

I nodded.

'Come,' said my father. 'I would discuss with you a plan I have, to go to the magistrates in Lincoln.'

As I baked bread and set to making the midday dinner with Kitty, they sat beside the fire, talking in low voices. Gideon, as a man of the cloth, would favour Father's plan, I was sure. Peaceful action rather than fire and violence. Which of us was right?

There had been no sign of Hannah or my mother this morning, after the disturbances of the night. Hannah was old and frail, but my mother was usually up and about her chores one of the first of us. For her to lie abed was a sign how badly she had taken Tom's injury. She appeared at the bottom of the stairs just as Kitty was laying out bowls and spoons for my pottage of bacon, carrots and turnips. I was shocked to see that my mother seemed suddenly to have grown old, yet she was twenty years younger than Hannah. There were dark pouches beneath her eyes and a careless strand of grey hair strayed from beneath her cap. She sank down on her chair at the foot of the table and I saw that her hands, loosely clasped in her lap, were trembling.

Kitty began to ladle out the pottage and I took a bowl of it together with a cup of small ale for Tom, slipping a spoon and a thick slice of bread into my pocket. It was difficult climbing the ladder in the barn with my burden and I had to make two trips. Tom was asleep, but stirred groggily as I squatted down beside him and set the cup of beer on the ledge made by one of the roof beams. I eased my arm under his shoulders and helped him to sit up.

'Did you sleep?'

'Aye.' His voice was muzzy, as if he had only half woken. He looked worse than he had done that morning.

'I've brought you a bowl of pottage.' I balanced the bread on his chest and handed him the spoon. He let it dangle limply, as if its weight was too much for him.

'Come, you must eat.'

He looked with complete indifference at the bowl I held out.

'Put it over there.' He nodded toward the cup of ale. 'I'll eat it later.'

'You'll eat it now, not leave it to go cold and greasy.'

I took the spoon back from him, and began to spoon the pottage into his mouth. He did not resist me and I thought of making some remark about feeding babes, but – seeing the exhaustion in his eyes – I thought better of it.

In the end, he took it all, and the ale, and most of the bread, and a little colour had come back into his face by the time I left him to return to my own dinner. The others were finishing as I warmed the pottage again and took my seat at the table.

'How is he?' Gideon asked.

'He has eaten his meal,' I said, keeping to myself that I had had to feed him. 'He seems very tired.'

Gideon nodded. 'That's often the way after a wounding. The body directs all its energy towards healing. I've seen it many times.'

With a jolt I remembered that for a while Gideon had served as minister with the local militia in the early days of the War. He would have seen many wounded men during those days of terrible, chaotic slaughter. After the militias were disbanded and the New Model Army formed, Gideon had come back to the Fens. He was not wanted in an army commanded by Puritans. Of course he had comforted the wounded and dying. I was ashamed that I had forgotten his own terrible experiences on the battlefield.

'You have seen musket wounds, like this of Tom's?' Father asked.

Gideon nodded. 'This is cleaner than most, and Hannah removed the bullet quickly. The bone is undamaged and the wound scoured out. The only thing to fear is if the bullet was dirty, or filth got into the wound in some other way, lest it turn putrid.'

'Hannah puts honey in her salves,' I said hesitantly. 'She says it is a sovereign cure for broken flesh.'

'So I have heard.'

'Has she eaten?' I was aware that I had not seen her yet, nor Nehemiah.

'Kitty took her dinner up to her.' It was the first time my mother had spoken.

'And Nehemiah?'

My father shrugged. 'He has gone to move his skerry down the delph to Baker's Lode, away from the encampment. He'll moor it nearer to where he lays his traps and walk over each day.'

'But his head–'

'He claims his poll is as hard as an iron cooking pot. He will not listen. He will go to Lincoln with me tomorrow, so at least I can keep a watch on him.'

The day carried on like any normal day and I was laying out the washing on the lavender hedge to dry when Alice came round the corner of the house. She was full of news.

'They have been searching the village,' she called, even before she reached me. Her Rafe had not been one of the party last night, but her brother had.

'Take an end of this sheet,' I said, 'and keep your voice down. Van Slyke's men? Have they seized anyone?'

She took hold of the other end of the sheet and we shook it straight before spreading it out over the hedge.

'Not yet. They beat little Rob Higson, to try to make him talk, but he wouldn't. He slipped their hold in the end and made for the Fen. They won't find him.'

'He wasn't there last night.'

'But you were?' She looked at me quizzically. 'What were you about?'

'Defending our lands,' I said, shaking out a pillow bere till it snapped. 'Why Rob?'

'Oh, I think he was the first child they caught, and they thought they could make him talk.'

She looked around the yard, which was quiet and sleepy under the sun, except for a few hens scratching. 'Where is Tom?'

'Somewhere they won't find him. Have they searched the houses in the village?'

'Indeed. Turned us upside down. Broke open linen coffers, smashed dishes, pulled down wall-hangings, pretending men might be hiding behind them.' She gave a furious snort. 'Villains and fools, they are. Everything is open to view. They had no need to wreck our homes. The men are mostly out hoeing in the fields, so they thought they could use violence against the women. The horses are all rested by now, of course. No sign of galloping through the night.'

I nodded. Blaze was back out in the pasture, under the drainers' very noses.

'I'd best go back.' She laid her hand on my arm. 'Be careful, Mercy.'

'I will. Like you, we are open to view, but my father and Gideon are inside, so perhaps they will be less ready to do damage here.'

When she had gone, I whistled for Jasper and cut across the fields to the pasture to call in the cows. I had no need of the dog, for the cows knew to come home at their milking time, but I felt safer with him beside me. As I herded them back along the lane, I noticed how the muddy surface, churned up by the drainers' activities, was pock-marked with the hoof-prints of our horses. Van Slyke and his men had only to follow them to find us. The thought chilled me, but at the corner where we had gathered, I saw that someone had been out with pick and shovel, breaking up the surface of the lane, so that the tracks leading back to the village and our farm were obliterated. Someone had had the foresight to come out early, to outfox the drainers. I was smiling as I drove the cows into their stalls.

But I was not smiling an hour later when van Slyke walked into the yard. He had six men with him, six large Hollanders. Perhaps he did not trust his Englishmen to hunt out their fellow countrymen. He went first into the house. I finished milking, carried the milk through to the dairy, but did not lead the cows back to pasture yet. I wanted to remain here to confront van Slyke and keep him away from the loft. We had hidden the ladder in plain view, around the back of the house, where my father was making much of pinning down a piece of the reed thatch which had worked loose. We did not want the ladder to draw van Slyke's eye up to the loft.

In the dairy I set some of the milk for cheese-making and unhooked two muslin cloths holding curds which had been hanging up to drain all night. I packed the curds into a large cheese-press, covered them with the lid, and laid a stone on top to weigh it down. Then I poured the rest of the new milk into the churn for butter-making, so that I could keep my hands busy when van Slyke came to the outbuildings. The men were not long in the house. My father had welcomed them in courteously, and no doubt had escorted them into every room. Soon they were crossing the yard. I had rolled the churn into the doorway of the dairy and sat on a high stool as I worked the paddle. To block the doorway to the barn would have been to invite suspicion, but from here I could watch where they went.

'Ah. Mevrouw Mercy, not so?' He stood square in front of me, younger than I had thought from a distance, perhaps of an age with Gideon Clarke, thirty or thereabouts. A good-looking man enough, in that heavy Dutch fashion. He doffed his hat to me, but still wore that supercilious expression.

I inclined my head very slightly. 'I am Mercy Bennington.'

'And your brother is Thomas Bennington. Somewhat of a leader amongst your young men, I hear. And both of you grandchildren of the famous Nathaniel Bennington.'

I held my tongue and worked the churn. The milk slapped the wooden sides, nowhere near coming to butter. I was sure that he was guessing when he said Tom was a leader. No one in the village would have named him. He was deducing from our grandfather's fame and our father's position as the most prosperous yeomen farmer in the parish. Reasonable enough. I did not take him for a fool.

'And where is he, this brother of yours? Meneer Thomas Bennington? He is not in the house. He is not in the fields, weeding the crops with the other young men. Is he catching eels? Shooting waterfowl?'

A knot had formed in my stomach. Could he have recognised Tom when he shot him in the dark? Surely not. I rested my hands from the paddle, and felt the lump of the lead bullet in the pocket of my apron. I cupped my hand over it, as if he could see through the cloth, and raised innocent eyes.

'My brother is gone to Lincoln market, two days since, sir. We think of purchasing a new bull for the breeding. Our bull was old and was slaughtered last Martinmas.'

We had contrived this story between us, Father, Gideon and I, to account for Tom's absence. There was a grain of truth in it. My father did plan to buy a new bull, though not yet.

Van Slyke studied me as I took up the paddle and heard the change in the milk. The butter was forming.

'Your pardon, sir.' I rolled the churn past their boots and into the dairy, then called across to Kitty, who was folding the dried washing.

'Come and finish the butter for me, Kitty. I must take the cows back to pasture.'

The men made a show of searching the dairy, but everything was open to view: the churns, the racks of drying cheeses, the big press of new curds. There was no corner where anything larger than a mouse could hide.

When Kitty had lifted the lid of the churn and scooped out the fresh butter to drain on the earthenware sieve, I went into the cowbarn and called Jasper after me. He circled the Hollanders, belly to the ground and growling low in his throat. One of the men aimed a kick at him, and I swirled around, ready to fight, but van Slyke shook his head at the man and said something in Dutch.

I turned the cows out of their stalls and made a noisy business of it, so that Tom would hear what was afoot and lie low. Jasper circled the cows, and I took up my stick. More slowly than usual, I herded the cows out into the yard, where they milled about. They were hearty beasts and some of the Hollanders retreated from them, looking nervous. Not countrymen, then, I thought. Van Slyke gave an order, again in Dutch and the men moved reluctantly into the barn, edging around the cows nervously. They picked their way amongst the straw and manure, peering into the stalls, and poking half-heartedly into corners.

'I must drive the beasts back to our pasture,' I said, turning a smile on van Slyke. 'Where you are camped. Usually the men drive them. It is difficult for me on my own. Perhaps you and your men could help?'

If he suspected my lie, he did not show it. He shrugged and jerked his head at the men. As courteous as good neighbours, we headed the cows out of the yard and up the lane. Even Jasper played his part, running along beside van Slyke as if he had known him all his life.

The next morning, Father and Nehemiah left for Lincoln. They were to take Nehemiah's skerry up Baker's Lode to the bridge that carried the old Roman road over the waterway. There they would meet the carter who regularly took Nehemiah and his baskets of eels on to Lincoln. That evening the eeler returned alone.

'Isaac has taken a room as the White Hart,' he said, 'and will hunt out a magistrate's clerk tomorrow, to ask what he must do to bring our case to court.' He shook his head doubtfully. 'I've never seen any man prosper at law but the lawmen themselves.'

He laid a worn purse on the table, which chinked faintly.

'This is for you, Abigail. For my board and lodging.'

'Nay.' My mother was flustered. 'You owe us nothing. If we cannot take in a friend who has suffered grief, what sort would we be? Keep your eel money.'

I left them arguing and went out to Tom. All day I had felt as though someone was watching the farm, though in truth I had seen no one. Yet I made sure that whenever I crossed the yard I was busy about some chore. Now I carried a broom and after using it to chase the hens into their house for the night, I swept the dairy floor vigorously before I went into the barn.

'So he has truly followed this plan of going to law.' Tom shook his head, just as Nehemiah had done. 'I think it foolish. Who will pay the costs? Does Father pay everything?'

'I don't know. Is it very costly?'

He gave a sarcastic laugh. 'Why do you think lawyers are always so prosperous, even when their clients have no shirt to cover their backs? Oh aye, it is costly. And the seasons of the year move more swiftly than proceedings at court. He must stay in Lincoln while the days and weeks drag by, and what shall we do in place of his labour? I cannot work yet. You cannot take on the labours of two men.'

'Kitty is hard-working and willing.'

'Kitty is a child, with arms no thicker than that broomstick. Mother has her own work. Hannah is too old to do more than a little about the house.'

'Nehemiah.'

'I grant you Nehemiah, but he will be most of the time at his eeling. He must needs fish, for it's how he gets his living.'

'At least we are at a quiet time. The fields are planted.'

'They will need to be hoed. We cannot expect our neighbours to take on our share.'

'I can hoe.'

'And it will be sheep-shearing soon, before I am able, I'm afraid. And then hay harvest.'

I turned away, trying to hide my tears. I knew that everything Tom said was true, and I agreed with him. How could I manage the men's work on the farm?

He reached out and patted my hand. 'I will do my best to recover quickly. Ask Toby and Jack to come and see me. After dark would be best.'

'Aye.' I hesitated. 'I feel as though someone is watching us, watching the farm, but perhaps it is just in my mind.'

'Or your guilty conscience?' He gave me a weak smile. 'You dealt very well with van Slyke yesterday, but it's wise to be cautious.'

Jack and Toby came to visit Tom two evenings later. I do not know what passed between them, but I found that nearly half our strips in the common fields had been hoed when next I went out to them, and when sheep-shearing came, they each gave me a day of their labour. Between us we sheared the whole flock. In earlier years I had helped with herding the sheep into the pens and driving them back out to pasture when they were clipped, but now for the first time I learned to wield the shears myself. Alice's husband Rafe was our champion shearer, and he came on the first day and took me in hand. I could not manage the older and heavier sheep, but he taught me how to heave the yearlings on to their backs between my knees, where they would suddenly become still, as if startled out of their wits. I nicked a few sides, and left some clumps of unsheared wool, but I grew better with each sheep and found that I loved the way the whole fleece would peel off at last, like a fat alderman shedding his fur robe. The naked sheep, full of skittish airs, would go leaping away, and I could throw the fleece over the hurdle to be bundled up by Kitty. Next year, I would be able to handle the full-grown sheep.

No word came from Father, but Nehemiah sought him out when next he went to Lincoln. He no longer went every week, for his catch of eels had fallen away. It seemed they did not like the disturbance caused by the drainers and many had taken themselves off to quieter waters. This time, however, Nehemiah had snared two dozen wild ducks and so returned to Lincoln soon after Father's arrival there.

'I have brought a letter from Isaac,' said Nehemiah, sitting down with us to evening supper. I was tired and grubby from the last day of shearing, and Tom was back amongst us again. The wound in his leg seemed to be healing cleanly, but he was not yet fit to work. However, he wanted to be seen about the farm, in case we were being watched. There was, of course, no new bull to show for his supposed trip to Lincoln, but we put it about that he had not found one to his liking.

My mother could read a little, though not well, and of late had needed to hold the paper out at arm's length. She needed spectacles, but they were a luxury she said we could not afford. She passed the letter to Tom. He read through it quickly, then shrugged.

'There is nothing to report. He has made the rounds of the magistrates' clerks, and they but pass him from hand to hand. He has some hopes of one Master Gillivray, but he is away at the Court of Common Pleas in London, and does not return for another week. He sends his remembrance to us all and will write again when there is anything to tell.'

The weather turned wet and windy after that, day after day beating down the grass in the hay medland. It was nearly time for hay harvest, but if the weather did not turn soon, we would lose it all. It seemed as though every year since King and Parliament fell out the very weather wept, spoiling the grain in the ear, beating the hay to the ground, festering mould in the crops, disease in the cattle and ague amongst the people. Tom was now able to help with the milking, but could not walk far enough to drive the cows to and from pasture, so that it fell to me twice every day. The rain had revived the poor grass in the area where the stock huddled, but it had turned the lane to a ginger-hued slurry and pocked the fields with plashes which shone dull pewter whenever the sun showed briefly through the clouds.

As I walked with the cows near the drainers' work, I saw that some of their ditches were filling with sluggish water, but also that the ground had grown so soft that when they tried to dig further ditches the earth collapsed and slithered back down into their holes as fast as they could dig them. Our own land was fighting back against them. In the end they took to their shelters, where I sometimes glimpsed them through their doorways dicing and drinking. Van Slyke strode about his muddy works, glowering, his boots sucking at every step.

At last the clouds cleared, the wind dropped, and we had fair weather. Tom managed to walk as far as the hay medland.

'The hay is fine and dry,' he said, dropping wearily into Father's chair. 'I've been into the village. We'll begin mowing tomorrow.'

'And the crop?' I said.

He shook his head. 'Not of the best. Some of it is so laid that it cannot be saved.'

'All things seem to conspire against us,' I said.

Every able-bodied man, woman and child from the village turned out for the hay-making. The survival of our beasts over the winter depended on the hay. If the supply was too little, it would mean more of the stock must be slaughtered at Martinmas, which meant reduced flocks and herds next year. This had happened four years running now. Little by little we were being stripped back to near poverty.

All day we laboured under a sun which – having hidden itself away so long – now blazed down on us. Under the shade of my woven straw hat, I swung a scythe along with the men as we worked our way in a rhythmic wave across the medland. The older women and young girls worked along the edges with their smaller sickles, while the old men followed behind us, raking the hay into rows. Babies were laid in the shade of the line of sallows that ran along Baker's Lode, the smallest children ran about getting underfoot and trying (unsuccessfully) to catch the rabbits which bolted ahead of our line of reapers. A few of the women tended the great flagons of beer and baskets of food, amongst them Alice, who sailed along like a Lynn wherry in full sail.

'There are still weeks to go,' she said with a laugh, when I scolded her for coming out into the heat and dust of the reaping.

'You look to me as though you might bring forth at any moment, here in the medland, with all the village gaping!'

At midday we downed tools and eased our aching backs amongst the babies under the sallows. I had snatched a drink from time to time during the morning, but now I threw back my head and drank and drank from an ale jack kept cool in the Lode, until I felt dizzy and had to sit a while to clear my wits. My head stopped spinning when I had eaten a slab of pigeon pie and an early apple. The apple was one of the drop-apples that fall from the trees in summer and tasted as sour as a lemon, but I liked its sourness on my tongue.

Gideon sat down beside me on the grass, a hearty helping of pie in one hand and a piece of cheese in the other. He had removed his clerical bands and untied the strings of his shirt at the throat, although he had not stripped to the waist like many of the men. He shone, bronzed in the sun, and to my dismay my heart leapt at the sight of him. When he had eagerly eaten both cheese and pie, he took off his straw hat and fanned himself with it.

'Hot work,' I said, reaching into the water for the ale jack and passing it to him.

'Aye.' He drank deeply and handed it back, but I felt I had drunk enough.

I lowered the jack into the cool water again by the length of twine tied to its handle. When I turned to speak to him again, I saw he was lying back amongst the long grass, his eyes closed. He lay very still, the only movement a pulse in his throat, where the sun had not yet caught the fair skin usually hidden from sight. I smiled and leaned back on my hands, dabbling my bare feet in the Lode.

By the end of the day the medland was cut and all the fit hay raked into wind rows to dry. The weather-wise amongst us swore that there would be three more days of fine weather to cure the hay. It was perhaps half the crop we would expect to take in a good year, but better than we had hoped for. Sore, exhausted, but fair content, we made our way home. Tom, who had scythed in the morning, but could not manage a full day, had done the milking by the time I reached home and I was so tired that I barely managed to eat a piece of bread and cheese before I fell into bed.

Three days later my aching limbs were almost recovered, but now we had to load the hay into carts and drive it to the communal tithe barn, where each family's share would be reckoned.

'I can drive a cart as usual,' Tom said.

'No, you cannot.' I was determined. He argued, but his heart was not in it.

So I drove our cart, taking over his role, first standing and packing down the hay as it was pitched up by the men, then bumping away over the stubbs to the lane and down into the village to the great barn. It was hard work for Blaze. The weeks of rain had left the lane a quagmire and the few days of sunshine had not yet dried it out. Blaze and the other horses struggled from medland to barn, pulling carts whose wheels soon became choked with casings of mud from the sludder in the lane, casings so thick the wheels would not turn but had to be dragged. At each end of the trip I poked and wacked at the mud with a heavy stick, but once in the lane the wheels became clogged again.

In all this time there had been no further word from my father, but we were not concerned. He had said he would write when there was news, and Tom had assured us that it would be weeks before any action was taken. The day after the hay was in, Nehemiah at last had enough eels to make the journey to Lincoln worth his while. He said he would look Father up and bring us back news.

'Tell Isaac to come home.' My mother twisted her hands in her apron and looked pleadingly at the eeler. 'Surely he can be sent for when he is needed in court? His place is here.'

'Indeed,' said Tom. 'I am still a poor worker and it is too much for Mercy, even with your help.'

'I will try,' Nehemiah said, 'but you know your father. He will not believe that matters will move forward unless he is there to see to it.' He picked up his baskets of eels and two brace of ducks he had shot the day before, and set off for his boat.

It was past nightfall when he returned, long after his usual time, so that we had begun to ask each other what had become of him. We were all sitting in the kitchen, Kitty scouring a pot she had allowed to burn earlier in the day, my mother and Hannah knitting woollen caps, which they could do without need of the candle set on the table, where Tom was reading a pamphlet Jack had given him. I was oiling my heavy boots by the light of the fire, for the weather had closed over and I could feel thunder in the air. I would have a wet and muddy walk for the cows tomorrow.

At last we heard Nehemiah's footsteps in the yard, slow and dragging.

I sprang up and Tom looked at me, frowning. We said nothing, but reached the door together. Nehemiah stumbled in. His coat was torn, the crown of his hat broken.

'Nehemiah!' Tom took him by the arm. 'What has happened?'

He shook his head at first, as though he could not speak.

'Why are you come so late?' I pulled off his wet coat and spread it over the back of a chair. The rain must have begun already, without our noticing.

'The trial was today,' he said. 'The hearing of your father's case. It did not come before a local magistrate. A judge had been sent from London.'

'Well?' In his impatience Tom shook the eeler's arm.

'There was another man there from London, a lawyer representing the adventurers, as they call themselves. The drainers. Cromwell's men.'

My heart began to pound, as if I knew already what he was going to say.

'This man talked and talked, lawyer's talk, I couldn't understand the half of it. Hours, it went on. Then it came your father's turn, or so I thought. There was no lawyer with him. That fellow Gillivray has never come back from London. But when your father got up to speak, the judge would not hear him. He said he had heard enough and would make his judgement.'

Nehemiah looked wildly round at us.

'He said the adventurers had won the case and sent Isaac to be held prisoner in Lincoln Castle, until he pays a fine.'

'A fine?' Tom said slowly. 'What fine?'
Nehemiah swallowed.
'Five hundred pounds.'
My mother cried out and fell senseless to the ground.

Chapter Five

My mother had been carried to bed, where she recovered her wits, but lay sobbing, Hannah sitting beside her and patting her hand from time to time. Hannah was the least disturbed of us, for she had no real notion of money. Five hundred shillings or five hundred pounds – neither made any sense to a woman who all her life had counted in pennies.

I came downstairs again to the kitchen, still too stunned myself to make sense of Nehemiah's news.

'I don't understand,' I said, coming through the door and confronting Tom and Nehemiah who stood by the dying fire, their hands hanging helpless. Kitty crouched on a stool in the corner, as unable to comprehend five hundred pounds as Hannah, but as sensitive as Jasper to the atmosphere of fear. The dog sat beside her and she ran his ears through her fingers again and again.

Neither Tom not Nehemiah answered me, so I threw a new log on the fire, sending a fountain of sparks up the chimney and turned to face them.

'I don't understand,' I said again. 'Father has committed no crime. He went to court to seek justice, to gain a judgement in our favour. How can the judge fine him? Fine him . . .' I gulped, then whispered, as if whispering could somehow make the words vanish, 'Fine him five hundred pounds? For what?'

Nehemiah was turning his sodden hat around and around in his hands. 'I don't rightly understand, Mercy. But I remember, before the War, there was men had fines and taxes laid on them by the courts. They had two weeks to pay, but the money was more than they earned in three years. Couldn't pay.'

'What happened?' Tom gripped the back of Father's chair as though he needed its support to keep himself on his feet.

'All their stock was rounded up and taken away. Their household goods too. You wouldn't remember, it must be twenty years ago or more, at the time of the first enclosures, when they stripped old Jeremy Freeman of everything. His wife was gone by then, and he had but the one son who wasn't right in the head.'

I shivered. Had I heard of old Jeremy before?

Nehemiah sighed and sank down on the bench.

'He smothered his son where he lay asleep, then walked out into the Fen. We never found sight nor sign of him. The Fen took him. They hadn't left even a slab of peat for his fire or a crust of bread for his dinner. Nothing in his house. Nothing.'

Tears were running down Kitty's face, but she didn't utter a sound. I knelt down beside her and put my arms around her.

'Don't worry, Kitty. We'll find a way through this.'

Tom gave me a bleak look. 'It would take ten years at the very least for us to pay off this fine. If we sold everything, stock, house, farm, all our possessions, we could not possibly pay it. I think that is what they are reckoning on. And perhaps the remembrance of our grandfather, who never lived to pay good coin for his misdeeds, perhaps that went into the scales as well.'

I turned to Nehemiah. 'Was there a term set for payment?'

'It must be paid in full by the fifteenth of August.'

There were tears running down my face now and I dashed them away angrily.

'Tom, what can we do?'

For once, he had no answer.

'There was such a crush in the court,' Nehemiah said, 'and men shouting that it was a disgrace and we fenlanders would not stand for it, that the officers drove us out.' He glanced across at his coat. 'They were rough and my coat was torn.'

'At least others supported Father,' Tom said.

'But what can poor men do against such men as these? That London judge, he'd made his decision before ever he came to Lincoln, I'll wager. They say it was Cromwell himself sent him.'

'Traitor,' I muttered.

'As we came away, they were saying that the constables, the sheriff's officers, will impound some of your stock as surety. And if Isaac is to eat in prison, you must send him food, or coin to buy it from the gaolers.'

Suddenly sharp into my mind came that image of my grandfather, huddled in the filth of Cambridge Castle. Now my father was come to a like fate, not for rioting but for seeking justice under the law.

'The stock,' I said, 'if they take our stock, how shall we survive?' I sprang to my feet. 'There is something we can do. Before they come, we must hide some of the stock.' I looked wildly round the kitchen. 'And food. We must hide our flour and cheeses and ale.'

'Mercy is right.' Nehemiah nodded. 'Hide what you can.'

'The draught oxen,' I said, 'and Blaze. Some of the sheep. One of the pigs.'

Tom stared at me. 'How can we hide the oxen? You are dreaming, Mercy.'

'We'll ask our friends. Rafe and Toby and Jack – surely they would be ready to say some of our animals are theirs?'

'It might be worth trying,' he said slowly. 'We cannot hide much or the constables would become suspicious, but we might be able to save some.'

'We must start now,' I said. 'Kitty, you and I will move sacks of flour and barley and oats into the hay loft. It hid Tom before. It can hide food now.'

'Rats,' said Nehemiah.

'We must risk rats. Some of our preserves too. And there are a few of the dried apples. Nehemiah, can you roll two of the ale casks out to the woodstore and hide them amongst the logs?'

He nodded.

'It's dark,' Tom objected.

'What if they were to come tomorrow? We must be ready.' I was seized with a kind of madness. 'Tom, you must go into the village now and put our plan to the others.'

'It's late.' He gestured at the dark square of the window.

I balled my fists and shook them at him.

'We must!' I was almost shrieking now and to silence me, for I do not think he shared my urgent panic, he lit a candle lantern and set out for the village. Nehemiah began rolling casks across the yard while Kitty and I hauled the heavy sacks between us to the barn and, panting and straining, up the ladder to the hay loft. We carried on until the first shower of rain turned to a heavy downpour and I dared not risk damage to our stores.

It was past midnight when Tom returned. I had sent Kitty to bed, and Hannah too, when I saw that Mother had fallen asleep at last, her face blotched and reddened with weeping. Nehemiah and I sat either side of the fire which had dwindled down to embers, for I did not think it worth making up. Nehemiah's chin was sunk on his chest and he snored gently through an open mouth. My own eyes kept falling shut but I was determined to sit up until Tom came home. My fear and horror at what had been done to my father had set light to a great anger in me.

The draught from the door brought me fully awake as Tom came in, blowing out his candle lantern and thrusting the bolt across the door. Usually we do not bolt our doors, but since the drainers had come, everyone took care to secure their homes.

'Well?' I asked.

He prised off his wet boots and I saw that his toe poked through one of his knitted stockings.

'They are willing to help us. Toby will mark a dozen of our sheep as his tomorrow. Jack will take Blaze into his barn, and the largest of the pigs. I have sold the draught oxen to Rafe.'

'Sold them!' I was horrified.

'They will work for the whole village, as they have always done. If we ever recover from paying this fine, Rafe will sell them back to us. In the meantime, I have the value of them in coin to put toward the fine.'

'How much?'

'Twenty-five guineas. More than they are worth. It is generous of Rafe. He has been saving to build a house of his own for Alice and the baby, but they both agreed our need was greater.'

I felt hot tears spring up in my eyes again, but however generous, twenty-five guineas would make little impression on five hundred pounds.

'Somehow we must get more coin. Is there aught else we can sell?'

'Eels.'

Nehemiah had woken.

'You must keep your eel money.' Tom was firm.

'And where would I go if you are turned out of the farm? We must help each other.'

We were all too exhausted to debate further that night and made our way to bed, but I lay awake, tense with worry, until a blackbird outside my window began to welcome the dawn, then fell into a restless sleep.

Tom and I shared the morning milking and then counted over the cheeses in the dairy. We had decided that we could sell half of them, though it would leave us short when winter came.

'If they take our cows, we shall have no milk, no butter and no cheese,' I said. 'We never thought of hiding the cows.'

'That would take some doing. Even if we tried to pass off some of our cows as belonging to one of our neighbours, come milking time they would give us away by coming home to their own barn.'

He was right. I could see no way out of the dilemma, but I was determined to find a way to save at least one of the cows. I helped Tom load half our cheeses onto a handcart so he could wheel it to the Sawyers' dairy. Each time Nehemiah took his eels to market, Tom would go with him, to sell cheese and take provisions for Father.

The officers from the Lincoln court did not come that day, as I had feared, and when I wasn't busy about my daily work or caring for my mother, I contrived to conceal a few more provisions in the hay loft, including several cheeses, but I had still not come up with a plan to save the cows. In the afternoon I carried four of my best laying hens in a basket to Alice.

She took both my hands in hers and kissed me. There were tears in her eyes. 'That it should come to this. Your father! How can they do such a thing?'

I shook my head. 'It seems they can do what they please. Was not the War fought to overthrow the tyranny of a king? It seems tyranny still stalks the land.'

Alice put my hens in a pen next to her own but separated from them by an osier hurdle, for if you put strange hens together they will fight as fiercely as cocks until they grow familiar.

'I will keep your eggs aside. Send Kitty every evening and I'll give them to her.'

I nodded, but could not speak. Perhaps with the kindness of friends we might survive.

'Come, sit with me a little before you go home. I've been baking.'

We went into the Coxes' kitchen, where Alice's mother-in-law, seated at her spinning wheel, gave me a nod. She was an austere woman, who rarely smiled and I felt a stab of guilt that Alice and Rafe's escape to a home of their own would be delayed many months because they had helped us. Despite windows and door standing open for air, the kitchen was hot and rich with the smell of baking. A rack of griddle cakes stood cooling on the table, beside a large slab cake stuffed with raisins, which Alice must have baked in the bread oven by the hearth, after the loaves were done. She patted the side of the cake.

'Cool enough to cut. Will you take some, Mother Cox?'

'Not between meals.' The woman's mouth turned down with disapproval.

Alice reached down two plates from the dresser and winked at me. 'We'll take these outside. Mercy, will you carry them?'

She followed me with two cups of small ale and we seated ourselves on a bench Rafe had built around an apple tree at the edge of the orchard.

'Very good.' I washed down a large bite of cake with a deep gulp of ale. 'Does she not approve of your baking, Mistress Cox?'

Alice laughed. 'Oh, she is ready enough to eat it when my back is turned. By tomorrow, the cake will be mysteriously smaller. She does not approve of *me*.'

She patted her stomach.

'Her first grandchild is coming sooner than she quite likes.'

'Are you well? Should you be standing in the heat, baking?'

'Hearty as a horse,' she said cheerfully. 'Now.' She patted my hand. 'What is to be done about all this?'

'I am frightened, Alice. The sheriff's men can take what they will. Even turn us out of the farm. We could lose everything. All for going to law.' I could not keep my voice steady and I felt my eyes blurring over. 'My father thought that going to law was the safe, the peaceful, decent thing to do. And look how it has turned out.'

Alice nodded. 'Rafe's father has endless stories of like treatment back before the War.'

'So has Nehemiah.'

'And they can really seize your property? Is there no way to appeal?'

'There may be. Tom has written to one of his friends at Grey's Inn, but it would take months, even years, to go through the courts. In the meantime we may be turned out to beg our bread.'

'You know it will not come to that. We – all your neighbours – will take you in, just as you took in Hannah and Nehemiah.'

'We cannot let you. Everyone has suffered, with the War and the years of bad harvests. No one has anything to spare.'

Besides, I thought, we have our pride.

'I have an idea,' I said slowly.

'What?'

'If Tom and Mother and Nehemiah can manage the farm without me, I thought I could hire myself out.'

'Hire out!' Her mouth fell open. 'You, the daughter of the biggest yeoman farmer in the neighbourhood! Wasn't one of your grandmothers a Dillingworth?'

'A great-grandmother. It was the Dillingworths I thought of.'

'You would work for them?' She looked horrified.

'I can cook. Or sew. I can read. Keep accounts. Besides . . .'

'Besides?'

'If Sir John had kept his promise and brought his lawyer from London to help us, my father would never have gone alone to take his case to court in Lincoln. I think Sir John is much to blame for this. He persuaded my father that the law would protect him. It is as much his fault as anyone's that we are come to this.'

'That may be a reason for seeking their help, but to hire yourself out as a servant to them . . .'

'I must swallow my pride. Anything I earn can go towards the fine. And it will mean one less mouth to feed at home.'

'I do understand, Mercy. But is there no other way?'

'I cannot see one. I will discuss it with Tom, then go to the Dillingworths some time in the next few days.'

I stood up, brushing the crumbs from my skirt. 'Thank you, Alice, and thank you for taking in my hens. Send word to me the minute you feel the child coming.'

'I will.'

She stood and put her arms around me. The smell of her baking still lingered in her hair and clothes, a comfortable smell of home and safety. I kissed her, picked up my basket and walked briskly away.

I did discuss my plan with Tom that evening, and he objected strongly, not on the grounds of his own continuing physical weakness but because it would shame us all if I became a servant to the Dillingworths.

'You cannot do this, Mercy.'

'I must. There will be a little money, and my board. We must contrive everything we can. And if I am there, in the Dillingworths' household,' I added cunningly, 'I may be able to persuade Sir John to act to help Father.'

I saw that this last argument was beginning to sway him.

'In any case, there may be no position for me. It will do no harm to ask.'

When Gideon heard of my plan, he was also opposed to it.

'Sir John may be our lord of the manor, and I know nothing against either him or his lady, save that they hold themselves a little too grandly, but there have been, well . . .' he looked troubled. 'There have been rumours about the son.'

I saw that it cost him a good deal to say this, but that he wanted to warn me.

'I have heard the rumours,' I said, slicing bread vigorously. He had agreed, reluctantly, to sup with us, but had insisted in exchange that we accept a side of bacon in return. 'I am not likely to have aught to do with the son.'

The rumours were plain enough. A girl from the next parish, Crowthorne, where the Saints lived, had worked as a kitchen maid at the manor. When it was discovered that she was with child, Lady Dillingworth had turned her out. Back in the village, she was shunned by her family and neighbours. The last we heard, she had set off for Lynn, hoping to find work, but nothing more had been heard of her. The general belief was that Edmund Dillingworth was the father of the child, but that would not have stayed Lady Dillingworth's hand. It was always the girl who must bear the guilt as well as carry the child.

'Be careful, Mercy,' Gideon said, reaching out and laying his hand on mine where it held the loaf steady. 'I do not like this plan of yours. Even if the Dillingworths offer you employment, it can do you no good. You will be humiliated. And how much can you earn toward the fine?'

I set my face stubbornly and drew my hand away.

'At least there will be one less to feed out of our stores,' I said. 'I do not see what else I can do to help.'

I thought I heard him whisper, 'Stay with us', but perhaps I was mistaken.

The next day I donned a clean gown of modest homespun and a plain apron without embroidery. I had washed my hair, which was not wise, for it was springy with curls and kept trying to escape from my cap. I set out for the manor house just after dawn, because the summer sun was turning fierce and I did not want to arrive hot and draggled.

The manor was ancient at its heart: a long central hall house perhaps two or three hundred years old, with wings added to east and west in the last century, making the shape of a wide letter H. More recently, a pillared portico had been added in the centre, incongruously framing the original doorway. Ivy climbed up the flint and brick infill between the timber framework and through the ivy leaves on the two wings dozens of panes of glass mirrored the sunlight. The central, older section had once had shuttered windows – not glass. Back in those old times even the Dillingworths had not had glass. But in Sir John's father's time these windows too had been glazed. The whole building glittered and seemed to peer down at me in contempt.

Off to the left, an archway led through to what I knew were the stables. On the right were the other outbuildings – a dairy, brewhouse, laundry, stillroom, and storerooms. There were no farm buildings nearby. The farm which served the manor was two fields away, so no smell or sight of beasts would trouble the inhabitants.

On the carriageway leading up to that imposing but slightly absurd portico I hesitated. I had been inside the manor a few times before, when the Dillingworths invited the better local families to some festivity. That had been before the War and all the disruption it had brought. I suppose I could not have been more than twelve when I was last inside the house. Should I knock at the front door, where I had always been admitted before? Or – since I was come to seek a position in service – should I go round by the courtyard on the right and look for the servants' entrance?

I decided that as I was coming partly to seek the help that Sir John had so far failed to give, I should go to the front. The pillars which supported the portico looked like marble from a distance, but when I drew near I realised that they had simply been painted to look like marble and some of the paint was beginning to peel off. As I passed them I tapped one with my fingernail and realised it was nothing but cheap wood, not even stone. The roof of the portico cut off the sunlight like a knife and I shivered slightly as I raised the stout iron knocker on the old hall door. This was wood, but honest wood, solid oak and clenched together with square-headed studs bigger than horseshoe nails.

My knock echoed inside the hall and my stomach flipped in dismay. It sounded too loud, too peremptory. There was a long pause and then I heard footsteps on the flagstones inside. The door groaned open and I found myself looking up into the face of the Dillingworths' steward. I remembered him now, from those earlier visits, and from seeing him once in conversation with my father. I felt a little spurt of hope. If he knew my father . . . Then it died, for the man was eyeing me in no very friendly fashion.

'Yes? What do you want?'

His tone was abrupt, even uncivil. Instead of intimidating me, as it was no doubt meant to do, it stiffened my determination.

'I wish to speak to Sir John,' I said, and was pleased that my voice betrayed no sign of nervousness.

'Oh you do? And who are you?'

'I am Mercy Bennington, daughter of Isaac Bennington.' I decided to attack. 'Great-granddaughter of Mary Dillingworth, your master's great-aunt.'

He looked sceptical at that, but clearly could not be sure how to treat me. With some reluctance he opened the door a little wider and stepped aside so that I could enter the great hall, which soared two storeys high. Despite the summer warmth outside, it was chilly here, and I shivered. He pointed to a spot beside the door.

'Wait there until you are sent for.' He swept away, keys clanking at his belt, and disappeared through a door into the side wing of the house on the left.

It was some while before he returned, which gave me time to regret my boldness in coming to the manor and to wish that I could bolt, but I could not bear the thought of the humiliation, having to admit to Tom that I had not had the courage to go through with my plan. Pride it was that kept me standing there.

At last the steward reappeared. I had remembered his name now, Master Rogers. He was said to be an honest man, even if he thought a little too well of himself. He jerked his head at me.

'This way. Sir John will see you.'

I was ushered along a hallway and into a room overlooking the formal gardens behind the house. I had never been in this part of the manor before, nor seen the gardens which looked very strange to my eye, with geometric patterns of low clipped hedges through which gravelled walks wound in perfect symmetry. Although it was full summer, there were few flowers except, at the far end of the garden, I thought I could make out a row of regimented rose bushes just coming into bloom. A garden of dark green yew and grey gravel. It was a depressing sight.

'Mercy Bennington, is it?' Sir John, more courteous than his steward, had risen from a chair behind a table near the window and stepped toward me. He sketched a slight bow, nicely calculated to be polite to my sex while marking my inferior status. Master Rogers withdrew, closing the door somewhat loudly behind him.

Sir John motioned me to a chair opposite his and we both sat. I found I was unable to decide how to speak, though I had been rehearsing what I would say all the way from home.

'And what can I do for you, Mistress Bennington?'

It gave me an opening. 'It is about my father,' I said. 'He took the case of the commoners to court in Lincoln, to prove the charter which entitles us to hold the common lands in the Fens in perpetuity.'

Sir John nodded, pressing the fingers of his hands together and raising them to his lips.

I grew bolder. 'Sir John, we have waited many months for word from your lawyer in London on this matter, and all the while the drainers are digging up our fields and destroying our crops. They have driven two people from their homes – Hannah Green and Nehemiah Socket. Their homes were burnt down and their possessions stolen. Hannah was struck in the face. Nehemiah was attacked and badly wounded.'

Still he did not speak, but cocked his head on one side.

'So at last my father decided he must take the case to court himself. And instead of hearing him, the judge passed judgement on nothing but the word of the adventurers.' I was losing control of my voice in the face of his continuing silence. 'They have thrown my father in prison and imposed a fine of five hundred pounds, which of course we cannot pay.'

There was a flicker in his eyes at that. I was certain that he already knew everything I had said, except for the size of the fine.

Now he sat back with a sigh and rubbed the knees of his velvet breeches.

'Mistress Bennington, what is it you want me to do? If you have come here to ask me to pay your father's fine, you have wasted your journey.'

He smiled, but the smile moved nothing but his lips, and there was a hard edge to his voice. I felt my face flush with anger and embarrassment, but I strove to remain civil.

'I have not come a-begging, Sir John. Except to beg you to urge your lawyer to act, and act swiftly, on our behalf. He seems to tarry forever over this matter.'

'Lawyers move at their own pace, Mistress Bennington,' he gave me a smile as condescending as his steward's looks.

'Not when they move to imprison a man who has done no wrong and came merely to seek justice.' I knew he would not like my impertinence, but I could not hold back the words.

'I will certainly write again to my lawyer. Will that satisfy you?' His tone was cool, dismissive.

'We would all be grateful, the whole parish, all the commoners, if you would do so.' I wanted to make it clear that I was not a sole petitioner, seeking help merely for myself.

He started to rise, but I held out my hand.

'There is one other matter.'

He sank back into his chair and I saw that he looked impatient, as though he felt I had trespassed too much on his time.

'My family cannot possibly pay the fine by the due date, which is the fifteenth of August. The officers of the court are likely to seize some of our stock as surety, which means it will be even more difficult for us to pay. So that we may pay at least in part, we must sell some goods, and I have decided to seek employment.' I swallowed. This was even more difficult than I had expected, in the face of Sir John's silence and look of disdain.

'I hoped that I might find a position here at the manor. I am lettered. I can keep accounts.' I was humiliated by the disdainful smile which spread across his face. How could I have been so bold? A man like Sir John would not employ a giddy girl to write up his accounts. He would have a young man not long down from Cambridge, like his son, or a responsible older man like Rogers. I stumbled on, feeling more and more foolish. 'I am a neat seamstress and a good cook . . .' My voice tailed off as his expression changed.

'It is Lady Dillingworth who supervises all household matters,' he said. There was relief in his voice. He would be rid of me now. He stood and rang a small silver bell which stood beside the papers on his table. Rogers entered so quickly that I wondered whether he had been listening at the door.

'Take Mistress Bennington to Lady Dillingworth, Rogers. She wishes to know whether my lady can offer her employment.'

Rogers's smirk told me that was no better than what he had expected of me. He jerked his head for me to follow and turned towards the door.

'You will not forget to write to your lawyer?' I felt I could risk Sir John's disapproval of my forwardness.

'No, no, you may count on it.' A look of annoyance passed over his face, but he remained coolly courteous. 'Good day to you.'

I made him a curtsey, nicely calculated on my part to show that I was not yet in his employ.

Master Rogers led me back along the corridor and stopped at the last door near the front of the house. He tapped, and on being answered stepped inside, shutting the door in my face. I could hear the murmur of voices from within, but not what was said. After a few minutes, Rogers opened the door.

'Lady Dillingworth will see you now.'

I stepped inside as pretty a room as I had ever seen. Where Sir John's room – his office or study – had been lined with bookshelves except where a few family portraits were hung on the oak panelling, the walls of this room were covered with paper, hand-painted with exotic birds and butterflies. Tom had told me of such paper he had seen in London, but I had never seen it myself before. There were small tables holding Delft bowls of pot-pourri, and vases of tiger lilies and flowers I did not recognise, like deep cups in shape, in white and yellow. I thought how strange it was to have a garden of gravel and cruelly trimmed shrubs, but flowers cut and dying in the house. The chairs were covered with damask, the cushions were worked in rich embroidered silks, and the colours were so bright and so profuse it made my head spin.

Lady Dillingworth herself was dressed in silks and sitting at her embroidery. I must have stood gaping a little too long, for she said brusquely, 'Yes? What is it you want, girl?'

I felt resentment rising in me, but choked it down. No one had ever addressed me so rudely, not even Rogers when he opened the door to me. I was, after all, a kind of cousin of the lady's husband.

'I am Mercy Bennington, Lady Dillingworth—'

'Rogers has told me who you are. What do you want?'

Unlike Sir John, she did not ask me to sit down.

I stumbled through the tale of the commons, the drainers, the court, my father, the fine. Her face showed complete indifference. Unlike Sir John, she did not suspect that she might owe us something.

'Well? This is all very . . . interesting, but why are you here?'

'My family must raise the money to pay the fine,' I said bluntly. 'I am seeking employment.'

'You wish to enter service at the manor?'

At that moment, it was the last thing I wished, but I nodded mutely.

'What can you do?'

Once again, I ran through my accomplishments. As with Sir John, I did not mention that I could herd and milk cows, make cheese and butter, and shear sheep.

Lady Dillingworth regarded me as though I was a rather inferior piece of fabric she was about to reject as being too coarse.

'Very well. You may start as under kitchen maid, on one month's trial. Come back tomorrow.'

She turned back to her embroidery. I felt a slow-burning rage at what was clearly a dismissal. Under kitchen maid! It was a post suited to a child like Kitty.

'On what terms, my lady? What wages?'

She turned astonished eyes at me, whether because she was surprised to find me still standing there or because I had dared to ask such a question, I did not know.

'Food and lodging. You will sleep with the other maids in the attic of the east wing. Two shillings a month and one day's leave a month.'

There was nothing I could do but curtsey and withdraw. Two shillings a month? How many months to reach five hundred pounds? More than my lifetime.

Rogers was waiting in the great hall, as though he did not trust me to leave without stealing something. He did not open the front door but led me into the east wing, down narrow passages and out through the kitchen, where several women and girls were at work, chopping vegetables and dressing meat. They stared at me as we passed.

'This is the door you will use in future,' the steward said, throwing open a door into the kitchen courtyard. 'And be here by six o'clock tomorrow morning.'

So he had been listening outside the door.

On the long walk home I had plenty of time to think about what I had done. My father, I knew, would be shocked that I could even consider hiring myself out as a servant to the Dillingworths. But under kitchen maid! I would be spending my time rising before all the rest of the household to light the kitchen fires, scrubbing the flagstones in the whole kitchen wing, plucking and gutting chickens and pheasants, scouring burnt pots, carrying all the heaviest loads, running hither and thither at the behest of all the kitchen staff. And I had told Sir John I was lettered and could keep accounts! Well, my pride had been well and truly humbled.

As I saw the familiar shape of home at the far side of the field, I quickened my step. I wanted to spend every minute left to me in those surroundings which suddenly seemed very dear. With my hand on the gate to the yard, a thought suddenly struck me. The girl from Crowthorne, the one who had been dismissed by Lady Dillingworth because she was with child – it was her place I was to fill. In the past I had paid little heed to my Dillingworth ancestry, but now a kind of shamed fury filled me. I decided that I would tell my family merely that I had a position with the Dillingworths, and not what the position was.

So abstracted was I by my own thoughts that it was only now that I noticed that all was not well about the farm. Firewood was scattered across the yard and distracted hens were wandering about. I could hear cows mooing in distress from the barn, needing to be milked. There was no smoke rising from the kitchen chimney. Suddenly alarmed I flew across the yard and into the kitchen. They were all there and looked up with frightened eyes as I burst in.

'Oh, it is Mercy!' Kitty ran to me and hugged me.

'What has happened?'

Tom was sitting in Father's chair, while Hannah bathed his eye. There was blood on his eyebrow and the area around his eye was reddened and bruised. Nehemiah was grimly washing bloodied knuckles in a bowl of water, while my mother made a pretence of slicing bread, but had to keep putting down the knife because her hands were shaking so much.

'The sheriff's men came,' said Tom. 'Ouch, Hannah, that's enough!'

'Keep still, Master Tom, while I salve this cut above your eye. It's a deep one.'

'You didn't fight them!' I said.

'Only got in their way a little,' Nehemiah said, 'but they pushed us aside. The one who hit Tom must have been wearing a ring, that's what cut his face.'

'They found the ale anyway,' said Tom, 'amongst the firewood. They've taken all the cows but two, and as many of the hens as they could catch, but your girls led them a dance and some got away.'

'Now they're off to the pasture for more of our stock,' said Nehemiah.

'Haven't the cows been milked?' I asked. 'They're crying out.'

'I'd just brought them in when the men arrived and they only left a few minutes ago. Leave it, Hannah. I must go to the milking.'

'I'll go,' I said. 'It won't take long if we've only two left.'

I wanted to see for myself how bad the damage was. I herded the hens back out of the yard to their run and threw them some grain, then I climbed up to the hay loft. It was undisturbed, so the provisions we had hidden there were safe for the moment. I climbed down again, feeling sick. Even if I had been here there was nothing I could have done that Tom and Nehemiah did not do, but I felt as though I had deserted them when they needed me most.

To my relief our favourite, Blackthorn, was one of the two cows still left to us, the other was an elderly cow, Kingcup, who was nearing the end of her useful life. Blackthorn as least would provide us with some milk. Or provide them – I reminded myself – the rest of my household. After tomorrow I would no longer be here. I carried the stool and pail over to Blackthorn and spent some time trying to calm her, but she was still distressed and it took me twice as long as usual to milk her. Kingcup had quietened by the time I had finished, but gave very little milk anyway. I carried the pitiful amount through into the dairy. They had left us one cheese. I was thankful that the ones we had marked for selling were already stored in the Sawyers' dairy. It would keep for winter food, or could be sold for coin.

But where would we be by winter? If the fine was not paid, would they seize the farm?

I went back into the barn and put my arms around Blackthorn's neck for comfort. Laying my cheek against her soft hide I could smell her sweet scent of hay and sunshine. She flicked her ear where my cap tickled it and snorted softly. As I stepped back I rubbed her head between her ears, and she turned her placid eyes on me, her mouth chewing quietly. I wished I could face the world with her calm grace. What would become of our other cows? Where would they be taken? I was not sure whether they would be impounded until the middle of August or sold at once.

For the moment I left the two cows in the barn, for I had no wish to encounter the sheriff's men rounding up our stock in the pasture. Back in the kitchen I lit the fire and laid out a simple dinner of bread and cheese. We could no longer expect to eat meat once or twice a day. Tonight we would sup on porridge.

'I have been to the manor,' I said, when we were all seated.

'And how were you received?' Tom said.

'Courteously enough,' I lied, 'and Sir John has made me his promise that he will write at once to his lawyer to move more quickly in the matter of the drainers.'

'Do you think he will keep his promise?'

'I think he would consider himself dishonoured if he did not keep it. That does not mean that his lawyer will indeed move more quickly.'

'And did you seek employment?'

At that the others turned towards me in astonishment, for I had spoken of my intention only to Tom and Gideon.

'Aye. I am to go tomorrow. To work in the kitchens.'

My mother drew in her breath with a hiss. 'Have they forgotten that my grandmother was their kin?'

'I reminded them, Mother. It will not be so difficult, merely doing what I do at home. I shall have board, and two shillings a month.' I decided I could not lie about that.

'Two shillings!' Tom gave a scornful laugh. 'What use is that?'

I flushed with anger. 'More use than nothing. It was the best I could get.'

I pressed my lips together to keep back a sob. I would not tell them how I had been humiliated. Already Gideon was proved right.

Chapter Six

On my hands and knees, scrubbing the kitchen floor with sand and lye, I could hear the other maids laughing as they picked up their tallow candles and headed up the narrow back staircase which led to the attic where we slept. As the least and last of the kitchen maids, it was my final task each evening to scrub the flagstones of all the mud and grease and spilt food of the day. And since everyone knew that I would scrub them until they gleamed, they were not overly careful about what they dropped as they went about the disciplined chaos that was the life of the manor kitchen.

I sat back on my heels and rested my wrists on my knees. I had been up since before dawn, when I had swept out the great kitchen hearth and built the fire for the day's cooking, fetched four buckets of water from the well in the yard, hung a pot over the fire to boil, and made porridge for the servants' breakfast. For a week now I had laboured in the manor kitchen, seeing daylight only when I fetched water or was sent for supplies from the storehouse across the yard, where the heavier barrels and sacks were kept. Much of my time was spent fetching and carrying, kneeling to tend fires or scraping pots of burnt residue to clean them. By evening, when I came to scrub the floor, my bones ached like those of an old woman. My knees were red and grazed, shooting pains ran along my spine, and the skin of my hands was raw and blistered. I had worked hard all my life, but at my own pace and in my own way. Now I knew how it must feel to be a packman's donkey, lashed and helpless.

The other maids resented me. There was little to resent that I could see, since I occupied the lowliest position amongst the servants, but they knew who I was. Some may even have known of my kinship with the Dillingworths. I had not spoken of it. In fact I had spoken very little, but I suppose they may have assumed that if I was kin and employed in such a demeaning post, it must be meant as some kind of punishment. Myself, I did not give Lady Dillingworth the credit for so much calculated thinking. She needed an under kitchen maid. I asked for employment. The solution was obvious.

Whatever their reasons, the other girls made my life unpleasant. In our attic, they allocated me the cot nearest the door, which was swept by draughts and next to the alcove where the pisspots were kept. In winter it would be bitterly cold, especially as I had but one thin blanket. At present, in the heat of summer, the stink was worst where I slept. Still it meant that when I had to empty the pisspots in the morning – another of my tasks – I had not far to go. I performed this service also for the family, which required some careful timing, as it had to be done when they had left their bedchambers, but I must keep out of their sight as I came and went.

There was much casual cruelty amongst the servants too. Hot pans would be accidentally knocked against my arm. Buckets of water I had carried into kitchen and pantries would be overturned. We slept in our shifts, our working gowns laid over the boxes we were each given to hold our few possessions. Three times in the first week my gown was screwed into a ball and thrown on the floor. One morning when I arrived to light the fire, I found that hot fat had been deliberately poured over the floor I had scrubbed the night before and had set hard. I had not finished scraping it away when the cook arrived. He boxed my ears for that.

Through all this, I said nothing. I would not allow them to bait me, but set my mouth and carried on as if I had noticed nothing. I sighed now, as I wiped up the worst of the wet off the floor, then took the broom and swept the damp sand out of the door and into the yard. Even the thought of my hard cot, which was too short and too narrow, seemed like luxury as I climbed the steep stairs to the attic, shielding my candle with my hand against the draughts which always seemed to find their way under the eaves of the attic. I undressed and folded my gown carefully, then laid it under my pillow. This had been my practice for two days now. They could not throw it on the floor without waking me first.

My prayers were incoherent, for I was too tired to frame my thoughts clearly. I prayed for Father, imprisoned in Lincoln. I prayed for my family at home on the farm. I prayed in a confused way about my feelings for Gideon. I prayed to be given the strength to endure and keep my temper. And I prayed for Alice, whose baby was due at any moment now.

Halfway through the next morning, one of the undercooks poked me in the ribs as I was scouring the cooking pots from the family's breakfast.

'Someone asking for you at the door,' he said, with a leer. 'Lover, is it?'

I did not answer, but dried my hands hastily on my apron and went to the door. It was Alice's brother Robin.

'Alice bade me come,' he said, looking nervously over my shoulder to the activity within. 'The babe is near. She begs you to come and sit with her.'

I too looked behind me.

'I'm not sure if I can come, Robin. I am to have but one day off a month, and I have not served a month yet.'

He nodded. 'Alice knows this, but–' he twisted his cap in his hands, 'things do not look well with her. The midwife says the babe is coming feet first, and Alice is bleeding too much.'

I reached out impulsively and touched his arm. 'I will come if they will give me leave. Tell Alice I am praying for her.'

He ducked his head, pulled on his cap and was gone.

I appealed first to the senior kitchen maid, Bess Whitelea, who gave me my orders.

'No, you may not have leave. Not until you have served your month.'

'But my dearest friend is having a difficult birth. She is like to die.' Putting it into words frightened me, making the possibility loom closer.

The woman shrugged. She wore a hard face. If she had come up through the regime I was enduring, this was understandable enough, but I would not be put off.

'Why should it matter when I take the day? I will still serve the month.'

'You do not have leave.'

I then appealed to the cook, Elias Walton, who brushed me aside and would not even hear me. Greatly daring, I knocked on the door of the housekeeper's room. When she called me in I stepped nervously through the doorway and explained my request.

'Mistress Atwood, my friend might die. We have been like sisters all our lives.'

She was kinder than most of the servants and smiled at me sympathetically, so that I could no longer hold back my tears.

'I am sorry, Mercy, but there is no way I can allow you to go. Neither Master Rogers nor her ladyship would permit it. I am truly sorry. I will pray for your friend and we must hope for the best. There is a midwife with her?'

'Aye,' I said dully, 'but it was the midwife who said there was danger.'

She rose from her chair and patted my shoulder.

'It is a danger all women must face. Now go back to your work. If you keep busy, the time will pass quickly and perhaps good news will come soon.'

I thanked her and dragged myself back to the kitchen. There was little danger than I would not be kept busy. Indeed my effrontery in asking for leave and even daring to speak to Mistress Atwood meant that I was driven harder than usual all day.

It was three days before I had news of Alice, then Tom sent a note by the carter who brought supplies to the manor.

Alice is delivered of a boy child, small but well enough. Hannah went also to attend on her, and matters were grave for a time. She lost much blood, but Hannah is sure she will recover. She is to keep to her bed for the next week. Gideon is away to Cambridge for the present, so the christening cannot be held until he returns. Alice sent word to ask that you take your day's leave to attend the christening, as you have promised to stand godmother to the child. We have not been troubled further by the sheriff's men and all is

*well with us. I saw Father last week and took him fresh clothes
and food. He has caught a slight fever but says he is better now.*
Your loving brother Thomas Bennington

I hoped that Tom was telling me the truth and not softening
the news to spare me, hoped that Alice was indeed recovering and
Father had no more than a touch of fever. All prisons are rampant
with diseases of every kind, from those carried in by the prisoners
themselves to those which breed in the damp stone and malicious
airs of a gaol.

So Rafe had got his son. I smiled. That was something to be
glad about. Old Master Cox would be satisfied and perhaps even
Alice's mother-in-law would unbend a little, now that Alice had
provided an heir.

I had stolen a few minutes free of tasks and gone into the
orchard beyond the kitchen outbuildings to read Tom's letter. As I
looked up from it, I saw someone approaching me from the back of
the stable yard. He was too close for me to hurry away without
seeming ill-mannered, so I stayed where I was, tucking the letter
into my pocket. It was Edmund Dillingworth, heir to the manor
and formerly Royalist soldier, though we did not speak of that in
these dangerous days.

'Mercy Bennington, is it not?' He had stopped in front of me
and was smiling easily, as if we were well known to each other. In
fact I had not seen him up close since I had come to work at the
manor. I had last spoken to him all those years ago, when I was
twelve and he would have been about sixteen and very conscious
of the difference in age.

I curtsied and lowered my eyes. 'It is, sir.'

'Come, cousin, no need to "sir" me. We are kin, are we not?'

I was so surprised I looked up. He was the first member of
his family to acknowledge the kinship and in the present
circumstances it was astonishing. Even more astonishing, given
what I knew of Edmund Dillingworth's reputation.

'Kin of a sort, I suppose. But now I am the lowliest of your
mother's maids.'

'That does not stop us being kin, though I do not understand
why you are here.'

'Perhaps you have heard of my family's troubles.'

'Many of us have troubles in these troubled times. I too have my troubles.' He gave me a rueful smile. 'Most of my friends and companions have fled to France. There would be a price on my head too, were it not for this distant cousinage with Cromwell, though I must lie low and keep out of sight.'

I could see that, for a man like Edmund Dillingworth, lying low must feel like being a hawk tethered in a cage.

'What should we do without kinship, cousin?' he said. 'It binds us all together. Why, I suppose you too must be kin to Cromwell.'

'I think not. Too many degrees separate us. I have no wish to be kin to him, if it is he who is bent on stealing our lands.'

'And it is that which is at the root of your family's troubles, is it? Come, walk with me, cousin Mercy, and tell me the whole of it.'

He held out his hand to me, but I shook my head.

'I must return to my work, sir. I had but a few minutes to myself to read my brother's letter.'

'Have no fear. I will make amends to Mistress Atwood. Come.'

He took my hand and tucked it firmly under his arm. I was fearful of the consequences, but I let him lead me through the orchard to a grassy seat at the far side, which had been contrived as a place to sit and admire the stream which ran clear under sallows on its way to the greater rivers of the Fen. After my weeks of loneliness and silence, it was a relief to talk of my family and how the whole parish was suffering at the hands of the drainers.

'And my father has done nothing to help?'

'Sir John wrote some months ago to his lawyer in London, but there has been no news. He has promised to write again . . .' My voice tailed off. I did not want to criticize Sir John to his son.

'But you do not know if he has done so, or whether the lawyer has acted on your behalf?' He read my answer in my face, and patted my hand, which he had kept tucked under his arm. 'Fear not, I will challenge my father tonight.'

I was alarmed. 'Please do not say that I . . .'

'I will go about it carefully, cousin. I'll say that I have observed the drainers and the damage they are causing, and ask what he has done about it.'

'You're very kind. But truly, I must go back to the kitchen. I must work out my month and be sure of my day of leave.'

'It is important to you? This day of leave?'

'My friend's first child is to be christened, and I am to stand godmother.'

'Your rector – Gideon Clarke? – still carries out christenings?'

With anyone else, I would have watched my tongue, but Edmund was a Royalist, had fought for the King. He would no more condone the Puritans' banning of Christian baptism and weddings than Gideon himself did.

'The Reverend Clarke continues to baptise and wed according to the traditional practices of our English Church,' I said, with a note of defiant pride. 'He believes any other form is wicked in the sight of God. As I do.'

The Dillingworths had their own chaplain and their own family chapel, where I worshipped on Sunday with the rest of the household. As far as I could tell, for he revealed little of his position, the chaplain too supported the traditional church, Queen Elizabeth's compromise with Protestantism. If he had been a Puritan, he would surely have given himself away in his sermons.

'Truly, I must go.' I withdrew my hand and stood up, brushing grass from my skirts.

'I will come with you and explain to Mistress Atwood that I delayed you.'

Later, I wished I had taken the punishment for the delay instead of allowing him to accompany me. Edmund returned with me through the servants' door, nodding and smiling to the other girls, pausing to speak to the senior kitchen maid Bess and the cook Elias, before bowing a farewell to me and calling me 'cousin'. As he disappeared in the direction of the housekeeper's room, the maids and undercooks and scullions whispered amongst themselves and directed looks at me whose significance I understood and did not like. I found myself flushing as if I were guilty, then inwardly berating myself for talking to Edmund

Dillingworth at all and for allowing the unfounded suspicions of the other servants to hurt me. I could not forget that other girl, whose place I had taken, and who might, by now, be begging pregnant on the streets of Lynn. But Edmund had called me cousin and treated me with affection and respect. I had nothing to fear.

At last the month was nearly over and Mistress Atwood confirmed that Lady Dillingworth had agreed to keep me on. It was little surprise. She would have found it difficult to find a stronger, harder worker in the parish to fill such a lowly position, which would normally be taken by a child of twelve or thirteen, not a grown woman nearly nineteen.

'You may take your day of leave when you wish, provided you give me three days' warning and it is not inconvenient.'

'Thank you, Mistress Atwood. I will wait to hear from my family.'

I did not mention the christening to her. I did not know in which direction her religion lay. Even though she had worked for the manor all her life, she might tend towards the view of the Saints. Many, like the villagers of Crowthorne, inclined that way, either from true conviction or because it was expedient to do so in a world where the King was a helpless prisoner and Cromwell and his cronies ruled in his stead.

Since our first meeting, Edmund had sought me out several times, although I tried to avoid his attentions, for it soon became clear that he was paying me more court than merely cousinly affection would warrant. I could not avoid him altogether and although he took my hand more than was necessary, and laid his hand in the small of my back, he did also take pains to tell me that he had made sure that his father had written again to the lawyer in London and expected an answer any time soon.

'Then we shall send these drainers packing, shall we not, Mercy?' He laughed gaily and picked me up by the waist to swing me over a clump of nettles in the orchard. He favoured the orchard, for it was out of sight of the house. I extricated myself from his hands.

'There is still the matter of my father's imprisonment. How can the verdict of the court be overturned? Nothing can be as it was until that is settled.'

'Oh, I am sure our lawyers have it in hand. But if your father is restored, you will leave us and go back home, so for my own part, I hope they will tally a long while.'

I could never be sure of him. He might call me cousin and appear to treat me with respect, but he touched me more than was right. Was he indeed courting me honourably? Lying on my lumpy straw mattress at night, I sometimes let myself toy with the idea of becoming mistress of the manor. That would be fair revenge for the way I had been treated here. Then I would take myself sternly to task. I did not wish to be wedded and bedded by Edmund Dillingworth. I certainly did not love him. And there came sometimes into his eyes a glint of something cruel, when I pulled away from him or ended our meetings abruptly. I even feared him a little.

Two days before the end of my trial month, word came from Alice that the christening was to take place on the following Sunday. It had been delayed further because Gideon had gone on from Cambridge to Canterbury about some church business and had but just come back to the village. Alice had been churched as soon as he returned, so she would be able to attend the christening herself. This was unusual, since the christening would normally have taken place within a few days of the birth and the churching later. I was glad Alice would be there to see her boy received into the Christian community with the proper rites.

I heard from Alice on the Wednesday and on Thursday gained Mistress Atwood's permission to go home for the day on Sunday. Although it was no more than my due, for I had worked at the manor my full month, the other maids seemed to resent even this small liberty of mine, and I found myself with additional work allocated to me, including washing the men servants' bedding, a dirty and heavy task. When it was done, I could scarce lift the buck basket to carry it outside, but no one offered to take a handle with me.

To one side of the orchard there was a dense beech hedge, pleached and woven to make a barrier between the orchard and the stable yard, which was not walled on this side. The bushes were sturdy, so we made use of them for drying the heavier items like blankets. The family's shifts and shirts – light fabrics which could be washed – were spread on the lavender hedge for its pleasant scent. Their heavy velvets and brocades were not washed at all, but left to grow sweaty and grubby, all outward show and inward stench.

I began to heave the wet blankets on to the hedge, an almost impossible task with no one to help. It was rare indeed for the men's blankets to be washed, even though they harboured bugs and dirt, and I knew the work had been devised for me out of jealousy. It was hot out in the full summer sun and I was growing hot and cross myself as I struggled, when I felt myself suddenly seized about the waist from behind. I had heard no footstep on the soft grass of the orchard, but I knew at once from the scent of him who it was.

'Let me go, sir,' I said, barely hiding my annoyance, for my hands were full of wet blanket and the front of my dress and my apron were soaked.

'Nay, cousin Mercy, your struggles become you. You are as pink as one of my mother's roses.' He tightened his grip and pressed his face against the back of my neck. 'You smell of roses too, and lavender. A veritable flower garden of delights.' His hands crept up to my breasts.

'Soap,' I said coldly, 'I scent the soap with rose water and dried lavender. And I wash regularly.' For I could smell his sweat and the harsh feral scent of him as he pulled me close. I tried frantically to think how I could rid myself of him without calling for help. I dropped the blanket to free my hands, but still could not break away from him.

'Come, Mercy. You have teased me long enough. I demand satisfaction, and as I cannot call you out, I must be satisfied another way.'

He pulled me away from the hedge and twisted me around so that I was facing him. I would have laughed at his ridiculous words if he had not been so strong and my fear so great.

'Edmund, this will not do. You cannot treat me as you treated that other poor child. Remember, I am Isaac Bennington's daughter and kin to your family.'

There was a flash of anger in his eyes. 'What do you know of some poor child? Do you mean that mean brat of a scullery maid? She was willing enough. And as for kin – let us become a little more intimate.'

With that he threw me on to the ground and lifted my skirts.

The child may have been willing, but if she was not, she would never have been able to fend him off. This time, however, Edmund Dillingworth had to do with a woman who had milked cows and sheared sheep. I might not be as strong as he, but I was strong enough to fight back. As he groped with the belt of his breeches, I brought up my knee and struck him hard in the groin.

He let out a cry of pain and fell backward as I scrambled to my feet. To delay him I grabbed the sodden blanket lying on the ground and dropped it over his head, then I took to my heels.

When I reached the kitchen, out of breath and with my dress and cap awry, everyone turned to look at me. There was a kind of expectancy about them, and I knew that they had told Edmund where I could be found. I glared at them, then turned to one of the scullions. My heart was pounding, partly from fear, but also from a rush of anger.

'Master Edmund is in need of assistance. He has met with a slight accident out by the beech hedge. And while you are there you can spread out the rest of the blankets to dry.'

They continued to stare at me as he went out, and I heard a snigger, quickly suppressed. To my surprise, sour-faced Bess Whitelea smiled at me.

'You may give me a hand with the pies for tonight, Mercy. You say that you have a light hand with pastry.'

It was acceptance of a sort.

I rose as usual before dawn on Sunday, but today it would be the turn of one of the other maids to light the fire and bring in water. I would not stay to eat with them, for I could barely wait to dress, so eager was I to be away. To my great relief, I had seen nothing of Edmund Dillingworth since that last encounter beside the beech hedge, and hoped he was taking care to avoid me. I ran down the stairs and out of the servants' door under the grey skies of the dwindling night. The birds were singing their hearts out – blackbirds and robins and great tits and thrushes and willow-warblers and black-capped tits. As I headed away from the manor I heard the boom of a butter-bump far out among the whispering reeds of the marsh, then a flight of oyster-catchers shrieked their way overhead. Instead of taking the road to the village, I went the shorter way, ploughing around the edges of fields and skirting the boggy fringe of the Fens, jumping over the smaller ditches and balancing my way over the logs which served as footways over the wider ones. My skirt was soon soaked a foot deep, but I cared nothing for it. I wanted to sing, and my feet kept bursting into a run.

The sky away to the east wore its first flush of gold, where the rim of the sun would just be rising above the sea, its rays reflected in the waves up to a perfect summer sky above. Where everything had looked silver and grey when I left the manor, a wash of colour was seeping over the world, as if an artist had passed his brush over a dull canvas with a tint of watery paint. Spread over the long grasses a gossamer of spiders' webs was crusted and jewelled with diamond drops fingered by the sun. The air was full of the beloved whisper of rushes, the immortal fenland song which poured through me, blood and bone. By the time I reached the edge of our farm, the pale green of the sallows stood out clear against the sky, the waters of Baker's Lode glittered, and away towards the commons I could see that the wheat – what was left of it – was brushed over with the faintest tint of gold as it began to ripen.

No one was yet stirring in the house. I had forgotten that we now bolted our door and laughed at the absurdity of it. I was shut out of my own home! I gathered up a handful of pebbles and made my way round the corner to look up at Tom's window. My first pebble missed, but the second hit the half-open window with a clink. No answer. I threw another. This one went in through the window and I heard a yelp. A moment later Tom's tousled head peered out.

'Mercy! We had not expected you as early as this.'

'I didn't stay a moment longer than I needed, but I'm shut out! Come down and unbolt the door for me.'

His head disappeared and I ran back to the yard. I heard the scrape of the bolt, then there was Tom, comical in his night shift with his bare legs poking out beneath.

'Your legs are grown very hairy,' I said.

He laughed. 'It must have been Hannah's salve she used on my bullet wound. Perhaps it is made from the fat of wolves or bears.'

'Bears, I should think.' I laughed from the sheer joy of being home again and hugged him hard. 'Is everyone well?'

'Well enough. Hannah and Nehemiah are valiant for their great age. Mother has never been quite well since Father was taken, but there is nothing really wrong. Just sadness and worry. I am quite recovered, as you can see.'

I could also see that his face had grown thinner.

'Off you go and dress,' I said. 'I'll make up the fire. Do we have oatmeal? I'll make some breakfast. I've had a walk of two miles from the manor.'

'Kitty put the oatmeal to soak last night. The fire is damped down, but there are fresh peats. I won't be long.'

He ran upstairs and as I revived the fire and hung the porridge over the heat to cook, Kitty came out of her room, carelessly dressed and rubbing her eyes.

'Oh, Mistress Mercy, you are home!'

She beamed at me and I hugged her, then held her at arm's length. 'The Lord save us, Kitty, you've grown a foot taller since I've been away!'

She giggled. 'Not really. But I think I *have* grown. I am twelve now.'

'So you are. Such a great age! Well, go and tidy yourself up and comb your hair. I will see to the breakfast. I am hungry as a wolf after my walk.'

Soon we were all sitting around the table and, apart from Father's absence, we might have been just as we were before the drainers came and all our troubles fell upon us. It seemed none of us wanted to talk about it and our conversation was all of simple, daily things.

'After the wet spring,' said Tom, 'the weather has been quite kind. The wheat is ripening up, and full in the grain.'

'Aye,' said Nehemiah, 'I walked the field yesterday, and I think the harvest will be no more'n a couple of weeks late.'

'How goes the eeling?' I asked.

'Not so bad. I go further afield. Away down Baker's Lode to the Nene and thereabouts. And Tom and me, we've been making baskets and hurdles to take to Lincoln market.'

'Regular traders, we are,' said Tom. 'We have a stall in the market now, usually sell all that we bring.'

'I heard Blaze in the barn,' I said.

'Aye,' said Tom. 'We thought it safe to bring him home again. I doubt the sheriff's men will be back.'

'And Hannah has set up a hive,' Kitty joined in. Once she would scarce have spoken at table, but she was growing up. 'She showed me how to weave a skep from osiers and we caught a swarm.'

'Aye.' Hannah reached across and patted Kitty's hand. 'I'll make a bee woman of the lass yet. I think my own bees have followed me here. They are wise, bees. They know more than people give them credit for. I swear these are my own bees come to me again.'

It sounded far-fetched. Yet the ways of bees are mysterious, and no one knew them better than Hannah. So our talk circled around what we would not discuss, but I was happy enough with that. Only my mother said little except, when we were clearing the table, she touched my hand and said, 'I am glad you are come home, Mercy.'

I was stricken, for I saw that she thought I had come home for good.

'Mother, I have only one day's leave. I am here just for the christening of Alice's baby.'

Her face crumpled. 'I thought . . . Oh, perhaps Tom did say . . .' She looked confused and it wrenched at my heart.

'Never mind.' I gave her hand a squeeze. 'We will have a fine day, with the christening and the merry-making at the Coxes'.'

The christening was to take place after morning service in the village church and we were then to adjourn to the Coxes' home where Master Cox planned to treat the village in order to honour the birth of his heir. I dressed carefully, glad to lay aside my rough working clothes and don my best skirt and bodice, with a lace collar I had worked last winter, and a matching cap. I drew on my finest stockings, knitted of delicate lamb's wool, and tied them in place with new garters of blue ribbon. I took up the delicate shawl I had knitted as my christening gift for the baby before ever I left for the manor. My roughened hands snagged on the fine stitches, reminding me how much I had changed. But as I went down the stairs to join my family I could pretend to myself that I was again Isaac Bennington's daughter, and no longer the lowliest kitchen maid to the Dillingworths. The sun was fully risen and there was never a cloud to cast a shadow as my family gathered and set out down the lane to the church and the baptism of Alice Cox's fine new son.

Chapter Seven

The Coxes' house was dressed for festivity. It lay in the village street, at the corner of the green, next to Ned Broadley, the carpenter, and across the way from Will Keane's smithy. Much of the village was already abroad, the women bustling in and out of the Coxes' house with platters and bowls of food, baskets of new cherries and flagons of ale. We had brought a cured ham, our last. We could ill spare it, but family pride meant we could not fail to contribute to the celebration. Trestle tables were being set up in the orchard behind the house by Rafe and other young men of the village, and Tom joined them, while Mother and Hannah found their way to the kitchen. Kitty ran off to join the other children. It was not often that she had the chance to see youngsters of her own age, and I soon heard her giggling with the village girls. As a parish foundling she had been looked down upon by the children of respectable families, but now that she had a trusted position in our household she could hold up her head. I noticed that Joseph Waters had already secured himself a sup of ale and a slice of pie, although eating was not to begin until after church.

I went in search of Alice and found her in the small bedroom she shared with Rafe at the back of the house. I felt a twinge of guilt again at the thought that they were still obliged to live with Rafe's parents. She had lost weight and her face was pale. As she came towards me, hands outstretched, I thought she even moved less easily than before.

'Oh, Mercy, it is so good to see you – how I've missed you!'

We hugged each other and I found I could not speak. I had feared for her so much.

'But your hands, Mercy! What have you done to your hands?'

'Oh, nothing but a little too much honest labour.' I tried to make light of it, but it was difficult to keep the bitterness out of my voice. I drew my parcel from under my arm. I had wrapped it in a piece of soft flannel and tied it with a bit of blue ribbon left over from my new garters.

'This is for my godson, but I do not even know what he is to be called.'

She gave me a wicked sideways smile. 'He is to be Huw.'

'Aha. In honour of his grandfather. Very wise.'

We both laughed as Alice untied the ribbon and unwrapped the shawl.

'Oh, this is so beautiful! You are a much better needlewoman than I am.'

I looked now at my ravaged hands and shook my head. 'Not any more.'

'They will heal. Surely they will heal.'

I felt the balm of Alice's perpetual sunny nature soothing me and realised how I had been holding myself tense as a strung bow all these weeks.

'Am I allowed to see Master Huw Cox the Younger?'

She dimpled and her pallid face flushed a little with pride. 'He is here.'

She led me over to a carved wooden cradle beneath the window and turned back the covers. The baby lay with his tiny fists above his head and his eyes screwed up in sleep. He had a tuft of reddish gold hair, but his lashes were long and black. I leaned over and smelled the new baby scent of him: soap and milk and that indefinable sweetness that all babies bring with them into the world.

'He has your hair.'

'Aye.'

'May I hold him? Or will it wake him?'

'He is very good and sleepy.' She laughed. 'At least in the daytime. Not at night. And I cannot keep him swaddled. See how he pulls his arms free, whatever I do.'

I lifted the baby gently, cradling his head in my cupped hand. They are so tiny, newborns, yet there is such a pulse of life in them. I held him against my shoulder, where he squirmed a little, gave a grunt, then curled into it as if we were one flesh. I laid my cheek against that golden hair and ached with envy.

'He's beautiful. You are so lucky, Alice.'

She sat down on the bed and passed her hand over her face, looking suddenly exhausted.

'I very nearly wasn't. For a time the midwife thought she must kill him to save my life. I had to fight her. I swore at her like one of Cromwell's troopers and said if there was to be any killing, she must kill me and save the babe.'

I thought of the village midwife, Meg Waters, a cousin of Joseph's. She was as big as the blacksmith, with muscles to match. It must have taken some courage to defy her.

'So what happened?'

'What happened was that Hannah Green arrived. She saved us both. Somehow she turned the baby, not right round but so he could come forth more easily. I'd lost a lot of blood then and I kept going in and out of blackness. I heard them arguing, Meg and Hannah, then Hannah took charge. After he was born, she dosed me inside and out, and eventually the bleeding stopped. She made me lie abed for a week.'

'You are still looking pale.'

'I'm much recovered now, though I tire easily. And the young master does not help, waking every hour of the night. Rafe has taken to sleeping in the kitchen.'

'How easy it is, to be a man,' I said.

'Indeed.'

I was reluctant to give up little Huw, but it was time to make our way to church. While Gideon had been absent in Cambridge and Canterbury, the villagers had been obliged to attend church in Crowthorne, where the minister was a fiery reformer, disliked by all of us. The Coxes would not have the baby admitted into the church there, under the new rules, and had made excuses to wait until Gideon returned to our parish, where the proper ceremony could be performed. Alice now wrapped Huw in my shawl and, just as she said, he pulled his arms free at once and curved them over his head. She tutted crossly.

'Don't worry, Alice. Why should he not have his arms free? We don't bind our lambs and calves. Why should we bind our babies?'

'Her ladyship will not be pleased.'

Her mother-in-law.

'She will not bother you in all this company. Besides, you are queen here. You have produced the heir.' Laughing, we walked downstairs and joined the company to go to church.

The summer sun filtered in through the east window I so loved, Mary holding out the white dove, the toddling Christ with his plump feet amongst the daisies. I let the words of the service wash over me and instead watched the shadows of the oak leaves dancing behind the scene. Beyond the very English field of daisies in the stained glass there was an improbable date palm and a very English church standing side by side on a little knoll. A stream ran down across the field and on its bank a hare sat up on its haunches, its paws dangling in front of its chest. It was as tall as the Christ Child and regarded him with interest across the water. I noticed, as I had never done before, that the Child was not looking at his mother but at the hare. He was stepping towards it, holding out his bunch of daisies. Perhaps he thought the hare would enjoy eating them.

My attention was caught by the final blessing, and we shuffled to our feet. Little Huw had remained docile in his mother's arms all through the service and I hoped he would maintain his good behaviour during the christening, though they do say that a child ought to cry when the baptismal water touches him. It is supposed to let out the Devil. I could not believe there was any Devil in that beautiful child.

Most of the congregation was leaving, bowing and exchanging a few words with Gideon at the door. They would finish the preparations for our merry-making while a small party remained behind for the christening – the Cox family (Mistress Cox leaning on her husband's arm, he on a stout stick) and the three godparents: Toby Ashford, Tom and I. We gathered around

103

the font, which was near the door of the church. A crudely hollowed stone, roughly circular, it was very ancient. Gideon thought it might even date from before the time that the Saxons converted to Christianity. There were strange carvings so old and rubbed that it was difficult to make them out, though with the tip of my finger I had once traced a horseman and something that might have been a mirror or a horse-collar. Later carvers had added Christian symbols, the Chi Rho and a cross with four equal arms. Someone had started to carve an inscription 'Deus no...' but had abandoned the hard granite. The stone itself was unusual, for we do not find granite around these parts.

Alice handed Huw to me and again he curled himself into my shoulder as Gideon, shining in a white surplice, began the baptismal services, holding Queen Elizabeth's Prayer Book open before him.

Wilt thou then obediently keep God's holy will and commandments, and walk in the same all the days of thy life?

Tom, Toby and I as godparents answered, *I will.*

When I handed the baby to Gideon, I thought I could hear the distant sound of galloping hoofs, but told myself it was my imagination. Who would be galloping through the village on a summer Sunday morning? The sound seemed to be coming from the direction of the manor, but onwards from here the road led nowhere except to our farm and the Fens.

We receive this Child into the congregation of Christ's flock, and do sign him with the sign of the Cross, in token that hereafter he shall not be ashamed to confess the faith of Christ crucified, and manfully to fight under his banner, against sin, the world, and the devil; and to continue Christ's faithful soldier and servant unto his life's end. Amen.

As Gideon was anointing Huw's head with the water from the font, his eyes sprang open in surprise and I saw that they were a deep blue. He did not cry out, but gurgled in pleasure and waved his fists in Gideon's face. Then I realised the very moment when Gideon also heard the horses. We looked at each other in alarm as he spoke the thanksgiving:

We yield thee most hearty thanks, most merciful Father, that it hath pleased thee to regenerate this Infant with thy holy Spirit . .

.

When he handed the baby back to me, everyone heard the disturbance. The horses were right outside. Men were shouting. There was a clatter as the horses pulled up, a jingle of harness, then the church door burst open and a dozen soldiers of the Model Army, carrying muskets and wearing armour, poured into the church.

We all shrank back, all except Gideon who stood unmoved beside the font, the Prayer Book in his hand.

'What evil papist practices are these?' A heavy-built man, clearly in command, strode towards us, pointing his musket at Gideon.

'Nothing but the baptism of a babe,' said Gideon mildly, 'according to the word of the English Church.'

The man, a captain, grabbed the book. 'This!' He waved it in the air. 'This Romish witchcraft is banned, as well you know, priest.'

He leaned his gun against the font and began to rip the pages from the book and throw them into the font. Gideon gave a cry and reached out to take the book back, but another soldier struck him across the face with the butt of his musket. Blood began to run down from his nose and stain the front of his surplice. Tom took a step forward, raising his fists, but at once several of the soldiers turned their guns on the three young men. The rest of us were clearly no threat. Mistress Cox had gone as white as milk and collapsed into the hindmost pew. Her husband, his legs trembling beneath him, sank down beside her. Alice had pressed her fist into her mouth to stop herself from crying out, but looked as though she might faint at any moment. I clutched Huw convulsively in my arms. The only one unmoved by the arrival of the soldiers, he held out his arms toward them.

My heart pounding, I tried to step closer to Alice, so that she could see the baby was safe, but at my first movement the captain picked up his musket and pointed it at me.

'Stay where you are!' He nodded to two of the soldiers and pointed at the window beyond the altar. 'Deal with that. And you! Tear down the rails and carry the altar outside for firewood.'

The men hurried to do his bidding. There was the crash of breaking glass as they swung their muskets against the window of the Madonna and Child. A few fragments fell to the floor, others outside, but large sections were held in place by the lead-work. Nothing deterred, they continued to smash it until the lead buckled and the east end of the church was strewn with a litter of jewel-like fragments. Then they turned to help their fellows heave the heavy altar out through the door and to stamp on the delicate carving of the altar rails, until they joined the broken glass in an horrific mosaic of destruction.

The captain swaggered up to the far end of the church and stirred the mess with the toe of his riding boot.

'Good,' he grunted. 'One less church of Rome.'

'We are not Catholics,' Gideon protested, as he wiped his bloodied face with the sleeve of his surplice. 'We are true to the English Christian Church. The church established under our Sovereign Lady, Queen Elizabeth.'

The captain walked back and stood over him.

'There are no kings or queens in England now. You are filthy recusants who disobey the orders of the government. You have been ordered, you and all your fellows, to cease these superstitious practices.'

He turned to the font, where the pages of the Prayer Book floated and then sank.

'Holy water? Holy shit!' He spat into the font. Then he unlaced his breeches and aimed an arc of piss into the baptismal water.

'Help yourselves, boys. As good a pisspot as I've seen anywhere.'

Laughing and making crude gestures, the other soldiers unlaced themselves and followed his example. Gideon threw himself forward, but was struck again and thrown to the ground, where he lay very still. Tom and Rafe both started toward the font, but were seized by the soldiers and pushed down to kneel on the ground with muskets to their heads. When Toby shouted out, he was forced to join them.

While their attention was distracted, I began to ease my way towards Alice, who stood trembling, gripping the back of the pew where the Coxes sat, as though she would collapse if she let go.

'Trooper Winter!' said the captain, 'fetch my horse!'

What did they plan now? They had defiled the font and wrecked the church. Did they intend to turn it into a stable?

One of the soldiers returned, leading a big bay stallion, who skittered sideways and rolled his eyes, frightened by the unfamiliar narrow spaces, and sensing the atmosphere of fear and loathing, as any intelligent animal will do. As he sidled away from the captain one of his rear hoofs came down hard on Gideon's hand. I heard him cry out. At least he was still alive. I watched as he struggled to get to his feet, then fell back again. I began to shake and clutched the baby more tightly in my arms, afraid of dropping him.

'Winter, give me your helmet.'

The trooper obeyed, looking baffled, but then the captain used it to scoop up some of the befouled water from the font.

'I baptise you Destrier,' he said, in a mock-pious voice, 'by the father, the son and the holy spirit, so help me, the Romish God and all his saints and angels and ghouls and hobgoblins.'

He poured the helmetful of water over the horse's head and the terrified animal backed away, dragging his reins from the captain's hand and rearing up. His front feet crashed down again, striking sparks from the stone floor, then he broke away and shot out of the door. The captain threw down the helmet.

'Fetch him back,' he said, and two of the soldiers ran out.

'Now,' he said, 'it is time we taught this recusant priest what it means to disobey Cromwell.'

I cannot speak of what happened next. I gave Huw back to Alice and buried my face in my hands. I could not look, but I could not stop myself hearing what they did to Gideon. At the sound of every blow, my stomach clenched. He was trying to keep silent, but his very body seemed to betray him into terrible, suppressed grunts. I raised my head for a moment and saw one of the soldiers raise a booted foot and kick him in the small of the back. Gideon's body arched like a broken doll. Then I saw the captain draw his sword and bring it down on Gideon's back. I clamped my arms over my head and a moan broke from my lips. At last everything was silent, except for the heavy breathing of the soldiers.

'Right,' said the captain. 'The rest of you can go now. Out with you.'

With the soldiers prodding us in the back with the barrels of their muskets, our pathetic little group was herded out to the village green. On the far side, guarded by more soldiers, the rest of the village had gathered, their faces stunned. One of the troopers was walking the captain's horse up and down to calm him. A sodden page from the Prayer Book was lodged in his mane.

As I stumbled into the sunlight, I saw that there was another mounted man with the soldiers. A man in elegant clothes which looked out of place amongst their buff coats.

Edmund Dillingworth made me an ironic bow, and smiled.

When the troopers and their informer had ridden away, people began to move slowly about, as if they walked in their sleep. Gideon had been left in the church. Dead or alive, we could not know, but I had to discover the truth and confront that horror in the church. I felt as cold as the ice-bound Fen in winter, and could not stop the shaking of my hands, but I found Kitty, keeping close to my mother and wide-eyed with fright.

'Kitty, you must find Hannah for me. Tell her to come to the church. Master Clarke is badly hurt. Then go to Mistress Cox's maid and ask for water and rags. Bring them to the church.' I was surprised that my voice sounded almost normal, although it seemed to come from a long way away.

She stood frozen, unable to move, so I gave her shoulder a shake.

'Quickly, Kitty!'

She ran off.

Alice and Rafe had taken Huw home. Tom and Toby were huddled with the other young men of the village, talking together in low but angry voices. Had they all forgotten Gideon? Or was he already dead and I too stupefied to see it? Reluctantly I turned back to the church, afraid of what I might find there. The door was half wrenched off its hinges and the interior was unnaturally bright.

108

Summer sunlight, untouched by what had happened here, flooded in from the doorway and the naked east window, where a few twists of lead and bits of coloured glass still dangled. I shaded my eyes against the light, and saw that the upper half of the hare swung in the breeze, as though he had hanged himself.

Gideon was lying face down in a pool of blood beside the font, curled up with his arms around his head as if he had tried to protect himself. His surplice was ripped off, and his torn shirt revealed the sword slashes across his back. His hair was a mass of matted blood. One shoe lay on its side, his stocking half pulled down, as if he had been dragged along the floor by his feet. My stomach heaved as I knelt down beside him, my skirt soaking up the blood. He must be dead already. One of the sword cuts ran deep into his left side and blood was pouring from it. Some vague memory stirred in me. Did not the blood stop flowing once a man was dead?

I reached out a shaking hand and felt beneath his ear. At first I could not tell whether I felt a pulse or whether it was the pounding of my own heart. Could it be that he still lived, despite these terrible injuries? A darkness rose around me and I knew that if Gideon were dead, something would die in me too. It burst on me with sudden clarity that this man was more to me than I had ever allowed myself to know. Surely there was a faint pulse there in his neck, no more than a faint flutter. Something fell on my hand and I realised that I was weeping. Angrily I brushed my eyes. This was no time for weakness.

There was a pulse, I was sure of it. I remembered the hay field and Gideon lying back in the sun, his shirt open to reveal the steady beat of his heart.

'Thank God,' I whispered. 'Thank God.'

I looked up as Kitty crept through the door. She carried a pail of water and a bundle of rags.

'Hannah is coming,' she whispered. 'The rector, is he dead?'

'Not yet, I think. Before all else, I must bind up this great wound in his side. Give me the rags.'

She crept a little nearer and set down the water and rags. Nervously she looked down at Gideon and gave a cry. 'Oh,

Mistress Mercy, surely he must be dead! How could they treat him so?'

'They were savages,' I said. 'Help me to tear the cloth into strips.'

We had made a length of bandage and I was trying to bind it around that terrible wound in Gideon's side when Hannah arrived. Kitty had struggled, unable to lift him enough for me to pass the bandage around his chest, but between the two of them they eased him far enough off the floor for me to pass my arms under and around, until I could secure it tightly. Still the blood soaked the cloth at once.

'I cannot stop the bleeding.' I turned frantic eyes to Hannah. 'What shall I do?'

'We must bind his head as well,' she said. Her calm voice steadied me. 'Then we must have him carried home. All my salves and potions are there.'

She ran her hand over his right arm, which I now saw was crooked at an unnatural angle. 'I think his shoulder is dislocated too, but we cannot set it here.'

'Kitty,' I said, 'run to Tom and tell him to find a litter – a sheep hurdle or a door – and some others of the men to help us carry Master Clarke to the farm. Quickly now. We must be quick.'

I was sure that with every minute that passed, Gideon's life was slipping away from me. Hannah gave me a sharp look as Kitty ran from the church.

'I'm sorry,' I said, not knowing why I was apologising. 'I don't know what . . .'

She reached out across Gideon's body and patted my hand.

'We'll take him home and care for him. The Lord looks after his own. Surely he will not allow this good man to die.'

'He allowed many good men to die in the War,' I said bitterly. 'Aye, and women and children too.'

I wished I had her faith. All I could hear ringing in my head was the sounds of the soldiers hacking at Gideon, and all I could see was Edmund Dillingworth, smiling upon his horse.

Tom came, and half a dozen strong men, and they lifted Gideon on to a sheep hurdle. We had bound the bloody mess that was Gideon's head, but his eyes were swollen shut. I could not even be sure that he still had eyes. Hannah told them to lay Gideon on his side, the side without the worst injury, and as we carried him out of the church, Alice came running with a blanket to lay over him. Her face was blotched with weeping.

'I know it is a warm day,' she said, 'but he has been so badly hurt. He may be cold.'

Her hands shook so much she could barely spread the blanket over him.

'He did this for my Huw, and now he may die for it.' She gave a great shuddering sob. 'This my fault, mine and Rafe's, for wanting proper baptism.'

'Go back to Huw,' I said, trying to sound calm. 'We will carry Gideon to the farm. He did what he believed to be right. You must not take the blame on yourself or little Huw.'

She nodded but stayed watching us until we passed round the bend in the lane, twisting her hands in her skirt, her face white and drawn.

'Rafe,' I said, for he was one of the bearers, 'go back to Alice and see that she rests. She is still weak. I will take your place.'

He nodded, clearly relieved, and gave up his place to me. I knew my poor strength could make little difference to the bearers, but I needed to be doing something.

As we drew near the farm, I ran ahead to make ready Kitty's bed, where we had nursed Nehemiah all those weeks ago. Then I stirred up the fire and put water on to boil. As the men lifted Gideon on to the bed, I climbed up to Hannah's room in the attic to fetch down her satchel of medicines. I caught up some of the wax-stoppered bottles arranged along the windowsill, unsure of what she would need. Hannah could not write and marked the labels with symbols known only to her, but I thought I recognised one or two she had used on Nehemiah's broken head.

When I came into the little room and saw Gideon lying there, mangled and bloody and pale as death, I thought my heart had stopped in my body. He could not surely live.

But Hannah was brisk, rolling up her sleeves and sending Kitty to bring the hot water. 'We must strip him, Mercy, to see how bad is the damage. His shoulder will need to be set and that great wound in his side must be sewn up. I do not like the look of his eyes.'

I shivered. I thought of Gideon's great love of his books. He would rather spend his meagre stipend on books than on food. What if he were to live, but be blind? Would he thank us for saving him? I pushed the thought away. There might be little chance of saving him.

Hannah made nothing of stripping Gideon to the skin, though I was embarrassed and felt he would not wish me to see him thus, but Hannah was right. To do our best for him we must put such feelings aside and I must behave as if this was some stranger, a soldier wounded on the field of battle.

The sight of him stripped was shocking, his whole body bloodied and bruised. Why had they attacked him so viciously? I had heard of other clergymen being beaten when their churches were smashed by the iconoclasts sent by the Earl of Manchester, but they were generally given a mild drubbing then turned out of their livings, to beg or go into exile. This beating was something much worse. I wondered whether it had been ordered by Edmund Dillingworth.

'We will set the shoulder last,' said Hannah, 'lest the shock of it wake him. It will be best for now if he remains out of his wits.'

We swabbed the injuries to his back and sides, using water into which Hannah had mixed one of her bottled potions which turned it the pale green of spring leaves. Then we spread them with one of her salves, binding up the worst but leaving others open to the air. She told me to fetch scissors and cut away Gideon's hair from the great wound in the back of his head. My hands shook so much she took the scissors from me and finished the task herself. We peered closely at the wound, but there did not appear to be any sign of splintered bone.

'His eyes,' I whispered. 'What of his eyes?'

Hannah looked grim, but did not answer. The lids were swollen and caked with blood which had dried to a hard crust. She shook her head. 'I cannot tell whether it is best to wash away the dried blood or to leave well alone. If we remove the scabs we may do more harm.'

I sank on to my knees beside the bed and slipped my arm under Gideon's neck. His eyes were a terrible sight.

'Surely we cannot leave them like this,' I said.

'Very well. You may bathe them very carefully. I must make up a fresh wash. This other is too strong for eyes. But first we must stitch the wound in his side.'

We had bathed and salved the wound along with the rest, but it continued to bleed, perhaps not quite as severely as before. I wondered whether he had any blood left.

'Fetch me a needle and some strong thread. Button thread, not your embroidery silks.'

I did as I was bid and watched, biting my lips and trying to keep down the heaving of my stomach as Hannah sewed great stitches to draw together the gaping sides of the wound. She had done about half when she stopped and rubbed her eyes.

'My sight is not as good as it was, Mercy. You will have to do the rest.'

I looked at her in horror. I had never done such a thing. How could I drive a needle through a man's flesh, draw that bloodied skin together as if I were sewing a pair of breeches?

'Here.' Hannah passed me the needle, thread and scissors. 'Don't waste any more time. Don't be squeamish, child.'

So I gritted my teeth and made the last six stitches, struggling against nausea and the shaking of my hands. When it was done, we wrapped a fresh bandage around his chest, and Hannah went through into the kitchen to make up the wash for his eyes. I put my arms around him and eased him over onto his back, and as I did so he gave a faint moan, the first sound he had made since the soldiers struck him down.

'Is that Mercy?' His whisper was so faint I had to lean close to hear.

'Aye, Gideon. You are back at the farm and Hannah and I are caring for you.'

'It is quite dark.'

'Your eyes are stuck together with dried blood. I'm going to wash them for you. We've bound your other wounds.'

He did not answer and I realised he had sunk back into his darkness.

When Hannah came I began slowly and carefully to wash away the dried blood. As I held Gideon's shoulders and head close in my arms, the blood and water ran down over my bodice until I was soaked to the skin and my dress stained a brownish red. When at last his eyes were clear I saw that although the lids and surrounding skin were bruised and swollen, the soldiers did not seem to have put out his eyes, as I had feared. There might, however, be permanent injury to his sight.

After I was done, we swathed his head in bandages, covering both his eyes and the wound on the back of his head. I was determined to stay with him so that if he woke again and feared the darkness before him, I could reassure him. There remained only the setting of his dislocated shoulder.

'Tom,' Hannah called, 'do you and Toby come here to assist us.'

They came cautiously through the door and I realised they had been all this while waiting in the kitchen. How much time had passed, I could not be sure, but from the fading light I realised it must be drawing towards evening.

Hannah explained what they must do to pull the arm out hard until the shoulder clicked back into place. Reluctantly I slid my arm out from under Gideon's shoulders and stepped out of the way. It happened quickly, but the jerk and snap as the damaged shoulder was reset turned my stomach and suddenly I could take no more. I ran from the house, across the yard and behind the barn, where I vomited until I was empty.

Back in the house I sank down for a moment on a stool next to the kitchen fire and wiped my mouth on the back of my hand. Toby must have returned to the village. Tom gripped my shoulder.

'You've done bravely, Mercy.'

'Do you think he will live?'

'Every chance, I should think, though it was a terrible beating. Why would they do such a thing?'

I shook my head. 'They were put up to it by Edmund Dillingworth.'

'I saw he was there. And I wondered why. Then I realised that if he wants to ingratiate himself with Cromwell's men, known as he is for having fought for the king, becoming an informer might be to his benefit. But how could he know Gideon was going to carry out a baptism?'

'It is my fault.' I began to weep. 'Fool that I was, I told him. I thought his sympathies lay our way. But I think he would never have betrayed Gideon, if I had not–'. I broke off.

'If you had not done what?'

I told Tom of Edmund's attempt to rape me and how I had kneed him in the groin, then made a fool of him before the kitchen staff. Before we could talk further, my mother and Nehemiah returned at last from the village and we had all to tell over of Gideon's injuries and how we had treated them.

'But, Mercy!' said my mother, suddenly alarmed. 'You must set off at once, or you will not be at the manor before dark. Did you not say that you had but this one day's leave?'

'I am not going back to the manor,' I said. 'I shall never return there.'

Chapter Eight

I turned on my heel to go back to Gideon, drawn to his bedside as relentlessly as the ebb tide sucking the waters of the Lode away to the sea. There was nothing more to discuss about the manor or the Dillingworths. I had driven all thought of them from my mind. Yet my mother laid her hand on my arm and fixed troubled eyes on my face.

'But you must go back, Mercy, it is your duty.'

I shook my head. At first I was surprised that my mother continued to urge me to return to the manor, since it was she who had thought at first that I had come home for good. But when I dragged my mind away from the small room and the silent, battered figure which lay there, I understood.

The custom of decades, and before my mother the custom of generations, had instilled in her a sense of duty and obedience towards the Dillingworths. I was employed by them. They had agreed to keep me on after my month's trial. I could not therefore of my own will walk away. Even her own relationship with the family counted for nothing. By marrying a yeoman – my mother's grandfather – Mary Dillingworth had demeaned herself and set her descendents lower down the social hierarchy than her own family. My mother could not see that the world was changing, that the old order had been disrupted for good. With a king dethroned and imprisoned, gentry families like the Dillingworths no longer stood on such sure ground as they had in the past. They could no longer command obedience. My mother would never understand this. Tom and I might read the tracts written by John Lilburne and his

116

friends, but we would never even try to make our mother understand.

Not that I attempted to reason or argue with her now. I simply said I would not return.

Tom looked at me and raised his eyebrows. I gave a faint nod. Let him tell her if he would. He led her to our father's great chair and settled her in it, with a cushion at her back, for we could both see that she was exhausted by the troubles of the day. He knelt down beside her and took both her hands in his.

'Mother, you must understand why Mercy cannot go back. Edmund Dillingworth tried to defile her.'

Her mouth fell open in shock and she uttered a faint cry.

'Do not worry,' I said. 'I managed to escape him. But he will not forgive me. And if I go back, he will attempt it again. Besides . . .'

I glanced again towards the door of Kitty's room, where Hannah was clearing away our bloody rags and basins.

'It was Edmund Dillingworth who brought the troop of soldiers to the baptism. They have wreaked havoc on the church and come near to killing Gideon.'

'What do you mean?' Her look of distress and bemusement wrenched at me.

'Did you not see him? Sitting upon his horse, watching everything and smiling his delight in all of it?'

She shook her head. 'I did not see him.'

'We think he did it for two reasons,' Tom said. 'He knew Mercy would be there, and that it was her friend's baby who was to be baptised. It was a form of revenge on Mercy. And by showing zeal for Puritan reforms, he buys himself favour with the authorities, to balance against his service on behalf of the king.'

My mother stared at him in confusion. 'I do not understand.'

Tom rose to his feet and patted her shoulder. 'Do not worry yourself about it, Mother. Mercy will not return to the manor and the Dillingworths will not expect it after what has happened here. Mercy, can you make us some supper? I for one have not eaten since early this morning, and I am sure Mother will feel the better for some hot food.'

I cast another anxious glance towards the open door of the room where Gideon lay. I wanted to be there, beside him, but Tom was right. We all needed sustenance at the end of this terrible day. My own stomach, I now realised, ached for food.

'Kitty,' I said, 'make up the fire and put on a pot of water to boil. I can contrive a pottage.'

I fetched onions and carrots from the store and met Nehemiah crossing the yard.

'I have milked the cows,' he said, 'and set the milk for your cheese-making.'

'Thank you,' I said. In all the confusion I had not realised how late it was, long past milking time. 'What is that you're carrying?'

'Rafe sent back our ham. The Coxes cut short the feast for the christening, seeing what happened. You had gone by then, but he knew we would be glad of the ham.'

'Oh, aye!' Now that I was back at home, the farm would need to feed one more.

In the kitchen I carved one thin slice from the ham and chopped it small. Kitty had already added a handful of last year's dried peas and the same of barley to the water, and when they had boiled for a time I stirred in the ham and the sliced onions and carrots, as well as marjoram and some mustard seed.

It was so late by the time we sat down to sup that Tom lit a rushlight so that we might see our bowls and cut the bread. I said nothing about the lack of candles. We were paupers now. I noticed that Tom and Kitty had made a store of rushlights from rush-heads gathered from the Fen and dipped in tallow. The light they gave was dim and the smell dreadful, compared with our usual wax candles, but we must make do with little and like it.

When we had supped I carried a bowl to Gideon in the hope that he might have woken, but he lay as still as a marble knight on a tomb, his breathing so shallow I had to lean close to detect it. With his head swathed in bandages he looked like some Saracen chieftain from the days of the Crusades. Until that moment I had been so caught up in caring for his wounds, I had not given myself time to think, but now I had to confront the truth. Despite all our care, despite the agony of my longing, he could still die. I

118

remembered him telling me once that more soldiers die of their wounds afterwards than die at the height of a battle. I bowed my head down and hid my face in the bedclothes.

Through the confusion of my thoughts I heard the others preparing to go up to bed.

'I will sit a while with Gideon,' I called, 'in case he wakes and needs anything.'

Tom brought in a fresh rushlight in its holder. 'You cannot sit in darkness.'

'Do not put it too near. Jesu, the stench is frightful!' I did my best to sound cheerful.

He laughed. 'You will get used to it. No fine beeswax candles here now, like the manor house.'

'I am well rid of it,' I said softly.

I saw his shadow nod on the wall.

'Aye,' he said. 'I do not think you would be safe there from Edmund. The bastard! That he should try to rape my sister!'

'He spoke me very pretty for a time. Called me cousin. The other servants were unkind, so for one of the family to acknowledge our kinship . . . I thought he was honourable. I thought I could trust him.'

'So you let it slip. About the baptism.'

'No. I told him freely, never thinking he was a danger. A King's man. Surely he would support the traditions and sanctities of the English church?'

'He is a brute, a lecher and a traitor.' Tom's voice shook with fury. It frightened me a little, coming out of the dark.

'Tom, you must not think of taking any revenge!'

'I would dearly like to.'

'We have enough troubles as it is, with Father in prison, our stock impounded, the drainers continuing their work unchecked. Promise me that you will not attempt anything against Edmund.'

He sighed. 'You have my word. For the present, at any rate. And the drainers are not quite unimpeded.'

'What do you mean?'

He gave the ghost of a laugh. 'No outright attacks any more. But tools go missing in the night. The bolts holding a sluice gate drop out and vanish into the mud. A remote section of a dyke collapses for no reason. Oh, we have learned to be subtle, never fear.'

I smiled into the darkness. 'I am glad to hear it.'

'Now I am going to bed,' he said. 'Shall I relieve you during the night?'

'No, do not trouble.'

I was jealous of my right to stay by Gideon's side and see to his needs.

Tom bade me goodnight and I heard him feel his way up the stairs, not bothering to light a taper.

Indeed, there was little I could do for Gideon. He continued to lie without movement, so that twice in the first hour or so I thought he had stopped breathing. I took his wrist in my hand to feel his pulse. It was faint as the beat of a moth's wing, but it was there.

After a time I kept his hand clasped between both of mine and resting in my lap where I sat on a stool pulled close to his bed. His hand felt clammy and cold, despite the warmth of the summer night. The rushlight smoked and flickered, and began to burn out, so I laid his hand gently back on his chest and got up to fetch another. My back was aching from sitting so long on the low backless stool. I stretched to ease it, then decided to heat a stone to warm the bed. I did not like the chill feel of his flesh.

We kept a few large flat stones which were used in the depths of winter to warm our beds, when ice formed on the inside of the windows in the rooms away from the fire. I heated one now, resting on a trivet at the side of the kitchen fire which I had fed to keep it burning strongly, for the heat from the kitchen reached partly into the bedroom. I had noticed that my family was now using nothing but peat, dug free from the peat moor, instead of more precious firewood. A wonderful boon for us commoners, peat. But it was said that, after draining, the peat moors would shrink and dry up, the peat turning to dust, so that we would no longer have this source of fuel. The draining of our Fens would not only rob us of much of our food – fish and eels and waterfowl – but of fuel to cook it and keep us warm in winter. The rushes and osiers would die away, so there would be no thatch or rushlights or hurdles or baskets or eel-traps. And if the common lands were enclosed and taken from us, where would we graze our beasts and plant our crops? I shivered at the terrifying thought of the bleak future which we seemed doomed to suffer.

When the stone was well heated through, I wrapped it in a cloth and slipped it under the blankets close to Gideon's feet. Like his hands they were icy, despite the covering of blankets. I lit a fresh rushlight and clipped it into the holder, wrinkling my nose at the rancid smell. I could not believe I would ever grow accustomed to it. The smoke, too, was choking and could not do my patient any good, but I needed some light in order to keep a watch on him.

With a faint groan I resumed my seat on the low stool, and smiled at my own weakness. 'You are become as creaking as an old dame,' I scolded myself aloud, then stopped, embarrassed by the sound of my own voice. I wrapped my skirts around my legs, for they too were growing cold. My skirts felt unpleasantly stiff and I realised that they were caked with Gideon's blood, which had hardened as it dried. I had worn my best skirt and bodice for the baptism. The stains would never come out. My mind shied away from the thought that these stains might be all I had left of him in years to come.

For greater comfort I untied the strings of my cap and laid it down on the bed, then unwound my head cloth and shook out my hair. As it tumbled around my shoulders I felt more at ease. I inched the stool into the corner made by the upper part of the bed and the wall, so that I could lean back, then I took Gideon's hand in mine again. Perhaps I imagined it, but his hand felt a little warmer, as though the blood had begun to stir again. But how much blood he had lost! As the minutes slipped by, his hand moulded itself to mine, flesh to flesh, so that I felt my own strength flowing towards him. My eyes closed, I tried to will him to life.

To sit up at night with a sick or injured person is to enter a strange half world, where the normal senses are distorted. In that dim, smoky light I could see little except the rough shape of Gideon under the blankets, but, as if to compensate, my hearing became sharper as I strained unconsciously to hear every breath he drew. Sometimes the breathing seemed to stop, or my hearing failed, and then panic would rise in my throat while I tried to still the sound of my own breathing, the beat of my own heart, leaning close to his face in the darkness until I caught again that faint whisper of breath.

When the sight of our eyes cannot overwhelm our other senses, the ability to pick out individual scents becomes sharper. Despite the rancid, burnt-fat stink of the rushlight, I could detect the black caramel smell of the peat fire and a lingering hint of our supper pottage in the air. As always, the kitchen held the dried memories of past summers in its bunches of herbs – mint and savoury, tarragon and thyme, rosemary and marjoram – while the ham, returned to its hook in the main beam above the fireplace, brought the promise of food to stave off starvation. The hot stone I had placed in the bed caused the blankets to give off the comforting scent of warm wool, which still held a touch of the lanolin from the raw fleece. It reminded me of the happy days I had spent sheep-shearing. It had been labour every bit as exhausting as scrubbing the manor kitchen floor, but it had been labour with a purpose, with a pile of fleeces at the end of it, the promise of wool to card and spin and weave and knit.

And although I could barely see Gideon as the rushlight burnt away and faded, I could feel his hand in mine. Warm, now, and supple, no longer feeling like the hand of a dead man.

As the rushlight went out, I must have dozed, for I woke suddenly from a terrible dream, my heart pounding in the surrounding darkness. I had been again in the desecrated church, the terrified horse charging down the nave, sparks flying from its hoofs, bearing down on me. Then I was on the floor and someone was gripping my head, forcing me to watch as the soldiers lashed Gideon with their swords. I saw them pound his face and the captain thrust his sword deep into his side. I struggled and struggled to cry out, but my throat was blocked, choked, as though a lump of rags had been thrust down it. My mouth was open, straining, gagging – until my struggles woke me.

For a moment I thought I was still in the church and my eyes had been bound so that I could no longer see, but then I remembered where I was. In my sleep I had slipped sideways, half off the stool, so that I was wedged between the stool and the bed, my left knee painfully pressed against the flagstones, my back twisted. I was still holding Gideon's hand in one of mine, clutching it convulsively. Awkwardly I crawled back up on to the stool. It was still the dark of the night, though there was a very faint glow showing through the door from the kitchen fire. I must get another light. I stumbled to my feet and felt my way into the kitchen.

As I lit another rushlight from the embers of the fire and carefully laid on a square of peat to coax it back to life, I heard the single sweet note of a blackbird somewhere nearby, probably on the roof of the cowbarn. For a few moments there was silence, then it sang again, a long, liquid waterfall of notes. It was answered by another blackbird, further away. Then the repetitive call of a great tit, remarkably assertive for such a small bird. A brief silence again, then a robin, a song thrush, a willow warbler. Although to my human eyes it was still night, not even the faintest grey in the sky, the birds knew that dawn was coming. I went over to the window and threw it open, the better to hear them. Such tiny creatures, their lives so brief and chancy, yet they sing in hope and belief that the dawn will come. They need no gods, no rituals of faith. Somehow in their small hearts they find the courage to go on.

I laid my forehead against the cold stone of the windowsill and closed my eyes. My body fell into a kind of deep stillness which somehow comforted me. The dawn would come. The day would break over this world of Fen and fields. Life would carry me forward, however uncertain the future seemed. I lifted my head and turned away from the window. Gideon will recover, and some day I will admit that I love him.

The rushlight was drooping in its holder. I straightened it, picked it up, and went back to my vigil.

Despite the brevity of my troubled sleep, I was fully awake now. I set the rushlight on the small coffer where Kitty kept her clothes and straightened the blankets which covered Gideon. They were pulled awry as though he had been restless, yet I had not seen him move since we had laid him down. I gazed at his bandaged head and face. When he did at last wake, he would be in darkness. He must not be alone when that happened, for he would have no idea where he was. After the beating he had endured, he might think himself imprisoned by the soldiers. And blind. I shuddered.

When I took my seat again and picked up his hand, it stirred in mine. I caught my breath. Would he wake at last? I pressed his hand and thought I felt some response, then it went limp again.

'Gideon?' I leaned close to him. 'Gideon, you are safe here. It is Mercy here with you. You are safe here at Turbary Holm. You have been badly hurt, but we have dressed your wounds. There is a bandage around your head, so you will not yet be able to see.'

I gulped. My voice sounded thin and scared. Gideon did not move or respond, but lay still like one dead.

For three days Gideon lingered somewhere in the borderland between life and death, and I veered between hope and despair. Each night I sat with him. Each day, reluctantly, I would rest for a time while Hannah watched over him, but soon I was back, taking up my position again on the stool beside his bed. My family did not comment on my determination to stay with him. Time enough to think on that if he recovered. I had confessed to myself that I loved him, but could not imagine that he could think of me as anything other than the child he had once taught. Several times a day and again at night, I tried to trickle a little small ale or one of Hannah's herbal potions between his lips. Most of it spilled on to the cloth I laid across his chest, but a little was swallowed, else I think he would have died in those first days.

During the night of the fourth day, he began to stir restlessly, uttering faint moans. When I tried to tuck the tangled blankets around him, he threw them off again. I felt the little of his brow that showed above the bandage. Where before he had been cold and clammy, now he was on fire. Should I call Hannah? No, I knew what to do. I fetched a jug of fresh cold water from the pantry and bathed as much of his face as I could reach, and the inside of his wrists. We had dressed him in a night shift of my father's, which hung loosely on him, for he was of much slighter build. I turned back the blankets and untied the strings at the neck. He was sweating profusely. Again I bathed what I could reach – his neck and armpits, the upper part of his chest above the bandaged sword slashes. When I had finished, I rolled the blankets to the bottom of the bed. Heat rose off his body so that I could feel it. I knew I must let the heat escape, but I did not like to leave him quite uncovered. From the coffer in the hallway, I lifted out a linen sheet which my mother had woven as part of my dowry. It was stiff but scented strongly of lavender, which aids sleep. I spread it over Gideon, not tucking it in but leaving it hanging loose. It seemed that already he was a little cooler.

I made up the kitchen fire and carried a cup into the bedroom. I was hot and thirsty and poured myself a cup of water. As if the clink of the jug against the pewter cup had at last penetrated that awful stillness, Gideon whispered, 'Water.'

My heart gave a great leap. I slid my arm under his shoulders and lifted him up. His body was still so hot in my arms that it burned me through my bodice.

'Here is water,' I said. 'Careful. I will help you drink.'

He sipped the water at first, then drank greedily. Despite my attempt to hold the cup steady, some of the water ran down over his chin and on to his shift. I set down the cup and with my free hand mopped it up with my handkerchief.

'Good,' he said. And after a pause, 'Is that Mercy?'

'Aye. You are at our farm. Quite safe.'

'I don't remember . . . What happened?'

'Later. Do not worry about it now. You were injured. But now you are recovering.'

'Very hot.'

'You've had a fever, but it is going down now.'

He lay still for a long time until my arm became numb and I thought he had fallen asleep again.

'Mercy,' he said quietly, in what was almost his normal voice, 'I cannot see.'

I felt tears prick my eyes, but I forced myself to speak cheerfully. 'You have some damage to your face and the back of your head. Hannah and I have bandaged you, that is all. It is night time anyway, and dark.'

'You have been sitting up with me?'

'Aye.' I pressed his hand. 'Have you much pain?'

He seemed to consider for a while. 'My head does hurt. And my left side. And my back.' He asked again, 'What happened?'

'It was a troop of soldiers. They broke in upon the baptism and gave you a beating.'

I thought it better not to tell him of the desecration of his church, but even so he became agitated and tried to sit up.

'The baby, Alice Cox's baby, he is safe?'

'Aye. They did not touch him.'

'And did I complete the baptism? It was not left undone?'

'You had just said the blessing. Little Huw is safely baptised.'

He sank back with a sigh. 'That is well.' His voice sounded blurred and a few minutes later I saw that he was asleep, truly asleep, and this time it seemed to be natural. I leaned forward and kissed him lightly on the lips, knowing that I would not wake him.

Then I rested my head against the wall and found myself also drifting off into a deep, untroubled dream.

The next morning Gideon was able to eat a little porridge and I realised that I must resume my normal work about the farm. I milked the two cows and set a batch of milk and rennet to start cheese-making. I churned butter, scrubbed out the dairy and cleaned the hen-hus. While I had been away at the manor house, Kitty had set one of the hens to brood a clutch of eight eggs and the chicks were now running about like balls of yellow wool on their stick legs. Alice had been as good as her word and sent the eggs from my best layers every day, so that, in this good laying season, the family had been living very largely on eggs and bread. We must preserve some for winter, however, so that afternoon Kitty and I set to and pickled a batch which we stored in an earthenware crock in the pantry.

Kitty was becoming a good little housewife and the next morning I decided it was time she learned to spin. My mother had been at her spinning wheel every day since I returned, for there still remained most of this year's fleeces to spin. Often we would simply send the untreated fleeces to Lincoln market, but this year, with times so hard for us, it was better to put in the labour spinning and weaving to sell the finished cloth, which would fetch in more money.

'Can you teach Kitty to spin, Mother?' I asked. It was something she could do sitting down, for I had been concerned, since I came home, at how she appeared to have aged just in the few weeks I had been away. 'I think she could manage a drop spindle now.'

'Aye. Fetch me yours, then.'

'I know where it is!' Kitty ran to the storeroom off the hall, where we kept our tools – spindles, loom and loom weights, carding combs, and the spinning wheel when it was not in use. Her eyes were sparkling at the thought of learning a new skill. Perhaps one day I would teach her to read. She was a clever little soul.

The two of them set to, Kitty on a stool at my mother's feet. It is far from easy to learn how to use a drop spindle. Somehow it seems impossible that something so simple can turn the raw fluffy wool into a fine twist which can be knitted or woven. To begin with Kitty got herself into a fine old tangle, but her fingers were slender and nimble. Quite soon she was spinning a thread which would not be fine or even enough for weaving, but could be used for knitting a man's woollen hat for winter. I left them to it, the eager child with her spindle and the skilled old woman at her wheel, and made our midday dinner.

Gideon wanted to come to table with us, but Hannah and I forbade it, fearing that his wounds might open if he moved too soon.

'Besides,' I said, spooning up his pottage for him as he lay in bed, 'you are not ready yet to have the bandages removed from your eyes. You must tolerate my nursing for a little longer.'

'You have been so kind, Mercy. Taking me in and caring for me.'

He reached out his hand towards me, and found my face. His fingers brushed back a strand of my hair that had escaped from my cap and he cupped my cheek in his hand.

'Nonsense,' I said briskly, glad that he could not see me blush. 'Of course we must care for our friends.' I was already beginning to worry that he might remember those intimate moments in the night, when I had held him in my arms.

Toward the end of the afternoon, when Tom had just returned from hoeing our portions of the common fields, Jack stepped through the door.

'You are all well?' he asked, looking around as if he was searching for something.

'All is well with us,' Tom said, looking puzzled. 'Why do you ask?'

'Come,' I said. 'You are looking very hot, Jack. Sit a while and take a cup of ale with Tom.' I had already fetched the flagon from the cool pantry, for Tom had come in complaining of the heat.

They sat at the table with their ale and I sat with them, taking up the mending of Tom's stockings which he always wore out quicker than anyone else in the family.

'I am just back from Crowthorne,' Jack said, wiping his mouth on the back of his hand. 'That's an excellent brew, Mercy.'

'Thank you.'

'Crowthorne?' said Tom.

'Aye. I drove over six of my ewes to sell to a fellow there. And there has been much talk.' He looked around him again. 'And here in the village too. They are saying that Gideon Clarke was killed by those troopers.'

Tom and I exchanged a look.

'And what are they saying about it in Crowthorne?' Tom asked.

'You know them for the rampant Puritans they are. Godly, they call themselves!' Jack snorted, and took another swig of his ale. 'So godly that they are rejoicing at Gideon's death. Saying that he practised ungodly superstitions, the way of the great Whore of Babylon. He deserved to die.'

I half started from my chair and opened my mouth to speak, but Tom shook his head at me.

'And what are they saying here in the village?'

'That they hope he lives and may be spirited away to somewhere safe.'

'Perhaps it would be well to put it about that he has died,' said Tom.

'Exactly what I was thinking.'

Jack followed my glance at the bedroom door. Gideon, I knew, was sleeping.

'Aye,' I said. 'We did our best, but his injuries were too severe.'

'You know, if there is any smuggling of a man to the coast, you can call on me,' Jack said. 'I have friends in Lynn, from the time I worked there on the boats.'

We both smiled at him, remembering Jack's adventures a few years before, and so it was agreed.

I got up and fetched bread and cheese and more ale.

'Any more news from Crowthorne?' Tom asked. The village was larger than ours and had been actively involved in recruiting men for the Model Army. News of the outer world generally reached there before it reached us.

Jack pulled a face. 'There has been more of the witch-finding. Matthew Hopkins and John Stearne have come this way again, just when we thought they had moved to Norwich and the coast.'

I shuddered. The panic spread by the witchfinders during the last months had reached even our remote village, though happily the men themselves had not. Places where all had lived in peace, neighbour with neighbour, were suddenly riven by terrible accusations of satanic practices. When children had died, crops had spoiled, cattle had run mad, it was all said to be the work of witches, where for generations these disasters had been attributed to visitations of the ague or the plague, bad weather, or beasts eating dangerous weeds.

The two men, Hopkins and Stearne, had moved up the east country from Essex, and as they moved, this poison of witchcraft moved with them, like the bow wave pushed out before a boat. Where the waters of daily life had been pure and untroubled before, now there was turmoil and turbulence, the waters poisoned. Accusations of witchcraft were worst in places like Crowthorne, where the people were led by a hell-fire preacher who spurred on their spite and suspicion. Old scores were being settled. The moving of a boundary stone in a grandfather's time was now being avenged by sending some poor innocent woman to torture and the gallows.

'Did you know that they swam a clergyman for a witch, and hanged him for it?' Jack said. 'And now they have declared an old woman of Crowthorne a witch. She is to be hanged.'

'So near to us!' Tom looked alarmed.

'Which old woman?' I asked.

'Agnes Pettifer. She's is the local wise woman and midwife. They say she has killed two babes and put a murrain on the preacher's cattle.'

'Agnes!' My heart began to beat fast.

'You know her?'

'A little. I have met her at Hannah's cottage a few times. They were girls together, when Agnes lived in our parish, before she married a Crowthorne man. They shared their knowledge of herbs and healing.' I shook my head. 'She was no witch, just a decent old body, a midwife, widowed these many years, who helped folk in need. She must have delivered most of the people of Crowthorne under fifty.'

'Well, they have turned against her now.'

'She would have stood against their new preacher,' I said slowly. 'She would not have tolerated his wicked nonsense. She was outspoken and probably did not watch her tongue.'

I thought of Agnes as I had last seen her, a few months before the drainers had come. She was a brisk, tidy woman, who wore her years more lightly than Hannah, for she made nothing of the long walk from Crowthorne. They had their heads together over some new way of preserving plums in honey with a little precious cinnamon stick. Two old women, discussing recipes.

'This is the work of that preacher,' I said.

'Aye. Likely,' Jack said. 'But it would have come to nothing if those two witchfinders had not arrived, prodding their staves and long noses into matters of no concern to them.'

'They are wicked, wicked!' I cried. 'Is there nothing we can do to help Agnes?'

Jack shook his head. 'She is already taken away to Lincoln a week ago. Likely she is dead by now.'

'It is a terrible place, Crowthorne,' Tom said. 'I would not have dealings with them, Jack.'

He shrugged. 'Now we are losing our grazing, I thought to sell some of my sheep. Besides, I need the coin. And the affair of Agnes Pettifer is not the only foul blemish on that place.'

'What else?'

'It seems that troop of soldiers is billeted in Crowthorne, those who broke up the baptism. They were posted there to come to the aid of the drainers if we should make another attack. They dare not billet them here.'

'I had heard they were there.'

'It seems they demanded that a whore be provided for them. Now, of course, in a godly place like Crowthorne there are no whores.'

'Of course.'

Jack glanced sideways at me, as if he might offend if he said more.

'Go on,' I said. 'You will not shock me.'

'Well, they needed to find someone. There was a parish foundling, a bit like Kitty, a girl of fourteen or so. Nell, they called her. A pretty girl. I've seen her. She was servant to the blacksmith's wife. Anyway, they forced her to go to the soldiers' camp and all the men slept with her.'

'Raped her, you mean,' I said savagely.

He inclined his head. 'You are right, Mercy. They raped her. And when she returned to the blacksmith's house the next day, they turned her away. The whole village drove her out with stones. She was now nothing but a dirty whore, and they would not let her live among them.'

'What is to become of her?' I could barely get the words out.

'I suppose she has become a vagrant, or gone to whoring in some town or other. 'Tis a pity, for I believe she was a good girl, before all this.'

She would be beaten from parish to parish as a homeless vagrant. And before long, no doubt, she would give birth in a ditch and probably die there. A child not much older than Kitty.

'How can they square this with their consciences, these *godly* people?' I spat it out, as if it was Jack's fault.

He held up his hands in protest. 'I am only the bearer of the story. No doubt they believe, as sure as they are Saints and Saved, that she – being born out of wedlock – was already one of the Damned.'

He got to his feet.

'Thank you for the food and drink, Mercy. But I think what should worry you more is the fate of Agnes Pettifer. If she was friend to Hannah, it would be best to warn Hannah to be on her guard. If Hopkins and Stearne come this way, she may be in danger.'

'I will warn her,' I said.

Chapter Nine

The next morning I took Hannah aside and told her everything Jack had said about the events in Crowthorne. In particular I warned her of the danger she might be in through her well-known friendship with Agnes Pettifer. It seemed she also knew the child Nell, and it was this that most upset her.

'The poor lass.' Hannah mopped her eyes with the corner of her apron. 'She was a good quiet girl, never a trouble to anyone. Very pretty, too, though I don't think she knew it. Now she is ruined. She should have come to our village, away from those devils who call themselves Saints.'

'At least she lives,' I said. I was not sure Hannah had understood what I had told her of Agnes. Besides, I was not so convinced our own village would have taken the girl in, after she had been defiled. It would have been different if she had been one of our own, but a girl from Crowthorne? Our neighbours are good people, but they are not without prejudice.

'We must pray for Agnes,' I said, 'and we must be watchful, lest anyone try to link you to her.'

'But she has but been taken to the assize at Lincoln,' Hannah said. 'Surely they will soon see that it is all nonsense, what they accuse her of.'

I was uncertain whether I should say more. I did not want to frighten her, but she needed to understand the seriousness of what had happened. I took both her hands in mine.

'Hannah, they will search Agnes for the marks of a witch. Anything can be taken as a sign. A mole, a mark on her skin. And if she does not confess freely, they will put her to the torture.

Under torture, who knows what a person will say to make them stop? What would I say? What would you say? If it is known you were her friend, they may come for you.'

Hannah smiled and shook her head. 'You worry too much, child. No one thinks me a witch. Nor will they think it of Agnes. It will all pass over like a summer storm.'

I could see there was no convincing her. When Nehemiah and Tom made their trip to Lincoln market the following day with their eels and baskets, they returned with word that Agnes had already been hanged. I could not bring myself to tell Hannah.

'However, one piece of good news,' said Tom. 'Hopkins and Stearne are away into Huntingdonshire with their filthy practices.'

That was good news indeed. Perhaps I had been too ready to worry about Hannah. 'And how is Father?' I asked.

Tom frowned. 'Not well. He has suffered a bout of the ague and now has a cough that will not leave him. The fellow in his cell is even worse. It is like to be gaol fever.'

This was worrying. In the close confinement of the cells disease spreads quickly from man to man, and gaol fever can be fatal. Worry for Hannah was overtaken by worry for Father. And the time for paying his fine was drawing ever nearer. Between us we had raised some of the money, but nowhere near enough.

With our church desecrated and its rector rumoured to be dead, the spiritual needs of our parish clearly came to the attention of someone somewhere, for we heard that the preacher from Crowthorne would be caring for us until a replacement could be appointed for Gideon, who was now relieved of his living, whether he was alive or dead.

Soon after he regained consciousness, Gideon asked me to go to his house to fetch away his belongings.

'Here are my keys,' he said, groping for them blindly in his breeches, which lay across the foot of the bed. 'I have a few spare clothes. And my books. If you could bring my books. If there is any food worth keeping, you must bring that as well, for I cannot go on living off the Benningtons' stores.'

I promised to bring everything.

134

'And in my bedroom, to the right of the fireplace there is a loose board under the candle table. Bring the box you will find there. I have a little money from my stipend. It will help us all.'

The next day, the day before the Crowthorne preacher was to make his first visit, I took Kitty and two large baskets, and we walked to the village. It was the first time I had been there since the day of the christening. We went first to see Alice. She was looking better, less fine-drawn and with more colour in her face. She held me close and wept a little.

'What a terrible day! My poor son, to have such a welcome into the world. I fear it will haunt him all his life.'

'You must not think that. He was properly baptised. Everything that happened, happened afterwards. He was untouched. See how well he looks!'

Already the baby had grown and he looked about him with eyes that focused and noticed everything. I had brought a pretty bunch of ribbons which I tied to the hood of the cradle and at once he began to reach for them.

'And Master Clarke?' Alice said tentatively.

'We are saying that, sadly, he did not survive the beating.'

She nodded, with a small smile. 'That is also what we are saying in the village, to any who come asking.'

'Has anyone come asking?'

'A few days ago. One of those troopers came. Rode about on his horse without dismounting. Looked down his long nose at us. We all shook our heads and said sadly that the rector had died.'

'Good. Kitty and I are going to fetch his belonging from his house before any intruder moves in.'

'Shall I come?'

'Best not. The less you know, the better.'

We found Gideon's house just as he must have left it the morning of the christening. No one else had yet been there. It was scrupulously neat, but simple to the point of austerity. The rector's house was intended for a married man with a family, but Gideon had used only three rooms: the kitchen, a bedroom, and a study, which must have been where he sat of an evening. It seemed a bare and lonely sort of place and I felt we were intruding. However, Gideon had asked us to come, so we must do as we were bid.

I felt curiously shy entering his bedroom, as though I had breached some barrier of intimacy. There were his few spare clothes carefully folded in a coffer, a pewter candlestick, and on a stool beside his bed one of those small Bibles that men had carried with them into battle during the War. I examined it curiously. It was stained and battered, the spine broken, not nearly so fine a volume as the prayer book the captain had destroyed. Still, it must mean something to him, so I laid it in my basket on top of his clothes.

There was very little in the kitchen. My mother had been right when she suspected that since his housekeeper had died he had not eaten properly. There were a few dried beans and some barley, half a dozen of last year's apples withered on a shelf, and an end of mouldy cheese. A telltale trail of crumbs and mouse droppings on the table showed where he had left part of a loaf on that last morning before coming to the church.

The study was better. Here there were two shelves of books, not just religious texts but poetry and a work on architecture and another on mathematics – books left, perhaps, from his time as a student at Cambridge. There were copies of his sermons, beautifully written in his fine Italian hand, a sheaf of paper, ink, and quills waiting to be sharpened, lying in a neat row beside a penknife. All of this was too much for our baskets.

'I'll find another basket, Mistress Mercy,' Kitty said.

I heard her ferreting about in the kitchen and she came back with a buck basket.

'Too large,' I said. 'We would draw attention to ourselves.'

I went out into the hallway where I had left the baskets of clothes and pulled out two belts.

'We'll tie the books into parcels with these,' I said, 'and put everything else with the clothes.'

When we were done, I looked around at the bleak little house and thought of Gideon sitting here alone on cold winter evenings. Then I remembered.

'There is something else,' I said.

I ran up to the bedroom and moved the candle table near the fireplace. The loose board was easy to see, not a very secret hiding place. Below it was a small carved box in a wood that looked like

136

yew. When I picked it up it rattled. I did not open it, but slipped it into my pocket. When I came downstairs Kitty looked at me enquiringly.

'Just something Master Clarke asked me to fetch,' I said. 'Come. We should manage if we take a basket each and a parcel of books each.' Suddenly I wanted to be away from there, as if we might be caught by the preacher from Crowthorne and damned for it.

I locked the door and looked around. The rector's house was set back behind the churchyard, away from the village street, and no one seemed to be about. Nevertheless, I led Kitty around behind the church and we climbed over the wall into the lane. I wanted no one asking questions.

Gideon was glad to have his belongings about him, feeling everything and shaking the box. Tom helped him dress in clean clothes and with his other injuries covered he would have looked his old self, had it not been for the great bandage about his head.

'I'm grateful to you and young Kitty for fetching my belongings,' he said. 'Whatever becomes of my living.' He sighed. I touched his hand lightly with mine, but could think of nothing to say.

We had told him about the imminent arrival of the Crowthorne preacher, but had not yet broached the plan Tom and Jack were discussing, of taking him to Lynn to find a ship for the Continent. First he must regain his health.

The next morning we were obliged to attend church under the new preacher. Our absence would have provoked suspicion and a severe fine. The whole household walked down the lane to the church: my mother, Tom and myself, Hannah, Nehemiah and Kitty. We left Gideon alone for the first time since the attack, but he assured us he would be safe on his own, and would bolt the door.

'And I have Jasper and Tobit for company,' he said with a smile. Jasper had taken to sleeping on the end of his bed in preference to his usual place beside the kitchen fire. Hannah's cat Tobit, an elusive creature, who spent much of his time watching for rats in the barn, had inexplicably taken to Gideon.

'I have never known him befriend anyone but myself,' Hannah said with a rueful laugh, the first time the cat was found curled up on Gideon's chest. 'It is a mark of great respect.'

As we neared the village, we saw our neighbours making their way towards the church. All were dressed soberly, as we were. Usually the village girls would adorn their dresses with a pretty lace collar for Sunday service, or tuck a rosebud under the band of their caps, but we were all afraid of the Crowthorne preacher, Reverend Edgemont, and dared display no finery.

It was the first time I had been in the church since that terrible morning. When I had come to Gideon's house the previous day I had turned my eyes away from the church, unable to bear the sight of it. But it must be faced.

Someone had swept away the broken glass and the splintered timbers. The last trailing strips of lead were gone from the window. Without altar or altar rails, and with the east window a blank space through which the wind blew, the ruined chancel of the church was stripped of its holy aura. The despoilers had been unable to shift the huge heavy bulk of the ancient font, but a dirty horse blanket had been thrown over it. There was still a large blood stain soaked into the flags of the floor nearby. In the centre of the church, below the step on which the altar rails had stood, a rough wooden platform with a lectern had been erected. We looked from one to the other in puzzlement at this, but it became clear when a big heavy-built man in a black robe strode in and climbed up to the platform.

This, then, was Reverend Edgemont.

I was too frightened, and my mind too filled with the memory of that last time I was here, to make much of his words. There was a great deal about how we were all sinners, condemned to ever-lasting Hell, and bitter accusations against our papistical practices, at which many of us stirred uneasily, but none dared speak. He quoted many fierce passages from the Old Testament and from the Book of Revelation, about killing and revenge and punishment. His words were full of anger and hate. I do not remember him mentioning Christ at all. The sermon went on for a very long time, so that the children became restless and one or two babies cried and were frantically hushed by their mothers. There was no singing, and the only participation of the congregation was the occasional 'Amen', muttered low and with little grace.

At last Master Edgemont swept away down the nave and out of the door. As we filtered out, slowly and without pleasure, we saw that he had not stayed to meet us, but was already mounted on a large black stallion and riding away in the direction of Crowthorne. I felt relieved that he did not wish to speak to us, and that it seemed he would not be making use of Gideon's house.

The congregation drifted away, without our usual Sunday greetings and cheerful conversation. I spoke to no one, except for a brief 'Good morrow' to Alice and Rafe. Tom raised his hand to Toby and Jack, but did not stop to speak.

Walking back up the lane to the farm, we were silent until we were nearly home.

'So,' said Tom at last, 'that is a taste of what we are to endure under the new regime. They take from us our lands and they take from us our decent English church. What will they leave us?'

'And to call us papists!' I said indignantly. 'Do they not know that Queen Elizabeth's church is a Protestant church?'

'Those folk,' Nehemiah growled, 'they think none but themselves have the right religion. They are the Saints and we are all the Damned. They will destroy the church of our fathers, or die doing it.' And he spat into the hedgerow.

Mother and Hannah, arm in arm, helping each other over the rough patches in the lane, said nothing. Nor did Kitty. She had plucked some stems of milk parsley and was twisting them into a garland. When she set it upon her head she gave me a mischievous grin.

'Am I condemned as a sinner, Mistress Mercy, if I wear flowers in my hair?'

I laughed. So Kitty had been listening to the preacher and had spirit enough to defy him and all his ways.

'I am sure that does not make you a sinner, Kitty. Will you contrive a garland for me?'

She did so, and we arrived back at the farm cheered by our small act of rebellion.

After we had dined – on cold pottage and bread, for we were now forbidden to heat food on the Sabbath – Hannah tapped me on the arm.

'I think it is time we removed the bandages from Reverend Clarke's face and head.'

I drew in my breath. As long as he was bandaged, we could pray that he still had his sight. Once they were removed, we could no longer hide from the truth.

I nodded. 'We will need warm water. The cloth is likely to have stuck to the blood. It will be a painful business.'

'Aye. The wounds will open again. I will fetch my salves.'

Gideon was up and dressed and had dined with us. He had become quite adept at finding his way about the kitchen and bedroom, and could eat unaided with a spoon if one of us cut up his food. He now sat down quietly on a bench beside the table, his clasped hands resting on its surface. The others went about their work, not wanting, I suppose, to witness what would be unpleasant and perhaps heart-breaking.

'So now we will know the truth, Mercy,' he said.

'What do you mean?' I was hesitant, unsure how much he guessed.

'You have tried valiantly to deceive me, but I know those men may have blinded me.' He reached out a hand in my direction and I took it. 'Don't grieve, Mercy. You and Hannah have done your best. If I am to be blind, it is God's will. Though I shall miss my books sadly. Perhaps you will read to me.'

I could not answer, thinking that soon he would be gone far away. My eyes filled with tears and I was grateful that he could not see me. Yet I also longed for his sight to be healed again, even though it would set the seal on his departure. My thoughts were in turmoil and I tried to concentrate on the task ahead of us.

Hannah came back and laid out her pots and bottles while I brought a basin of warm water to the table. She stirred in some honey for healing and something from one of her bottles, then nodded to me.

'I'm going to soak the bandages, Gideon,' I said, 'so they will come away more easily, but I'm afraid we may hurt you.'

'I'm ready,' he said. 'Don't trouble yourselves. I know you will do your best.'

It was a messy and grim business. Once the cloth was soaking, I cut through the knots with a sharp knife and began to peel it off. The first layer came away quite easily, but as I came closer to the skin, the bandage was stiff and rigid with hardened blood. I took my sewing scissors and cut away as much as had come free, then soaked the inner layer. Nothing would soften the caked blood.

'I'm sorry,' I said. I could not keep a sob out of my voice. 'I will have to cut it away piece by piece. It is going to hurt.'

He tried to pat my hand, but missed. I drew my hand away, for I could not bear him to touch me. I must think of this as a task to be done, like assisting the birth of a lamb or slaughtering a pig. This was not the flesh of the man I loved which I was going to tear.

Hannah looked at me in concern. 'Shall I do it, Mercy?'

'No.' I gritted my teeth. I must not be a coward.

Little by little I cut the rest of the bandage away from the back of Gideon's head. He bowed forward to help me, and I found myself forced to cut away large patches of his hair as well. At last it was clear, and we could see the wound. I gave a sigh of relief. It looked clean. Part of the scab had come away with the cloth and it was bleeding, but there was no pus, no foul matter. Hannah leaned over and sniffed.

'Good,' she said. She scooped up one of the salves and spread it over the wound.

Gideon gave an involuntary grunt. 'That stings!'

'It stings,' she said, 'but it will speed the healing. 'Now your face.'

This was what I was dreading. The cloth around the sides of his face came off quite easily as I cut it away, but that left the part over his eyes. My hands were shaking now, and Hannah laid her hand on my arm.

'Are you sure you can do this?'

'Aye.'

I took a deep breath. Again I soaked the cloth until it was sodden, but it was still stiff with blood.

'I cannot cut away any more, Gideon. It is too close to your eyes. I will have to peel it away. I'm afraid it will hurt.'

'Do it,' he said. 'You must.'

He managed to speak quite calmly, but I saw that he clenched his fists.

Carefully, slowly, I peeled away the stiffened cloth over his right eye. It was free at last. The skin around the eye was bruised and blackened, but the eye itself looked intact, although it was shut. I threw the dirty cloth into the fire and began to ease back the remaining portion of bandage over the left eye. This was more stubborn. Gideon caught his breath and bit down on his lower lip. He was trying not to cry out and I struggled to hold back the whimper that rose in my throat. At last it came free.

The left eye was horribly swollen, the upper and lower lid stuck together with a mass of yellow crusted matter. Some of the lashes had been torn away by the bandage, which as well as being bloody was also caked with the same yellow matter, some kind of hardened pus.

The whimper broke through my lips in spite of myself. Slowly Gideon opened his right eye. He smiled.

'I can see,' he said. 'One eye at least is sound. How is the other?'

'Not good,' I said.

Hannah examined it carefully. 'You must wash away all that yellow matter, Mercy. I will make up more of the potion, a little stronger this time.'

When she brought the fresh mixture I sat facing Gideon and slowly began to soften and wash away the hideous crust. All the while he watched me steadily from his good eye, which I found unnerving. At last it was done and with difficulty he managed to open his left eye, although it was still badly swollen. The white of his eye was bloodshot.

'Can you see with that eye?' Hannah asked.

I could not speak. I sat with my hands fallen useless in my lap, trembling from fear of what I might have done. I could not believe that the bandages were off at last.

Gideon covered his right eye with his hand.

'I can see a little with the left eye, but it is blurred.'

'Give it time,' Hannah said. 'It will be better when the swelling goes down.'

Gideon let his hand drop over mine.

'It is over, Mercy. Thank you for your courage.'

Then he smiled radiantly. 'I can see! And why are you wearing that milk parsley in your hair?'

Foolishly I began to weep. I ran from the room, that they might not see me.

I needed to escape from the house, from the farm. I headed up the lane, then turned off along the edge of the wheat field, following the raised bank of the drainers' new ditch. Since I had returned from the manor I had ventured nowhere but the farm and the village, so the changes here were startling. In the centre of the field the wheat was growing strongly and turning gold. Harvest would not be long away. But here where the drainers had been at work a wide swathe of the field along the drain was churned to mud, the wheat stalks trampled under foot, the unripe grain spilt and smashed. At the very least, a third of the wheat crop would be lost.

Standing with my feet amongst the spoilage, I gazed over the field in dismay. What gave these men the right to destroy our food in this way? The last few years had seen terrible harvests. This year the spring had been late and cold, and we needed every ear of wheat, every grain of barley and pod of beans to stave off starvation. With the hem of my apron, I dried my tears, as anger flooded me. In my fury, I tore off my garland and threw it in the ditch, where it floated on the muddy water, spun slowly round, then began to drift in the direction of Baker's Lode. That meant water was moving from further up the ditch, from the Fen where Hannah's cottage had stood, and draining down towards the Lode and thence to the river and the sea.

I tried to imagine what the Fen would look like if all the water was drained away. Its marshy land, home to thousands of water fowl, would become, I supposed, some sort of grassland, with here and there the raised clumps which were now islands. The open meres, dotted across the marsh, would be hollow dips in the grassland, the fish and eels dead or driven away. I looked down again at the ditch. The water was dense with mud, unlike the clear streams running along the natural ditches and ancient lodes. It struck me suddenly that this new ditch might also be draining water from the wheat field where I stood. That would mean that the crop was starved of the moisture it needed for the grain to plump up.

Picking my way through the wheat until I was in amongst the undamaged stalks, I bent down and scooped up a handful of the soil. It ran dry through my fingers like sand. I broke an ear off the nearest stalk. The leaves were beginning to take on that yellowish tint of ripeness. The ear was small, and as I ran my thumbnail along it, breaking off the individual grains, they fell on my open palm like tiny hard peppercorns, withered and dry. So even the scarce wheat they had left us would be poor.

Back at the edge of the ditch, I followed it down to Baker's Lode and climbed the bank, near where Tom and I had stood all those months ago, watching van Slyke and his men begin their surveying. From here I had a clear view of the barley field, over the narrow bridge, on the far side of the Lode. I caught my breath.

The further half of the barley field had vanished. Like the work of genii in an old tale, a village had appeared. There was a neat row of houses, well spaced. I counted eight. Beyond the furthest one, two more were being built. Not some ramshackle huts erected by wandering folk. These were sturdy half-timbered houses with lathe and plaster infill. Smoke rose from brick chimneys. And, unbelievably, each house had an enclosed small-holding of land fenced in around it, cut out of our barley field. There were cows. There were pigs. I saw children. A woman spreading washing on a fence.

Thinking I must be dreaming, I rubbed my eyes. No, it was all still there. What was more, I saw van Slyke come out of one of the houses and stand talking to someone in the doorway. He gestured with his arm in the direction beyond the houses and I saw that the drainers were now at work there, cutting across the very centre of the field planted half with beans and half with peas.

I was suddenly very afraid. Not only was our land being torn apart, but now there were strangers suddenly settled upon it, as though they had every right to be there. I turned and stumbled down the bank, heading back towards the farm. Did Tom know of this? He had said nothing. But then, we had all been so preoccupied with other matters. I needed to get home as quickly as possible.

'Jack saw two houses,' Tom said. 'Just before you came home. He challenged them, asked what they were doing there, but could not make them understand. They spoke no English. He thought they were Dutchmen, or maybe French.' He ran his fingers through his hair. 'Jesu, eight houses! And two more building.'

'But where have they come from, these people?' I asked. 'They are not the drainers. I saw women and children. Livestock. They are making farms.'

'It's what they did on the Bedford Level,' said Nehemiah. 'Brought in foreign settlers. Gave them lands to rent, all the rents to be paid to the adventurers.'

'That is the whole purpose of these schemes,' Gideon said. 'The investors have no intention of farming the land themselves. They bring in these land-hungry foreigners as tenants. For the small investment of draining our land, they have rich rewards.'

I had never heard Gideon speak so worldly-wise before. The four of us were sitting around the table in the kitchen, where my mother was continuing to teach Kitty to spin. Hannah had gone out to fetch in the eggs.

'How do you know this?' I asked, curious.

'There was much talk of it in Cambridge when I was there. Do you remember that I told your father that a friend of mine had seen the documents authorising the new drainage plans? He has been following the activities of these adventurers for ten years now. He explained it to me. And riding down to Cambridge I have seen some of these new settlements.'

'How can they do such a thing?' I felt helpless in the face of this outrage.

Tom shrugged. 'With authorisation from Parliament, they can do as they please. And even Parliament is losing control of the nation's affairs. A few men of power can ride roughshod over all the rest.'

'But what must we do?'

145

'Best to move carefully for the time being,' Gideon advised. 'We must work to free your father before all else. Leave the drainers until that is done.'

I was glad that he said 'we', but how much longer would he be with us? And how long would it take us to pay Father's fine? During that time these Hollanders could build a whole town on our fields.

Nothing was heard from the manor about my absence, nor was there any word from Sir John about his London lawyer. I think by then we all knew that it would come to nothing. We wondered whether Sir John had ever written to his lawyer at all. In the meantime we lived frugally, attending Reverend Edgemont's hellfire services on Sunday. Gideon regained his strength and most of the sight in his left eye, though it would always be affected by the soldiers' beating. He was restless.

'You must keep out of sight,' I told him anxiously, when I found him wandering up toward the Dutchmen's settlement. 'You know that we have reported you dead. It will spoil everything if you are seen.'

'I do try to occupy myself with my books, Mercy,' he said, turning back with me toward the farm, 'but I feel so useless when all of you are working so hard.'

'You must get your strength back,' I said, swallowing painfully, 'if you are to sail for the Continent.'

He took my hand. 'I do not want to go, Mercy.' He looked at me so keenly I felt weak. His eyes were clear now, with no visible sign of injury.

'I do not want you to go,' I said, 'but it is the safest way, for all of us.'

The previous evening Tom and Jack had opened to him their plan that they should take him to Lynn, where Jack's friends amongst the seamen would help him find a ship to travel to France or the Low Countries. There he could join the other exiles who had fled there after the War. From the start it was clear that Gideon was reluctant to go, saying that it was a kind of desertion and he had never been a King's man, but Tom pointed out at once that now we had spread the news of his death, we should be in danger if it was discovered that we had lied.

We still spoke of 'after the War' as if it were done with, but from time to time news filtered in that perhaps the War was not finished after all. There was other bad news. The witchfinders were busy again, crisscrossing the Fen country, hunting out those they believed to be witches and condemning them on the flimsiest of evidence, often nothing more than some tall story by a spiteful neighbour.

All of this seemed far away, however, when what concerned us most was Father's continued imprisonment and his poor health. And there was the wheat harvest to gather in, what was left of it. After that, the barley and the beans and the peas, if the interlopers had not stolen everything. Until the wheat was ready, we all worked hard at doing everything we could to raise money for the fine. Kitty knitted caps from her spun wool, Mother and Hannah wove lengths of woollen broadcloth. I made cheeses until my arms ached, and in the evenings knitted several fine shawls like the one I had made for little Huw. Tom and Nehemiah continued with their making of baskets and hurdles, and even recruited Gideon, though he was not a man of his hands and proved uneppen. Hannah's bees were well established in a skep in our small orchard and she had hopes to take a fair quantity of honey soon. Each week Tom and Nehemiah travelled to Lincoln market, carrying our produce, together with the eels and any waterfowl they had managed to net or shoot. Instead of depending on Nehemiah's carter friend, they now borrowed a cart from Rafe and harnessed Blaze to draw it, since our own cart had been confiscated by the sheriff's men. The money for the fine grew slowly. We all pretended it would be enough, but knew in our hearts it would not.

When it came time for harvesting the wheat, everything else was set aside. As for the hay harvest, every able-bodied soul from the village turned out. Most of the women and older men had not seen the damage to the wheat, for it was the younger men who hoed it to keep it free of weeds. We were a sober and silent company as we set to, without the usual banter and jollity. At least the weather kept fine. As the crop was so much smaller than usual, we finished the whole field in two days, and at the end of the second day I stood in the adland where Alice and I had climbed off the harrow, all those long months ago, and looked out over the rows of stooks standing amongst the stubbs. Once the sheaves had been carried in and the gleaners had finished, we would turn the stock on to the field to graze on the stubbs and manure the soil, but would we be able to crop this land next year? Perhaps even now some surveyor was marking out boundaries on a map, allocating this part to one rich man, that part to another, and subdividing it into holdings for strangers.

Threshing and winnowing the grain would last many weeks and we would all take our turn at it, but it had hardly begun when Jack arrived at our house one evening. He pulled a folded paper out of the breast of his jacket.

'I have heard from one of my friends,' he said. 'There will be a packet leaving Lynn for the Low Countries in three days' time. We must make ready to take you there, Master Clarke.'

Gideon gave me a troubled glance and I lowered my eyes to the shawl I was knitting. Though my heart beat fast, I would say nothing. What mattered was that he should be safe.

'Let us go tomorrow, then,' said Tom. 'What do you say, Gideon?'

'If you think it best.' Gideon was polite, but not eager.

'I have thought,' said Jack, 'if you borrow Rafe's cart, and load it with your goods as you do when you go to Lincoln, we can carry them to Lynn market. Say that you think you will get a better price there and I go with you because I know people in the town.'

'That seems a good plan.' Tom nodded. 'It's a fair way, though.'

'Aye. It will take us two or three days altogether, going and returning, with time between to find the ship and sell our goods. I'll bring some of my fleeces as well, to make it all the more convincing.' He grinned. I could see that for him it was no more than an adventure, like the months he had spent at sea.

'Will you need to conceal Gideon?' I asked.

'At first, aye. Until we're well away from here. But it should be easy. We can hollow out a space amongst the goods. Then once we are out of the parish and on the road for Lynn, you can come up for air.' He sketched a little bow at Gideon, who smiled, catching a little of Jack's light-hearted enthusiasm.

I slept badly that night and rose early. Jack would come soon after dawn, driving Rafe's cart with his own horse. They would then harness Blaze and later in the day I would ride Jack's horse back to the village. I set about putting up a basket of food and a flagon of ale to help them on their journey, but my heart was full of regret.

When I had covered the basket with a cloth and stirred up the fire to make breakfast, Gideon came out of his bedroom.

'I'm sorry,' I said. 'Did I wake you?'

'I slept very little,' he said, sitting down at the table. 'I do not like this running away, but I see that it may be safer for you all if I go.'

'Have you packed your belongings?'

'I shall take very little. A few clothes and my Bible. I am leaving the rest of my books here for you, Mercy.'

'I do not want you to go!' The words burst out of me, despite myself. I threw myself down on the bench opposite him, but I could not look him in the face.

'Mercy.' He reached across the table and took my hands. 'Look at me.'

Reluctantly I raised my eyes.

'I am much older than you. I shall be thirty next year. But . . . if we ever come out of this . . . if it is possible for me to come back . . . if there is no one else in your life . . . will you allow me to speak for you?'

I felt the colour rising in my cheeks, but I did not turn away.

'Aye,' I said.

He rose from his bench and without realising what I was doing, I found I was standing before him.

'Oh, dear heart,' he said, 'I have watched you grow from a lovely child to a woman who fills all my thoughts, the one person I want to spend the rest of my life with, and you send me away.'

Tears were streaming down my face, but I could not brush them away, for he had both my hands firmly gripped in his.

'I don't send you away, but you must go,' I whispered.

Then his arms were around me, holding me so tightly that our bodies merged and our lips were together. Dear God, stop Time's flow. Let me hold him forever.

Jack arrived and suddenly everything was happening too fast. The cart was loaded with the goods for market, the horses were changed over, the goodbyes said. Tom took the reins and I passed the basket of food up to Jack. Gideon climbed into the back of the cart and wormed his way down amongst the fleeces and bolts of cloth. He gave me one last look, but did not speak. Then they were gone.

I turned and climbed up to the attic and threw open the window that overlooked the lane. I watched until the cart was out of sight and the dust of its passing drifted down to the ground. He was gone.

Chapter Ten

They returned from Lynn nearly three days later. In the early evening Tom rode Blaze into the yard after leaving Jack and the cart in the village. Both man and horse looked exhausted.

'Poor Blaze,' Tom said, stroking the horse's neck. 'It has been a hard few days for him. The road from here to Lynn was in a bad way, uncared for since before the War, I'd say. Rutted and pitted with holes, mile after mile. And the cart was heavy with all our goods.'

He led Blaze into the barn and lifted off his harness. I fetched a bucket of bran mash and another of water. The horse drank thirstily, then buried his nose in the mash. I began to rub him down with a handful of straw where his coat was stiff with dried sweat.

'Then when we reached Lynn we could find no decent livery for him.' Tom hung the harness on its peg and sat down on an old cask, stretching out weary legs. 'The town was overflowing. It was market day, but there were also crowds of people like Gideon, intent on finding ships to leave England. And the same ships were bringing in foreigners – whole families with their bundles and even livestock. Lynn is where they are coming into the country.'

'So what did you do?'

'Found one of Jack's old shipmates. He's a fisherman by trade and let us tether Blaze in the yard at the back where he has a smokehouse. The poor horse has had to stand on cobbles the whole while. I'm surprised he's not lame. We slept on the floor of the fisherman's house. Not much more than a hut, in truth. They're poor men, those fishermen.'

'And Gideon has gone on board the ship?'

'The next morning we found the ship, the *Brave Endeavour* – a brave name for a small packet, not much bigger than an inshore herring buss! She was not to sail until the day after tomorrow, so Gideon stays with the fisherman until then.'

I did not like to think of Gideon lingering in Lynn. If he must go, why then, let him go. I would rather think of him safe in the Low Countries than lurking like a thief in Lynn. At least, that was what I told myself.

'Did you sell our goods?'

'Aye, and did well.' Tom patted the front of his jerkin, which gave a satisfying clink of coin. 'We should make the trip more often, did it not take so long. We sold everything and at good prices too.'

'So now what do we do? Will Gideon send word when he is safely in the Low Countries?'

Tom shook his head. 'I told him, better not. Remember, he is a dead man by all reports.'

I felt a flash of anger. It seemed that Gideon had said he would send word and Tom had undertaken to forbid him. How dare he! Now I could hope for no news, good or bad. Who could tell when or if it would be safe for him to return? I might never see him again. I pressed my lips together and scrubbed harder at Blaze's back. Startled, he threw up his head and gave me a reproachful look.

'Good lad,' I said, rubbing him between the ears and throwing down my lump of dirty straw, determined to hold back my tears. I turned to Tom. 'Come. We have kept your supper for you. I thought you would be home tonight.'

While Tom ate, I cleared away the rest of the supper dishes, then sat down opposite him.

'I went over to look at the settlement again today. They have started to build another row of houses, forming the other side of the street, with their holdings stretching out behind them. And at the nearer end of the street they have begun what looks as though it might be a church. At this rate the settlement will soon be larger than the village.'

'It cannot go on.' Tom pointed his spoon at me. 'We will have those foreigners out of here. What right have they to settle on our commons? Tomorrow I'll go to the village and talk to the other lads. I think it's time we moved to greater efforts. These last weeks we have done only minor damage, childish things. They care nothing for it but go on relentless as a flood. And all the while destroying our food. That wheat we harvested will make poor flour.'

I nodded. 'I took my turn at winnowing today. The grains of wheat are hard and dry as stones.'

'And how much of the barley have we lost to this settlement? A third? A half? Now they are digging up the bean field.'

'It is not just that they destroy the growing crops. The soil is drying out. It will turn to dust.'

'I know.' He began to beat a rapid tattoo with his spoon on the table top. 'That our wetlands should turn to desert! There's an irony for you!'

'What will happen when the winter floods come? I do not believe this van Slyke and his men understand what happens here then.'

We both fell silent. I knew that Tom, like me, was thinking of our Fen country in winter. When the rains came, all the watercourses in the land to the west of us – higher ground which sloped down to the Fens – would fill up and rush down towards us, bringing flood waters and the precious silt that fed our fields. As the high winter tides rose in the German Sea, the rivers which drained into it would also back up. Between the sea and the wolds, all our low-lying land would flood and remain flooded until it drained naturally, slowly, in spring. We fenlanders were used to this. We harvested our crops and laid them up, brought in our animals to the barns or a few high-standing pastures, and prepared to be cut off from much of the rest of the world until the floods receded. This was our way of life. This was how our ancestors had lived since the beginning of time. Where there were man-made ditches and lodes, these had been constructed slowly, over centuries, by men who had watched the movement of the waters during a lifetime. Bit by bit they had learned to manage the water, to live with it and respect it. Where the floods needed the relief of a drain they studied where to place it, always working with the water. For a flood is a mighty beast, perhaps the most powerful element God has placed on this earth. These fly-by-night drainers, with their heedless ditches and arrogant ways, understood nothing of this. If you do not respect and fear the power of the flood, you will drown.

The next morning Tom went off early to the village, leaving the work of the farm to the rest of us. After milking and cleaning the house, I set to and tidied the room where Gideon had slept. I lifted the blankets and pressed them against my face, trying to draw in the essence of him. Although he had taken his clothes, he had indeed left his books for me, all except the Bible. I turned them over now, running a caressing hand across their covers. Holding what he had held, I felt closer to him than I had done since he had left. I had never before owned books of my own. In the house we had our family Bible, Foxe's *Book of Martyrs*, and a few chapbooks Tom had bought in London, mostly folk tales but also some ballads. As well, Tom had several of John Lilburne's tracts. Now I was the richer by a library of my own. How wisely Gideon had judged his gift.

As I opened them and read a few paragraphs here and there, something slipped out of the book on architecture that I had noticed in Gideon's house. I stooped to pick it up. It was a folded paper packet with my name written on the front. I could tell from the feel of it that it contained coin. Opening the paper I saw that Gideon had written a short note on it.

Mercy, I am leaving this with you to be put towards redeeming your father's fine. It is little enough, but it may help to make up the amount, so that you may bring him home from his wicked confinement. You will always be in my thoughts, however far away I may be, however long. Pray for me, dear heart. Gideon Clarke.

I sat down on the bed and wept. Gideon had beggared himself, gone penniless into exile to help us. Dear heart, I thought.

Tom did not return until after we had eaten dinner, but refused food, saying he had shared a meal at Toby's house.

'We are resolved to make another attack tonight,' he said, looking round at us. 'We can no longer sit still and do nothing but a few minor pranks. This time we will attack the settlement, set up so brazenly in our barley field.'

'Tom, I wish you would not do this,' Mother said. 'Your father would not like it.'

I saw from Tom's expression that he thought Father was in no position to forbid it. Besides, these months in the Lincoln prison were likely to have changed his mind.

'Mother,' he said, kind but firm, 'if we do not act, soon there will be no fields to feed us and no pasture for our beasts.'

'Aye, and no meres for fishing. No waterfowl to trap. The eels driven away,' Nehemiah growled. 'I am with you, Tom.'

'I am glad of it,' he said, 'but I do not think you should come tonight. We will likely have to make a run for it. Our actions won't go unnoticed.'

Nehemiah made a face, but conceded Tom was right. He was still strong and hearty for his age, but he could not run swiftly.

'And I will come,' I said.

'No, Mercy!' My mother was clearly deeply upset. 'Remember what happened the last time you took part in one of these dangerous capers.'

'It is not a caper,' I said stubbornly. 'This is war. A war to protect our livelihood. Besides, it was not I who came off worst last time.'

'She speaks truly, Mother,' said Tom. 'I was the one who took the bullet and without Mercy I might have fared far worse. She may come, if she takes care.'

'Thank you.' I did not try to hide a slight touch of sarcasm in my voice. Tom could not stop me if I chose to go.

We were not yet a month past the summer solstice, so darkness was late coming. Our farm was the meeting place, being the nearest to the settlement, and one by one our friends slipped in – Toby and Jack, Alice's brother Robin, half a dozen others. Even Rafe, despite his changed status as a married man and a father.

'They are all of a piece,' he said to me, as we waited for full dark. 'These drainers and settlers and the soldiers who defiled the church and that evil preacher Edgemont. We used to have a fine way of life here. Prosperous, comfortable, at peace with the Fens and with God. Yet they would destroy it all.'

'I agree. But does Alice approve your coming?'

'Aye. She would have come herself, were it not for Huw.'

'I shall get ready,' I said.

Up in my bedchamber I dropped my skirt and petticoat to the floor and pulled on a pair of Tom's breeches, which I had begged him to lend me. If it came to running, I would impede them all, clumsy in my skirts. Tom was slender, but a good six inches taller than I. The breeches were too long until I had rolled them over at the waist and tied them firmly in place. I tried walking up and down in them. They felt strange, but my movements were freer than they had been since I had worn short skirts as a child.

I came downstairs to be met by curious looks.

'Best you don't let Master Edgemont see you like that,' Jack said. 'Else you'll know for sure you're damned to the eternal fire!'

'Do you have darker head gear, Mercy?' said Toby. 'That white cap will give us away. There is a quarter moon tonight.'

'Of course.' It was stupid of me not to have thought of it. They were all wearing dark clothes. My cap was the only pale garment amongst us. I ran back upstairs, pulled off my white cap and headcloth, and looked around for something dark. There was nothing I could find quickly. But my hair was brown and would not show in the dark. I would leave it uncovered, a sure sign of damnation for Reverend Edgemont. Bare-headed and wearing man's breeches!

When I went back to the kitchen, Jack gave a whistle at my tumble of loosened hair, but Toby silenced him with a frown. We were ready now, and would go on foot over the fields, the others leaving their horses in the yard so they could ride quickly back to the village afterwards.

Between us we carried a variety of tools. Our plan was to destroy the buildings, not harm the people, so we carried axes and billhooks and pitchforks and scythes. Anything that could be used to pull down thatch, break timbers or tear away lath and plaster. It was a mild summer's night. Even if the people found themselves suddenly homeless, they would not suffer exposure to the weather. So I reasoned. As we set off, creeping silently in twos and threes toward the barley field, I felt a small pang of guilt, thinking of that woman I had seen spreading her washing on a fence. There had been a small child playing around her feet with some toy. At that distance I was unsure whether it was a girl or a boy. The woman was not so very different from Alice, the child perhaps two years older than Huw. Still, they had no business here, putting up their houses on our commons without so much as a by-your-leave. None of these people had come anywhere near the village. Were they afraid of us? Or was it because they knew they did wrong, and were ashamed to show their faces?

As we came within sight of the settlement, we could see light shining in the windows of some of the houses, and at that my anger grew, for I could tell by the quality of the light, a bright clear yellow, that they lit their rooms with beeswax candles. And we, who belonged here, were driven to make our light from rushes gathered from the Fens, dipped in our melted tallow – those rushlights which burned dull and smoky, leaving such a stench that even by day our rooms and clothes reeked of it. The sight of those wax candles was enough to strengthen my resolve.

As we crossed the bridge over the Lode, the men were whispering together. Those who were deemed the swiftest of foot were sent off to the far end of the settlement, where they would attack the furthest of the completed houses. Tom and I, with Robin and Toby and two others, remained at the nearer end. We would attack the nearest house. It had been the first built and was by far the largest. It must be the home of the leader of the settlers. Next to it stood the framework of the half-finished church, a crucifix of timber uprights, with cross beams joined in with hefty tongue and groove joints. Overhead the curved roof beams soared higher even than the largest house.

There was, as Toby had said, a quarter moon, which gave us enough light to make out the outline of the settlement quite clearly, now that our eyes had adjusted to the night. There was a sweet scent wafting over from the bean field, which lay up wind from us, and the rich damp smell of newly turned earth from the drainers' ditches and the foundations of a new house pegged out beyond the church. Was there to be no end to this settlement?

Something rustled in the grass just in front of where I was kneeling. A field mouse or a vole, or possibly a snake. I hoped it was not a snake. I hate them, with their slithery ways. However much I argue with myself that a grass snake is harmless, they still make me shudder and recoil. I peered closer at the spot. In the faint light I saw a small dark shape, not much larger than my thumb, and as it turned for a moment towards me, the moonlight caught two bright eyes. Then they whisked away, there was another rustle and it was gone. A field mouse.

We waited in deep silence so that I thought my heartbeat was loud enough for the others to hear. My hands clutching a long-handled scythe grew slippery with sweat, so I laid it down and wiped my palms on the seat of my breeches. Then came the call of a barn owl from the far end of the settlement. Three times. Then a pause. Then three times more. It was the signal that the others had reached their appointed spot. Tom gave a nod, which we could just make out in the dim light, and we rose to our feet.

Now we were running towards that large house. My task was to reach up with the scythe and pull down the thatch, while Tom and the others attacked the main timbers of the frame with axes, except Robin who was wielding a pick to prise off the plaster infill. This was not one of the houses which had shown a light, so the people must all be abed. Somewhere up under the thatch, I thought, as I tugged helplessly at it. I seemed to make no impression. The noise the others were making would soon rouse the whole settlement.

Then I felt my scythe snag on the binding of the thatch and catch firm hold. I dragged at the scythe with all the strength I could muster and suddenly bundles of thatch were cascading down around me. It was the dried reed thatch we use in the Fens and it is apt to be dusty. As I was showered with it, I began to cough. Next to me Robin had prised away one large section of plaster and started on another. To my shame, I began to feel excited with the glory of destruction. We would drive out these people who dared to set up their houses on our fields!

I moved along, past Robin, and attacked another section of thatch. Already I had exposed part of the roof beams and now that the thatch was loosened, the next section came away easily. There were noises now from inside the house – a child crying, someone shouting. Then a candle was lit, casting its light through the great hole I had made in the roof. A woman screamed. The thud, thud of the axes made the whole structure shake. These houses had been constructed hurriedly and were not so well jointed as the framework for the church. There was a cracking as one of the corner uprights split. The upper half tore away from the roof and collapsed like a felled tree, bringing part of the roof structure down with it. Tom and Toby jumped out of the way just in time. From the other end of the settlement I could hear the noise of more breaking timber and now the whole place was astir, with shouts and screams.

There was the sound of a door crashing back against its frame from the far side of our house.

'Tom!' I shouted, 'they're coming!'

Tom put his fingers in his mouth and gave a piercing whistle. I heard the pounding feet as those from the other end of the settlement ran toward us. I pulled down a last bundle of reeds, shook it loose from my scythe and turned to flee. Men were running toward us now, big men, some with muskets. We had not thought the settlers would be armed and carried no weapons ourselves. I scrambled toward the edge of the field, tripped and fell full-length. Someone fell on top of me and I gave a yell. I thought it was one of the pursuers, but it was Tom.

'Jesu, I've fallen on your scythe.'

'Come on!'

Robin and Jack were hauling us to our feet, but Tom fell back down again.

'My leg! I've hurt my blasted leg!'

Jack got an arm under Tom's shoulder and heaved him up again.

'Help me, Robin! Mercy, don't wait. Run!'

And we all ran as if our lives depended on it. Perhaps they did.

With my scythe over my shoulder, I ran, but not fast. I was fearful of tripping again and a fall with a scythe is dangerous. I might cut off my own head. As I scrambled up the lode bank and across the bridge, then dropped down into the lane, I could hear running steps ahead of me and the sound of Robin and Jack dragging Tom along behind me. He yelped with pain as they jumped down after me and began to man-handle him along the last stretch to the farm.

At last we were through the gate. The yard was a melee of men and horses, Jasper barking, Nehemiah at the open kitchen door shouting, 'Be off with you, quick, before anyone comes!'

I leapt out of the way as Rafe and Toby clattered past me and out of the gate. In moments everyone was gone except Jack and Robin, half dragging, half carrying Tom into the house.

'Go!' I said. 'Go! We can manage now.'

As the sound of their horses' hoofs faded away down the lane, I closed the door and leaned on it, gasping for breath. I was still clutching the scythe and let it drop to the floor. Mother, Hannah, Kitty and Nehemiah were looking from me to Tom, who had collapsed into Father's big chair. His breeches were ripped and blood was pouring down his leg.

Mother moaned. 'Not again. Oh, sweet Jesu, not again.'

Hannah took charge. 'Kitty, run and fetch my basket of salves.'

'Which ones?'

'Bring everything, I haven't time to explain.' She turned to Mother. 'Abigail, can you heat water? We will need to wash that leg.'

I saw now that as well as blood Tom's leg was covered with mud and leaves and even fine gravel, which must have come from the bank. Trying to get my breath, I said, 'I'll heat the water.'

Hannah shook her head and leaned near. 'Better for her to be busy.'

Nehemiah fetched a pail and brush and began to clean the blood from the floor and out in the yard, where the moon cast barely enough light for him to see. That trail of blood would lead straight from the settlement to the farm. I followed him outside.

'What can we do to hide the signs?'

160

'We can clear it here in the farm, but how far back does it go?'

'Right to the settlement.'

'Did they shoot at you?'

I realised now what I had been too confused to understand before, that there had been the sound of shots as we had run away, but none of us had been hit.

'No, I tripped and Tom fell over me. He landed on the scythe.'

Nehemiah shook his head. 'It will be deep, then.'

We stood looking up the lane. There was no sign of anyone following, but it was also too dark to see if there were traces of blood.

'I'll go up there at dawn,' Nehemiah said, 'and hide any marks.'

'Do you think you can?'

'I must,' he said grimly.

Back in the house we found that Tom had been laid on the bed so recently vacated by Gideon. His breeches had been removed and I saw that the injured leg was the same one that had been shot before. The previous injury had healed, but the skin over the scar was thin and pink, fragile as an eggshell. And like an eggshell it had broken. By the worst of luck the scythe had cut across the scarred area, a terrible deep slash that showed the white of bone and turned my stomach. Even Hannah was pale as she bathed it. I knelt beside the bed and took Tom's hand. He was awake, but his face was drawn with pain.

'Oh, Tom, I'm so sorry. If I hadn't been so stupid and tripped . . .'

'It wasn't your fault,' the words came out with difficulty. 'The ground there was broken and uneven. Anyone could have fallen. Better my leg to meet the scythe than your neck.' He tried a weak smile and I squeezed his hand.

'Come, Mercy,' said Hannah. 'We must stitch this. There is no other way. You must be brave, Tom.'

I do not want to remember the next hour. Mother fled to her chamber and even Kitty and Nehemiah, both of whom were stout-hearted, found tasks to keep them busy, well away from us. It seemed as though, ever since the drainers had come in early spring, Hannah and I had spent our time tending the injured. Nehemiah, Tom, Gideon, now Tom again. I thought I had become hardened to it, but I had not.

At last we were done and the mess of bloody rags and red-stained water cleared away. Tom had drifted into unconsciousness from pain and loss of blood. Hannah sank down in Father's chair, suddenly looking dreadfully old and frail. Soon she would no longer be able to do this. It was too much for her. I brought us both a cup of the strong beer, usually kept for feast days. We drank it gratefully and I began to feel less shaken. I saw that Nehemiah had removed my scythe and Tom's axe. I was glad of another man about the farm, for with that leg, Tom would be helpless for weeks. And Nehemiah had shown a quick and practical turn of mind tonight.

Hannah's head was nodding and her eyes drooped.

'Come,' I said. 'I'll help you up the stairs to bed. Then I'll sit with Tom.'

Tom was restless in the night, calling for water, then sleeping fitfully and crying out in his sleep. I had resumed my old place on the stool at the bedside, hoping I might doze a little, but my senses were too alert after all that had happened. I kept seeing the house coming down around us and thought of the people inside. One of those who had cried out had been a child, and a woman had screamed. In spite of my anger at the settlement, I began to feel a little ashamed. We had not stopped to ask ourselves how these people came to be here. They seemed to be poor tenant farmers. Who had brought them? Who had told them they could settle on our field? The more I thought about it, the more I was convinced that some great men were behind it, as they were behind the whole drainage of the Fens. Perhaps it did indeed go all the way up to Cromwell. They were exploiting these poor Hollanders just as they were exploiting us. Yet the strangers could not be allowed to settle here on our common land. Someone must have brought them into the country with promises of land they could farm and, whatever our rights in law, it was going to be difficult to evict them now they were here.

I must have fallen asleep at last, for I woke to the sound of lashing rain against the window. It was still dark. Outside I could hear the wind getting up. The previous day had been exceptionally hot, the sort of day which often preceded a thunderstorm, but we had been so preoccupied with our attack on the settlement that I had not thought about the weather. I got up from my stool and went into the kitchen to check that the window there was secure. It was half open and as I reached out to close it I jumped in shock as the whole sky was lit up by flash after flash of lightning, followed almost at once by thunder so loud I could feel its vibration through the soles of my feet.

I pulled the window to, and as I did so, the lightning flashed again, illuminating the whole yard in a bluish glow. I saw that the barn door was open. In our haste to set off we had failed to close it and Nehemiah had been so occupied with cleaning away the blood he must have forgotten it. Blaze hated thunderstorms. He would panic and start kicking the sides of his stall. He might hurt himself. There was nothing for it. I would have to go out there and close the barn door. I hooked Tom's coat down from its peg on the wall and slipped it on. It hung down low and the sleeves were too long, but it would keep the worst of the wet off me. The wind fought me for the door, but at last I managed to open it and step out into the yard. The wind nearly threw me off my feet and by the time I was halfway across the yard my hair, still uncovered, was sopping, blowing across my face in a wet tangle.

Before I even reached the barn, I could hear Blaze. He was kicking out and giving shrill whinnies of fear. I slid into his stall, avoiding his hoofs, and began to talk to him, stroking his head and neck, and laying my cheek against his shoulder. After long minutes he grew calmer and stood still, though tremors continued to run over his skin. I forked down fresh hay into his manger, which he began tentatively to eat, rolling a nervous eye at me from time to time. When at last he seemed quiet, I slipped away, closing and bolting the door.

The storm had not abated one jot. If anything, the wind was stronger, sweeping me towards the house so that I could barely stay on my feet. The orchard trees were lashing their branches in the storm like the wild dervishes dancing through some eastern tale, and despite the noise of the storm I could hear the pattering of apples dashed to the ground. Even our apple harvest was to be taken from us. I fought again with the door, then stood leaning against it in the sanctuary of the kitchen, water streaming from my hair, my shoes making puddles on the floor. I realised with a jolt that I was still wearing Tom's breeches.

Despite the noise of the storm, which continued to light up the kitchen with those violent flashes, no one else seemed to have woken. I prised off my shoes and laid Tom's coat over a bench near the fire to dry. When I looked in on him, I saw that he was sleeping more quietly now, so I took a rushlight and climbed up to my chamber. There I discarded the breeches and pulled on the petticoat and skirt I had left in a heap on the floor. Either Hannah or Kitty turned over in bed in the attic room above me, but did not wake.

Back in the kitchen I laid the breeches next to the coat to dry. Feeling a sudden pang of hunger, I cut myself a slice of bread and topped it with a piece of cheese. It would mean less for tomorrow, but fear and danger, dressing Tom's injury, and now the storm, had left me feeling that hours had passed since I had last eaten. As I suppose they had. I took my seat on the stool again and ate my bread and cheese slowly, to make it last.

Gradually the storm began to blow itself out. At least, I thought, all this rain will have washed away any traces we left when we fled from the settlement.

The storm lasted for two days, and we saw no one outside the household. I hoped the people whose houses we had destroyed had been able to take shelter with their neighbours. On the first morning Nehemiah trudged through the dropple to the pasture and brought back the cows for milking. After that, we decided to keep them in the barn until the storm had passed. Gradually it blew itself out and on the third day a watery sun broke through. Everywhere the ground began to steam, a mist from the evaporating pools rising like smoke.

'I wonder how the new ditches will have dealt with the rain,' Tom said. He was out of bed, refusing to lie like an invalid, though his leg was heavily bandaged and propped on a low stool.

'After milking I will go and see,' I said. I did not tell him that I also planned to take a careful look at the settlement, from a distance.

As I had expected, the new ditches were filled almost to the top, water roaring along like raging rivers. Usually when we had one of these heavy summer storms, the peat moors would absorb most of the water. They were like sponges. The ground would become even more water-logged, the open meres would spread their boundaries, but by and large the water would be contained. The fields and meadows, which stood a little higher, would be soggy for a day or two, but not enough to give the stock foot-rot or cause the crops to go mouldy, because the excess would soon drain into the Fen.

Now, instead of this natural dispersing of the water, it was being channelled from the Fen into the new ditches. I skirted round the place where the ditch which had been dug across the pasture met Baker's Lode and saw a group of men struggling with their new sluice gate. They seemed to be having trouble opening it against the pressure of the water. When they did, there would be a surge of water down Baker's Lode. If there was too much, it might even overflow the banks and flood the fields, including the area where the settlement had been built. There would not be enough to endanger our farm or the village, but in the future, when the winter storms came, who could tell?

On a high point of the bank along the Lode, I stood and looked over at the settlement. The large house we had attacked had collapsed in on itself. We could not have done that much damage, but the subsequent rain would have weighed down the broken thatch and further undermined the weakened frame, until the hastily built house had given way. I could not see the furthest house clearly, but one whole wall had fallen outwards and lay in pieces on the ground. I retreated quickly, not wanting any of the settlers to catch sight of me.

When I reported back to Tom what I had seen, he smiled in satisfaction.

'Good. We have taught them a lesson, then.'

'Do you think it will make any difference?'

He shrugged. 'It will show that we mean business. That we will not give up until we are rid of these drainers and intruders.'

I was not sure, but I was too tired and saddened to argue with him.

The lane between the farm and the village was deep in sludder, an impossible quagmire, which gave us an excuse not to attend church on Sunday and endure Reverend Edgemont's tirade. It was another two days before we saw anyone from the village, then Toby came wading through the mud to enquire after Tom.

'And how does the leg fare?' Toby asked.

'Well enough.' Tom answered cheerfully, though I suspected that he was still suffering a good deal of pain. The slash to his leg, cutting through the flesh which had already been damaged once, was very deep and would take a long time to heal.

'So you managed to stay away from Reverend Edgemont's sermon on Sunday.' Toby looked from one to the other of us keenly, and I realised that he had some news to impart. Disturbing news, it seemed.

'That was a fair old storm we had. Not just thunder and lightning and rain, but a fierce wind.'

'Aye,' said Tom. 'Mercy says it has flattened the barley. That will be another crop running short this year.'

'That's the truth. But it damaged more than barley. That ship you went in search of, at Lynn – the *Brave Endeavour*?'

My heart gave a lurch. We are not sea-goers hereabouts, apart from Jack's three years' adventure. I had not thought about how the storm might affect a ship. Suddenly I was aware of the danger such a small ship must face on the wild German Sea.

'The *Brave Endeavour*, that was the name. What of her?'

'It seems she set out, two days after you left Lynn. That was the day the storm broke. The day we went to the settlement.'

'Aye, it was.'

'It seems the captain was reluctant to sail, for he could see a storm was brewing over the German Sea, but there were some passengers travelling with him who were particularly anxious to leave the country. Gentlemen who had served in the King's forces. They paid him well to leave as planned, despite his worries.'

'What happened?' I burst out. What did I care who else was aboard? 'Has something befallen the ship?'

'They sailed on the afternoon tide and were out to sea when the storm broke. It was a northeast wind and it's a small ship, poorly rigged. They fought the storm for several hours during the night, but in the end they had to make a run back to port with the daylight.'

'They were safe?'

'Safe enough. Torn canvas, a broken spar. She will not sail again for a week or so, but no one was lost or injured.'

I gave a sigh of relief, but why did Toby look so serious?

'It seems that one of the Dillingworths' servants was sent on business to Lynn, and he came back with a strange tale to tell. He announced that he had seen a dead man walking. Gideon Clarke was alive and seen on the street in Lynn.'

'So our lies will be discovered,' said Tom with a worried frown.

'Worse than that. Edmund Dillingworth went to Reverend Edgemont and told the tale. They put their heads together as to how this might have come about. The preacher announced it in church on Sunday.'

Toby looked from me to Hannah, who was alternately knitting and dozing by the fire.

'Reverend Edgemont has declared that the rector was known to have died. As he now lives, he must have been raised from the dead, and such can only be accomplished by witchcraft. He claims that those who treated the rector practised witchcraft, and has sent for Matthew Hopkins and John Stearne. He declares that Hannah Green and Mercy Bennington are to be taken up for witchcraft.'

Chapter Eleven

'That is madness!' Tom said, although I could see panic in his eyes. 'They have merely discovered that the tale we spread abroad of Gideon's death was a lie. It will mean trouble, but surely not serious trouble.'

'Aye, it is certainly madness,' Toby said. He spoke calmly, but there was an undertone of dread in his voice. 'However, it serves their purpose to pretend they believed Gideon *was* dead, and now has been raised from the dead.'

'Purpose? What purpose?' Tom shifted uncomfortably in his chair and lifted his leg with both hands into a better position.

'Edmund Dillingworth has a purpose,' I said quietly. 'He wishes to do me harm. But why should he wish to harm Hannah? And why would Reverend Edgemont support him?' I was determined to keep my voice calm, but terror was filling me, blood and bone, like an icy flood.

'Edgemont has his own purposes,' said Toby. 'Our village and our traditional beliefs are like a thorn in his shoe. If he cannot convert us to his Calvinist ways – and I think he sees now that he cannot – why then he will punish us, make an example of us. We shall be known as a den of sacrilege and witchcraft.'

I drew in a sharp breath. It made sense. These extreme reformers, with their hellfire and their conviction that every man, woman and child was either saved or damned from birth, were most zealous in hunting out any who did not conform to their way of thinking. Any old country practice – like our simple bringing in of the May – was accounted blasphemous. Old superstitions about signs of good and bad luck, even weather lore, were seen as the workings of the Devil. If they could sniff out witchcraft, they would do so. There had been no talk of finding witches amongst us until Hopkins and Stearne had begun their searches, yet suddenly dozens of witches had been discovered and hanged, all over our Fen country, sometimes on the flimsiest of evidence. And above all where the most extreme sectaries lived. What evidence had been produced against Agnes Pettifer? We had never heard. But Crowthorne and Edgemont could not rest satisfied with one witch. They must come amongst us and spread the poison of their accusations here. All of this flashed through my mind, but as if I were thinking of someone else, not myself.

Up to that moment I had been trying to consider Edmund Dillingworth and Reverend Edgemont rationally, but suddenly, like the rush of water when the sluice is opened, I truly understood the fearful news. They were seeking me. And Hannah. It could not be long before they would arrest us. Now I was submerged by sheer terror. My whole body began to shake.

'How long do you think,' I asked Toby softly, 'before they come for us?' I could not blot out that terror from my voice.

He looked at me compassionately. 'They have sent for the witchfinders. They will probably wait until they come, with their men-at-arms. That way Edgemont and Dillingworth can accomplish their purpose, but at arms' length. If you are proved innocent, they can maintain their lack of involvement.'

I swallowed. It would depend on where the witchfinders were at present, how long it would be before they came amongst us. Not long, though.

Tom half rose from his chair, then fell back. 'We must hide you, both you and Hannah.'

'Aye,' said Toby, 'though I do not know how it is to be done.'

I glanced across at Hannah, who had fallen asleep, ignoring our talk.

'I could hide, I suppose, or live rough out on the Fen, but she could not.'

We all studied the old woman. In recent weeks she had grown older. It was as if, having left behind her sturdy independence in her cottage by the Fen, she had let down her defences against the creeping onset of old age. Living protected amongst us at Turbary Holm, she was losing the battle. I remembered how exhausted she had looked after we had dressed Tom's wound. No, Hannah could not take to the life of an outlaw, hiding in the Fen from pursuit.

'Hannah cannot go, and I cannot abandon her.'

'At least we may save one of you,' Tom said.

I shook my head, though my heart clenched with fear. 'I cannot abandon her.'

We had not long to wait. Before dawn on the fifth day of August, we were woken by a loud hammering on the door. I knew at once what it meant and made myself hastily ready, while Nehemiah went to answer the door, grumbling and delaying as long as he could. I dressed in clean linen and my simplest gown, wrapping a fresh cloth around my head and tucking my hair out of sight beneath my cap. The previous night I had bathed in a wooden tub before the fire, washed my hair and pared and scrubbed my nails. I wanted my appearance to be as far from the perceived image of a witch as possible. Clean and neat, I felt able to face the witchfinders' men, although I was unsure how long I could keep up my courage.

After supper last night, Tom and I had discussed what we should do about the payment of Father's fine, which was due in ten days' time. I handed over the money Gideon had left me. Together with what we had managed to save and to earn with our dealings at market, and from the sale of the oxen, we had about two-thirds of what we needed.

'What will happen if we cannot pay all?' I said.

'I do not know. Perhaps he will be bailed for the rest. I will be told when I pay the fine.'

'You cannot go yourself, not with your leg as it is. Send Toby or Rafe.'

He shook his head and would not discuss it further.

Now he limped across the kitchen floor to the bottom of the stairs as I came down. I tried to give him a calm smile, but my lips trembled.

'They are here,' he said softly.

I nodded, not trusting my voice.

Above me on the stairs I saw Kitty, her face white with terror and her hands pressed against her mouth. I had warned her what was going to happen and told her she must take on more of the work about the farm. With Hannah and me gone and Tom injured, a heavy burden would fall on her young shoulders.

'Kitty,' I said, 'tell Hannah to come down. We must go now.'

She nodded and flew back upstairs to the attic.

We had explained everything to Hannah the day after Toby had brought us the news, but she still refused to believe that anything serious could happen.

'You will see, child,' she said, patting my hand, 'it will all come to nothing. We are no more witches than . . .' she searched for a suitable comparison. 'Than Cromwell himself! It is all nonsense.'

In some ways I was glad of her robust scepticism. It would give her strength in the ordeal that was to come. I had told her eventually of Agnes Pettifer's death, but even this had not shaken her. She put it down to the wickedness of the people of Crowthorne, which had somehow by-passed the proper findings of the court. I did not know how to argue against this, for I was ignorant of how the courts proceeded in the cases of witchcraft.

I smoothed down my apron over my skirt and walked ahead of Tom into the kitchen. There were four men there, large men with swords, wearing some sort of official livery. It seemed excessive to arrest two women. One, who seemed to be their captain, confronted me.

'You are Mercy Bennington?'

'I am.'

'You are arrested on a charge of practising witchcraft, in particular raising from the dead one Gideon Clarke, a recusant priest.'

'Gideon Clarke was never dead,' I said steadily. 'Nor is he a recusant.'

'Do not answer back, you slut!' He struck me across the face.

I was so startled I shrank back, my hand over my mouth. I tasted blood, where my teeth had been driven into my lower lip.

'How dare you strike my sister!' Tom had come up behind me. I cast him an imploring look. I tried to signal with my eyes: Don't provoke them.

It was too late. The captain slammed his fist into Tom's jaw and sent him sprawling on the floor, his injured leg twisted beneath him. I had hoped the arrest could be carried out quietly and now everything was going wrong. Hannah came into the room, followed by Kitty. They both looked frightened when they saw Tom on the floor and me with blood on my face. Behind them Mother and Nehemiah crowded in, Mother as white as bleached linen, Nehemiah looking as though he would attack the guards at any moment.

I went to Hannah and took her arm.

'Come, my dear,' I said. 'We must go with this gentlemen. Do not be afraid.'

I led her towards the door. The last I saw of my family was Kitty and Nehemiah helping Tom to his feet.

Outside there were four horses. I had expected a cart of some sort. How did they plan to carry us to wherever we were going? Were we to ride pillion? It was soon clear what they intended. One of the other guards brought a rope and bound my wrists together, then fastened the other end to his stirrup iron. Another tied Hannah to his horse. We were to be made to walk at the horses' tails, like condemned criminals. But how far? Hannah would manage as far as the village, but I doubted whether she could go much further.

We set off. Although they walked their horses, it was a fast pace. We stumbled along after them. The lane to the village was still deep in mud after the heavy rain and I could not pick up my skirts, which were soon draggled and muddy. As we reached the village, I wondered what my neighbours would make of us.

They stood before their houses in silent anger. Early as it was, they were all there. They must have heard the men ride through on their way to arrest us.

'Shame!' Someone shouted. 'Those women are innocent.'

The captain looked round quickly, but could not see who had spoken.

'Courage, Mercy!' I knew that voice. It was Alice.

172

'We will pray for you. These devils shall not harm you.' That was Toby.

The captain drove his heels angrily into his horse's sides and increased the pace. We had to half run to keep up, or the rope burnt into our wrists. Even so, it had given me courage to hear what they said. If any were called as witnesses, they would speak for us.

When we reached Crowthorne, it was a different matter. By then Hannah was exhausted, falling down every few yards, so that our whole procession had to stop while she got to her feet again. Her dress was covered with mud and her cap awry. At last she had begun to understand what was happening to us. Her eyes were wide with terror.

I had been to Crowthorne only twice in my life. Once, when we were children, Tom and I had made our way there out of curiosity, to see what it was like. That was before it became such a reformist place, but even so the local children had threatened us. The second time was on my way to work at the manor, when I had gone round by the lane to keep my shoes and skirts tidy, instead of over the fields.

Now, as we were dragged through Crowthorne, the inhabitants here had also come out to watch us pass, but with very different intentions. The guards slowed down, deliberately, I realised. The people jeered at us.

'Filthy witches!'

'Spawn of Satan!'

'May you burn in hellfire!'

Then they began to pelt us with fistfuls of mud and dung, with stones, even with eggs. As an egg burst on my shoulder, I thought it strange that they should be so wasteful of food, but then I realised from the stink that it was rotten.

At last we were through Crowthorne and once more on a country road. We passed the lane which led to the manor. From here it was unknown territory. I risked speaking to the guard ahead of me.

'Where are you taking us?'

'Lincoln,' he said, without turning his head.

'Lincoln! This old woman cannot walk all the way to Lincoln.'

'She should get the Devil to fly her there, then.'

One of the other guards laughed.

After a minute or two he added, 'At the Roman road there's a cart waiting, so you need not fear for the old witch. Master Hopkins wants you both alive. He can have more entertainment out of you that way.'

I bowed my head, feeling sick. What kind of entertainment would that be?

At the old Roman road, we were heaved into a dirty cart drawn by a mule, but our hands were left tied. I did what I could to make Hannah comfortable, but it was little enough. There was not even straw in the cart for us to sit on. From the smell of it, recently it had been used to transport pigs. I managed to ease Hannah until she was lying with her head on my lap. She was exhausted. One of her shoes had fallen off, but we had not been allowed to retrieve it, so her left foot was cut and bloodied. I wondered why they had not brought the cart all the way for us, but guessed they wanted to make a spectacle of us, to frighten our neighbours and entertain the people of Crowthorne, who could congratulate themselves on their saintliness. And all the time, to humiliate us.

When we reached Lincoln at last, we drove through the streets, attracting some stares, but no one paused in their daily business. They must be accustomed to such sights. The road wound up a steep hill towards huge ramparts, which must be the ramparts of the castle, so high I had to crane my head back to see to the top of them. I had never before seen walls so high. To the right a vast church reared up, which must be the cathedral. The holy and the profane, cheek by jowl, crowned the city of Lincoln. The cart was driven under the castle gatehouse, and we were tipped out, Hannah barely able to stand. At the sight of those grim, massive walls, my courage began to falter. Somewhere in here my father had languished for months. How long would we be held here before they questioned us? I remembered that Toby had said we would not be arrested until after the witchfinders Hopkins and Stearne had arrived, so that must mean they were already here, or expected soon.

'Come along with you.' The captain jerked his head and two of the guards led us after him, dragging us by the ropes, like cattle.

The ropes had already rubbed the skin of my wrists raw and as the man jerked the rope it dug painfully into the sores. I managed to find my feet, tired as I was, and followed him, but Hannah collapsed on the ground in a faint. The captain grunted in annoyance, but it was clear that this was no pretence.

'Two of you, carry the old witch,' he said, and set off for a round tower over to the left of the vast castle courtyard.

We were taken through a heavy door, studded with great nails, and then down damp and slippery steps with led below ground. I managed to keep my footing with difficulty, but the men carrying Hannah took little care and struck her head once against the stone wall. At the bottom of the steps there was an iron-barred gate and a turnkey who opened it, looking curiously at us. I saw his hand creep up to his head as though he would cross himself, then he thought better of it and wiped his nose with his hand, as if that had been his intention all along.

Beyond the iron gate was a narrow corridor smelling like the mud stirred up from a stagnant pool, with doors on either side. Halfway along, the turnkey stopped before one that was open.

'This one is free,' he said.

'In you go,' said the captain, giving me a push so that I fell to my knees.

Seeing that they were going away, leaving me alone there, I held up my bound wrists. 'Will you not unbind me?'

He laughed. 'Be thankful we have not chained you. Not yet.'

As the door began to close, I cried out, 'You will not separate us? Hannah is old and ill, she needs to be cared for.'

'Leave two witches together? Never. No knowing what devilry you may get up to.'

The door slammed and I heard the key turn in the heavy lock.

I do not know how long I stayed in the cell. It was entirely empty, not even a straw palliasse on the floor. No window, just a small hatch in the door, through which a dim light filtered. It must have been late afternoon when we reached Lincoln and I supposed by now it must be night. I realised that I was hungry, for I had eaten nothing since the previous evening, but hunger was the least matter to worry about. I wondered where Hannah was. In one of the other cells along this corridor, or had they taken her somewhere else? If she was still out of her wits, they could do no good questioning her.

After what seemed like many hours, during which I sat on the damp stone floor with my back against the wall, I heard footsteps outside the door. I strained to hear voices, but there were none. Then there came the grinding of the key in the lock, a rusty sound of metal on metal. The light of a candle lamp dazzled me after the long dark and I raised my bound hands to shield my eyes.

'Get up.' It was a different man, not one of the guards who had brought me here. A middle-aged, fatherly-looking gaoler, who seemed out of place in these grim surroundings.

I scrambled unsteadily to my feet. He jerked his head for me to follow him, and led me back down the corridor to the iron door. As we passed the other cells, I wondered whether Hannah was in one of them, or perhaps my father. Tom had never told me exactly where in Lincoln castle he was held. We ascended the steps, then crossed the courtyard to the other side, to a long rectangular building. It was full dark now. I tripped once over the trailing rope and nearly fell. The man put his arm under my elbow and held me up, not ungently.

Inside I was led into a large room which was brightly lit with many candles. There was a table, where two men sat, and three old dames stood together in the middle of the room, near a single chair. The gaoler who had brought me untied the rope, bowed to the two men, and withdrew, shutting the door quietly behind him. I flexed my fingers, which were numb, and saw that my wrists were bleeding and swollen.

Two of the women seized me by the elbows and marched me to the centre of the room. All of the women were elderly, with hard, self-righteous faces, dressed in the severe garments of practising Puritans. With a shock I realised who and what they were. Searchers. They would strip me and search for witch-marks on my body. Despite my determination to be brave, I began to shake.

They pulled off my cap and headcloth and searched my scalp, their bony fingers raking through my hair. They twisted my head this way and that, to examine my neck from every angle. All the while, they said nothing.

Apparently there were no marks to find on my head and neck. I knew what was to come next, and tried to turn my back on the watching men, but one of the women, tall as a man and strong despite her age, forced me round again. She untied my apron, then the strings on my skirt and petticoat, which slid to the ground. Another unlaced my bodice and pulled it roughly off, twisting my arms behind my back. They removed my shoes and peeled off my stockings, breaking one of my ribbon garters as they did so. I was left in nothing but my shift. Two of the women grabbed my shift and started to pull it over my head, but I began to fight back, pulling it down again to hide my shame.

The big women slapped me hard across the face. 'None of that. We'll have it off, will you or not.'

There was a sound of ripping as they dragged off my shift and I stood naked, there in the centre of the room. In my humiliation I raised my eyes and stared straight at the men. I will defy them, I thought. Let them try to outface me.

Both men were younger than I had expected. One was small, neat and dapper, a pile of paper before him and a quill in his hand, ready to take notes. He looked at me lasciviously, with a moist eye. His red lips curled in a smile as I was revealed in my nakedness.

The other man, taller and thin, though also young, looked ill. He was pale and his eyes were sunken and bruised-looking. From time to time he coughed into his handkerchief, which he folded and hid, as though he had coughed up something unpleasant. I sensed that he too took pleasure in my nakedness, but that he was too tired or too ill to savour it to the full.

The three women began to examine my body, poking and prodding every inch of my skin, even into my most private parts. I felt my face flush with rage and humiliation, but I would not cower before them, nor plead. I threw back my head and continued to stare straight ahead at the two witchfinders. The smaller man saw my defiance and I watched him make note of it.

At last the big woman spoke.

'We can find no witches' marks, Master Hopkins.'

The thin man, the one who appeared to be ill, gave a brief nod.

'Very well. You may go.' He looked at me. 'You may dress yourself.'

My hands were shaking as I pulled my shift over my head. One sleeve was partly ripped out and my fingers caught in the tear. I heard one of the men laugh. As quickly as I could, I donned the rest of my clothes, making a clumsy knot in the broken garter. At last I stood fully clothed, though I knew my clothes were disarranged and my hair, hastily bundled under my cap, threatened to fall down again.

The smaller man, who must be John Stearne, shouted, 'Guard!'

I felt a spasm of hope. They had found no marks on me. Was I to be released?

One of the men who had arrested us came in, carrying a large coil of rope.

'Bind her,' Hopkins said.

The guard forced me down on to the chair, then pulled my arms behind it and tied them together. He carried the rope round my throat and back again, so that I could not bend my head forward without choking. Then he passed the rope under the seat and bound my ankles to the legs of the chair.

'Now, Mistress Bennington,' Hopkins said, 'you will remain here and you will be watched, to see whether any of your imps or familiars visit you.'

'I have no imps or familiars,' I protested. 'I am a yeoman's daughter and a good Christian. You have no right to treat me thus.'

'It is sad, is it not, brother,' said Stearne, 'when a woman of good family turns to the devil? An unhappy sign of these most unhappy times.'

Hopkins ignored him and stood up, coming to stand close before me.

'I will have your confession out of you, woman. Be sure of that. However long it takes, and by whatever means.' He fixed on me the eyes of a fanatic, burning in his gaunt face. 'It is my mission from God, our Holy Father, to root out this pernicious growth of witchcraft which has spread over this land like a choking vine. Be sure. You cannot hide from me.'

I think he would have said more, but he began to cough, great racking coughs which shook his emaciated frame. He fixed on me a look of hate, as though he believed I had occasioned his illness, then turned and left the room.

Stearne bustled about, a fussy, lesser man, one of those who must always make themselves appear more important than they are. He consulted with the guard, who nodded and left.

'Now, woman,' said Stearne, 'you will be watched. As soon as you are ready to confess your loathsome deeds, your pact with Satan to raise the dead, you have but to speak and we will come to record your confession.'

'I am no witch. I have made no pact with Satan. I have never raised the dead. Master Clarke was injured, but never dead. We nursed him back to health.'

Stearne struck me across the face and I saw that he took pleasure in it.

'Do not deny it. It has been attested that the man was dead and is now alive. Speak only when you are ready to confess.'

With that, he bustled to the door, strutting peacock of a man that he was. He was met there by the guard returning with more candles, and by two women and a man. These, I thought, must be the Watchers. I licked away blood, where Stearne's blow had opened the cut on my lip again. When Stearne and the guard had left, the Watchers came in, each carrying a chair and cushions. They meant to make themselves comfortable, then. One of the women went out again and returned with a tray on which stood a pitcher, some cups, and plates of food. My stomach groaned in anticipation. Perhaps they were going to feed me at last. But no, they arranged their chairs in a semicircle in front of me and sat down, the man in the middle. He doffed his hat and they all lowered their heads.

'Dear Lord,' he said, 'help us in our righteous work this night, that we may bring this woman out of the clutches of the Devil and all his works. May you guide us to the truth, in the name of Christ our Saviour. Amen.'

'Amen,' the women echoed.

'And I pray that the Lord God will guide you to the truth, that I am no witch,' I said. 'Dear Lord, open their eyes. Amen.'

The man stared at me angrily. 'Do not utter your blasphemies here, woman. Do you pray to your master Satan?'

'I pray to our Lord God in Heaven,' I said wearily. 'And to Jesus Christ, our Saviour.' But I regretted my outburst. It would do me no good. I saw that if Matthew Hopkins thought he could force me to say what he wanted to hear, then both the witchfinder and the Watchers could twist whatever I said to suit their own purposes. My only safety lay in saying nothing. I clamped my jaw shut. Very well, I would not speak.

The time dragged slowly. After a while, the three Watchers helped themselves to food and drink, but none was offered to me, though I was becoming very thirsty. As the candles burned down, more were lit. I could not doze, for whenever my head fell forward, the rope around my neck throttled me and brought me quickly awake. And with my arms twisted behind my back, it felt as though they were being wrenched out of their sockets. The pain began to burn in my arms, my shoulders, my neck and head.

The Watchers seemed accustomed to sitting like this, their eyes fixed on me. I wondered whether they were allowed to sleep in the daytime, else this punishment of forbidding sleep, the *tormentum insomniae*, was as harsh to them as to me. After my long vigils of sitting up with Gideon all night, I did not find the wakefulness that first night difficult, had it not been for the pain. By the time light began to filter in through the windows and the candles were burnt out, I was tired, but it was nothing I could not endure. It was the pain that preoccupied me. By now, my legs, too, were numb.

With full morning, Hopkins returned.

'Anything?' he asked the man.

'Nothing, sir, but a blasphemous prayer.'

'Aye?' Hopkins was interested.

The man repeated what I had said, with perfect accuracy, but Hopkins shook his head.

'Not enough. Give her to drink, then be off.'

One of the women held a cup to my lips with tepid water. As I could not incline my head, much of it poured down on to my bodice, but what little I managed to drink moistened my mouth and relieved my thirst a little.

The Watchers left and Hopkins sat before me. Now he was so close, I caught the rank smell of his sickness, sweet and sour together, and a smell of blood. That is what he has been spitting, I thought. And there was something else. A strong smell of onions. Consumption, it was a sure sign. He cannot have long left. Yet he will drag me down with him.

He began to question me. How long had I had congress with Satan? Did he visit me at night to sleep with me in sin? What were my familiars? What harm had I worked on my neighbours? Who else was in our coven besides myself and Hannah? It was known I was an intimate friend of Alice Cox, was she part of the coven? It was also known that we were intimate with Agnes Pettifer, who was already confessed and hanged for a witch. How had I raised the great thunderstorm which had recently swept the country? Would I confess to having laid a curse on the private parts of Master Edmund Dillingworth?

At that, I nearly broke my vow of silence and could only with difficulty keep myself from laughing. So that was what he had told them! To knee a rapist in the groin was now the work of a witch! Oh, Edmund Dillingworth was carrying his revenge too far. But I must not speak.

After a time, Stearne took over. His questions were more prurient, and he touched me intimately several times, but all I did was glare at him, though it was difficult not to flinch. Three times during the day I was given a drink, but no food. When night came, the witchfinders left and the Watchers returned. This time they carried iron probes, of the kind sometimes used on cattle. I thought they were going to torture me, but as the night wore on, I discovered their use. By letting my head lean a little to the side, I found the rope did not choke me and I would begin to slip into blessed sleep, despite the burning agony of my body. Every time, one of the Watchers would drive a probe into my side to wake me up.

This second night I was beginning to suffer from the lack of sleep. Moreover, my limbs and back were becoming even more numb from being tied with ropes so long. For long stretches I could not feel my feet at all, then sensation would flow back into them with excruciating pain, as if they were being stabbed with a dozen knives. The whole of my spine was a burning pain. All this time I had not been allowed to relieve myself. To my shame, my clothes were soaked with urine.

For whole minutes together, I would seem to sleep, although my eyes were open. My mind wandered away from the great bare room, lit by flickering candles, and from the three people watching me. It was as though I moved inside a dream, a kind of shell which held me, within the outer shell which was the torture room.

The next day the questions continued, first Hopkins, then Stearne, then Hopkins again. Their voices braided together, a meaningless sound. My ears had become deaf, my hearing turned inward to the drumming of my chained blood, the shrieks of my paralysed limbs. No longer did I need to struggle to keep silent. My tongue cleaved to the roof of my mouth and my thoughts were as scattered as leaves in the wind. No words came together to form meaning. That night as the Watchers came, the door stood open and I heard a distant screaming, but my blurred mind made no sense of it.

That night – I think it was that night, the third, or the fourth, but perhaps it was the fifth – I watched the Watchers as their heads began to balloon above their shoulders. Their mouths gaped and their eyes bulged. Then all the flames of the candles joined and danced about me, like the flames of a funeral pyre, such as I have read about in Tom's chapbooks of strange tales from the Indies. At first I watched the Watchers with interest, and wondered whether they knew their heads were like to explode at any moment. But I could not tell them. I must not speak.

Perhaps I *had* bewitched them. Perhaps I was indeed a witch after all. I found myself shaking with inward laughter. All this time, I was a witch and did not know it! Gideon had been killed by the soldiers, lain dead in my arms, and by my witchcraft I had brought him back from the dead! I felt a surge of terrible power, and I broke free from my bonds and rose up into the air, where I looked down on the body of that poor, misguided girl, Mercy Bennington, who sat chained by the agony of her mortal body, while I could fly away. Away from the pain. Away from the questions. Away from the screams I could hear, nearer and more distinct.

My mind tumbled down from the ceiling and collided with my body again. The male Watcher had fixed me with a keen stare. Had I uttered something, without realising? For I knew now that those screams came from Hannah.

A cold sweat had broken out all over my body and I began to shake. My teeth rattled together in my head and I could not grip them tight enough to stop the sound.

'Liz,' said the man, 'fetch Master Hopkins.

The younger woman rose from her chair and shook out her skirts, then went quickly from the room. The man fetched a cup of water and held it for me to drink, but clumsily, so most of it ran down my chin. A little managed to find its way between my clattering teeth and down my throat.

It seemed a long time before the woman Liz returned, bringing Matthew Hopkins, who had dressed hastily and carelessly, but his eyes shone with excitement. He drew the man aside and they spoke together, but I could hear them.

'She went into a fit, and we saw her imp fall from her mouth and run across the floor.'

The older woman nodded. 'Aye, a black imp, in the form of a rat. I saw it with my own eyes.'

I wanted to shout, 'They lie!', but I would not speak.

'And you, Liz?' Hopkins said. 'Did you see the imp?'

I watched the younger woman struggling with her conscience. At last she shook her head. 'No, Master Hopkins. I must have looked away. Certainly the witch had a fit, but I did not see the imp. It must have been there, but the dark, the shadows . . .' Her voice trailed away.

One of them was honest, it seemed. Through the fogginess of my brain I thought: That is good.

'Very well.' He became brisk. 'Goodman Thomson, untie the witch. Then walk her for the rest of the night. That will make her speak at last.'

With this he left. Back to his warm bed, no doubt, though I heard him coughing as his steps receded. The man Thomson began to tackle the knots in the rope, but they were damp and swollen with my sweat and blood, so at last he drew out a knife and sawed through them, strand after strand. I stared at him. While Hopkins was there, my head had been briefly clear, but now there seemed to be a buzzing in my ears and my sight was blurred. After what seemed like hours, the last of the ropes dropped away and I fell forward out of the chair, striking my face on the floor. My arms were so numb I could not put them out to save me.

'Come, on your feet!' Thomson took hold of my right arm and pulled. I gave an involuntary shriek.

'Careful!' The woman Liz knelt down beside me. 'She will not be able to move. You must wait.'

She rolled me over and began to rub my arms and legs, not with any great kindness, but as if she were dealing briskly with an injured animal. The pain as my frozen limbs came back to life was like nothing I had ever felt before, as if thousands of knives were piercing my whole body. I drew in air in great shuddering gasps. The other woman knelt to help Liz and between them they brought some movement back to me. The man stood impatiently tapping his iron probe against his leg, waiting for them to finish.

At last they got me to my feet, though my knees buckled and my right ankle turned over.

'We must walk you,' Liz said. 'It will help.'

The women took an arm each and began to walk me up and down the full length of the room. The flames of the candles wavered and flickered with the disturbance of our movement, and our shadows danced grotesquely on the walls. Gradually I gained control over my limbs, until I was able to stand and walk by myself.

'Enough,' said Thomson. 'Let her go.'

The women stood back.

'Now you must run,' he said. 'Quick now. Run to the end of the room and back.'

I stared at him. I thought my torment had stopped, but it seemed another was beginning. As I did not move, he struck my back with his probe, holding it like a whip.

'Run!'

He ran me up and down that room as the sky grew pale outside the windows and the sun came up. Again my mind seemed to separate itself from my body and watched this poor shambling creature stumbling and weaving across the floor, like an injured beetle. In a coolly detached way, I felt sorry for the foolish woman who would not speak, would not confess that she was a witch. Why not speak, and end this torment?

Some time later, Hopkins and Stearne came into the room together and dismissed the Watchers, who seemed glad to go, for they had been kept there much longer than usual. As they went, I sank to the ground, for I could not move any more. I wished I could faint, as Hannah had, but my body would not give me that respite.

Hopkins came and stood looking down at me, where I sprawled on the floor.

'So, you have still not spoken, even though they have seen an imp spring from your mouth. Will you admit your devilment now, to spare yourself more torment?'

I stared up at him, but kept my lips, dry and sore as they were, pressed tightly together.

'Very well. Tomorrow we will swim you, as final proof.'

'But we do not need it,' said Stearne, and I saw that he rubbed his hands together.

'No, but we will observe the rules, that there can be no doubt before the magistrate.'

In my foggy brain I could not understand their meaning. What did Stearne mean, that they did not need final proof?

As if he read my thoughts, Hopkins smiled.

'Hannah Green has confessed herself a witch, admitted to many crimes. And she has declared you her fellow witch, who did bring back Gideon Clarke from the dead.'

He began to cough again, and I saw that his handkerchief was stained with blood. When he could draw breath, he squared his shoulders, like a man who is pleased and proud at having accomplished some difficult but worthy task.

'We hanged her this morning.'

Chapter Twelve

I was returned to my cell, though I was barely able to walk across the courtyard and down the slippery steps. It was the same gaoler who escorted me, the one who had fetched me to the questioning. He said nothing as we made our stumbling, weaving way back to the prison, but he went slowly and supported me with a strong arm under my elbow.

When we reached the cell, I saw that a straw palliasse had been laid on the floor and there was a pisspot in the corner.

'I will bring you food,' he said.

I sank down on the palliasse and laid my head on my folded arms, trying to think. Why this sudden small measure of kindness? Perhaps it was to satisfy the magistrates, who might be suspicious if the accused witch was brought before them in too terrible a state of body. Any fearsome state of mind would be understood as normal for a witch. But now my thoughts could shy away no longer from what they had told me.

Hannah had betrayed me.

I could not shake those words from my mind. Perhaps they lied? But no. I thought that whatever Hopkins's fanaticism drove him to, he had his own strict code. Had he not chided Stearne, saying that the proof they had was not enough? No, Hannah had indeed betrayed me. Declared me for a witch.

I began to sob then. All that I had endured was for nothing. And tomorrow they would swim me. It was well known that when suspects were swum, they almost always floated, which meant that the water rejected them as vile witches. I could not swim. I could not dive under the water, as Tom or Jack or any of their friends could do. If I floated, there was nothing I could do to save myself. I would hang.

How could Hannah betray me? All my life she had been one of my dearest friends, a comfort, a solace, a rock on which I depended. If of late I had looked after her more than she had looked after me, it was through her increasing old age. And that gave me pause for thought. Her body was weaker than mine. She was fragile. Her bones would break easily if they had tied her as they had tied me. And her mind had grown more frail of late. In her firm refusal to believe any harm could come to us, there was a kind of shrinking from the truth. When the truth and the agony of the torture had been visited upon her, it had proved too much. How could I, in my young strength, condemn her? And now she was dead.

I heard the gaoler returning and wiped my eyes on my dirty apron. He came in bearing a tray on top of a stool, which he set down beside me. There was a jug of ale and a basin of water, as well as a plate of cold meats and an early apple. I looked up at him in surprise.

He gave me a tentative smile. 'Eat,' he said, 'and wash yourself. And then sleep. Sleep all you can. You must gain strength for the swimming.'

Was he mocking me? 'Thank you for the food,' I said.

He glanced behind him at the open door, then crossed the cell and softly closed it. I wrapped my arms around myself in fear. What did he intend?

He came back and squatted on the floor beside me.

'Listen,' he whispered. 'You know that if you float, they will take it as proof you are a witch, and hang you?'

'I know.'

'But you see, you women with your long skirts, they fill with air and hold you up. Like a bubble floating on the surface, see?'

I stared at him. Why was he telling me this?

'That means innocent women are declared guilty. But if you sink, you are proved innocent. Can you swim?'

I shook my head.

'Then there is only one way. You must fill your pockets with stones. They will drag you down and all will see that you are no witch.'

'I shall drown instead.'

He shook his head impatiently and glanced over his shoulder. 'You must stay under the water for the count of thirty, then empty the stones from your pockets. You will rise then, but it will be enough.'

'The river will sweep me away.'

'No. They tie a rope around your waist to pull you out. They don't want you to drown, witch or not.'

I gave him a wan smile. 'It is a clever notion. But where will I find stones?' I glanced around the cell. 'There are none here.'

'I will bring them when I fetch you tomorrow for the swimming.'

'Why are you doing this? If they discovered you, surely they will accuse you of colluding with a witch.'

He sat back on his heels. 'My cousin Will lives in your village.'

'Will the blacksmith?'

'Aye. He has told me everything, how your people pretended the rector was dead, to get him safe away. How you and Hannah Green were no more witches than he was. Besides . . .' He passed a hand over his face. 'The girl I was to marry, a girl here in Lincoln. These witchfinders took her for a witch and hanged her. She was no witch!'

His voice cracked on a sob and I reached out a hand and touched his arm. 'They are devils, these witchfinders,' I said.

'Aye. And think they do God's work.' His voice was grim.

He got easily to his feet and I realised he was younger than I had thought. Not much older than Gideon. His troubles had aged him.

'Eat now, and sleep. You must be strong for tomorrow.' And with that he left.

I washed first, cleaning my face and hands in the basin, then drying them on my apron. There was nothing I could do about the state of my urine-soaked clothes, but I reflected wryly that the river would wash them clean tomorrow. At least the cleansing water on my face seemed also to wash away some of the confusion brought on by my lack of sleep. The walk in the open air through the courtyard and the conversation with the gaoler had helped to clear my mind a little, though I was exhausted, all my joints shrieking with pain and my head pounding. Despite all this, I realised I was hungry and looked now to see what he had brought me.

The food was simple but fresh and hearty. A beef pie, packed with meat and onions and dripping with gravy that ran down my chin. Three cold sausages. A boiled onion. A slab of pease pudding. I wolfed it down like a beggar child who fears the food may be snatched away. The ale was decent stuff, not as good as my home brew, but passable. The flagon filled the cup three times. As I bit into the apple, a ginnet, sharp and a little under ripe, I wondered whether the gaoler had given me his own dinner. The food was surely too good to be wasted on a prisoner.

Could I trust him? He seemed honest enough and what was there to lose in trusting him? It was too great a problem for me to solve in my present fuddled state. I lay down upon the palliasse with the half-eaten apple still in my hand and fell at once into a sleep as deep and dark as a well.

I do not know how long I slept, but when I woke the light filtering in from the corridor was dim and flickering, so I supposed it must be night and the light was that of a candle lantern. With a groan I sat up. All my limbs had stiffened while I slept, so that I could hardly move. I had lain on the remains of the apple. I could just make out that it had turned brown, but I ate it anyway. Then I discovered that the gaoler must have been in the cell while I slept, for the first tray had been taken away and a new one was now on the stool.

With difficulty I managed to get to my feet and walk about the cell. I knew that if I was to survive tomorrow's ordeal I must get some movement back into my arms and legs, so I forced myself to walk round the perimeter of the cell ten times. Then I used the pisspot and sat down again on my bed.

This time the man had brought me bread and cheese. The bread was fresh and I tore lumps off it with my teeth. It was a rough, coarse loaf, but the finest white manchet bread could not have tasted better for me then. There was a good sized piece of cheese, a local cheese, white and crumbling, with a strong tang. It was wonderful. There was more ale and another of the apples.

I devoured everything, then walked around the cell again and again. Although I still ached all over, I was beginning to move more normally. As I walked, I went over in my mind the plan the gaoler had suggested. He would bring the stones to the cell and I would put them in my pockets. Walking to the river, I must be careful not to let the unnatural swing of my skirts show. If I could keep my hands down by my sides, I could perhaps hide that.

Then something struck me. Did they not tie a witch before throwing her into the water? Right thumb to left foot, left thumb to right foot. A kind of parody of a crucifix. Even if they did not notice the stones when they were tying me, I could not possibly pull the stones from my pockets when I was trussed like a bird on the spit. The stones would drag me down, well and good. I would be judged innocent. But I would drown before they pulled me out.

In despair I threw myself down on my bed again and wept. I could refuse to take the stones, but then I would most certainly float and be condemned as a witch. That meant hanging, and hanging was not always swift. Better to drown, adjudged innocent, than hang and cast shame on my family.

These thoughts kept me awake, until at last I slid into a troubled sleep, in which I fought some force which closed about my throat. Afterwards, I did not know whether, in my dreams, I had been drowned or hanged.

I woke early the next morning, but I could tell it was already day by the quality of the light coming through the grill. No longer a lantern but a stray beam of daylight which found its way down the prison steps. The door at the top must be open. A few minutes later, the gaoler entered. He was wearing a heavy coat, unseasonable for August, and carried a bowl of porridge, which steamed slightly.

He left the door ajar and whispered as he bent to pass me the bowl, 'Turnkey out there.'

I took the bowl, but he motioned to me to put it on the stool. Then he drew out of the deep pockets of his coat two large, flat stones, each about twice the size of my palm and about two fingers thick. I slid them into the pockets on each side of my skirt and they lay flat and heavy against my thighs. He had chosen well. Large round stones like cannonballs, which was what I had expected, would have pulled my skirts out of shape.

As I stood up, the stones swung a little back and forth. I tried walking across the cell. If I took fairly small steps and kept my arms down at my sides, I could prevent them swinging too much.

He nodded and smiled, then laid his finger to his lips and turned to go. Urgently I needed to tell him what I had realised in the night, that I would not be able to remove the stones once I was tied. I tried to mime this for him, so that the turnkey would not hear, bending over and crossing my arms so that my hands touched the opposite feet. Then I made a gesture of despair. He nodded and smiled. Could he not understand?

I was about to risk saying something, when the turnkey came to the door.

'Hurry the witch along,' he said. 'She's wanted in half an hour.'

'Eat up, can't you?' the gaoler said roughly. 'There's no time for your tricks.' And he winked at me.

They left me to eat my porridge, but I barely tasted it as I spooned it down, feeling sick at the prospect of what lay ahead. The same gaoler came back with another and with the turnkey to unlock the outer door. The gaoler tied a rope around my waist, which must be the line they would use to pull me out of the river, alive or dead, innocent or guilty. As we came out into the courtyard I was dazzled by the bright sunlight of full day. It was the height of summer and there were birds singing from nooks and crannies around the battlements of the castle. A male blackbird flew across my path as we approached the outer gateway, with a beak full of food. It must be rearing a second brood, I thought, for the first would be fledged by now. Somehow, that gave me hope. It seemed a positive sign, a good omen.

The two witchfinders were waiting for us just outside the gate, surrounded by their liveried guards, including those who had arrested Hannah and me. Beyond them a crowd of curious citizens peered in our direction, come for the fun of watching a witch swum. And behind them the cathedral raised its tower heavenwards, indifferent to these devilish doings. Enclosed by the crowd, we walked down to the river in a chorus of jeers and curses. I kept my hands at my sides, though the street was so precipitous I wanted to spread my arms to keep my balance.. With the two gaolers walking on either side of me, I hoped no one would notice the stones, and wondered whether the second gaoler was privy to the plan.

Until we reached the river Witham, my mind was occupied with walking normally and concealing the stones, but now suddenly faced with the fast-flowing river, I was terrified. The whole plan, the stones, the contrived sinking into the water, seemed like madness. I was going to drown. I would die in that river, and within the next few minutes. I turned aside, gagging. The porridge I had eaten was there in my throat, a horrible lump.

The gaolers guessed what was amiss with me, for I suppose I was not the first. Swiftly they shoved me to the side of the path, keeping well back as I vomited into the verge. Several people in the crowd laughed. As I lifted my apron to wipe my face, I saw Matthew Hopkins's look of disgust, and I wondered whether he fancied he had seen imps jumping out of my mouth.

We reached the river bank. Now was the moment when they would tie me crossways.

'Bend over,' said the gaoler. 'Put your left hand to your right foot.'

He slipped a loop over my thumb, tightened it, then passed the rope round my ankle twice.

'Now the other hand.'

He brought the rope back to my left ankle, passed it round twice, then caught up my right thumb. Doubled up like this, I could see nothing but my own soiled skirt hem. I prayed then, prayed that the end would come quickly.

Though I could see nothing, I could feel heavy bodies bumping around me. Muffled by my skirts, Hopkins's voice said, 'Are you sure she is securely tied?'

'Aye, sir. This isn't the first witch I've trussed for the swimming.' He sounded surly but confident.

Then someone lifts me and hurls me into the air. I strain my head back, free of my skirts. I seem to float there, time suspended. Perhaps I really am a witch and I can fly. There is the castle, where I have been held, I know not how many days. There is the cathedral, reaching up to the summer sky. There are the busy streets which I know only from tales told by Nehemiah and Tom. There are the crowds of grinning strangers. To them I am not a woman like themselves. I am a source of entertainment, a brief diversion from their hard lives. I am no more than a bear, set upon by dogs, or a cockerel, fighting desperately to the death. I am nothing. There is the gibbet, with two bodies swinging from it. Is one of them Hannah? Like Hannah, I am going to die. I know now that the gaoler's plan is a foolish device.

Sweet Jesu, I gabble, take me into Heaven. I have not done what they say I have done, but I am going to die anyway.

And as though in answer to my prayer, time moves on. I am falling towards the river, brown and filthy with the towns ordure.

As I hit the river hard, I draw in a deep lungful of air.

And the waters close over my head.

I am sinking down and down into the thick waters, my clothes are sodden and clinging. No chance that I will float like a bubble on the surface. The stones are doing their work. He said to count to thirty, but I cannot think how to count. What use is it anyway? I spin at the end of the rope, like a fish on a fishing line. My lungs are burning, bursting. I will have to draw breath soon and I will draw in water and then I will die.

An end of rope slaps me hard against the face and I twist away. The river is pressing against my head, my ears are full of its sound. Then my right arm floats up in front of me. I am dreaming. My right hand is tied to my left foot. It cannot be there. I try to see my hand through the murky water.

My hand is free! I realise that the rope which hit me was the rope that fastened my right thumb. The gaoler had not tied it securely. Frantically I grope for my right pocket. The wet cloth fights me and I must breath, I must breath. At last the stone comes free and I feel it tumble past my leg. Desperately I try to reach my left pocket, twisting my body until my back shrieks with pain. If I can just free the stone . . .

It comes away at last and slips from my fingers, catches in my skirt and is gone, but I cannot last out any longer. My body is out of control. My mouth opens and I gasp. Not air, but water. And the darkness takes me.

When I saw the light again, I was lying on the bank, face down, with my head turned to the right, away from the river. At first I could see nothing but feet. There was a line of feet belonging to the witchfinders' guards, who seemed to be keeping the crowds back, away from the bank. Closer, near my shoulders, I saw a pair of mended boots which I recognised as those of the gaoler who had befriended me. Beyond him were the witchfinders themselves, together with a pair of expensive boots in fine red leather. For a long time I lay there, my mind filled with nothing but the contemplation of boots.

Then I realised that someone was pounding my back. I wanted to tell them to stop. My back was still painful from my long hours bound to the chair and from the twisted way they had tied me before they threw me in the river. Strange. I seemed to be lying flat, so my left arm was no longer tied to my right foot. Stop hitting me, I cried, but no words came out. Instead a gout of water rushed out of my mouth and nose. I began to choke, for the water was drowning me again. I gasped and drew in a little air. More pounding. More water bursting out. I began to cough and tried to roll over, tried to sit up.

'Keep still.' It was the gaoler again, His voice, I thought carefully, was attached to his boots, and it was he who kept hitting me.

'Hurts,' I croaked. 'Don't. Hit.'

'Have to get the river out of you.'

He hit me again. Then I could sense him standing up. I closed my eyes. It would be pleasant to go to sleep here. The grass was soft with moss and I was so tired. Despite the sun, I shivered. I was very wet. 'Drowned rat,' I said. It came out as a whisper.

He bent down and whispered back, 'Keep your mouth shut.'

All right. Keep my mouth shut.

'So this one's innocent, then, sir.'

'It would seem so.' It was Hopkins's voice. He was disappointed. 'What do you think, sir?'

In my fuddled brain I worked that out. Someone Hopkins called 'sir' must be of higher rank. Who?

It was too difficult.

'Are you sure you tied her properly?' Hopkins's voice was sharp with suspicion.

'Oh, aye, sir!' My gaoler's voice was warmly confident. 'Tied dozens of them in these last months.'

'It seems the water embraced the woman.' It was a new voice, cultured and slightly bored. 'We adjudge her no witch.'

I opened my eyes and squinted sideways, twisting my neck to look up. The owner of the fine boots wore a red alderman's gown and a magistrate's chain of office. He was looking down at me as though he were appraising a horse of dubious parentage which he was contemplating purchasing, but had decided against.

'Get up, woman.'

I tried to get up, but fell back to my knees.

'They're weak after the swimming, sir,' my gaoler said knowledgeably. 'She'll need help.'

He put his arms under my armpits and heaved me to my feet. I realised he was also checking that the stones were no longer in my pockets. I managed to stay on my feet, though the world seemed to tip sideways and I felt myself sway. Hopkins looked disappointed, but also seemed even more ill than he had before. Stearne peered at me suspiciously, but I realised that he did not dare to contradict the magistrate.

'Let her go then,' said the alderman. 'You have caught one witch, the one you hanged. This woman must be an innocent neighbour.' He glanced around at the crowd. 'Be off with you! Back to your work.'

The people began to melt away, some looking a little shamefaced, others disappointed that the whole episode had ended so tamely. The alderman turned on his heel and walked away, the crowd parting like water before him. The witchfinders and their guards followed behind. In a short time there was no one left on the bank with me but the two gaolers.

'Here, Jim.' My gaoler picked up a coil of wet rope which had been lying underneath me. 'Take this back.' The other man looked as though he would say something. 'And keep your mouth shut.'

The man called Jim nodded, gave me the ghost of a smile, and headed back to the castle carrying the rope.

'What is your name?' I said, when we were left alone.

'Maybe better you don't know.'

'I'll tell no one. I want to be able to remember you in my prayers. You saved my life.'

He gave a shy grin. 'All right, then, Mistress Bennington. I am Abel Forrester.'

I was Mistress Bennington again, though I felt I no longer fitted my name, standing there dripping with foul river water.

'I thank you, Goodman Forrester, with all my heart. I don't know how you contrived to tie me so that my hand came free.'

'Like this.' He took a length of twine from his pocket and with a quick few turns knotted it around my thumb. 'You see, you are tied fast. Now move your thumb a little.'

I did so, and the twine fell away.

'Magic!' I said.

He shook his head and looked at me gravely. 'Do not utter that word here, at such times as these. There is no magic. When I was a lad I served on the King's ships for a time. I learned every sort of knot, for they intrigued me. On a ship you sometimes need a knot which can be unfastened quickly.' He bent to pick up the twine and stuffed it back in his pocket. 'If they had swum my Cecily, I might have been able to save her, but they tortured her till she confessed. She was not as strong as you.'

'I grieve for you,' I said.

'It is done now.' He looked away in the direction the witchfinders had gone. 'I think one of them is being punished by God and I am glad of it.'

'Hopkins? That is consumption that is eating him away. And I also am glad of it.'

Suddenly, despite the sun, I shivered violently. 'What must I do now?'

196

'Get out of Lincoln as quickly as you can and make your way home.' He gave a harsh laugh. 'We do not provide a means of transport for the innocent, only the arrested or condemned. I will escort you to the city gate so that you are not set upon. The people are not happy when a swimming fails.'

We started to walk through the streets of the city, parallel to the river, towards the gate where Hannah and I had been brought in the cart. I stumbled once or twice and my shivering grew worse.

'I hope you may not have caught some disease from the evil humours of our stinking river,' Abel said.

'I did swallow some of the river.'

'You did.' He grinned. 'I'm sorry I had to hit you, but it is the only way to get the water out.'

'Something else you learned as a sailor?'

'Aye.'

'I think it is my wet clothes that make me shiver.' Indeed I was leaving a wet path through the streets like the trail of a giant slug. And clouds had begun to pile up, shutting out the sun. 'I have no clothes with me and no money to purchase any. I must walk briskly and hope they dry on me.'

'Aye, that is best. Keep going as long as you can before you stop to rest, as far from the city as possible.'

We had reached the gate and the bridge over the river. Unbidden, tears filled my eyes. This man, this stranger, had risked so much for me. I curtseyed deep to him, as if he were a gentleman.

'I shall always remember you, Goodman Forrester, and pray for you and for the soul of your Cecily.'

Looking embarrassed, he made me a clumsy bow. 'God go with you, Mistress Bennington.'

'And with you.'

I turned away and passed through the city gates, setting my feet on the road home.

The city gates opened on to the bridge over the Witham, leading to the old Roman road, so I knew I had only to follow it until I met the lane which led eventually to Crowthorne. I would not risk walking through there, however, but would bypass it, cutting through the fields. But the junction with the lane was a long way away, at least three days' walk if I had been strong and healthy. In my present weakened state it was bound to take longer.

There were people about along the first stretch of the road near the city, which was lined on both sides with new houses, where Lincoln had burst beyond its ancient perimeter. The people stared at me. No wonder, in my draggled, filthy clothes, my cap and headcloth long gone. I had torn my skirt trying to free the stone from my left pocket and it gaped, showing my underskirt. Before long I had to hide behind a bush at the roadside and knot my broken garter again, for my stocking was falling down. The clouds were building up further overhead and I could feel rain coming. Not that it mattered. I could hardly be wetter than I was already.

I trudged on through the darkening afternoon, so weary I was hardly aware of where I was going. Had the old road not lain across the country in a straight line, swinging neither to right nor left, I might have wandered off, but the way lay clear. Somewhere in the back of my mind I realised that I was hungry and regretted that I had vomited up the porridge I had been given that morning. Unless I could beg food somewhere, I would have nothing to eat until I reached home. I was thirsty too. Vomiting up the river water had left my throat raw and sore, but for the first few miles of my journey I passed no clear stream or village well where I could drink.

Sometime in the late afternoon the rain came at last, a slow mizzle at first, more mist than rain, but as the sky grew darker so the rain came down heavier, until at last it fell in grey sheets. My clothes had dried a little by then, though they were patched with river mud. Now I was soaked again to the skin.

I did not know how far I had come. My legs ached, but I was sure my pace had been so slow that I had covered little ground. There were thick hedges here on either side of the road and it was some time since I had passed through the last village. It was the best shelter to be found, so I crawled into the base of the hedge, where sheep or deer had hollowed a shard through, and crouched under the lowest branches of a hazel tree. I found a dock leaf in which a little rain had gathered and drank it thankfully. There were

198

small clusters of nuts on the hazel, barely ripe yet, but I broke them off and prised the nuts from their husks. How to free them from their shells was more difficult, but I found a couple of stones and pounded them until at last the shells cracked. There was little sustenance in the tiny nuts, but I ate them gladly, chewing them slowly to give myself the illusion that here was food indeed.

All this effort had exhausted me. I curled up in my prickly bed, laid my head on my arms, and fell asleep. Once or twice in the night I woke when the pains that still lingered in my limbs and back became too acute. There were furtive rustlings in the hedge – small creatures like field mice or roosting birds – but they seemed to have accepted my presence. When I had eased my painful body into another position, I fell asleep again.

I was woken very early by the dawn light filtering through the hedge into my face and the sound of the birds giving voice, welcoming the day. It had stopped raining, but my clothes were sodden with the rain that had penetrated the hedge and the heavy dew which now lay over everything. Before I started on my way again, I gathered as many of the hazel nuts as I could reach and shelled them so I could fill my pockets with a little food to take me through the day. All the leaves of the hedge were wet and I was driven to licking them for water.

Before climbing forth again into the road, I peered out to make sure there was no one about, for I did not want to be taken for one of those mad creatures who are turned away from their villages and live wild in the woods. When I saw the road was clear, I scrambled down from the hedge and set off walking again, picking leaves out of my hair as I went. It was tangled and as wild as any mad woman's, though I tried to comb through it with my fingers.

In the next village I came to, I asked at the first house for bread, saying that I was a poor traveller, robbed, and trying to get home to my village, but the door was slammed in my face. I did not try again. That night, having eaten the last of my nuts, I could not find anywhere to bed down, so I simply kept on walking, until sometime in the night I lay down on the verge and slept there.

The world was becoming a very strange place. The road was no longer straight, but swerved first this way and then that. The trees leaned over me and threatened to fall. And the line between land and sky was blurred and wavering. I no longer tried to find food, but from time to time thirst drove me to seek water. One day I found a clear stream running beside the road. I lay down on my stomach and scooped up the water, drinking like a thirsty horse. I cupped water and poured it over my head, which had grown very hot. I touched my cheeks and forehead with my wet fingers and they were so hot I thought they would sizzle, like fat in a hot pan. That set me laughing and I lay there by the stream, laughing and laughing until my sides hurt.

Everything after that was blurred. Days and nights merged into each other. Sometimes I felt as though fire was licking at my limbs. They burn witches in Scotland. Hanging in England. Burning in Scotland. Sometimes my very limbs were frozen into ice, so that I could not lift my legs but rolled into a ball under a hedgerow. My mind was filled with terrifying visions, in which water closed over my head and I fought for breath until a thin scream broke from my lungs. Once, I saw Gideon walking down the road in front of me and I stumbled after him, begging him to stop, but he walked on, dwindling into the distance and did not look back.

I do not know when I reached the crossroads with the lane which would take me to Crowthorne and eventually to my village, the crossroads where they had loaded Hannah and me on to the cart. I stepped from the raised ramper on which the Roman road was built down on to the rutted lane. Somehow my feet took me along the lane without any conscious thought. I looked down at my feet. One. Two. One. Two. Step after step. I noticed that the sole of my right shoe was flapping loose. When did that happen? I had no memory of it. My face was so hot, sweating. I tried to wipe it with my apron, and found that my apron was gone. I stopped and turned slowly around. No sign of it. Where had I lost it?

Staggering a little, I turned back again. My feet seemed to know where to go, so I let them lead me, thinking of nothing except how hot I was. One step. Then another. And another. And another. There was smoke ahead, rising from cottages. I shook my head to try to clear it. Something told me I should not go there. My clever feet – they knew where to go. Over the stile to the left, and along a faint path which followed the edge of a field. It was difficult walking here, the ground rough with tussocks of grass and stones. The sole of my shoe clung on by the last few nails. I stopped and looked at it for a long time, then I took it off and put it in my pocket. That was better. The shoe no longer caught on every rough place on the path, but now I went dot and carry, with one shoe and one stocking foot. I stopped again and took off the other shoe and put it in my pocket. Now at least my feet were the same. My stockings were little protection, for they were full of holes.

I crossed the field and then another.

My whole body was on fire and my head ached, but through the buzz in my ears, one clear thought reached me. That house ahead was my home. I climbed over the wall that ran along the side of the field into the lane.

Aye, this was my lane, my home. A few more steps and I would be there.

There was the gate into the yard. The barn. The hen-hus.

It was very quiet.

Somehow I knew it was milking time. Someone should be bringing in the cows. Should I go and fetch the cows?

I reached the gate into the yard and leaned against it, for it was almost too much to lift the latch and open the gate. Slowly I managed to open it and stepped through.

Why was it so quiet?

Then Nehemiah came out of the barn. I could not hear his steps, but that must be because of the buzzing in my ears.

'Mistress Mercy!' he cried out, and looked at me in horror.

'Why is it so quiet?' I said.

Then it went black.

Chapter Thirteen

The room was filled with the sound of bees. I lay flat, gazing up at the white-washed ceiling. My whole body felt slack, as lifeless as the cool linen sheet that covered me. I wanted to do nothing but listen to the bees hovering outside the open window and study that ceiling, whose bumps and cracks were as familiar as the palm of my hand.

Indolently I lifted my right hand and regarded it thoughtfully. It seemed unchanged. I let it drop back again.

The bees were busy in the late honeysuckle that grew up the outside wall of my chamber. They loved the sweet flowers, their creamy trumpets filled with nectar which they would turn to honey. Hannah's bees. I knew there was some reason I should not think about Hannah, but my mind would not focus on the thought.

There was a fluttering of wings just outside the windows and the shrieks of hungry nestlings. House martins always nested under the eaves there, and this year the parents had built a second mud nest adjacent to the first, to rear a second brood, like a householder with a growing family building another wing to his house. As my ancestors had added to this house.

I knew where I was. This was my own chamber, where I had slept since I was a child first out of the cradle. Everything about me was familiar. My narrow bed. The way the ropes beneath the mattress creaked when I moved. The coffer holding my clothes. Two joint stools, one of them beside my bed with my Bible laid on it. A small table where I kept a few childish treasures – a pretty pebble, a kingfisher's feather that changed colour as you turned it in the sunlight.

The house martin returned and the nestlings shrieked again, demanding to be fed. I smiled and stretched out my arms. Then I frowned. There was something strange about my arms. They were too thin. I peered at them. No question, they were my arms, yet they looked unfamiliar.

There was a gentle tap on the door.

'Aye?' I said. My voice came out in a weak croak, but the door opened. Kitty put her head round it and beamed.

'Oh, Mistress Mercy, you are awake at last!'

She ran over to the bed and fell on her knees beside it.

'You have been so ill.'

'How did I come here? I remember reaching the gate, and Nehemiah crossing the yard, then nothing.'

'You fainted. Nehemiah and I carried you up here. Your clothes – they were terrible, torn and filthy. I have washed them and mended them as best I can, but they are hardly fit even for rough work.'

I looked at the sleeve from which my odd arm protruded.

'You dressed me in my night shift.'

She blushed. 'I washed you and tried to make you comfortable, but you have had the sweating sickness for more than two weeks.'

I remembered then confused dreams and a feeling of burning in the fires of Hell.

'You said terrible things,' she whispered, her face pale. 'You kept saying "They burn witches in Scotland" and "I am going to drown, I am going to drown." It was very frightening.'

I reached out and patted her hand. 'But I did not drown. Or burn.'

'And Hannah? What has happened to Hannah?'

I took a deep breath. 'Hannah is dead, Kitty. We must pray for her.'

Tears welled up in her eyes and spilled over. 'I feared that was so. She was kind to me.'

'And to me.' I resolved then that I would never let it pass my lips that Hannah had betrayed me. She should rest in peace.

'Kitty, could you bring me a drink?'

'Of course. And something to eat?'

203

I realised that I was hungry. 'Aye, that would be kind. But something soft. My throat is very sore.'

'The apothecary said that you had an infection of the throat as well as the sweating sickness.'

'You have had an apothecary to me?'

'Aye.' She seemed suddenly nervous. 'I will fetch you some buttered eggs and small ale.' Then she was gone.

We could ill afford an apothecary, I thought. Where had Tom or Mother found the money? Or Father? My heart gave a sudden leap. If the fine had been paid, or most of it, was Father home again?

Kitty soon returned with a tray and helped me to sit up so that she could balance it on my lap, but she seemed flustered and anxious to go back to the kitchen, so I did not try to keep her. The ale slid comfortably down my throat, my own good brewing with its familiar flavour, enhanced with the herbs I used. The eggs were soft and rich with butter. They slipped easily down and the warmth glowed inside me. I lifted my Bible from my bedside stool and laid the tray in its place. Tired from even the small effort of eating, I lay back, with my hands folded over the Bible on my chest, and fell asleep again.

When I woke the light had changed. It was softer and the bees must have retired to their skep, though the young birds still demanded food. How hard the birds work, I thought, during the few intensive weeks when they breed. Then somehow those tiny creatures must survive through the winter. Surely this new brood was very late to be still unfledged. How could they hope to survive? Inexplicably the thought of those nestlings freezing in the snow made me weep.

A little later Kitty tapped again at my door and asked if Nehemiah might come to see me. I was surprised that he should come, rather than Tom or my mother, but I nodded.

'Of course. Can you help me sit up?'

The tray was gone from beside my bed. I laid my Bible back on the stool and ran my fingers through my hair. It was not tangled any more and I realised Kitty must have combed it for me. She slipped away.

'Mistress Mercy? How do you find yourself?'

Nehemiah came in and stood twisting his cap in his hands.

'Take a stool, Nehemiah. I thank you for helping Kitty bring me up here.'

He moved the other stool near the bed and sat down with his hands planted on his knees.

'I thought we'd lost you then, when you fell down in the yard. Didn't hardly seem to be breathing. And once or twice since then . . . You've been bad, mistress.'

'I had a bad time in Lincoln,' I said.

'Can you tell me about it? And about Hannah? Kitty says she is dead.'

I nodded. Then I told him everything, from the time we were taken away from the farm until I had collapsed at his feet. Everything, except how Hannah had betrayed me. At the end of it he scrubbed his face with his cap and looked at me in horror. He had turned pale when I told him of Hannah's death and of how I had been tortured.

'Jesu! That they can do such things, to folk who have done no wrong. Is there no justice?'

'Very little, it would seem. Though I think the witchfinder Hopkins will not be able to persecute many more. He is dying of consumption.'

'May the devil take his own!' His anger shone in his eyes.

'Aye, indeed.' I considered for a moment. 'Yet somehow I feel he believed he was doing right, doing God's will. The other man, Stearne, I'm not so sure. I think he tortures and hangs women for pleasure.'

'A strange kind of pleasure that must be.'

'Something is twisted in his mind.'

We sat silent for a time. Then I said, 'But you must tell me all that has been happening here. I do not even know what date it is.'

'It is the seventeenth of September.'

'So late! I must have been a long time ill.'

'Aye. And we do not know how long you were on your journey home from Lincoln.'

'I do not know myself. Is the harvest in, then?'

'What there is of it. The barley. And the beans and peas are pulled, and the haulms ploughed in. Kitty is salting beans now, for winter.'

'Has there been more trouble with the drainers?'

He looked uncomfortable at this. 'More skirmishes, aye. Our lads pulled down another of those pumping mills, and broke up part of the settlers' church.'

That was some satisfaction. I was beginning to feel tired and wondered why Nehemiah had come to see me in my chamber, something I would not have expected him to do, unless he was anxious to hear what had happened in Lincoln from my own lips.

'What has happened about my father's fine?'

He did not answer at first, but sat staring at the floor, crushing his cap between his big hands. The knuckles, I noticed, were swollen, and the skin cracked and sore-looking.

'Tom rode to Lincoln to pay the fine,' he said at last, 'three days after you were taken. A week before it was due.'

I sat up straighter. 'What? But his leg, the deep wound in his leg?'

'Aye.' He gave a deep sigh. 'He would go, we could not stop him.'

'And is Father freed?'

Still he would not look at me. My heart began to beat more quickly and suddenly I shivered. I knew something was terribly wrong.

'Master Tom went to the court, or the magistrates' office, or wherever he had to go, and he paid them all the money that had been saved toward the fine.'

I nodded.

'When he had handed over the money, they said that the debt would be recorded as paid and the stock returned. He was pleased, because that meant Master Isaac could come home.' He cleared his throat. 'Then they told him your father had died a week before, of the gaol fever.'

I let out a cry, and pressed my fist to my mouth. While I was lying there in Lincoln Castle, my father was already dead. And Tom had come, had been nearby.

'They could not say where your father was buried, only in some unmarked pauper's grave. And they would not let him see you.'

My father gone. I would never see him again. His temper and bluster were often near the surface, but they concealed the deep underlying kindness of his nature. I thought how I had sat on his lap as a child while he told me stories of his youth and of my heroic grandfather. It was he who had insisted that I learn to read and write, for he said there was a new world coming, when women would need these skills. Tears filled my eyes, and I felt about for my handkerchief.

'Thank you for telling me, Nehemiah. It cannot have been easy. But I am surprised Tom did not come to tell me himself.'

A desperate look had come into his eyes. 'He cannot manage the stairs.'

'His leg is still bad, then?'

'He reopened the wound, riding to Lincoln and back. He came home like a madman. Then he led the attack on the mill, as if he was possessed.'

He drew a deep breath and his words came out in a rush. 'The wound festered. Gangrene.'

'Tom is not dead as well!'

'No, no. But we had to fetch the barber-surgeon from Peterborough. He cut off Tom's leg. He burnt the stump. Cauterising, he called it. And painted it with tar. It has healed now. But Tom cannot manage the stairs.' The last words came out limply, as if they were all that mattered.

I fell back and began to sob uncontrollably. My strong brother, always the leader, the fastest runner, a fine horseman. His leg cut off. And my father dead.

Nehemiah must have left, but I did not hear him go.

In the end I fell asleep from exhaustion and sorrow, for when next I woke early daylight flowed through the window. I realised now, what I had not seen the previous day, that there was that slight change in the light that comes as the year turns from summer to autumn. Even the young birds were quiet in their nest as I lay

207

gazing again at the ceiling, but without the empty calmness of the day before.

When Nehemiah had brought me his heavy news, I could take nothing in but wretchedness, but now I realised that our lives must change. How did Tom manage? With a crutch? I had never known a man with one leg. Could he walk at all? One thing was certain, he could never again work the farm. A man with one leg might perhaps milk a cow. He could weave baskets and eel traps, and perhaps – with help – even fish. But he could not plough or sow or hoe or reap, he could not thresh corn, he could not drive cattle or pitch hay or ride a horse. With Father gone and Tom unable to work, how would we survive?

Soon afterwards, Kitty brought me breakfast and I asked after Tom. I could see that she was relieved Nehemiah had broken the news to me.

'He has two crutches that Nehemiah made for him. At first his armpits became very sore, but I made some cushions for the tops, padded with tufts of fleece, and now he says he is much more comfortable.' She flushed with pride.

'He can walk with them?'

'Not to say *walk*, Mistress Mercy, but he hops about. He gets better at it every day.'

'He is sleeping downstairs in your room off the kitchen?'

'Aye. That's best. I – I'm still in Hannah's room.' The words caught in her throat, but she went bravely on. 'I'm a strong worker, Mistress Mercy. Nehemiah and me, we've kept things going, but I'm fair glad you are back again.'

'You have been truly wonderful, Kitty. Both of you. Nehemiah said you were salting the beans.'

'Aye. I must get back to it now. And I've pickled more eggs.'

'I will get up today and come to help you.'

Her brow creased in a frown. 'Are you sure you should, mistress? You must still be very weak.'

'I am sure I can sit at the table stringing beans.'

In truth, when I tried to get up and dress myself, I found I was indeed very weak, but at last I made my way on slightly shaky legs down to the kitchen.

Kitty was sorting beans on the table and Tom was sitting in Father's great chair, with his crutches propped against it. I could hear Nehemiah shovelling litter from the barn. There was no sign of my mother. Tom gave me a rueful smile.

'They have told you, then?'

I went over and kissed him on the forehead. 'They have told me. Oh, Tom!' I could not keep the tears from my eyes.

He reached out an took my hand. 'And what you have endured. We thought we had lost you.'

'As we have lost Father.'

He nodded. 'They waited until I had handed over every penny we had saved, and then they told me. In law, I do not know whether they had the right to the fine after Father was dead. Dead in their prison, of gaol fever contracted there.'

I shook my head. 'I do not know what are the rights of it. But I want no dealings with courts and magistrates for the rest of my life.'

I sat down on a bench, for I found I was more tired than I expected. 'And you? How do you manage?'

He smiled at me cheerfully. 'Oh, I get by well enough. I shall win no races, but I make my way about the place. See.'

He struggled to his feet, holding on to the back of the chair, then took up the crutches one at a time. Swinging himself forward on them and his one good leg, he crossed the kitchen and came back. The left leg of his breeches was caught up short with pins.

'You see, I am fine and hearty.'

He eased himself down into the chair again and I noticed beads of sweat on his brow.

'Good,' I said, doing my best to smile. 'Now, Kitty, give me some of those beans.'

As I began to string and slice the beans, then pack them down tight into a crockery jar between layers of salt, I said, 'Where is Mother?'

Tom and Kitty exchanged a look.

'She rises late,' Tom said. 'She'll do a little spinning later. She . . . she has been troubled in her mind since you were taken, and then when I brought back word of Father's death. She has become very forgetful.'

209

And she will be troubled by your loss of a leg, I thought, but did not speak my thoughts aloud.

'Our stock has been returned,' said Tom, 'all except one calf, which they say died, though I think they lied. It was our best calf.'

'All our stock?'

'Aye. And our cart. Our friends have returned the beasts they cared for amongst their own. Alice brought back your hens last week. We have everything except the yoke of oxen. Rafe tried to return them, but I said him nay, not until we could pay back the money he gave us.'

'Of course.' I nodded. 'But the work on the farm . . . ?' It was good news that the stock was returned, but that would mean more to be undertaken by any who were able-bodied.

'Kitty and Nehemiah have worked from dawn to dusk. And I can milk, if someone stalls the cows for me. Joseph Waters has been doing day-labour for us too, in return for meals. He seems happy with the arrangement.'

'Now I am home I can take on my share.' I rammed down the layer of beans to make my point.

'Only when you are well enough. You are as thin as a stray cat.'

'Thank you for that.'

He laughed. 'Oh, Jesu, it is good to have you home. I do not know how you survived. I am not sure I would have.'

'I am not sure how I did. Certainly I would not have survived the swimming without the help of the gaoler, Abel Forrester. When I can walk that far, I must go to see his cousin Will.'

Kitty and I worked at salting the beans until dinner time and finished them. Mother came down then and looked at me in surprise, as thought she did not know me, but she said hardly a word, sitting down after the meal at her spinning wheel. Kitty set all up for her and she sat spinning all afternoon. In the evening I went out to collect the eggs and shut the hens away. Even walking the short distance across the yard proved to me that it would be some time before I could walk to the village and see Alice.

As I came in and set the basket of eggs on the shelf, a thought occurred to me.

'Is Reverend Edgemont still acting as our preacher? I am not sure I can walk as far as the church, and he may come in pursuit of me again.'

'No, they have appointed a fat little fellow from Peterborough,' Tom said. 'Not a ranter like Edgemont, but a time-server, who will bend with the wind. He knows you were found innocent and that you have been ill. He will not trouble us.'

'Good. I suppose you cannot go so far yourself.'

'Not yet. But I am getting stronger every day. The sawbones told me that if I went to Lynn or London, I could have a wooden stump made, like the ones they make for injured soldiers and sailors. I shall do that one day.'

'Will that make things better for you?'

'I could manage with one crutch then. Aye, it would be better.'

He leaned back in his chair and I could see that for all his brave talk he was tired and in pain.

'There is another piece of news that will interest you,' he said.

I looked up from the rabbit I was cutting up for the evening's pottage. Nehemiah had brought it in while we were slicing beans.

'What is that?'

'Edmund Dillingworth has disappeared from home. Some of the manor servants mentioned it in the village. He has not been seen since the beginning of September. No one knows where he has gone. Into exile with other Royalists? Or perhaps there is some new gathering of King's men.'

'We are well rid of him.' I chopped the meat savagely.

'There is also,' he said quietly, 'no news of what has become of Gideon Clarke.'

I was too tired, too numb – even too frightened – to question him further. That vision I had seen as I dragged myself home from Lincoln, Gideon walking away from me until he vanished, felt like an omen. Gideon was gone for ever and I felt as though I had lost a limb as surely as Tom had.

The next few weeks went by quietly enough, taken up with the usual tasks of autumn, preserving as much food as we could for winter. Nehemiah salted down eels and smoked both eels and fish. He had always done this in his own smallholding, and sold some of his produce at Lincoln market. Now none of us wished to go near the city. He said he would store his produce for our household and exchange some of it in the village for other goods. He found an old hollow stump somewhere out on the Fen and wheeled it back in a barrow, then he fitted crossbars inside to hold the fish, strung together in pairs, and made a roof of tightly woven green willow branches, which would let the smoke gradually out at the top. I watched him make a fire of wood chippings in the bottom of the stump, then, when it was low and smoking to his satisfaction, he hung the fish in the smoke and fitted on the top.

'I remember watching you do this when I was a child,' I said.

'Aye, you were always a curious little thing, wanting to know how everything was done.'

'How is the fishing now? Since the drainers moved over towards Crowthorne?'

He shrugged. 'Poor. The wild creatures do not like their homes disturbed, whether they are flesh, fish or fowl.'

When I was strong enough, I walked to the village, taking with me two hearty cakes stuffed with some of our precious dried fruit. One I gave to Will Keane the blacksmith and his wife, sitting down with them to recount the story of the way Abel had helped me.

Will shook his head sadly. 'I am glad you are safe, Mercy. Abel is running a great risk, although he says he will only try to help those he believes are innocent.'

'I think he does it for the sake of the girl he was to marry.'

'Aye,' said Will's wife. 'He loved Cecily dearly and courted her a long time before her father would consent. Then this frenzy of witch-hunting began. She was no more a witch than you or I, but some of their neighbours disliked her mother, who had a sharp tongue on her, and they accused mother and daughter both of witchcraft. They confessed under torture.'

'There was a packman came through a few days ago,' Will said. 'His pony had cast a shoe and I saw to it. He said the witchfinder Hopkins had gone back to where he came from. Somewhere in Essex. And died there.'

'Not soon enough,' said his wife.

I was relieved to hear it, but not surprised, and wondered whether Stearne would carry on without the more senior man.

The other cake I took to Alice, to thank her for caring for my hens and sending the eggs every day. Without them there had been days when we might have starved. She insisted we sit out in the orchard with a slice of my cake and a drink she had made some months ago from elderflowers and mint. It was the very bench where we had sat before Huw was born. He lay now on the grass at our feet, trying to roll over.

'Soon he'll be crawling,' I said.

'Not yet a while!' She laughed. 'Aye, and then he will be into everything, like his father.' She beamed at me, and touched my arm. 'I cannot say how glad I am you are safe, Mercy. I thought I should die when they took you away. So many they have killed, those witchfinders, most of them innocent, I'll be bound. Perhaps all of them. And then that terrible journey you had, coming home, ill and starving. You are still so thin.'

'I grow fatter every day,' I said, more cheerfully than I felt. 'But, oh, Alice, I do not know how we will fare, with Father gone and Tom . . .'

'I know,' she said. 'Rafe and I have been discussing this. It will be apple harvest soon, and we will come to help you. Then at Martinmas Rafe and Jack are going to come for your autumn slaughtering. You and Nehemiah cannot do it on your own.'

Tears sprang into my eyes. I seemed to cry easily these days, as though all my iron control during the torture was breaking down now.

'Thank you,' I said.

We sat silent for a long while, watching Huw there on the grass. He was a very noticing child, gazing at a humblebee flying past his face and a yellow butterfly swaying as it perched on the seed head of a grass stem. The sun through the branches of the fruit trees cast dancing leaf shadows over him. I saw his eyes follow their movement.

'I think he is going to be a very clever child, your Huw.'

'Of course.' She dimpled. 'How could he not be, with two such parents! But you, Mercy, how do you fare? I think you have been marked by these last terrible weeks.'

I sighed. 'I sleep badly and I have dreams. I try to forget, but perhaps I never shall.'

I watched the yellow butterfly leave the grass stem and hover for a moment over Huw. He smiled and tried to reach out to it, but with a flick of its wings it was gone up into the apple tree overhead.

'Tom says there has been no news of Gideon.' I did not look at her, but she took my hand.

'Jack has been to Lynn twice, on the excuse of trading there, but really to get word. It seems that after the *Brave Endeavour* was driven back into port by the storm, she needed repairs, which took several weeks. There were no more ships leaving for the Continent at the time, so Gideon was forced to wait about in the town. That must have been when he was seen by the Dillingworths' servant.'

I nodded. 'But that was back at the end of July.'

'Aye. It seems the *Brave Endeavour* was ready to sail again about month later, but by then Gideon was not to be found. She sailed without him.'

'What can have become of him?'

'No one knows. Perhaps he saw the manor servant and decided to go into hiding.'

'But then why did he not rejoin the ship? By now he would have been safe from persecution in the Low Countries.'

She shook her head. 'Perhaps he found another ship, before the *Brave Endeavour* was ready to sail, but Jack thinks someone would know.' She squeezed my hand. 'You care for him, don't you?'

I nodded. Those foolish tears were filling my eyes again. Would I never cease weeping? 'Aye,' I whispered, 'I care for him. I want to be sure he is safe.' I paused, then I looked at her. I had spoken of it to no one, but if I could not tell Alice, I could hardly acknowledge it to myself. 'Before he left, he asked me – if he is able to return – he asked if he might speak for me.'

She nodded. 'I've long thought he cared for you, but I was not sure about your feelings for him. You never spoke.'

214

'I used to think of him as my father's friend. He is older than I, a learned man . . .'

She gave a scornful snort that made me laugh through my tears.

'I think it was only when he was so badly injured and like to die, that I realised how much I loved him.'

'It's when we fear we may lose someone that we understand how much they mean to us,' she said. 'How our lives will be the poorer without them. You must be brave. There has been no news that he has come to harm.'

She gave me a quick hug. 'It is time that boy is fed, or he will be grizzling. Can you fetch in our cups and plates?'

I nodded and wiped my eyes.

Apple harvest came and with the help of Alice and Rafe and Joseph we picked everything, though the cold early spring had meant not all the blossom had been pollinated, so it was a smaller crop than usual. The next few weeks Kitty and I worked from morning to night, slicing apples for drying, preserving apple jelly and apple butter, gathering blackberries for apple and blackberry jam, and making pickles with apples, sloes and rosehips. Tom was able to help by sitting at the kitchen table and sorting out the perfect apples that would keep best. These Nehemiah and Joseph stored, wrapped in straw, in the apple loft over the dairy. Like the dairy it lay on the north side of the farm buildings, which kept it cool except in the hottest weather.

We had barely finished with the apples when Martinmas was upon us, the traditional season for slaughtering the animals which are not to be kept over winter. Any rams not suitable for breeding would provide mutton, cows past lactation and male calves would provided beef, and most of the pigs would be slaughtered. Pigs are particularly valuable because they are the source of so many different kinds of meat, all of which, if it is properly prepared, keeps best of all.

As they had promised, Rafe and Jack came to help with the slaughtering, but so did Toby (who had plenty of stock of his own to keep him busy) and Will the blacksmith. Will brought word that his cousin Abel had left his employment as a gaoler in Lincoln and would be coming soon to join him at the smithy.

'His father was a smith too, like mine, and married my father's sister. Abel grew up at the forge in their village, but went off to better himself in Lincoln.' He smiled grimly. 'Not that it proved much of a betterment. He says he is much out of practice at the anvil, but he used to be a great hand at the finer work, making tools and the like. I'll be glad to have him.'

It was good news, for ever since he had helped me I had feared that Abel would be discovered and punished, perhaps even hanged.

With so many men to do the work, I did not have to help in the slaughtering myself, for which I was glad. Not even the most hardened farmer can say that it is a pleasant business, to cut the throat of an animal you have reared and cared for. At least my hens were safe. They were too valuable as layers to be killed for meat.

As it was, Kitty and I had work enough to keep us busy all the day long and even into the night, with the carving and salting and smoking. Our hands grew chapped and sore from the salt and saltpetre we rubbed into the preserved meat. The fire in the kitchen must be kept burning hot but smoky for the hams and muttons hanging in the chimney, till our eyes smarted and watered and our clothes and hair stank of smoke. For two weeks we could think of nothing but the preserving of the meat, until at last all was done. We ate well all the while, from the scraps and the blood puddings and the humble pies and other produce which would not keep over the winter.

At last we were able to scrub down the kitchen and wash ourselves and our clothes. All this time my mother had kept to her chamber, where she had continued with her spinning, well away from the smoke and stench of our work. Every day she seemed more confused. She could not remember whether she had eaten, even when she had just left the table. Sometimes we would find her wandering around at night. Once she had crossed the yard and begun to walk towards the Fen. Much of the time she did not recognise us. In particular she seemed not to know me since I had come home, though sometimes she called me 'Elizabeth', the name of her sister who had died as a young woman. I was said to resemble her.

The morning of our great wash-day, Kitty and I carried a heavy buck basket out to the hedge and were spreading out the clothes to dry when I saw a soldier on a horse, followed by six men on foot, approaching up the lane. My hand flew to my mouth. The last time men in uniform had come to the house, it was to arrest me.

'Good morrow, mistress,' the officer said, doffing his cap to me. His tone was polite but not deferential. 'Is this Turbary Holm?'

I dried my hands on my apron, for they were damp from the washing, and walked over to the gate. 'It is. And who are you, sir?'

'Sergeant Whickers, billeting officer.'

I realised then that the men wore the uniforms of the Model Army, not the somewhat ostentatious livery of the witchfinders' guards.

'Billeting officer?' I looked at the six men in alarm.

'Aye. We have been posted to this neighbourhood because of troubles in the area.'

'Troubles? What troubles?'

Foolish of me. I had been so caught up in the Martinmas slaughtering I could not think what he meant.

'Attacks on the work of the licensed drainers, mistress. Destruction of property. Injury to persons and works. Riots and disturbances. We are here to keep the peace.'

I said nothing. To keep the peace? No, to protect the speculators and enclosers.

'Six men have been allocated to this farm.' He drew a folded paper from the breast of his buff coat and held it out to me. His expression was condescending, as if he thought I could not read.

I took the paper and scanned the list. Altogether fifty men were to be quartered in the parish. Fifty! Almost half the entire population of men, women and children in the village! And indeed six were marked down to us. I handed the paper back.

'Fifty men in our parish,' I said. 'That is a great many. There are already soldiers at Crowthorne.'

He was clearly surprised that I could read and that I had calculated the total for the parish so quickly.

'It is felt necessary.'

'And how are they to be fed, these men? The harvest has been poor this year, after the bad weather. And we have lost at least half because the drainers have destroyed our crops in the field.'

He frowned. It was clear he was not used to a woman standing up to him.

'The billeted soldiers must be fed by the population. It is the ruling of Parliament. You will be issued with chits to reclaim the cost of the soldiers' food from the military commissariat.'

He spoke glibly. I could guess what those chits would be worth. Nothing. Even if we could discover where to take them.

'And besides the local riots here,' he said, 'there is word that there may be a nest of King's men nearby.'

Edmund Dillingworth again. Were we never to be rid of him?

'The only known Royalist hereabouts has disappeared months ago,' I said coldly. 'You will find none here.' And no one too keen to support the Puritan ranters either, I thought, except at Crowthorne.

He shrugged. 'I am simply carrying out my orders. These are the men allotted to you.' He looked down at the soldiers. 'You will report for duty each morning on the village green in front of the church, starting tomorrow.' With that he turned his horse and rode back down the lane.

The men and I looked at each other. They were all quite young, some as young as I or younger, two perhaps of an age with Tom. They looked tired and cold, and as though they did not much care to be marching about the country, billeted amongst civilians to guard foreigners. A bitter November wind was getting up. Kitty would need to weigh down the washing with stones or it would blow away.

'You had best come inside,' I said grudgingly. 'This way.'

And the six of them followed me across the yard to the house.

Chapter Fourteen

The billeting of the soldiers in the parish did nothing to promote peace. Instead, the problem of feeding the men put such a strain on our resources that it brought even more anger and restlessness. The previous year had been one of the worst for farming within living memory. It was said that many in the towns had starved to death. I knew of none in our parish who had perished from starvation alone, but disease had also swept through the country in the autumn and the beginning of winter, much of it carried by soldiers coming home from the War. Ague, plague, and sweating sickness had carried off many all over England, especially those who were already weakened by lack of food. In our own parish we had been spared the plague, thank God, but Nehemiah's brother, another old bachelor fen slodger, had died of ague, and Alice's cousin, a little girl not yet eight years old, had wasted away from the sweating sickness and the bloody flux. Her father had been press-ganged into the army and blamed himself for bringing the sickness back with him. He had fallen into a melancholia ever since and was hardly ever seen.

Short supplies during last winter had meant some were forced to eat rye bread made with grain spurred with ergot, a black rot which has terrible effects on those who eat it, causing fits and strange visions. Those afflicted feel that their skin is being pricked all over with pins or, in the worst cases, flayed. The milk of nursing mothers dries up and those who are already weak can develop gangrene which brings on death.

The wheat crop had been battered in the fields and the grain was thin and lank. Two of the poorest cottars in our village had been forced in despair to eat their seed corn, leaving them with nothing to plant for this year. In the spring, Gideon had given them his, saying that, as a single man living alone, he had plentiful supplies and could go a year without planting, which I now knew was untrue.

We had all been forced to forage for nettles and dandelions and even beech leaves to eke out our pottage, and some had ground up roots to stretch their flour for bread. And although the weather had been better this year, the loss of so much of our crops to the enclosures meant that we would all need to tighten our belts over the winter. We foresaw a bleak future ahead of us.

So when fifty soldiers were thrust into our homes, where our precious supplies were limited, and we suspected that we would have to give them free quarter, whatever the talk of 'chits', resentment grew quickly. My first concern was to find room for the six allocated to us. I told Kitty to move her belongings down to my room. We would share and I would lodge the soldiers in the two attics. We spent most of the day unpicking a number of the canvas sacks we use for storage and then sewing them together to make large sacks for palliasses. These I handed to the soldiers.

'There is straw in the barn. You can stuff them with that. Then bring them to me and I will sew them shut.'

I looked at them dubiously. 'Do you know the difference between straw and hay? You must not take the hay. We need it as winter feed for the cattle.'

'I know the difference, mistress.' It was a decent-looking fellow, one of the older ones. He seemed less surly than the others.

'Good. Well, make sure you use straw.'

When they had gone to the barn I returned to the kitchen and sat with my head in my hands.

'How are we going to feed them?' I said to Tom. 'Six big hungry fellows. How long do you think they will be here?'

Tom shook his head. 'Until they think there will be no more attacks on the drainage works, or until they are needed to fight the King's forces again. It seems the War is not concluded after all. I do not think you need to feed them royally.'

I gave a bitter laugh. 'I have no plans to do so. I meant to feed our household enough, but frugally, just enough to get us

220

through the winter. Now we may run out of food before the spring. And spring is always a hungry time.'

'Surely they will be gone by then.' Kitty looked up from where she was helping my mother who was in a tangle with her spinning. Ever since the men had arrived she had been agitated and frightened.

'I hope so. I must fetch in the washing. It has been so cold, everything will still be damp.'

As I walked across the yard to the hedge, the soldier who said he knew straw came towards me, with his palliasse hoisted over his shoulder.

'I've seen to it that they haven't touched your hay, mistress.'

'Thank you.'

'And I'm sorry we're visited on you like this. Not all of us want to be here, policing our own people and feeding off you. I was forced into the army myself, and so were some of the others.'

'What's your name, soldier?'

'George Lowe, mistress. I've a wife and two children in Middlesex that I've not seen for two years. All I want to do is go home. I'm tenant on a smallholding there, and I don't even know if my wife has been able to pay the rent. We thought the War was over and they would give us leave to return home, but they keep us on. They haven't paid us a penny for months, and they only feed us by foisting us on people like you.'

'Well, Goodman Lowe, my name is Mercy Bennington, and this affair of draining and enclosing our lands has already cost my father his life and my brother the loss of his leg. I have little sympathy with any who protect the speculators who are stealing our land.'

'No blame to you there.' He gave me a sympathetic smile. 'We've had trouble with enclosures in my own village, though I know nothing about the Fens.'

I turned away to the hedge. 'Only the fenlanders understand the Fens,' I said, 'but these Londoners and Dutchmen will cause a disaster before they are done.'

'Any help you need about the farm,' he said, 'you just tell me, and me and the lads will give you a hand.'

In the next few weeks we were proved fortunate in the men billeted on us, more fortunate than most of the village, where some fights broke out, especially after the men had been drinking in the yelhus. We had none of that trouble with our men. The other older man was called Seth, and the youngest, a boy of fifteen, was Ben from London. Aaron and Jem were also Londoners, while Col was Lincolnshire born, but had lived all his life in Peterborough and knew nothing of our fenland ways. George himself was a private soldier like the rest, but he was respected by them and kept them in order. Each morning they went off to the village, where they drilled and had weapons practice, or were sent off to guard various portions of the drainage works. This meant that during the day we were mostly free of them, but I had to feed them every evening, and it was beginning to encroach on our winter supplies.

As December drew in and the weather grew colder, everyone in the parish brought in the stock to the barns and higher ground. The glebe land behind the church – where Gideon would have sown his corn if he had not given it away – was the highest ground in the parish. By long practice, all the parish sheep were wintered there until after spring lambing and the pigs until farrowing. We drove our sheep and pigs there with the rest, Nehemiah and I assisted by George, together with Aaron and Ben. These two knew nothing about stock, but they were willing enough, if a little stupid.

'Why do you put the animals here,' one of them asked me, the young lad called Ben, with ears like jug handles and big clumsy hands. 'There's more room in that field where they were.'

'There used to be much more room, before the drainers dug a ditch across it,' I said bitterly. 'We bring them here because in winter all that part floods. The water comes down from the hills and the Fen spreads out over most of the farmland. The village and our farm become a sort of island, though we can sometimes get through the lane to Crowthorne and the Lincoln road. Not always though. Sometimes we're cut off till spring.'

His mouth fell open and he looked frightened. 'You mean we'll be caught here, surrounded by water? Maybe not be able to get out?' There was a note of panic in his voice.

'Aye. That could happen. Unless you're posted somewhere else before the floods.'

I noticed that our new rector, fat little Reverend Apsley, was listening. After all the sheep were herded on to the glebe land and settled down to graze, he took me aside.

'Is that true, Mistress Bennington? Could we be marooned here?'

'Quite likely, sir,' I said cheerfully, enjoying his look of panic, which mirrored the soldier's. 'About three winters in four we're cut off. As for this winter, with all the damage the drainers have done, who knows what will happen? I suspect the floods will be far worse, because they are draining the water away from the peat moors, which are supposed to absorb most of the waters. You may find yourself climbing the church tower for safety.'

I could see that he did not know whether or not I was exaggerating, but he was worried.

In the past we had had little to do with the people of Crowthorne. And little love for them either. But now that the drainers had moved into their parish, it seemed as though we might come to have common cause with them. They had taken no part in our earlier attacks on the works and the settlement, but now they saw that they too were threatened with the loss of their lands and the food we all garnered from the Fens. And like us they also made traps and baskets and hurdles and thatch from what grew there – the sallows and reeds and sedges. It had taken them months to awake to the dangers, but now we began to hear about one or two incidents of collapsed ditches and a broken sluice gate here and there. Van Slyke was not one to ignore even a minor attack and I was soon told by George that trouble was brewing.

'It is nothing to do with us,' I said. 'Crowthorne is a different parish. There has been no trouble here for weeks.'

He gave me a curious sideways smile. I wondered whether he knew about what had happened here earlier in the year, and the part Tom and I had played in it.

'It's a word of caution only, mistress, that I'm giving you. For I do not think our captains make a distinction between the two parishes. It's all one drainage scheme, you see, for this part of the Fen, so to them an attack is an attack. People may suffer for it.'

He said no more, but soon afterwards Jack visited us one day when the soldiers were away on duty, bringing news that someone over Crowthorne way had pulled down a pumping mill, like the one we had burned in the spring.

'They gave us no help before,' he said, 'but it's bold of them to do it right under the noses of the soldiers.'

His tone was admiring and I sensed that Jack, always ready for mischief, wanted to go back on the attack again. Tom slapped the arm of his chair in frustration.

'And I can do nothing. Are you planning anything, Jack?'

He shook his head. 'Not yet. We will wait and see what the soldiers do. It seems those on guard near the mill let off some shots but hit no one.'

'I believe the soldiers take little pleasure in it,' I said. 'They think they are not in the army to protect rich men's interests against the farmers of ancient commons.'

It was not long before we discovered what the captains of the two troops had decided – the captain in charge of the soldiers who had been posted to Crowthorne some months before and the one commanding the troops now billeted on us.

Without warning, a contingent of soldiers descended on the glebe land and drove away a tenth of the sheep, making no distinction between the owners. They were taken to a disused farmyard which had been commandeered in Crowthorne for a pinfold. The pigs were not moved, perhaps because the soldiers found them too cantankerous to handle. The next day, a troop came to our farm, none of them the men who were billeted with us, and took possession of four of our cows. As soon as they were gone, I rode Blaze into the village, which was a milling chaos of soldiers, cattle and protesting villagers.

Toby ran up to me and caught hold of my bridle. 'For Jesu's sake, Mercy, get that horse out of here or they'll take him too.'

'Why are they doing this?'

'They are punishing everyone in the area. It will cost us ten shillings to redeem each sheep and thirteen and eight pence for each cow. Jesu knows how much for a horse. They know we cannot pay. They will sell the stock to the settlers, to the profit of the projectors. Now go, before you lose Blaze!'

I turned Blaze so sharply he reared in alarm. A slap on the rump from Toby sent us careering up the lane to home.

The next day when our soldiers were gone from the farm, Jack rode into the yard. I was cleaning the hen-hus, but I dropped my shovel and tied his horse to the fence. In the kitchen he flung himself down on a bench while I fetched beer. My mother, looking alarmed, gathered her skirts about her and hurried from the room, though she stumbled and nearly fell. Kitty ran to her and helped her up the stairs to her chamber.

'I'm sorry,' Jack said, 'I did not mean to alarm your mother.'

'She is very confused these days,' Tom said. 'So much has happened to our family, and now these soldiers living with us. She doesn't understand who they are and why they are here.'

I set down beer for them both.

'She's grown suddenly old,' I said, sitting down next to Jack. 'I remember your grandmother.'

'Aye.' He smiled sadly. 'Such a sharp mind and then one year she became like a child again, babbling about Queen Bess as if she were still alive. In the end she could not even feed herself.'

'I would rather die young than sink into a childish dotage,' I said fiercely.

Tom looked at me over his beer. 'Be thankful that you have survived this far. You may even live to be twenty.' He turned to Jack. 'Now, I think you have something to tell us.'

Jack leaned forward. 'We have been speaking to some of the men from Crowthorne.'

I raised my eyebrows in astonishment.

'Aye, you may look like that, Mercy, but their stock has also been taken, and they are no happier than we are. We are going to have a football game.'

'Football! The godly folk of Crowthorne would never play at football!'

'Ah, desperate times.' Jack laughed.

'It was a device they used down in the Great Level,' Tom said slowly, 'in our grandfather's time.'

I looked at him in puzzlement.

'You would not remember, Mercy. You were scarcely more than a babe. They would call for a football game and in all the confusion, divert the guards from seeing what was happening elsewhere. Make an attack under cover of the game.'

I could see that might work. Football games between villages were vicious affairs with no rules. Often violent, they could end in serious injuries. Any number could take part, chasing an inflated pig's bladder up and down a street until one team carried it off or everyone lay wounded.

'You aren't planning another attack, are you?' I said. 'Surely we have suffered enough, with our stock impounded.'

'If we do not take action before the end of the week, all the stock will be driven off to Lincoln market and sold there. You know we cannot pay to redeem them.'

'But how –'

'We will play the football game in the street outside the pinfold. There are soldiers guarding it and we will make sure there is so much noise and hullaballoo that they will take notice of nothing else.'

I began to see where this was leading. 'So while they are distracted, others will release the stock?'

'Aye. And herd them home. Most of the young men will be at the football, so . . .'

'You want me to go with the other party? Bring out the stock?'

'Are you willing?'

'Aye.'

'Mercy,' said Tom, 'it will be dangerous. You have suffered enough already these last months.'

I glared at him. 'And that is why I am prepared to fight back. Have they not done us enough harm already? I will gladly come, Jack. Who else is to be there?'

'I thought you could take Nehemiah. And Will says he's too old for the football, but not too old to herd the stock. There will be two, perhaps three, from Crowthorne. Best not to be too many, or you will draw attention to yourselves. You would come as if to watch the game, then slip away.'

I nodded. 'Have you seen where the stock is held?'

'I went there yesterday. They are in an open cobbled yard, not shut in a barn, which will make it easier. At the back of the yard, away from the street where we will play, there is an old fence. The whole place is neglected. It should not be too difficult to pull it down, at least enough to make a gap wide enough for the beasts.'

'I'll take Jasper,' I said. 'He's good at herding sheep.' The dog, hearing his name, looked up at me and wagged his tail. 'Will it be difficult to find the place?'

'One of the people from Crowthorne will show you. You had best go mounted, and bring the beasts back over the fields, not by the lane.'

'Of course. That may be a little slow, but the crops are all in, there will be no harm done.'

I felt a stirring of excitement. At last we would be doing something to fight back. The injustice that had been done us, impounding our stock when we had not even been involved in the latest attacks, infuriated me.

The football game was planned for two days hence. I was not happy to wait until then to find the pinfold and the place where the fence was weak, so I persuaded Jack to take me there the next day, once our soldiers had gone on duty.

'Like army scouts,' I said cheerfully, 'spying out the enemy's territory.'

'Hmph.' Jack was still unconvinced, though he had agreed when I said I would refuse to help unless I could see the place first.

'It is not that I do not trust the Crowthorne people to show us the way. It is in their interest as much as ours,' I said. 'I feel we will waste less time, be more certain of success if we know exactly what we are to do beforehand.'

'Perhaps,' he conceded. 'But we must take care not to attract attention.'

'I think we should go over the fields to Crowthorne. Work out the best way to drive the beasts back.'

That is what we did, starting from the village, through a gate which would allow us to bring the animals from the fields into the street. We both carried baskets and stopped to gather nuts and rosehips and late bullaces from the hedges as we went. Like any frugal country couple, we were harvesting the last of the wild provender before the worst of winter set in. There had been a heavy downpour during the night, so our shoes and the bottom of my skirts were soon soaked.

As we drew near Crowthorne, I saw where new drains had been cut through their lands in the weeks since I had stumbled across them on my journey back from Lincoln. The smell of sodden grass and wet mud was everywhere. Fortunately for our plan, the abandoned farm was on the edge of the village, adjacent to the fields. We stopped some distance away and Jack was able to point to the rotten fence which bulged out at the back of the yard. Even from here I could see that it would be no great barrier.

'Careful!' I said. 'Someone is coming.'

We turned aside to the hedge and began foraging about amongst the leaves. Unfortunately, there was little here to gather, though our baskets already contained enough to display our honest activity.

Two soldiers were approaching from round the side of one of the farm buildings. They were coming straight towards us. Suddenly Jack threw his arms around me and began kissing me enthusiastically. Taken by surprise, I nearly fought back before I realised what he was about. I relaxed and put my arms about his neck.

I heard one of the soldiers laugh.

'Just a courting couple. Take care, lass,' he shouted, 'he only wants one thing.'

'Aye, unless you've a bit for us too,' called the other one.

'Be off,' said Jack, laughing, 'and leave me and my girl in peace. She'll not look at anyone else.'

'That's what you hope! Good luck to you, mate.' They turned and went back to the pound.

'I'm sorry, Mercy,' Jack said. 'It seemed like the best thing to do.'

'I know.' I straightened my cap, which had fallen half off. I was somewhat breathless.

'Not to say I didn't enjoy it.' He gave me a wicked grin and I blushed.

'We've seen enough,' I said. 'Best be off, before they suspect something.'

We made our way back across the fields. I took note of the best route for the animals, while Jack whistled merrily all the way home.

The football game was planned for the end of the next working day, when all the young men of both villages would be free to take part – farmers and craftsmen, labourers and apprentices. The yelhus keepers from both villages had set up stalls on each side of the main village street in Crowthorne and beer was flowing freely. I saw Reverend Edgemont looking on with disapproval as his parishioners indulged in this ungodly habit, but our little Reverend Apsley was enjoying himself with the rest. I had suspected that his rosy countenance owed something to the bottle.

I wondered whether either man was privy to what was afoot, but thought they had probably been kept in ignorance, lest their consciences prick them into giving everything away. If so, they were probably the only inhabitants of the two villages not to share in the knowledge. It seemed everyone had turned out, to fill the street with crowds and make as much noise as possible. Children ran everywhere, dodging in and out of the bystanders. Women with babies tied in shawls on their breasts were admonishing their husbands. I caught sight of Alice with Huw, over near our beer stall. She gave me a tiny nod, but did not draw attention to me. Even the old people of Crowthorne were here, sitting on stools set out before the houses and looking eager for the game to begin.

I had ridden Blaze over early and left him tied up just outside the village, near the gate to the field where Jack and I had encountered the soldiers the previous day. Nehemiah had followed on foot with Jasper on a lead. Will would meet us here and I caught sight of him now in the crowd, talking to Jack. They were joined by two older men I did not know, who must be the locals who would drive away their own beasts. Daylight was fading fast on this winter afternoon. It was a rawky day, with a mist curling up from the Fen, as it usually did at this time of year. Provided that it did not become too thick, it would make our task easier.

The two crowds of young men were being marshalled to the opposite ends of the street by Toby's father and a local man. Another man I did not know was holding the pig's bladder, ready to throw it into the empty middle of the street when all was ready. I began to work my way to the back of the crowd. Will and the others had already disappeared.

When I reached the spot where I had left Blaze, Nehemiah was waiting. He untied Blaze while I loosened the strings of my skirt and let it drop. Underneath I was wearing the pair of Tom's breeches I had borrowed before. I was even thinner now, but I had spent time the previous evening taking in tucks at the waist so that they fitted better. I rolled up my skirt and pushed it into the satchel I had fastened behind my saddle, having taken out the small billhook I had brought to help in breaking down the fence. Nehemiah had another tucked into his belt.

'Ready?' he said.

I nodded. We led horse and dog through the gate and closed it carefully behind us. We could hear shouting from the centre of the village, but it was still only sporadic. The game itself had not started yet. I knew they were taking it slowly, to give us the most time possible. My heart was beating so hard I could feel it in my throat as we made our way up the edge of the field behind the houses to the yard where our animals were impounded. Would all the guards have gone to watch the match, or were some still at this end of the yard, conscientiously continuing their duty?

As we neared the rotten fence, where Will was already waiting, a great roar broke out from the village and I knew that the pig's bladder had been thrown into the street. Both teams would rush toward it and whoever managed to seize it would be guarded by his own men and attacked by the other team. Nothing was barred, save the use of weapons – fists, feet, teeth, elbows, all could be used to gain possession of the bladder. I prayed that, caught up in the excitement of the game, they would not forget that they were supposed to make it last as long as possible, secretly passing the bladder from team to team, so that it went up and down the street, neither side gaining the upper hand.

As soon as the noise started, we attacked the fence. As well as our billhooks, Will had brought a long-handled chisel, which he inserted between the boards to prise them apart. The two Crowthorne men had concealed crowbars in the long grass, with which they heaved at the base of the fence. We exchanged no words as we worked, but I saw them looking at me askance. It appeared Jack had not warned them that one of us would be a woman, and a woman wearing breeches at that. But there was no time for argument or recrimination. The fence was indeed rotten in places, but still sturdy enough to resist us. I began to sweat with the effort and with nerves, despite the December cold and the damp of the thickening mist.

At last two of the planks fell forward, catching one of the Crowthorne men on the foot. He cursed, using language Reverend Edgemont would not have approved. Will pulled them away and threw them to the side.

'After the beasts are out, we should replace the fence,' I said. That will fool them for a while. No need to make it plain where the beasts got out.'

Will nodded. 'I've a pocket full of nails. I can tap it back into place.'

'Why bother?' said the man whose foot had been hit. 'All we want is to get our stock back.'

'Strategy,' I said firmly. 'To put them off the scent.'

'Petticoat government,' he muttered. 'I'll not take my orders from a woman.'

'You need not concern yourselves,' Will said calmly. 'I'll see to it while you drive your own beasts home.'

They did not try to argue further, for at that moment a great shout went up from the football game and the rest of the section of fence fell down. Hoping the noise did not mean the game was over, I helped Nehemiah pull the remaining planks to one side, so the animals would come to no harm, while Will and the other two men made their way cautiously into the yard.

The noise of the crowd had started up again – luckily, for the animals were milling about in distress, making plenty of noise themselves. We could only hope the guards would think they were disturbed by the game. Nehemiah let Jasper off his lead and I

231

whistled to him, sending him to round up the sheep. The foolish creatures were running from one side of the yard to the other, but Jasper soon had them gathered together and heading for the gap in the fence. Once they were through and Nehemiah was helping the dog sort our sheep from those belonging to Crowthorne, I darted into the yard and found Blackthorn. She lowed plaintively, butting her head against my chest. I put an arm round her neck.

'Come, girl,' I said. 'Good girl. We're going home.'

As I led her out of the yard, all the other cows followed, as they will do when they are driven in for milking, the local cows as well as those from our village. As we reached the fence there was another loud burst of shouting and some of the cows shied away. Will, coming up behind with one of the other men, spread out his arms. Between them they turned the cows back and they followed me into the field. Nehemiah was already halfway across it with Jasper, herding our sheep into the mist. The Crowthorne man who had complained of me was driving the rest of the sheep off in the opposite direction.

There were about twenty cows altogether, twelve belonging to our village. The local man and I soon sorted them, while Will began knocking the fence roughly together again. Before he turned away, the local man gave me what amounted to a smile in Crowthorne.

'I'm sorry for what Ephraim said. You're a brave lass.'

I grinned back. 'Perhaps our villages have more in common than we thought. We must all stand up to these enclosers.'

'Aye.' He nodded. 'Good luck to you. I hope you come home safe.'

Almost at once he was lost in the mist. I stowed my billhook away in my satchel and took out a length of rope. The cows were already beginning to wander off, enjoying the taste of fresh grass after being held in the cobbled yard. I passed a loop around Blackthorn's neck, making sure it would not tighten and throttle her. I remembered suddenly Abel Forrester and his talk of sailors' knots. The other end of the rope I tied to my left stirrup.

'Are you done?' I asked Will.

'Nearly. You get on your way. I'll follow you and see none of them stray.'

He gave me a leg up and went back to his fence. As I turned Blaze to follow the edge of the field where Nehemiah had gone before, Blackthorn began to plod after me. Our other three cows fell in behind her, then five or six more. I hoped the others would follow or that Will would be able to find them, for the mist was thickening into a true fog now. I had explained the route to him, which Jack and I had worked out.

I was forced to keep Blaze down to a cow's pace, although every instinct shrieked to me to get away from there as rapidly as possible. In some ways the mist would help, hiding us if anyone came looking soon, but it would be easy to lose some of the animals. I was glad I had thought to bring Jasper, for he would be able to round up any stray sheep which Nehemiah could not see. For myself, I was forced to depend on the cows' natural instinct to follow one another. They would also have some homing instinct, wanting to return to their own farms, but I was not sure whether they would sense the way, being so far from their own village.

The noise of the football game was fading away, either because it was muffled by the fog or because it had become impossible for the teams to see, forcing them to abandon it. As soon as it was over and the crowds dispersed peacefully, the soldiers were bound to resume their duties. Would they notice at once that the animals were gone, or would the thick fog lead them to believe that they were simply huddled in some corner? It had been a large farmyard. The soldiers might just patrol the outside and – seeing no break in the fence – would not realise what had happened until the mist cleared or someone came to feed the animals.

As we were crossing the second field, Blackthorn stumbled, and I realised that my anxiety had made me increase Blaze's pace. I stopped, so that she could recover, then moved on again, slowly, slowly. It was impossible to see more than one cow behind her now. I could only put my faith in the dull persistence of kine.

At the end of the second field I opened the gate, which Nehemiah must have closed. I left it open for the cows still following. Now we were in the third and last field, one belonging to our village. Nearly home. One of the cows loomed up out of the fog and passed me at the shambling trot a cow can manage when she chooses. This was one, perhaps, who sensed home was near. Blaze and I groped our way forward after her, already swallowed up in the fog. Even Blackthorn was picking up the pace now, crowding behind Blaze so that he jigged sideways and flicked his tail in annoyance.

The gate into the village street wavered into sight. It was closed, with the cow leaning over it, mooing anxiously. Two figures loomed up and opened the gate. I saw that one was Nehemiah. The other, to my surprise, was Rafe's father, leaning on his stick.

'This is one of ours,' Master Cox said. He looked up at me, his expression a comical mixture of disapproval and relief. 'Have you all the cows?'

'I hope so. It's difficult to tell in this fog. Most of them were following me and Will was chasing up the stragglers.' I turned to Nehemiah. 'Are the sheep safe?'

'Aye, all herded back into the glebe land. Thanks to Jasper here.' He reached down and patted the dog. 'I'd have lost a few but for him.'

'Best let me through,' I said, for they were blocking the gate. 'The cows are crowding my horse.'

We counted them as they came through the gate. Including the Coxes' cow, which had ambled off toward their house, there were ten.

'Aye, I thought two had wandered off,' I said. 'I hope Will has been able to find them in all this.' I waved my hand at the blanket of fog.

Our own four cows stayed placidly near me, tearing at the grass verge. Master Cox drove off two to their owner at the end of the street, while Nehemiah led one to the yel-hus and another two to Jack's house. Still there was no sign of Will. Nehemiah returned and leaned on the gate, while Blaze fidgeted under me. I was beginning to worry.

'I hope the soldiers have not caught Will. Apart from three sheep, none of the stock are his, but we needed him to fix the fence.'

I told Nehemiah what we had done after he left.

'Some fool,' he said, 'that fellow from Crowthorne. "I'll not take my orders from a woman." ' He imitated the man's surly tone.

I laughed. 'The other fellow apologised for him. He won't be the first to object to petticoat government. Or the last. There have been pamphlets written and published, giving dire warnings against upstart women who forget their place, now that the world is turned upside down.'

He was silent for a while. 'Have you thought what you will do, Mistress Mercy? Now that Tom cannot work the farm?'

'I don't know. For now, we must just survive the winter if we can. In the future? I do not know. With Father dead, the farm is Tom's now. He must decide.'

'Would you run the place yourself?'

'Do you think I could?'

'What have you been doing, lass, ever since you recovered from what they did to you in Lincoln? Aye, I believe you could run the farm.'

'Would you stay? Or would you rather go back to a holding of your own? You are like family now.'

He looked down and shuffled his boots. 'I'd be glad to stay,' he said gruffly, 'if you want me.'

'Hey!' A voice came out of the fog. 'I heard voices. Is the gate there?'

'Will!' I called. 'Jesu be thanked! We feared you were taken.'

He materialised out of the fog like a ghost, driving two cows before him with a hazel switch. He was mired up to the waist in mud, his boots squelching with every step.

'What has happened? You look half drowned.'

'That b'yer lady cow of Rafe's!' He pointed his stick menacingly at the cow which was pushing past Blaze through the gate. I saw that she was muddied halfway up her sides.

'She led me a merry dance, right down to the far side of that second field. And it's all gone to bog.'

'Bog?' I said. 'There was never bog there before.'

'Well, there is now. It has started to flood, weeks before time, and by the look of it, I'd say it hasn't just happened. The works over that way have turned the water.' He looked around. 'Jesu, where's that cow now?'

'Headed home,' Nehemiah said. 'Whose is this other one?'

'The widow Peterson's,' I said. Can you take her back, Will? I want to get our cows home before our soldiers come back.'

We parted, Will herded the last cow down the village street while I headed Blaze up the lane towards the farm, leading Blackthorn, Nehemiah and Jasper following behind and urging the cows along when they showed signs of stopping to graze.

At last a faint glow from the kitchen window showed where the farm lay through the fog. Nehemiah drove the cows into the barn, while I removed Blaze's tack and fed him.

Tom and Kitty looked up expectantly as we came in, kicking off muddy boots. For the first time I realised that my clothes were sodden from the dense fog. I stood with my back to the fire and began to steam like a kettle.

'Done?' said Tom.

'Done,' I said. 'Now we see what will happen when they find their stolen animals gone.'

Chapter Fifteen

Jack arrived soon after Nehemiah and I had finished the milking, though the four cows which had been impounded gave little milk, still distressed after their ordeal and the long walk home. After we had bedded them down and I had checked again on Blaze, we crossed the yard by the light of a rush lamp just as Jack rode through the gate. He followed us into the house.

In the brighter light, he was a sorry sight. His right eye was blackened, his upper lip burst and bloody, his clothes torn and dusty. But his eyes were alight with triumph.

He clapped me on the back as if I were one of the village lads, though I was now decently dressed again in clean skirt and bodice, my apron as white as the milk in my bucket. 'We have beaten those bastards,' he said, 'begging your pardon, Mercy, Kitty.' He looked around and saw that my mother was not there, for she had taken to her bed early, confusing the dark of a December evening with the middle of the night.

'We certainly got the stock safely away, but how went the football game?' I said. 'I think you have suffered.'

'Nothing to speak of. We kept it going until you couldn't see from one end of the street to the other. In the end we let them win, when we thought you must be safe away. We must challenge them to another game, and this time we will beat them fair and square.'

'I doubt Reverend Edgemont will permit another game,' Tom said, with a wry smile. 'I am surprised he allowed this one to go forward.'

'They told him nothing about it. It was only when all the crowds gathered that he realised what was happening, and by then it was too late to stop it.'

He turned to me. 'You had no trouble, then, Mercy?'

'One of the Crowthorne men took exception to a woman being of the party, but that was all. Will mended the gap in the fence before we left, so it should be some time before they discover how the stock escaped.'

'In this fog, that will take some days.'

'Two of the cows strayed on the way back, but Will rounded them up. He says that middle field is turned to bog at the far side.'

'You didn't mention that.' Tom turned a worried look to me.

'I haven't had time. He thinks the drainage works over at Crowthorne have already caused flooding. Jesu knows what will happen when the winter floods come.'

They digested that in silence.

'We could attack the works again,' Jack said slowly.

Tom shook his head. 'I cannot think that would achieve much. No one can know now how the water will behave. We must wait and see, once winter brings our normal floods. Then we will know where the drainers have caused the most damage, concentrate on those parts of the works.'

'Perhaps you are right.'

Nehemiah nodded. 'Before all this happened, we always knew where the water would flow, and where was safe. Now everything is a mystery, in God's hands.'

'What I do not understand,' I said, 'is where Sir John stands in all of this. It was back in the spring, after Father and the others went to see him, that he said he had written to his lawyer. Surely there was that ancient charter which guaranteed our rights to the commons in perpetuity? The commons cannot mean so much to him as they do to us, for they form only a small part of his estate. But he does have some common rights. Does he not want to protect those?'

'I've long thought Sir John never wrote to his lawyer,' said Tom.

'And I.' Jack nodded.

'But why?'

238

Tom gave a mirthless laugh. 'Perhaps, like Cromwell, he has turned his coat. Perhaps he has shares in this drainage project.'

'Do you really think so?' I was shocked. I knew Edmund Dillingworth for what he was, but I had always believed Sir John was an honest man and as lord of the manor would protect the people of this area.

'It could be so. We shall know, someday, if we see him take over our stolen land. There would be more profit to him in owning the land outright than in his small share of the commons.'

I studied Tom without responding. These days the fight seemed to have gone out of him. I could not imagine how it must be to have lost a leg, but I suppose he felt unmanned, as well as weak and frustrated. And still in pain. He spent most of his time sitting in our father's great chair beside the fire. Although he could, with some difficulty, manage to help with the milking, he seldom offered now, leaving it to Nehemiah and me. He told me once that he was still aware of his leg, as if it were there. He would feel a pain in his calf or an itch in his foot, and bending over would discover, as if for the first time, that the leg was gone.

That evening our soldiers returned much later than usual. As I served them their supper, bacon and turnips warmed over, with bread I had made fresh that morning, I heard them discussing their day.

'They need not have kept us searching in the dark,' Seth said. 'As if we could find anything in this thick fog and a night as black as a bag over your head.'

'Aye,' said Ben, the jug-eared boy. 'But that was a fine football game before! Best I've ever seen, and we've had a few in London.'

'I wonder whether they knew there was to be a game,' Aaron said. 'And got the animals away while we were watching.'

'But we never left the gate of the pound,' Ben said. 'How did they get past us?'

The other man shrugged. 'Witchcraft?'

George, I noticed, did not join in the discussion.

'Anyway,' Ben said with a sigh, 'they will have us hunting again to tomorrow, so I heard tell.'

George turned to me. 'Mistress Bennington, these fogs on the Fens, how long do they last?'

I considered. 'When the ground is already as wet as it is, and at this time of year, it could last four or five days. Perhaps as long as a week.'

'You see,' said Ben, 'they'll have us out there in this blasted fog, going round in circles, and we'll find nothing.'

Indeed I hope not, I thought.

Later in the evening, when I was about to bolt the door and go upstairs, I caught sight of a lantern moving back across the yard from the barn. One of the soldiers must still be abroad, though everyone else in the household had gone to bed. I sat down to wait. I could hear Tom thumping about in the small bedroom and occasionally cursing, but by now I knew better than to offer to help him.

George came in. He bolted the door and blew out his lamp, then sat down across the table from me.

'I have washed down the cows' legs,' he said. 'They were covered in mud and would have given you away. Cows kept in a barn for the winter would not be caked in mud.'

I stared at him. 'You knew!'

'I guessed. Then I counted the cows and found the right number restored, with four of them bearing traces of a muddy journey. Do not worry.' He smiled at me. 'I'll tell no one. It was cleverly done. I doff my cap to you.'

'How did you know about me?'

'Oh, I have heard of your exploits. You have nothing but my admiration.'

'You may get into trouble.'

He shrugged. 'I don't intend to stay around to get into trouble. I'm going home. I miss my wife and children.'

'But how can you?'

'By rights, my term of service is up.'

'By rights, the common lands belong to us. The rights of poor people are worth little. If you go without leave, it will be desertion. You could hang.'

He spread out his hands in a gesture of despair. 'I never sought to join the army, and when I was forced to, I thought: Very well, we are fighting the King to better the lot of the ordinary people of England. But now, is our lot any better? Look what is happening here in the Fens. And the men behind it nowadays are not courtiers and aristocrats. They are the very men who told us soldiers that we were fighting for freedom.' His tone was bitter.

'I'm going, and going soon, while the fog lasts. I can slip away from the search party and head south for Middlesex.'

'George.' I reached across the table and laid my hand on his arm. 'South of here lie nothing but Fens, and the Fens are dangerous, never more dangerous than in the fog. Even a fenlander would not try to cross the Fens in fog. You must not run the risk.'

He shook his head. 'I'm a countryman, Mistress Mercy. I can find my way.'

I kept trying to make him understand, but he was stubborn and would not listen.

The next day the soldiers were away early to join the parties searching for the missing stock and Nehemiah went off to Peterborough market. At the farm we went quietly about our daily business. I checked the four cows and saw that George had made an excellent job of washing them clean. The fog continued to lie heavily over the land, a thick sea fog rolling in from the German Ocean with a taste of salt and seaweed in it. It lay like a sodden blanket over our wetlands. With a winter sky above and a watery landscape below, the fog had nowhere to go. Everything outside was dripping. Indoors the fog seemed to penetrate the very rooms and fill our lungs.

The one excitement all day was a raid by a fox on my hens. Slipping in under cover of the fog, it managed to carry off one of my best layers. Although the panicked cries from the birds sent me running outside, I was too late. I caught a glimpse of a white-tipped tail vanishing under the gate before the predator was lost to sight. In case he decided to come back, I shut the hens away for the rest of the day.

The soldiers returned earlier than usual, soaked to the skin and out of temper. Five of them.

'Finally saw sense,' Col said, 'those bastard officers. Realised we'd find nothing in this blasted fog.'

Four of the soldiers stamped upstairs to change into dry clothes.

'Bring your wet things down,' I called after them. 'You can dry them by the kitchen fire.'

Ben had lingered. He watched me as I began to set up the loom. I had promised to teach Kitty to weave and these long winter evenings were as good a time as any.

'Mistress Mercy,' he said, squeezing his wet cap nervously between his hands so that water dripped on the floor.

'Aye?'

'George has not come back with us.'

'I noticed.'

'I'm feared he may have done what he threatened. Deserted and headed for home.'

I dropped the heddle rod I was holding and turned to him.

'What? Are you sure? I warned him the Fens are dangerous.'

'You knew as well, then.'

'He told me last night that he wanted to go home. It's Middlesex he comes from, isn't it?' I said.

'Aye. Is that south of here?'

'South, but with miles of Fens to cross first.'

'I think he's gone.' The boy looked pathetic, his great ears red with the cold and his nose dripping. He was not so stupid after all, and he had a kind heart.

'You get out of those wet clothes. I'll see what I can find out.'

As soon as he had gone upstairs I turned to Tom, who had been listening to all this.

'What do you think?'

He shrugged. 'Why should we care what becomes of him? One less mouth for us to feed.'

'George is a decent man. And we are in debt to him.'

I told Tom about my conversation with George the night before, and how he had washed down the cows, so that they should not give us away. He gave a whistle and grinned.

'That was clever of him. And a kindness. I suppose many of these soldiers do not care for this present posting.'

I untied my apron and took down my cloak.

'I'm going to ride into the village and see whether anyone there has seen him. And try to get help to search for him.'

'You are not planning to go out into the Fen – in this fog!'

'Someone has to. If he has set off heading south he'll be in the Fen as soon as he crosses the pasture. I warned him, but I don't think he believed me. I'll see if Jack or Toby will come with me.'

'Mercy!' Tom said as I opened the door. 'I forbid you to go!'

I closed it softly behind me, pretending I had not heard.

I did not bother to saddle Blaze, but rode him bareback down to the village. If George was out on the Fen, every minute counted. The news I gathered there was as I feared. The soldiers billeted at the Coxes' house said that the six men billeted with us had all set out along the lane to the farm, but they had noticed one lingering behind the others. Six had set out and only five had arrived. George had given the others the slip somewhere between the village and the farm. That meant almost certainly that he had taken the branch of the lane that led to the pasture and the drainers' rebuilt pumping mill, where Hannah's cottage had once stood.

I went next to Jack's house, where he lived with his widowed mother. They were just sitting down to an early supper and invited me to join them. I shook my head, explaining why I had come. Jack stared at me incredulously.

'You want me to come and search the Fen in this fog, for a missing soldier? After all they have done to us? Mercy, what have we been fighting for?'

'This soldier is different,' I said. 'Forced to join the army, forced to stay on past his term. He just wants to get home to his family. Besides, he has helped us.'

Once again I explained how George had concealed the evidence of our muddy cows.

'Jesu!' said Jack. 'I never thought of that! I must wash down our Bessie and White-Leg.'

'So will you come with me? You know the Fen as well as anyone, except Nehemiah, and he is not back from Peterborough market yet.'

Jack shook his head. 'I'm sorry, Mercy, but I will not come. If it were one of us, I would, but not for some soldier.'

243

'One of us would not go out on the Fen.'

'More fool him. I'm afraid he will already be drowned by this, you must know that. It is an hour at least since the soldiers came through.'

'Then I shall have to go alone.'

'Don't be a fool, Mercy!' He scrambled to his feet, knocking over his stool, while his mother sat gaping at the pair of us.

I ignored him and ran from the house. He was right. George could already have drowned. There was no time to waste trying to persuade someone else to go with me, only to find this same hostility to the soldiers. I used the milestone outside Jack's cottage as a mounting block and set Blaze cantering back up the lane to the farm.

Back at home I shut Blaze hastily in the barn, not even stopping to take off his bridle. I knew Nehemiah would notice it when he came home. In the kitchen I paused only to change into my high winter boots and to collect the rope I had used to tie Bluebell to my stirrup.

'Well?' said Tom. 'What has happened? Has he deserted? In anyone from the village coming?' He began to struggle to his feet.

'Later,' I said. 'Stay there.' I caught up a lantern with one of our precious wax candles and flint and tinder. 'Come on, Jasper.' I whistled, and the dog followed me out of the house.

Out in the yard I struggled to light the lantern, but my hands were shaking so much it took me four tries. I knew that what I was doing was foolish, dangerous, but I was driven on by a sense that somehow I owed this to God, who had sent Abel Forrester to save me when all hope was lost. It was my time to repay the debt.

I tied one end of the rope to Jasper's collar and knotted the other around my waist. A dog has a better sense of safety in the Fen than any human being and I did not want to lose contact with him. Then we were through the gate and running by the short way I had so often taken in the past to Hannah's cottage. If George had followed the lane from the village, I had some hope of shortening the distance between us, though he would still be ahead of me. Even knowing the way as well as I did, I stumbled several times and fell once, extinguishing the lantern. It took me even longer this time to relight it.

Wait! I said to myself. This will get you nowhere.

I stopped a moment to slow my breathing and think calmly. No roads ran south of the village, only the lane that petered out at the pasture. Normally anyone wanting to travel south would go north first to Crowthorne, then across to the Roman road which led to Lincoln, but would turn south there, instead of north. The Romans had built it on a high causeway, a ramper skirting the fenland. George, however, would not go that way, past the army camp, where he would be seen and stopped. He was a countryman and believed he could travel cross-country, avoiding the roads. Despite my warnings, he clearly thought the Fen was no more difficult country than his own Middlesex. I knew nothing about Middlesex, except that it was near London. I imagined it to be a rolling countryside of neat little farms and tidy woodlands. What could a man like George know of our vast acres of peat bog interspersed with chains of ponds and larger meres? What looked like solid ground could tremble as soon as you stepped on it and suck you down in minutes. As children we were brought up on tales of men sinking into the Fen, never to be seen again. And there were boggarts and jack-a-lanthorns and ghosts out there. Safe indoors by the fireside it was easy to enjoy the tales Hannah used to tell, not quite believing in them. But out on the Fen, it was a different matter.

I slowed my pace to a fast walk and managed to avoid any more falls before I reached the pasture. I crossed it carefully, avoiding the new ditch. The pasture seemed much wider than usual when I could not see across it, then suddenly the pumping mill loomed up in front of me, like one of Hannah's boggarts. I gave a yelp before I realised what it was. The sails hung motionless in the still air, reaching out like great arms overhead. In the heavy fog, with no breath of wind stirring, the pump would not be working. Had the drainers thought of that? It would mean that, at the moment, water was not being pumped out of the Fen. It might even mean that water which had been pumped into the new ditch would drain back. Even as a fenlander, I could not be sure. The ways of water are mysterious, no one really understands them. If the mill had dried out this end of the Fen, the level of the peat moor might have sunk, because it was said that the new drainage schemes caused the peat to shrink. In that case, water from the meres might flow over the shrunken peat and change the whole landscape of the Fen. On the other hand, if the fact that the mill had stopped pumping meant that water had flowed back over the lowered level of the peat, that too would have altered everything.

I had been into the Fen in daylight, in summer, with Hannah to fetch herbs that grew there and I tried now to picture in my mind the pattern of safe ground one could follow. The pasture lay on slightly raised ground, not more than a foot above the level of the Fen beyond, but just behind where Hannah's cottage had stood there was the beginning of a path, reinforced with ancient woven hurdles, preserved by the dark peaty water. Hannah used to say that the path had been made by fairies, but Gideon said it was the work of our ancient ancestors who had first settled this land long ago.

No, I must not think of either Hannah or Gideon.

Calling back Jasper, who had been investigating some interesting scent, I skirted the mill and raised my lantern. The light barely reached a few yards, reflected back weirdly off the fog. Everything was changed since the cottage had been demolished and the cider apple tree cut down. Then I saw the two large, flat boulders which formed steps down from the edge of the pasture to the path.

Sending a prayer for help up into the grey mass overhead, I stepped down into the Fen.

Would George have investigated the way south? Despite his refusal to take seriously my warnings about the dangers of the Fen, I though he was, on the whole, a careful man. Only a careful man, with foresight, would have thought to wash the mud off our cows. A careful man, with foresight, would have found an opportunity to investigate the first part of his route south.

Jasper was sniffing eagerly along the line of the path reinforced by the hurdles. He tugged at the rope and I followed him. Although I could see only about six feet in front of me, I knew I could follow the path for about half a mile into the Fen. I had never been further than that with Hannah and did not know how far it extended. At first the path seemed the same as I had remembered it, but then we reached a great patch of liquid mud which spread in all directions, hiding the path.

I stopped. Jasper tugged at me again, sniffed again at something on the ground. Squatting down beside him, I held the lantern over the mud. There was a trail of fresh footprints. They must have been made by George. No one else would have come this way, in this weather. And they were indeed fresh, because the mud was so wet that water was already filling up and obscuring the prints. Cautiously I stood up again and began to follow them. The path must lie beneath this part of the mud, because it had borne his weight, therefore it would take mine. I followed slowly, keeping a sharp eye on the prints, which were fading fast.

Then, to my horror, I saw that the prints led to a great scrabbling in the mud, where they had sunk in deeply. I groped around until I found a stone and tossed it into the middle of the disturbed ground. There was a sucking noise and the stone disappeared from sight. I realised that I had been holding my breath and let it out in a gasp. Jasper had run ahead, vanishing into the fog. The rope stretched between us, and I gave thanks to God that I had thought to bring it. Sliding my feet carefully ahead of me, one by one, along the line of the rope, I followed the dog, skirting the churned area of mud. The ground, for the moment, was firm under my feet. Had George been sucked into the bog, like the stone?

Ahead, Jasper had sat down and was waiting for me, looking as pleased as if he were out for a normal walk. Then I saw, half-hidden by his tail, more of the footprints. George must have managed to regain his footing and found the path again. Slowly we resumed our careful walk. We came to the end of the mud slurry. In the dark and fog I could not be sure, but I thought the path continued for some way yet, though here the ground was the usual deceptive rough grass and moss, interspersed with the clumps of the taller fen grass that we call hassocks and which we dry for lighting fires. This is the terrain which is so dangerous, because what looks like firm ground can collapse beneath your feet. As there was no more of the wet mud, there were no more footprints, so I was not even sure whether I was following George, though I could still sense the hurdles beneath my feet, from the way they bounced slightly when stepped on.

I also sensed that it was getting darker. In the fog it had been dull all day, but now whatever winter light had been in the sky above the fog was seeping away. Soon I would have true darkness to contend with as well as the Fen and the fog. Slowly I felt my way further along the path. Now it curved to the right, on the very edge of a large mere. A moorhen, startled by us, gave a loud cry and flew up from the water. This was as far as I had been with Hannah. We would come here to gather the mare-blobs that grew along the fringes of this mere. She used them in several of her cures, saying they were a sovereign remedy for many ills.

Did the path go any further? When I had discussed the path with Gideon all those months ago, I had said that I thought it might have been made by those ancient people so that they might fish in the mere, but he disagreed.

'Why go to all that trouble, when there is easier fishing nearer to hand? No, there must have been some other reason. Perhaps they thought it was a place sacred to one of their pagan gods. Did you not say there is an island in the mere? Very remote and inaccessible?'

I remembered that now. I could not see as far as the island, but the thought of some ancient, terrible god frightened me. I crossed myself in the old way, which would have had Reverend Edgemont damning me as a recusant.

'Jesu, protect me,' I whispered. And I crossed my fingers against any evil lurking here. Yet somehow the remembered sound of Gideon's voice steadied me. I could hear it now, as clearly as if he stood beside me in the cold and fog. His voice was warm and reassuring, wrapping me round. I had the strength to do this, I told myself. There are no evil spirits here, only the memories of ancient times. And the only dangers are the physical ones, the sink holes of the bog.

I knew the path went a little further and felt my way along it, round the bank of the mere. I still had a horrible feeling that I was being watched, either from that unseen island or from behind the clump of sedges that grew on the bank, with their feet in the water, but I scolded myself and went on, one cautious step after the other.

Then Jasper, running enthusiastically down to the edge of the mere, startled another moorhen, which rose with a clap of its wings, disturbing other roosting birds.

Suddenly, I thought I heard a faint call in the distance ahead of me.

'George!' I shouted, holding up the lantern. 'George, are you there? It's Mercy Bennington.'

My voice seemed to bounce off the fog, echoing around me. The call came again, but seemed to come from a different place. Not only was the fog blinding me, it was distorting sounds.

'Jasper, seek, boy.'

I patted him on the rump encouragingly. He stood up and trotted off into the fog. I lost sight of him at once, for it was much darker now, but the tug on the rope guided me to him.

'George, where are you?'

'Here.'

This time I heard him more clearly. Jasper seemed to be heading in the right direction, but we were moving away from the part of the path I knew.

'Easy, Jasper.' I prodded the ground with the toe of my boot. It squelched and sucked. No hurdles here. We had come to the end of the path. The dog pulled again, but I held him back, feeling my way cautiously forward. Ground that would support a dog might not support me.

'Mercy?' The voice was much nearer now.

'I'm coming. I have to feel my way.'

'Be careful. I'm in the bog.'

Jesu. Was he sinking?

Suddenly Jasper stopped. I held up my lantern. The spit of ground on which we stood was surrounded on three sides with sodden peat and water. One step on to that and we would both be drawn down into the Fen. Where was George?

'Here.'

I turned. The light from my lantern just reached to an isolated hassock rising up from the peat. George was sitting there, clinging on to the long grass. Between us stretched impassable bog.

'How did you get there?'

'Jumped. I thought I could jump from one of these islets to another, and get across the bog that way.'

'Well, jump back, then.'

'I've twisted my ankle, or broken it.'

'You're a fool, George.'

'I know.'

Suddenly very weary, I sat down on the last bit of firm ground. Jasper yearned towards George, but I held him close.

'What are we going to do,' George asked humbly. 'Will you fetch help?'

'Just let me think.'

I did not want to tell him that no one might want to help.

'I'm going to try something,' I said. 'I'll send the dog across to you, with the rope. It may not work. If the peat won't support him, I'll have to pull him back. If he can reach you, do you think you can hold on to the rope while I pull, and crawl or slide back across the peat? I don't think you will sink as quickly lying flat on your stomach as you would standing up. But I can't be sure. We'll have to be quick, or you *will* sink.'

'I'm willing to try. I'd better throw my pack over to you.'

I saw then that there was a knapsack lying beside him on the hassock. He must have had it hidden somewhere, ready for his journey.

'All right. Throw it.'

He flung the knapsack and I caught it, then laid it behind me on the firmer ground.

I stroked Jasper's head. The peat might not hold him and I might not be able to save him. 'Good boy,' I said, and pointed to George. 'Seek, seek.'

Jasper trotted happily out on to the black, sucking peat. He hesitated a moment, then ran on, leaving a trail of footprints that filled immediately with water. Luckily the rope was long enough to reach. He jumped up on George, licking his face.

'Good lad,' George said, hugging him. I could hear a break in his voice and realised how terrified he must have been, alone here in the Fen, waiting for the end.

'Untie the rope from his collar, and tie it round your waist,' I said. 'Then send him back to me. I don't want him getting tangled up in the rope.'

Jasper ran halfway back to me, stopped again, then ran on. There must be a quag there in the middle. I hoped I had the strength to pull George out if he sank into it. Throughout the Fen there were these particularly dangerous bits, bottomless, they were said to be. There was nothing here to help me, no tree stump, not even one of the ancient bog oaks which dot the Fen, so old they have turned to stone. If there had been a stump I could have run the rope around it to give me more purchase, but there was nothing.

'Ready?' I called.

'Aye.'

Even as he said it, the candle in my lantern flickered and wavered. I had not thought to bring a spare. If it burnt away, finding the way back would be even more difficult.

'Stretch yourself out along the bog as far as you can in my direction, and hold on to the rope with your hands. I'll start pulling at once. If you can, try to crawl, or squirm across.'

'Right.'

Cautiously he lowered himself on to the bog on his stomach. That took some courage, I thought. Immediately I pulled in the slack rope. He began to crawl towards me as I hauled, but he was beginning to sink. Jasper barked excitedly.

The distance was about thirty feet. Although he sank a little in the first half, it was only a few inches. As he crawled and I pulled, it seemed to be going well.

Then he reached the part where Jasper had hesitated and I felt the pull on the rope as the bog began to suck him down. I backed further away, hauling on the rope which was burning my hands, beginning to slip away from me. George was thrashing about, no longer able to crawl. I tightened my grip on the rope. Then inexorably I felt myself being dragged towards the bog.

I drew in a great sobbing breath, leaning back and digging the heels of my boots into the soft ground. George's legs had disappeared. Then he made a last desperate heave, throwing himself somehow forward. I took a step back, moved one hand further down the rope, then the other. With a horrible sucking sound, the bog released him and he crawled the last few feet to the firmer ground where I stood.

I crouched down and held out one hand to him, keeping tight hold of the rope with the other. He could still slip back. He grabbed my hand and crawled up the slight slope, collapsing beside me. Jasper ran about barking, but George and I were too exhausted to move.

'In my knapsack,' he croaked at last. 'Bottle of beer.'

My hands were shaking so much I could barely unfasten the buckles. My palms were rubbed raw and bleeding. I found the squat green bottle and passed it to him. He rolled over and sat up.

'God's bones, that was a near thing. You saved my life.'

'We aren't out of this yet. We still have to get back out of the Fen.'

He pulled the cork out of the bottle with his teeth, dropped it into his palm and took a long swig. Then he passed it to me. I drank thankfully, though the beer was inferior stuff, something issued to the soldiers. Then I remembered the flickering candle and scrambled to my feet.

'We must go. My lantern won't last much longer. Can you walk?'

'Maybe you should leave me here. This seems firm enough.'

'No, I think the water is rising. You'll have to lean on me.'

I suddenly realised that the fog must have been lifting for some time. I had been able to see George across quite a wide stretch of bog, much further than I had been able to see when I first entered the Fen. But now full dark was coming on. There was a wind rising too, and with it there arose the voice of the Fen, the whispering susurration of the rushes. This was the Fen I knew and I welcomed it.

I passed the bottle back to him. 'Cork that and put it away. We must go now or I won't be able to find the way. And untie the rope from your waist. I need to tie Jasper again.'

He fastened his knapsack while I secure the end of the rope to Jasper's collar, then I helped George to his feet. He gave one yelp, quickly bitten back. I got my right shoulder under his armpit and picked up the lantern with my left hand. It was not going to last until we were out of the Fen.

The journey back was almost worse than the journey out. Although I knew that the path would take us back to the pumping mill, I was not sure I could keep to it once the lantern went out. George limped along as best he could, but I had to support much of his weight and before long pain was shooting through my shoulder and back. Jasper, having decided that he had had enough of this adventure kept running ahead and nearly jerking me off my feet when the rope tightened around my waist.

The candle finally went out as we reached the slurry of mud across the path. We had hardly spoken, but George said now, through gritted teeth, 'I nearly fell in the bog here.'

'I saw. Wait a minute. I'll need to feel for the hurdles with my feet, to find the right place.'

At last we were across the mud and it was easier to feel the path underfoot. There was no moon to be seen and the sky was so clouded over that – even with the fog lifted – there was not a glimmer of starlight to help us. After what seemed like hours groping our way through the darkness, I was able to make out the pale glimmer of the mill's sails rising ahead and above us.

'We've reached the pasture,' I said. 'Are you all right, or do you want to rest?'

'Best not,' he said, with a faint echo of a laugh. 'If I sit down now I probably won't get up again for a week.'

I untied Jasper and let him run free, then we struggled on. Never had the distance across the pasture and along the lane seemed so far. Although the lane was not the shortest way, I thought it would be the least difficult for George. I could feel that he was at the end of his strength, as I was.

We were halfway along the lane when the mizzle I had felt in the air began to come down, softly at first, then in great sheets, like a river in flood. We were both already plastered with mud, but now we were wet to the skin in minutes. My cloak, which was good woollen broadcloth, soaked the rain up at first, then let it through, and grew heavier and heavier.

At the turn in the lane leading up to the farm, Jasper ran ahead and out of sight. Not much further now, I told myself, but I was too exhausted to say it out loud, to encourage George. As we drew near the farm, I saw a light approaching us. With Jasper jumping around his feet, Nehemiah was coming down the lane, holding up a lantern.

'Thank God, Mercy,' he said. 'Thank God.'

I nodded.

'George,' I said, and my voice came out in a croak, 'George has damaged his ankle. Can you help him?'

Nehemiah took George's weight from me, and it was like the weight of the world being lifted. I could stand up straight again, though I could barely put one foot in front of the other.

Somehow we were all in the kitchen. Tom, his face white and his eyes red and staring, stumbled to his feet, grabbing his crutches.

'Thank God,' he said.

'We're all thanking God,' I said.

'You are mad.'

'I know.' I fell, rather than sat, on to a bench and closed my eyes.

For the first time since we had reached the pasture, George spoke.

'She saved my life.'

Chapter Sixteen

W e all slept late the next day. The other soldiers had woken while we were talking in the kitchen and we had passed off what had happened as an accident in which George had damaged his ankle. I stayed out of sight in Tom's room so that they should not see the sorry state of my clothes, but I could hear them examining the injury. General opinion pronounced it a sprain and not a broken bone, but George would not be able to attend the morning muster.

With all the disturbance and broken sleep, the soldiers had to make haste to leave in the morning. I could hear Kitty cutting them bread and cheese, but decided I had no need to get up. I turned over in bed and fell asleep again.

When I finally came downstairs I was still muzzy-headed. The day was dark as evening, and I saw that the rain was continuing to fall in torrents from great roiling clouds overhead. It looked as though we were doomed to a glut. Tom and George were sitting on either side of the hearth, George with his bandaged foot propped on a pile of cushions. Despite a good fire, the winter chill and damp had invaded the kitchen. Kitty was spinning. The half-assembled loom chided me with forgetting I had promised to teach her to weave. Of my mother and Nehemiah there was no sign.

As I came through the door, George struggled to get to his feet but I motioned him to sit. I rubbed my eyes which were still blurred with sleep.

'I'm sorry I have slept so late. I must go for the milking.'

'Nehemiah has done it,' said Tom, 'an hour past. We left you to sleep.'

'I will make you some breakfast, Mistress Mercy.' Kitty left her spinning and ladled porridge from a pot keeping warm on the hearth, then laid out bread and honey.

She kept stealing furtive glances at me as I ate. I wondered what they had told her of what had happened last night, for although she had woken when I went up to our shared room, I had told her not to get up. This morning I had noticed that my muddy and sodden garments had disappeared. It must have been Kitty who had taken them away. They were probably soaking in the scullery now, for it would be difficult to wash away the stains from the bog.

'Where is Mother?' I asked.

'She wanted to stay abed,' said Tom, 'so we left her to lie. She seems unsure whether it is day or night.'

I looked around the room, where they had three rushlights burning.

'It is so dark it truly is difficult to tell. Do you think it has been raining this hard all night?'

'The lane was already awash when the lads left,' George said. 'They'll not be pleased, hunting for stock in this.'

Tom and I exchanged a glance. If the lane was awash, it meant the winter floods were coming early. At this time of year high tides could also rush up river a long way inland in our flat country. We would need to be on the alert.

When I had finished eating, Nehemiah came in, tipping water off the broad brim of his felt hat onto the floor. Kitty clicked her tongue in annoyance at the dirty puddle and got down on her knees to mop it up.

'Sorry, Kitty,' he said, 'but it's b'yer lady terrible out there.'

He prised off his muddy boots by the door and walked to the fire in his stocking feet. Jasper followed him and shook himself hard, so that water spat and hissed in the flames.

'Did you feed the hens?' I asked.

'Aye, and kept them shut in the hen-hus. It's no weather for them to be outside.'

'A day to keep busy indoors,' I said. 'Kitty, you can help me put the rest of the loom together, then I will show you how we string it.'

She beamed at me. Soon we were busy setting up the warp threads, each weighed down with a small pottery loom weight.

The rest of our soldiers returned after midday, their captains having decided that it was a fruitless waste of effort, trying to search for the rescued stock in a rain storm so heavy it was near as bad as the fog had been. The lads were happy enough playing at cards and dice, while Tom got out Father's chess set and began to teach George and Ben how to play. From time to time Ben glanced from George to me and back. It was clear he was curious to know just what had occurred out on the Fen last night, but feared to ask. Kitty and I worked away at the loom. By bedtime she had managed to weave about two inches of rather lumpy cloth which would be good enough for a blanket. I praised the speed at which she had learned and she blushed with pleasure and pride.

For days it continued to rain with a relentless persistence that we usually saw only in the worst winters. Often it fell as sleet, or even snow, but the ground was so wet the snow did not lie. It melted at once, adding to the water spreading everywhere. After the second day the soldiers were ordered to stay indoors until the rain ceased, which meant more meals to be provided. They were becoming more like members of the household now, no longer resented – though still hungry. Nehemiah taught Col how to milk, the others carried in logs and peat for the fire. We all stayed together, crowded in the kitchen, for it was very cold, with an east wind blowing, and we benefitted from each other's warmth.

My mother kept to her chamber, Kitty or I taking her meals to her there. We lit a fire in the small hearth, for she felt the cold. Mostly she stayed in bed, although she was not ill in body. When we could persuade her to get up and dress, she would sit in a chair by the window, her hands in her lap, staring out at the relentless rain and sleet. She seldom spoke, but when she did she seemed puzzled and could not tell who we were. Once she threw her dish of pottage at me, scalding my hand and smashing the dish to fragments. Then she began to weep.

I knelt beside her and put my arms around her. 'Don't worry, Mother. It was an old dish, it does not matter.'

She shook her head and raised a tear-stained face to me. 'Who *are* you? I thought you were my sister Elizabeth, but your voice is different, lower.'

'I'm your daughter Mercy, Mother. Surely you know me? I believe I look a little like Elizabeth.'

Again she shook her head. Her eyes were frightened. 'I have no daughter. I am not married yet, though Isaac has come courting. He was to come today. Where is he?'

'It is raining very hard,' I said, trying to keep my voice steady. 'Perhaps the lane is flooded.'

That seemed to satisfy her.

'Aye. That will be it. The lane is flooded.'

I gathered up the broken pieces of the bowl and as I crept out of the room I could hear her saying, over and over, 'The lane is flooded. The lane is flooded.'

I told Tom quietly what had happened. 'Her mind is going.'

'She thinks she is a girl again, I suppose.' He gave a great sigh.

'Back to the time when she was happiest. I remember how it was with Jack's grandmother. In the end she thought she was a child and went searching for her dolls.'

'It is a terrible thing.'

'Aye.' Suddenly a sob escaped from my lips. 'I just wish she could remember that I am her daughter and I love her.'

He laid his hand on mine, but there was nothing he could say to comfort me.

Ten days after George had set off to cross the Fen, it was still raining, though it was mostly sleet now. The hens had stopped laying and the cows were giving little milk. George could walk without limping now, though he still favoured his bad ankle. Nehemiah had walked twice to the village and I had ridden there once on Blaze, but apart from that we had seen no one outside our own small household. We were all becoming restless, especially the soldiers. As fenlanders we were accustomed to being cut off from the rest of the world in winter, but usually the weather allowed us to see more of our neighbours in the village. Kitty and I spent so long at our weaving that we finished an entire blanket and started another. When Kitty was at the loom I knitted woollen caps for all the men, even the soldiers.

Then on the eleventh day Toby rode over to see us.

Running his hands through his hair, draggling with wet despite his hat, he said, 'Are we to have Noah's Flood? It begins to look like it.'

'How are matters in the village?' Tom asked.

'Wet. Those two cottages along the Crowthorne road, the ones furthest from the village, they've a foot of water indoors. We can't get through to Crowthorne any more.'

'It's early in the winter for that.'

'Aye. And I'll tell you something else. That little plump hen of a clergyman, Reverend Apsley – he's gone.'

'Gone?' I said. 'What do you mean, gone?'

'He told us in his last sermon that he wasn't staying here to be swept away on the floods. He was going back to Peterborough.'

'I teased him once that he might have to take refuge in the church tower,' I said. 'I hope it wasn't my words that drove him away.'

'I don't think it needed that,' Toby said. 'The man is a coward. And he likes the comfort and safety of a large town. Not for him the life of the Fens!'

'He's no loss,' Tom said. 'I would it were safe for Gideon to return.'

'And I,' said Toby.

I kept silence, though I wanted to cry out: *But where is he? What has become of him? Is he still alive? What if his injuries have exacted their toll in the end?*

In my heart I was sure that I would know if he had died, but the fear never left me.

'There's something else,' Toby said. 'A few of us have been out scouting around. Baker's Lode is higher than I've ever seen it. And Jack rode all the way to the river, though the water in the fields was up to his horse's knees. He thinks the river will burst its banks soon.'

My head went up. This was dangerous news indeed.

'What about all the new ditches?'

259

'Full and getting fuller. The pumping mill over where Hannah's cottage used to be is sending more and more water along from the Fen. And the one over at Crowthorne must be working by now as well. It will all be heading towards us.'

We thought about this in silence. Crowthorne stood on slightly higher ground than we did. Not much, but enough to determine the flow of the water.

'Do they man the mill?' I asked. 'The one in our pasture?'

'They did at first, but when they moved over to Crowthorne they only sent a man over every few days to make sure it was working. Now, it seems, the drainers have left, saying they cannot work in this weather.'

'But that means the mill will go on moving the water from the Fen to us. It has to be stopped!'

'Some of us should go and stop it!' Tom half rose from his chair, then fell back, a look of angry frustration on his face.

'I don't understand how these pumps work,' Toby said, 'or I'd gladly try to reach it and attempt something.'

'Will might know,' I said.

'He might. We'd probably need to break in. They'll have the place locked up.'

'Crowbars,' said Tom. 'Mallets to smash the locks.'

At that moment we all heard a loud noise out in the yard, shouting and screaming. I realised that while we had been talking I had half heard something in the distance. Nehemiah was out there with the soldiers, shoring up one wall of the barn which was being undermined by the rising water in the yard, now a foot deep. The cows and Blaze were standing in water in the barn. The hens at least could take refuge on their perches.

Toby and I went to the door, Tom hobbling behind us. The yard was full of people. Where had they all come from? Nehemiah was there, making shooing gestures with his hands while the soldiers looked on, astonished. There were whole families there, families with children, all of them carrying bundles. A few dogs ran about their feet. One woman had a hen under her arm, another held a singing bird in a cage.

From their clothes, I knew who they were – the men in those wide baggy breeches, the woman in caps much bigger than ours, with large flaps at the sides of their faces. It was the people from the settlement. What were they doing here?

I threw my cloak around my shoulders and stepped outside, realising at once that I should have put on my boots as the water rose over my shoes and filled them.

'What is the matter?' I said to Nehemiah. 'Why have they come here?'

'I don't know, Mistress Mercy. I can't make these foreigners understand.'

'Do any of you speak English?' I raised my voice, as though I thought that would help. It did at least quieten them a little.

One of the older men stepped forward. 'Me a little, Mevrouw.'

'Why have you come here?'

'The stroom, the river, he come in our house.'

'The water in the field, you mean? That field always floods in winter. You should never have built there.'

'Water in field, ja, that come, it is a week. Now the river, he come.'

He made a sweeping gesture with his hand.

'You mean the river has burst its banks?'

'I not understand.'

'The river,' I tried to think how to explain. 'The river, he – it – isn't where it was? The river gets very wide?' I spread out my arms.

'Ja, ja. He is very wide. Come fast into our house. Take our sheeps. We run. Here it is higher.'

Not much higher, I thought.

I turned to Tom and Toby. 'If the river has burst its banks there, the flood will be here soon. We'd better send them to the village.'

'It won't even be safe there for long,' Toby said. 'The only ground likely to be safe is the glebe land and the church.'

'We'll send them there. Ben,' I called, 'take these people to the village and get them on to the glebe land. You know, where the sheep are.'

'I know, mistress.'

I turned to the Dutchman. 'You go with this boy. He will show you a safe place. Not here. The water will be here soon.'

He nodded and directed a stream of Dutch at the other settlers. They bowed their heads submissively. The shouting and screaming had stopped, except for a few children who were still crying. For the first time I felt sorry for them. Brought to a strange country, almost certainly on false promises, merely to be exploited by rich men. And now flooded out of their homes.

'Go quickly, Ben. As fast as you can get them to move. Then stay there with them.'

'I'm going to warn them in the village and find Will,' Toby said. 'We'll see if we can stop the mill pumping any more water on to us from the Fen.' He ran to his horse and was off down the lane before the settlers had started after him.

'We'll need to move our stock,' Tom said.

'The cows will have to go to the glebe land too.' I laughed a little wildly. 'It really will be like Noah's Flood.'

'Nehemiah,' Tom said, 'can you drive the cows to the village and up to the glebe land?'

'Aye, I heard what you were saying, Master Tom. I'll get one of the lads to help me.'

I ran into the house. 'Kitty, come quickly. The river is flooding, coming this way. Nehemiah is taking the cows to the village. I want you to help me carry the hens into the attic. They should be high enough there.'

We ran to the hen-hus, splashing through the water in the yard, which already seemed higher than it had a few minutes ago. The hens were restless, aware something was happening, but we stuffed them into the carrying baskets without much care for their feelings. It took us two trips. Tipped out of the baskets, they scuttled about the attic floor amongst the soldiers' untidy belongings. Polly squatted at my feet, looking at me reproachfully out of a sideways yellow eye. Elderly, a little tattered now, and hardly laying any longer, she still remained precious to me for Hannah's sake. We closed the attic door on them, leaving them pecking at the grain we had scattered.

'Tobit,' I said. 'Have you seen Tobit?'

Kitty shook her head. Tobit lived his own separate and secret life, and was nowhere to be found.

'I hope he uses his feline sense to find a place of safety.'

We climbed down the ladder to the first floor.

'Mother!' I said suddenly. 'What are we going to do about Mother? She can never walk to the village in time.'

'Could she ride Blaze?' Kitty asked. 'I've never seen her ride, but . . .'

'She hasn't ridden a horse for years. But if she went two to a horse . . . Oh, if only Tom could ride!'

'You could take her, Mistress Mercy.'

'No, I have more to do here. Go and get her up and dressed in something warm, then bring her down to the kitchen.'

When I reached the kitchen myself, I found that the water was already six inches deep on the floor. I waded across the yard to where Nehemiah and Tom on his crutches were persuading the reluctant cattle to leave the barn. Nehemiah had a loop of rope around Blackthorn's neck and was leading her to the front. Jem followed behind with Jasper as they set off down the lane.

'Kitty is getting Mother ready,' I told Tom. 'We thought someone could take her to the village on Blaze. She will be safe in the church.'

'You could take her.'

'No, I think it needs to be a man. A strong man, in case she turns violent. Beside, I've had an idea.' I turned to the remaining soldiers. 'Can one of you ride?'

'I can.' It was Seth.

'Get Blaze and saddle him. I need you to take Mistress Bennington to the village. Do you think you can do that? She is, she is . . .' The words stuck in my throat.

'Don't you worry, Mistress Mercy. I'll manage her.'

He had Blaze ready in the yard when Kitty and I brought my mother out. She seemed dazed and stared at the lake which spread across the yard and the lane, joining them in one featureless mass. Seth mounted and George lifted my mother up to him, where he settled her in front of him, between the reins. She looked suddenly tiny and frightened.

'Where is Isaac?' she cried out. 'Is Isaac coming?'

263

'We're all going to the village, Mother,' I said. 'To get away from the flood. We'll see you there.'

They began to move off.

'Kitty, you go with them. Mother will need someone she knows.'

'Don't you need me here?'

'It's more important for you to look after her.'

She nodded, then ran after the horse. I saw Seth lean down to speak to her, then she took hold of his stirrup. Good, that was sensible. If only they could reach the village in time.

'You must go too, Tom,' I said. 'You know you will be slow. I can catch you up.'

'I am going nowhere until I know what you are planning, Mercy.'

Only Tom and I, and three of the soldiers were left in the yard now – George, Aaron and Col.

'I've remembered that old dyke, down near where Baker's Lode meets the river. When we were children – do you remember? There was a worse flood than usual one year. I think it was in '39. Father and the others opened the sluice gate to the old dyke and it carried off some of the water from the Lode into that part of the Fen, to stop the river bursting its banks. It's lower than we are here. It could help to hold back the flood until Toby and Will stop the pumping mill. If they can.'

'That was eight years ago. It's never been opened since. The sluice will be rusted and the wood swollen. Nobody could move it now. Besides, the river has already overflowed.'

'It's worth trying. Before even more water pours out of the river.'

Tom freed his hand from one of his crutches and grabbed me by the shoulder. 'I forbid you to do this, Mercy. With Father gone and Mother . . . weakened in her mind, I am responsible for you. It would be deadly dangerous to go down there, into the teeth of the flood. You will drown.'

'I've survived drowning once. And being sucked down by the Fen. See, I lead a charmed life!'

He ignored my bantering tone and shook me.

'No! Mercy, please listen!'

264

'If it seems too dangerous, we will come back. You'll come with me, won't you, lads?'

'Aye,' said George. 'We'll see she does nothing foolish, Master Tom.'

I jerked my shoulder out of Tom's grip and ran across to the barn.

'We need tools. Anything you can find that will help us break down the old sluice gate. It won't matter if we destroy it.'

A few minutes later we were wading back the way the settlers had come, with a motley collection of tools – two axes, a crowbar, and three pitchforks. I would not look back at Tom, standing frustrated and alone in the yard.

'Start walking to the village, Tom,' I called back over my shoulder. 'We'll catch you up before you are there.'

A little further on I stopped to remove my sodden shoes and stow them in my pockets.

'I'll keep my footing better without my shoes,' I explained to George. 'I didn't have time to put on my boots. The soles of my house shoes are too slippery.'

As we neared Baker's Lode, we could feel the slight rise in the ground under our feet, which meant we had reached the embankment.

'Careful now, I said. 'Don't step into the Lode by mistake.'

The water was up to our knees now and I wished I had had time to don breeches again, for my sodden skirts were dragging me down.

'Wait while I find the top of the bank.'

I felt my way up until I reached the flat top of turf. The water tugged at me, trying to pull me away, so I curled my toes to get a grip of the ground. The view from here was terrifying, glimpsed through wavering curtains of sleet. In every direction the flood covered the land. Here and there a line of sallows or poplars, apparently growing out of the water, marked the course of one of the old ditches which fed into the Lode. Across what used to be the barley field, the tops of the settlers' houses poked above the flood, which had now reached the windows of the upper stories. The water swirled ominously around them, carrying several dead sheep.

'All right. Come up carefully now. No further than this or you'll be in the Lode.'

The three men climbed up beside me. They all looked terrified, even George. I suppose that for anyone who lives where land remains land and water flows where it is supposed to, our shifting world where land and water blend and change places must seem like some cold version of Hell.

'Where is this sluice gate you spoke of?' Aaron asked.

'Not far. Over there.' I pointed across the Lode and down towards the river.

'You mean it's on the other side of this . . . this "Lode"?'

'Aye.'

'But how can we get across?' George asked. He looked down at the line of fast-flowing water at our feet which marked the Lode.

'If you were a fenlander, you would vault across, but as you're not, we'll go over the foot bridge, just before the sluice.'

He looked dubiously in the direction I had pointed. 'I don't see a bridge.'

'It's there. Or it will be if it hasn't been swept away. The water must be a few inches over it now, but we can feel our way across. It's just a flat plank bridge, no side rails, so we must be careful not to stray off the edge.'

All three of them looked at me now as if I were mad. Perhaps I was. I ignored them and began to follow the bank along the edge of the barley field and past the settlement, feeling my way with the handle of a pitchfork. It was becoming very cold. The sleet was now mixed with large flakes of snow.

'Somewhere here.'

I stopped. To my relief, I could see the top of the old sluice gate on the far side of the Lode. Over there the ground was wet, but not yet flooded, for it stood higher than the land on this side. The line of the old relief ditch ran clearly away out of sight, still empty except for a dribble of rain water in the bottom. It would provide an escape for the water coming down the Lode, augmented by all the water pumped from the Fen. If we could open that escape route, the level would drop in the Lode and it would ease the pressure on the river, until the pumping mill was stopped and prevented from drowning us all.

To the left of the sluice gate the far end of the foot bridge showed, just rising out of the Lode. In the centre it was covered by no more than three inches of water.

'There is the bridge,' I said, pointing with my pitchfork. 'It will probably be slippery, but if we're careful it should not be difficult. I'll go first.'

'With your permission, mistress.' George put me firmly aside. 'I will go first. I'm the heaviest of us. The bridge may have been weakened by the flood. If it holds me, it will hold the rest of you.'

He set off across the bridge, using the axe he carried to steady himself against the invisible planks. That was brave of him, I thought, after what he had endured in the bog.

'It seems firm enough,' he called back to us from the other side. 'But be careful. It is slippery and the water tries to pull you off.'

I realised that my wet skirts made me even more likely to be dragged away than the men. I went next, clutching my skirts tight around me with one hand, and feeling my way with the handle of the pitchfork. My feet found the other bank, and I was over. The other two followed me.

George was already examining the portion of the old sluice gate which projected above the level of the Lode. On the far side, where the ditch led away, we could see the whole gate, bulging as the weight of the water pressed against it. The men immediately started discussing the best way to break it down. I realised that, having brought them here, I could leave the work to them. They would know what to do. I was suddenly very tired and sank down on the end of the bridge, wet as it was. I could hardly be much wetter. I smiled wryly to myself. I seemed to have been spending much of my time lately in sodden clothes, battling with water in one form or another.

The men began to chop at the planks with their axes, but seemed to be making little impression. These old sluice gates are made from oak and are as hard as iron. After a while they paused and tried to prise the hinges loose with the crowbar. There was a plop as part of a hinge fell into the mud in the bottom of the ditch, then another. Still the gates remained firm.

I heard them muttering, 'This one is giving a little. Get the end of the crowbar in there, Col.'

Aaron said, 'Aye. It's going! Over here, George. See if you can break this hinge.'

The water was coming down the Lode as fast as ever. I wondered whether Toby and Will had been able to break into the mill and stop the pump. Even if they had succeeded, it would be some time before all the water from the drainers' new ditch and the upper part of the Lode had flowed through here.

Suddenly my attention was caught by movement on the far side of the Lode, though it was difficult to see, now that the sleet had turned finally to whirling snow. It might be one of the settlers' animals, seeking higher ground. Then I realised it was a man. A man swinging himself painfully forward on crutches.

'Tom!' I shouted. 'What are you doing here? Get back! The men have nearly broken down the old sluice gate. There's no need for you to come.'

I was so angry with him. Why could he not accept that he could no longer do what he had always done? That he could not always be my protector? Oh, it was hard for him. I knew it was hard, but now he must go back to the village.

I do not know if he heard me, but he ignored me. He was nearly at the bridge now. I stood up at the near end of the bridge.

'Go back, Tom! The bridge is very slippery. You cannot cross it on crutches.'

Behind me I heard a loud splintering sound.

'It's going! Watch out!

There was a crash. I twisted round and saw the men jump back, away from the sluice. Some of the timber fell into the Lode, sending a fountain of water up, then whirled away toward the river. The rest must have fallen into the ditch.

'It's partly blocked at the bottom,' George said, 'but see, some of the water is already pouring through.'

We could all see it. The amount of water flowing down to the river would be reduced soon. Although that would make no difference to the flood which had already poured over the fields, drowning our farm and creeping towards the village, it would lessen the force of the overflow from the river.

'Stay there, Tom, we're coming back.'

I crossed back over the bridge more quickly than I had crossed it first, still using my pitchfork to steady myself, glad of it, even though it had not been needed to demolish the sluice. The three soldiers followed me.

'That was well done.' Tom was grinning, standing on the Lode embankment, where several inches of water covered his one foot and the ends of his crutches. 'I can see the water flowing into the old ditch already.'

Then disaster struck. Tom leaned over to peer through the snow. His crutches slipped on the muddy bank. He pitched forward into the rushing water of the Lode and was swept away.

Chapter Seventeen

Everything happened so fast. One moment Tom was there on the embankment, the next he was gone. One crutch floated on the shallow water round our feet, the other spun round and round, following him down the Lode. I saw his head sink, then rise again.

'Can he swim?'

George was beside me. He had dropped his axe and was stripping off his buff coat.

'He used to be able to swim.' My hands were pressed against my chest. It was as though something had struck me there, driving out all the air. I gasped. 'He used to swim. Before he lost his leg.'

George nodded. 'Get down along the bank, lads. In the direction the water is flowing.'

We all stared at him blankly. For a moment we could not understand what he meant, then as one we began to plough our way through the knee-high water. I tripped over George's axe, then picked it up, not knowing why.

He checked to see that we were doing what he wanted, then turned away from us and leapt into the Lode.

'God's bones!' Aaron cried. 'They'll both drown!'

'Can he swim?' I tried to see either of them in the water, but the snow was too thick. Then George was there, level with us.

'I don't know,' Aaron said.

Col stood gaping in horror.

'I think he can.' I waved the axe to where George could be seen, his head above water, carried steadily downstream, a little ahead of us now. He was moving more quickly than we could, but

270

of course the water was flowing that way. I could not seem to think clearly.

'Careful with that axe, mistress,' said Col. 'You'll have one of our heads off.'

We were almost at the point where the Lode met the river when I caught sight of Tom. He had managed to grab the crutch, using it to help him stay afloat. He was making an attempt to swim back against the current, but he was barely holding his own.

'Tom!' I shouted, 'we're here. Keep swimming. George is coming for you.'

I don't know whether he was too far away to hear me, but George was drawing nearer and I think at that moment Tom saw him.

The roar of the water and the blinding snow storm made it almost impossible to see and hear what was happening, But as we came level with the two of them, I could just make out that their heads were close together.

The three of us stopped, staring down helplessly into the muddy water. George had hold of Tom's left arm now. His right was still hooked over the crutch. For an agonising minute they both began to be swept away towards the river, but slowly, slowly they held their position against the current.

'Over here,' Aaron called. 'We're here. If you can get to the bank we can pull you out.'

Time seemed to slow down.

I thought: They cannot make it. One man crippled, the other weighed down by his heavy clothes. And his boots. Why did he not take off his boots?

But, of course, there had been no time.

We watched, unable to help, as they inched toward the bank. They were almost here.

'Reach up with the crutch and we can pull you out with it,' said Col.

They were beside the bank now. With his free hand George had grabbed a tuft of grass that showed just below the surface of the Lode. In normal times it was part of the embankment that would be above water. Tom managed to lift the crutch up along the bank and Aaron reached out to catch hold of it. I threw down the

271

axe and seized him round the waist, so that he too would not fall in. On his other side Col stretched out his hand to Tom's free hand as George tried to push him upwards.

Then they had hold of Tom and were dragging him up over the embankment. He sprawled, sitting up to his waist in the water.

'Give us your hand, mate,' Aaron called down to George.

I looked around for the pitchfork, to give him something to hold on to, then realised I must have dropped it back by the bridge, when I picked up the axe. I half turned. Should I go back for it? But the men weren't waiting. Col was kneeling, trying to grab George's free hand. His other hand was still gripping the clump of grass.

Then suddenly, unbelievably, the clump came away from the bank in a swirl of mud. George made a lunge towards the reaching hand. And missed.

The waters took him and swept him out into the faster current of the river, and he was gone.

A kind of panic seized us then. Leaving Tom where he was, we struggled down to the river, but there was nothing to be seen. Although the river had overflowed into the barley field and beyond, the central portion, the river itself, could still be made out as a strip of angry flowing water, carrying branches and broken planks and dead sheep past so quickly we could hardly see them before they were gone.

The two men looked at me helplessly.

'What shall we do, mistress? You know these waters.'

I shook my head. I could barely speak.

'I fear he's gone, unless he can get ashore further down river.'

I knew it was unlikely, with the river raging as it was.

'We'd best get your brother home,' Aaron said. 'In this cold he'll not last long, soaked through like that.'

I nodded. I looked back over my shoulder at the river, filled with horror and a kind of shame. If Tom had not come, if we had been quicker, stronger, understood better what to do . . . But it had all happened so fast. Turning our backs on the river, on George, seemed like the worst betrayal.

We made our way back to Tom, who was barely conscious. I picked up the crutch.

'He'll not be able to walk, mistress.'

'I know. But can you carry him?'

'We'll manage. Carried enough injured men after battle, we have.'

They made a kind of chair by linking their hands and wrists and eased Tom's arms round their necks, though I thought he hardly knew what was happening to him and would not be able to hold on. I waded behind them, ready to put a steadying hand on his back if he should start to slip. The water was still up to our knees, but did not appear to be getting any deeper.

As we reached the near end of the bridge, I saw George's army coat caught on a small gorse bush. It was wet, as all our clothes were wet, but not soaked through like the rest of Tom's clothes. I draped it round his shoulders. A sorry little procession, we set off through the driving snow, which was growing heavier every minute. The wind was getting up, blowing hard in our faces. It must have shifted direction to the north. Snowflakes clung to my eyelashes and my clothes, forming a kind of breastplate on the front of my bodice. I tried to clutch my cloak together to fend off the wind and the snow, but it kept slipping out of my frozen fingers, whipping behind me in the wind.

I do not know how long it took us to reach the farm. It seemed to take forever. Every so often the soldiers had to rest and change the grip of their hands. I stumbled along, numb with the horror of all that had just happened. George would probably wash up, along with the dead sheep, where the river met the sea. Somewhere I had never been. Even if he had managed to keep swimming, the cold would surely kill him. I hoped it would not kill Tom. My hands and my bare feet were so cold that they had lost all feeling. Snow was filtering down the back of my neck and along my spine. We had to grope our way blindly along the embankment, then, at the end of it, down across the lower ground in what I hoped was the direction of the farm. Once off the embankment, we found the water reaching our thighs. And we still had to reach the church.

At last the buildings of the farm loomed out of the snow. We were on the right track and once on the lane, even though it was underwater, it would be slightly easier to move along. My home stood marooned amid the water like a lost ship. I just wanted to turn in there, to find refuge, but it was pure folly. The water would be two or three feet deep on the floor. We could not light a fire to get warm. We would have to carry on to the village.

The men stopped for a few minutes, leaning against the gate. They were both white with exhaustion and I felt guilty that I was not strong enough to relieve one of them. If only Tom had not followed us out to the Lode! But what was the point of wishing that? If wishes were horses, Hannah used to say, then poor men would ride.

'Not far now,' I said, trying to sound cheerful. 'There will be food and warmth in the village.' I hoped I spoke the truth. They both gave me shaky smiles and heaved Tom up again.

It must have taken us twice the usual time to reach the village, we were so tired. Finally the church took solid form through the snow and the gathering dark, and we could hear the mingled chorus of animals from the glebe land. Light shone from every window of the church.

'Wait here a moment,' I said. 'I want to see whether the village is flooded and whether we should go on.'

I went forward a few yards till I could see down the village street. It lay in a slight dip beyond the church, which – with the rector's house and the glebe land – stood on the highest ground in the parish. Not a single light showed from any of the village houses. The water reached halfway up to the ground floor windows.

No help there, then. I went back to the men.

'Everyone has gone from the village,' I said. 'They'll be in the church.'

We turned off the lane and started up the slope to the church. I held the church gate open and the men manoeuvred themselves and Tom through it. Tom looked more dead than alive and my heart clenched with the fear that we had reached help too late. As we climbed the path to the church, we rose up out of the flood, like some grubby parody of Venus rising from the waves. The last few yards of ground in front of the church were deep in snow, which was settling here above the water line. We could hear a Babel of voices from inside. My hands were so cold and so numb I fumbled helplessly with the heavy iron ring of the door latch. At last I managed to lift it and swing the door open, and stood blinded by light and deafened by noise.

It seemed every face turned towards us together, as though they were all joined to a single string. There was a moment of silence, then the noise broke out again, louder than ever. A small shape detached itself from what seemed a huge crowd and flew to me.

Kitty threw her arms around me, sobbing. 'Oh, Mistress Mercy, we thought you were dead!'

I hugged her, unable to speak.

'But Master Tom, what has happened to Master Tom?'

'He fell in the Lode.'

I saw Nehemiah helping the two soldiers to ease Tom on to a bench.

'These two men,' I said, 'Aaron and Col, they've saved Tom. They need dry clothes and warmth and food. Tom must be stripped. Are there any blankets?'

I gradually became aware that a fire had been lit in a brazier in the middle of the nave. In the church! There was even the smell of meat cooking. There were so many people here. All the villagers. The settlers. The soldiers.

My two soldiers had disappeared, drawn in by their fellows. Jack's mother and Mistress Cox – of all people – were wrapping Tom in blankets. I hadn't seen them remove his clothes, but my head was swimming. I must have lost a few minutes somewhere. It was too bright and too noisy. Too many people crowding around, all talking at once.

Kitty was tugging at my arm. 'Come, you must take off those wet clothes. And your feet are bleeding.'

I looked down at my feet in puzzlement. They were bare and leaving bloody footprints on the flag stones of the nave. I remembered that I had taken off my shoes, but it seemed my stockings were gone as well. It was improper of me to show my feet like this. Must cover up my feet. I took an unsteady step forward. Two strong hands reached out and took mine.

'Mercy, you are safe.'

I shook my head. Now I knew I was lost in some weird dream. That was Gideon's voice. Gideon's face in front of me. Gideon could not be here, holding my hands. Gideon was far away. In the Low Countries. Or was he dead and I was dreaming of ghosts? I felt the whole church tip sideways as the floor swung up to meet me.

I was lying on the floor in one of the small side chapels. I remembered Gideon explaining to me once that before the Great Reform, each of the side chapels – and there were four – had been dedicated to a saint. They had each an altar and a statue of the saint, before which a lamp burned perpetually. There had been brightly coloured wall paintings as well. He had seen a portion of one once when some plaster fell away.

'They were plastered over a hundred years ago.' I could hear his voice telling me. 'In the time of the boy king Edward, son of Henry. He was a zealous reformer. The statues and side altars went earlier, in Thomas Cromwell's time.'

All they had left us was the stained glass window of Mary and Jesus and the hare sitting up and watching the toddling Child.

No, that was wrong. The window was smashed. I remembered that now.

There was something else. The font. Very ancient. That was it. A font which might once have been something else. I needed to remember something about the font. Something to do with Alice.

'Alice.'

'I'm here, Mercy.'

I opened my eyes to see Alice's worried face bending over me.

'What was it about the font?' I frowned. 'I can't remember.'

She looked startled. 'At Huw's christening, do you mean? Those foul soldiers brought by Edmund Dillingworth. They pissed in the font.'

'That's right.' It was a relief to have it explained. 'Filthy brutes. But our soldiers saved Tom. And George drowned.'

'I know, Mercy.'

'Edmund Dillingworth tried to rape me. He wanted revenge.'

'Don't think about it. Here, drink some more of this.'

She lifted me up and propped a cushion under my shoulders, then held a cup to my lips. Hot spiced wine. I drank gratefully.

'Am I drunk, Alice?'

'Just exhausted and confused. And you struck your head on the corner of a bench when you fainted, though Gideon managed to stop you hitting the floor.'

'Gideon? Don't be silly, Alice. You're confused. Gideon went to the Low Countries. There was a ship, the *Brave Endeavour*.'

Perhaps it was Alice who was drunk, not me. It was strong, that wine.

'The ship was blown back by the storm. And then you and Hannah . . .' her voice trailed away.

'I'm not a witch,' I assured her.

'I know you aren't. You were even proved innocent.'

'That's right. They tried to swim me and I nearly drowned. Like George.' I began to cry. 'All he wanted was to go home to his wife and children.'

'I know.'

'He was a good man. He saved Tom.'

'Aye.'

'Tom!' I said, trying to sit up further. 'Is Tom all right?'

'He's wrapped up warm and he's been eating. Kitty is fussing around him like a mother hen.'

'She's a good child. She can't be blamed for being a foundling, whatever they say.'

'Nobody blames her. You've brought her up like your little sister.'

'It was my mother took her in. Mother came here safely? Kitty was with her.'

'She's safe. All the village is safe. And Toby and Jack managed to break into the pumping mill and stop the machine. There's still water being pumped down from Crowthorne, but if they can get through in the morning, they're going to try to break in there as well.'

'Fenland riots,' I said. 'We're a bad lot. Always known for troublemakers.'

'We'll just keep on fighting.'

'Aye. Just keep fighting.' I felt my eyes closing and slid down again.

'Get some sleep.' Alice tucked a blanket around me.

The next time I woke, the church was quiet, except for soft breathing and a few snores. It was dark, though further down the nave several candles had been left burning. I was aware of many people around me and outside the church a great silence. The wind must have dropped and left behind that particular silence which means that thick snow is falling relentlessly.

There was a heavy weight on my chest. As I stirred, it shifted and I felt a faint vibration against my skin. My hand met soft fur and as I stroked it, a paw reached out and patted my face.

'Tobit,' I whispered. 'I knew you were a wise cat.'

My hand resting on his back, I fell asleep again.

I woke next when the first grey daylight fell on my face from the window in the side chapel. Tobit was gone.

'The Mary chapel,' I said softly. 'That's what it is. I remember now. Gideon said this was the Mary chapel.'

'Aye, I did.'

I was even dreaming his voice now. Alice was confused last night, or I was confused listening to her. I closed my eyes and felt my hand taken in a large warm one.

'Father?' I said.

'Go to sleep.'

The third time I woke, all the village cocks in the glebe land were competing for dominance. No one could sleep through that. Someone was still holding my hand. I rolled over awkwardly, for the floor was hard and I was stiff.

Gideon was sitting beside me, holding my hand and smiling down at me.

I shook my head to drive away the fantasies of the night.

'I'm still dreaming. Or everyone is dreaming. Gideon went away into exile.'

'But I came back.'

I tried to sit up but I was too stiff and fell back clumsily. He put his arms around me and lifted me up. Then he kissed me. His lips were warm and real, and I found myself clinging to him, kissing him, but weeping too.

'Are you so sad to see me?' He was laughing and brushed away the tears from my cheeks with his thumb.

'I thought I had lost you for ever.'

'In the end, I couldn't do the cowardly thing and hide away in exile. I went to London to plead to get my living back. I was kept dancing on a rope for months, but failed in the end. It was only when I arrived in Peterborough on my way home that I heard the terrible news about what had happened to you and Hannah.'

'Poor Hannah,' I said. 'I loved her.'

'I know.' He kissed me again, and I curled up against him, feeling the warmth and strength of his arms around me.

'What happened then?'

'I heard there were soldiers billeted everywhere and thought I might bring more trouble to everyone if I showed my face here. I kept out of the way, until I ran into Jack a few days ago in Peterborough market. He told me there were different soldiers billeted here now and he thought the floods were coming. He also said my replacement as rector had run away. I remembered your father telling me how the church used to be the place of safety when the floods were really bad in his childhood. I thought I could help, but I told Jack to say nothing for the moment.'

There was beginning to be movement in the church, people getting up and shaking out blankets. I heard the clank of an iron cooking pot and realised I was ravenously hungry.

'Have you heard about Tom? About his leg?'

'Aye, Jack told me. And I was here when you all arrived last night.'

'I don't know what will become of us. Father is dead, Mother is losing her mind, and Tom cannot work on the farm. I'm afraid of the future.'

He smiled down at me. 'That doesn't sound like you. Fear is not something I link with your name.'

'I've been somewhat too bold, I think. If I had not insisted on going to break down the old sluice gate, Tom would not have followed us and fallen in the Lode, and George would not have drowned.'

'They tell me you saved his life in the Fen.'

'And a brave man saved my life in Lincoln.'

'In this terrible age of the world,' he said, 'so many dead, brother fighting against brother, father against son, the English church destroyed by these rampant Puritans, innocent women hanged as witches – in spite of all this there are still private acts of kindness and courage. We have to cling to that and hope for a better future. I cannot believe that it is God's plan that there is nothing in prospect for us but a blood-stained future.'

'Mercy?' It was Alice, carrying Huw and giving me a knowing smile, seeing me sitting there in Gideon's embrace.

I began to scramble awkwardly to my feet and Gideon put a strong arm around my waist to help me. For the first time I realised I was not wearing my own clothes from the day before. Someone had dressed me in a voluminous night shift, that looked as though it might belong to Jack's well-rounded mother. My feet had been bandaged and my hair hung loose. I picked up my blanket and wrapped it round my shoulders, for modesty's sake.

'Tom wants to speak to you,' Alice said.

'Has something happened?' I was instantly apprehensive. 'He isn't dying? Mother, is mother safe?'

Alice patted my arm and Huw looked at me with wondering eyes.

'Tom is well. He seems none the worse for being half drowned in the Lode. Your mother is just as she has been lately. Some of the village goodwives are sitting with her. They've all known each other since they were girls and can talk to her about those days. I think it has eased her mind a little to talk to them.'

'More than I can do,' I said sadly. 'She does not even know who I am.'

She squeezed my arm. 'Come. Speak to Tom.'

Gideon steadied my stumbling steps as Alice led us out of the side chapel and down the nave to where two benches had been pushed together near the font to make a bed for Tom. His back was propped up against the wall and he was laughing with Jack over something. I felt a brief stab of anger. Did he not know that a good man had died because of his folly in following us to the sluice? But I was so relieved that he had not died as well that I pushed the thought away.

'Mercy!' Tom held out both his hands to me and I took them. 'Thank God you are safe. I think we all nearly died. Then Alice said your mind was wandering in the night.'

'I struck my head, she told me. And I was exhausted.'

'And grieved for George.' A sudden spasm passed over his face and I saw that he was full of shame and guilt for George's death.

'Can you sit? Gideon, is there somewhere for Mercy to sit?'

Gideon carried over another bench and set it beside Tom. As he turned away, Tom put out his hand.

'Please stay, Gideon. I may need your help.'

Gideon sat down beside me.

'Help with what?' I said.

Tom considered for a moment, putting his thoughts together.

'What I did last night was stupid. More than stupid. Wicked. I should never have followed you, putting you all in danger. I cannot forgive myself for what happened to George.'

I bowed my head, but did not answer. The memory of last night flashed before my eyes and I clenched my fists.

'Since . . . since I lost my leg, I've tried to pretend to myself that it does not matter, that I could continue my life as if nothing had changed. I persuaded myself that with time I could do everything I used to do, work the farm, carry on Father's legacy.'

'Tom–'

'Hear me out, Mercy. As I said, I was stupid. I was deceiving myself. Of course I cannot work the farm. I can barely help with the milking, and then only with Nehemiah covering up my failings.'

'Tom–'

'Please, Mercy.' He drew a deep breath. 'I have been thinking again of what I intended after I left Cambridge. I want to go back to Grey's Inn, to train to be a lawyer. A lawyer can still practice if he has a wooden leg, and in London I can buy a leg of the very finest quality!' He smiled bravely.

I did not know what to think at first. This was not what I had been expecting, if I had thought at all.

'But . . . I thought you said that London was corrupt, the courts and government controlled by a small faction who are bent on ousting all the honest men?'

'All the more reason for the honest men to fight back. If I can no longer fight in the Fens, I will fight in the courts. If not a rioter, then a lawyer for the rioters.'

'Always known for troublemakers,' I murmured.

'Well, you may carry on making trouble, Mercy.'

'But what will become of the rest of us?'

'I am going to make the farm over to you. I know that you are as capable of running it as ever I have been. Why, in this world turned upside down, even great ladies have taken to running their estates, and they have not your skills.'

I laughed. 'You flatter me.'

'No.' He reached out again and took my hand. 'Shall we do it, Mercy? Each of us carry on the fight in our own way?'

I glanced sideways at Gideon. Tom saw me and turned to him.

'What do you say, Gideon?'

'I say that Mercy is a strong woman who will do whatever she sets her mind to. And only she can decide. But whatever she decides, I will be beside her, if she will let me.'

All around us the church was filled with the murmur of voices. Children, recovered from the fears of the night before, were playing knucklebones in the aisle. Outside, winter was closing down. Soon all of these fenlands would lie under a sheet of ice.

I looked from one to the other of them and smiled.

'We will carry on the fight,' I said. 'Troublemakers. Every one.'

THE AUTHOR

Ann Swinfen's first three novels, *The Anniversary*, *The Travellers*, and *A Running Tide*, all with a contemporary setting but also an historical resonance, were published by Random House, with translations into Dutch and German. *The Testament of Mariam* marked something of a departure. Set in the first century, it recounts, from an unusual perspective, one of the most famous and yet ambiguous stories in human history. At the same time it explores life under a foreign occupying force, in lands still torn by conflict to this day. Her second historical novel, *Flood*, first in the Fenland Series, based on true events, takes place in East Anglia during the seventeenth century, where the local people fight desperately to save their land from greedy and unscrupulous speculators. The second novel in the Fenland series, *Betrayal*, is set partly in East Anglia and partly in London. *This Rough Ocean* is a novel based on the real-life experiences of the Swinfen family during the 1640s, at the time of the English Civil War.

Currently she is also working on a late sixteenth century series, featuring a young Marrano physician who is recruited as a code-breaker and spy in Walsingham's secret service. The first book in the series is *The Secret World of Christoval Alvarez*, the second is *The Enterprise of England*, the third is *The Portuguese Affair*, the fourth is *Bartholomew Fair* and the fifth is *Suffer the Little Children*. A sixth novel in the series is due in 2015.

http://www.annswinfen.com

Printed in Great Britain
by Amazon